PRAISE FOR *GIRLS OF GLASS*

"Excellent . . . Readers who enjoy having their expectations upset will be richly rewarded."
—*Publishers Weekly* (starred review)

PRAISE FOR *IT ENDS WITH HER*

"Once in a while a character comes along that gets under your skin and refuses to let go. This is the case with Brianna Labuskes's Clarke Sinclair—a cantankerous, rebellious, and somehow endearingly likable FBI agent with a troubled past. I was immediately pulled into Clarke's broken, shadow-filled world and her quest for justice and redemption. A stunning thriller, *It Ends With Her* is not to be missed."
—Heather Gudenkauf, *New York Times* bestselling author

"*It Ends With Her* is a gritty, riveting, roller-coaster ride of a book. Brianna Labuskes has created a layered, gripping story around a cast of characters that readers will cheer for. Her crisp prose and quick plot kept me reading with my heart in my throat. Highly recommended for fans of smart thrillers with captivating heroines."
—Nicole Baart, author of *Little Broken Things*

"An engrossing psychological thriller filled with twists and turns—I couldn't put it down! The characters were filled with emotional depth. An impressive debut!"
—Elizabeth Blackwell, author of *In the Shadow of Lakecrest*

BLACK
ROCK
BAY

OTHER TITLES BY BRIANNA LABUSKES

Girls of Glass

It Ends With Her

BLACK ROCK BAY

BRIANNA LABUSKES

THOMAS & MERCER

Published by Thomas & Mercer, Seattle

www.apub.com

Amazon, the Amazon logo, and Thomas & Mercer are trademarks of Amazon.com, Inc., or its affiliates.

ISBN-13: 9781542004244
ISBN-10: 1542004241

Cover design by Rex Bonomelli

Printed in the United States of America

To Deb and Bernie
For your unconditional support, always.
And for, thankfully, being nothing like the parents I
write in my books.

PROLOGUE

St. Lucy's Island, Maine
Then

The whimper was a quiet thing, broken and almost lost to the wind battering the outside of the lighthouse. But it was enough, just enough, to pull Mia from the fog, despite the sly promises of numbness that oblivion offered.

Everything was soft and blurry when she opened her eyes. *That's not right,* panic whispered.

There was something in Mia's hand, slick and metal and sharp, and her fingers convulsed around it as she tried to blink the world into focus.

A razor blade.

It was nestled in her palm, fresh droplets of blood gathering in its divots. It hadn't hurt, though. That slice of its edge into her flesh when her grip had tightened. Why hadn't it hurt?

The whimper. *The whimper.* There it was again. And a rustle, the drag of fingernails against wood. Another person.

Mia shifted, the starlight slipping in behind her enough so that Monroe Bell's face was bathed in silver.

The girl was sprawled on the floor, not far from where Mia sat, her dull eyes pleading for something. Help, probably. Because of the blood.

The dark sludge of it pooled beneath Monroe's body, the wood, already saturated, unable to absorb any more.

Monroe's lips quivered, struggling to wrap around words without success.

Maybe if Mia got closer. She pushed to her knees to cross the small space between them, but her hand slipped when she tried to brace herself. More blood. This time hers—from the weeping gash at her wrist.

"Why?" The question when it finally came was whispered, but it jolted Mia from her daze.

The razor clattered on the floor as Mia crawled toward Monroe, her knees scraping against the hardwood. It didn't hurt. Why didn't anything hurt?

"Come on." Mia fumbled at Monroe's shoulders, trying to lift her up into a sitting position, not really sure why but knowing she couldn't just leave her like that, a broken doll, horrifying in its pliancy. "Come on."

"Why did . . . ?" Monroe tried again, her eyes locked on Mia's face. But she didn't work at all to help Mia's efforts.

"Come. On." Mia's fingers dug into Monroe's shoulder, hard enough to leave bruises had there still been enough blood left in the girl's drained body to rush to the blown capillaries. The roughness wasn't enough to shake Monroe—she was lax, mostly unresponsive, her head lolling back and to the side. The directive—*come on*—had stopped making sense, if it ever had, but it was the best Mia could do. Monroe was looking for answers, and there were no answers here. None that Mia had, at least.

The last thing Mia remembered was drinking whiskey down by the black rocks. With Cash.

Cash. Nearly dropping Monroe back to the floor, Mia shifted, her eyes sweeping the small room, the corners, the shadows, the hiding spots, for signs of another body.

No. No.

Because there it was. A hand, an arm. But it wasn't Cash.

Asher. No.

The anguished howl she just barely recognized as coming from herself pulsed against the walls, returning in vibrating waves that slammed into her chest.

"Why did . . . ?" Monroe's voice was fragile, but still it managed to slip through the pain that held Mia in its grasp.

Monroe. Focus on Monroe. It was too late for Asher.

Mia was all but holding the girl in her lap now, rocking her as she would a frightened child.

Too late for Asher. Too late for Monroe.

No. Not too late for Monroe.

"Why . . . ?"

Why what? *Why what?* Again, the anger flared, and she wanted to shake the girl into answering. *Why what, Monroe?*

Instead, she petted at Monroe's hair, trying for comfort.

The fog's tendrils slid along the edges of her skull again, whispering promises of silence, of escape.

Mia looked at Asher instead of giving in to them.

Pale cheeks, so pale. Not like the ruddy chapped pink he'd get from running through the woods, from getting teased, from giggling after three too many shots of whiskey. Long arms and legs, uncontrolled now, so much like in life, where he'd flop on a bed, on the ground, in the back seat of a car, his body almost graceful in its uncoordinated movements. Fingers curled toward Mia. Reaching for her. Like he always had since they were kids. Best friends forever.

"Why did . . . ?" Monroe tried again, and it brought Mia's attention back to her. It had to be the last time; it had to be. Her lips were white at the edges, almost so white they were blue.

"What? Why did what?" Mia asked. If these were Monroe's final words, Mia would at least hear them.

Then with one last shudder, an inhale, an exhale, Monroe met her eyes.

"Why did you do that?"

Mia stilled. Then a shudder. An inhale. An exhale.

"Shhh. Shhhh," she whispered as Monroe slipped into the darkness.

Now

The bloated hand disappeared beneath each whitecap, only to knock against the bow of Greg Lawson's boat in between the swells.

The paleness of it stood in stark contrast to the boat's cheerful red bottom, and Greg could only stare, a lobster cage still in his tight grip. Icy droplets of ocean spray slashed at his exposed cheeks, tangled, and then froze in his beard. The dock beneath his feet rocked, but muscle memory born from spending forty years on the sea kept him upright. It was the only thing that did.

"Oi," Brandon called from the helm. "Stop pissing around. It's freezing out here."

Greg finally remembered to breathe. "Get down here."

The curse Brandon shouted back nearly got lost in a gust that swept along the crests.

"Get. Down. Here."

Another wave, and something more solid than a hand bumped the boat.

The cage crashed to the deck, bouncing off the rope that lay coiled at Greg's feet as he crossed himself.

"What the blessed hell are you doing down here?" Brandon stopped in front of Greg, his eyes the only thing visible beneath his slicker's hood and the scarf he'd wrapped high around his face.

The rush of saliva was an early warning sign that the rolling in Greg's stomach shouldn't be ignored.

In a quick move, he spun toward the side, away from the hand, and heaved, his body desperate to rid itself of that image, of what it meant.

When he was done, he wiped his chin with his sleeve, a sour taste still lingering on his tongue. "There's a body."

"What?" Brandon yelled it like he thought the wind might have twisted the words into something that couldn't be possible.

"There's a body," Greg said again, pointing to where he'd last seen the fingers trailing along the red bottom, clutching at it, begging for help that was coming far too late.

Finally, the younger man caught on.

When Brandon glanced back toward Greg after peering over the side, there was a hardness in his eyes that Greg recognized. Young men around here were like that. Had to pretend to be tough, even when they were scared shitless. "Let's get it up."

They worked together with the efficiency they'd mastered hauling in cages up and down Maine's coastline. Brandon was the one to grab the fingers first, in an obscene parody of hand holding.

Greg plunged his own glove into the water, searching for something to latch onto.

Water-swollen flesh gave beneath his fingers, and he gripped it tight so it wouldn't disintegrate. "Got it. Pull up."

Brandon nodded once and then wrenched his arm back at the same time Greg hauled what he presumed to be the body's thigh up and over the slight lip of the boat.

They staggered beneath the sea-laden weight of their burden before dropping it to the deck. The head bounced against the same rope the lobster cage had earlier when it had slipped from Greg's numb fingers.

"Hell." Brandon hadn't let go of the body's hand but took three shuffling steps back to avoid it landing on his feet.

"You can let go," Greg said quietly, watching Brandon's face, where a determined mask had slipped into place. "You can let go."

It took another moment, another deep, shuddering breath, before Brandon let the body's arm fall to the deck.

There was a sickening thud as the limb slapped against the hard plastic.

Only then did Greg get his first good look. It was a man on the younger side. Thirties maybe. Late twenties. Though his face was puffy, he looked familiar. Not an islander. But not a stranger.

No other defining features stood out, no tattoos or deformities. Just an average guy with apparently shit luck.

"We better call the mainland," Greg said.

The body lurched to the side as a wave slammed into the boat, and Brandon finally lost the contents of his stomach to the ocean.

CHAPTER ONE

Mia

Black Rock Bay, Maine
Thursday, January 17

Detective Mia Hart sank deeper into the warmth of her field jacket as the ferry's engine roared its displeasure with the choppy bay. It had always been tradition for her to stand at the bow and watch St. Lucy's come into sight, no matter the time of year or how painful the weather.

"You're insane," Detective Izzy Santiago yelled as she came shoulder to shoulder with Mia. Izzy was off-balance as only a kid raised nowhere near a boat could be, and she bumped into Mia with each wave.

"Go back inside," Mia urged her partner. "I won't think any less of you, I promise."

As Izzy angled her bare and vulnerable face away from the wind, she shivered beneath a thin winter coat that was useless against Black Rock Bay's merciless bite.

"We're almost there, right?" Izzy asked, ignoring Mia's suggestion.

Mia traced the blade-thin scar on her wrist through layers of gloves and jackets and long johns before turning her eyes back in the direction of St. Lucy's. "Yes."

Even as she spoke, the Bell mansion, which sat as an imposing sentry on the island's northern cliffs, began to take shape, cutting through the thick mist that had settled into Black Rock Bay. Soon they would be able to see the lighthouse to the west.

A briny tang hung heavily in the air, coating Mia's nostrils as she inhaled, and she concentrated on the soft expansion of her lungs instead of the way her skin suddenly felt too tight stretched across her bones.

It had been fifteen years since she'd been back to St. Lucy's, yet she could still count the seconds it would take for the smooth, white slope of the lighthouse to emerge from behind the jut of cliffs after the ferry passed the mansion.

Izzy whistled, low and impressed, when it came into sight, the water-slick black rocks lending a bleak, ominous look to the scene. "It's like a scary postcard."

Mia laughed, amusement cutting off the anxiety that had been coiling in the depths of her belly, winding tighter with each minute they crept closer.

Izzy was good for that, easing the tension. They'd been partners for only about two months, ever since the woman had transferred up from Dallas under apparently less-than-ideal circumstances, but Mia liked her.

She was a few years younger than Mia's own thirty-one and about half a foot taller than her. She was loud and sarcastic, often leaning into the self-deprecation that was the cornerstone of her humor. Her spiky pink hair, tattoos, and piercings had proved to be an asset more often than not, letting them blend into places where Mia struggled not to look like a cop.

And Mia was endlessly entertained by the born-and-raised Texan discovering the delights of winter in Maine.

"I didn't pack right, did I?" Izzy asked as the channel into port created a particularly vicious wind tunnel. "I'm going to freeze this entire time, and you're just going to sit there and laugh at me."

"Go back inside."

Again Izzy didn't listen. "We're meeting the coroner at the ferry landing?"

"Yes." Although "coroner" was a generous term. St. Lucy's was so small that it didn't have basic emergency services like a police department or a dedicated medical examiner. Sammy Bowdoin, whom Mia still thought of as Stoner Sammy B., the island's doctor/veterinarian/coroner, had been able to write up a basic report on the body the local fishermen had pulled from the bay, but it was rudimentary at best. From what Mia could tell, Sammy hadn't even gotten dental records or fingerprints back yet to make an official ID, and if the vic had been carrying a driver's license, it had been lost to the sea. They knew who he was only because Sammy had recognized him from the time he'd spent on the island.

Robert Twist. The name was one of the few concrete details they had in the case. Twist was a small-time journalist who had, according to Sammy, arrived on St. Lucy's sometime before Christmas, then disappeared a few weeks later. No one on the island probably would have given him a second thought had his body not been dragged onto that fishing boat.

The rest of the information they had was bare bones, at best.

Mia had called the magazine Twist usually pitched to, and the editor there hadn't been able to give them anything more than what they already knew. The man was a freelancer, and the place was small enough that they didn't pay for expenses beforehand. Twist hadn't even hinted at what he was working on or why he was going out of town.

"He's pretty secretive," the editor had told Mia. "Paranoid someone's going to scoop him."

But there was secretive, and then there was their vic.

Twist didn't have an emergency contact on file with the company, and a search for a family member or friend turned up zilch. In fact, the man's digital footprint was almost nonexistent, save for a website with a simple listing of his articles. None of the outlets he worked with even had a picture of the guy. The best they'd been able to find was a years-old pixelated snapshot. For what it was worth in the modern world, they might as well have been hunting a ghost.

Frustrating as it was, the dead ends gave Mia something to focus on apart from the burning, acidic knot that had pulsed beneath her breastbone ever since Gina Murdoch, Rockport's police chief, had handed over the Twist case, eyes dark and watchful as Mia took the file.

Mia's thumb found her scar once more, a weak attempt at self-soothing.

"Do you think it was murder or suicide?" Izzy asked.

Mia's mind tripped, caught in the past for half a heartbeat, her nail digging into the skin at her wrist. "What?"

"Twist." Izzy bounced beside Mia, her voice distant and considering, seemingly oblivious of the stumble. "I mean, if it looks like a suicide, swims like a suicide, quacks like a suicide . . ."

She waved her hand to fill in the rest. *Then it was suicide.*

Dropping her hands so that she could rest her forearms on the ferry's railing, Mia stared down at the dark water that lapped at the bow.

They'd had this conversation already but always ended up in the same place. Still, Mia was willing to go through it again. Sometimes the repetition helped.

"Gunshot through the soft palate's not exactly common for homicides."

"Right." Izzy touched her nose, pointed at Mia, and then cursed, shoving her hands back into her pockets. "But, the ocean."

The ocean. That part niggled at Mia, burrowing under her skin, an annoyance she couldn't ignore. And, God, did she want to ignore it.

If Twist had killed himself, as it looked like on first glance, they could easily wrap up the case, fill out the proper forms, do their due diligence—and then get the hell off St. Lucy's before Mia had to deal with all the reasons she'd left in the first place.

Suicide. That's all it would take, a simple ruling. Her body leaned into it with an eagerness Mia couldn't trust.

But. The ocean.

"How'd he end up there?" Mia whispered, as though if she said it quietly enough maybe the question would go away, maybe Izzy would forget that little detail, maybe Mia would.

"In a thin undershirt and trousers," Izzy filled in, because of course she remembered her lines to this particular conversation. It was this discrepancy that punched a hole in their beautifully constructed suicide theory.

Maybe Twist had been drunk enough to explain the lack of proper clothing. Alcohol wasn't called a liquor jacket by college kids everywhere for no reason. But if he *had* been planning on shooting himself, wouldn't he have just stayed inside the cabin? Why would he have gone outside in the cold anyway?

Mia didn't have an answer yet, though she knew Izzy was getting restless. Maybe they were thinking too much like the cold-case detectives they were, making things complicated where they didn't need to be. Maybe their leaps of logic were unsupported by the circumstances. Maybe they needed to step back. Like Izzy said, it looked like suicide, and it probably was suicide.

For now, though, their hands were tied. They hadn't even seen the body yet, let alone gotten a feel for any of the rest of the evidence. Until they got a better handle on it all, there was little else to debate. Murder or suicide? It was too early to make the call.

Izzy knew it, too, Mia knew, because this was where the conversation ended. She pivoted, as she had every time they'd reached the impasse before. "So what's the game plan, boss?"

It was something else they'd gone over a dozen times, but Mia didn't mind. She wondered if it was a particular tic with Izzy, or if the woman was trying to find her footing, feeling a bit untethered by the general lack of information in the case.

"We'll talk to the seaplane pilot," Mia said. "This ferry only runs once a month, so the reporter probably had plans to get off the island somehow. Or he was booked to be on this one, and we'll be able to get the records for that."

"If his departure was planned for anytime soon, maybe the killer was trying to stop him from leaving St. Lucy's?" Izzy easily followed Mia's train of thought.

"We'll also want to check out the cabin he was renting. If we're lucky, we'll be able to access his computer or notes."

If Twist's death had been a homicide, his notes could at least give them a place to start for a motive.

Mia bit her lip. Knowing why Twist had come to the island, what sore spots he'd been poking, would have been helpful. Going in blind was unsettling, another handicap when they would already have enough trouble getting anyone on St. Lucy's to talk to them.

People on the island didn't like outlanders, didn't trust them, especially not someone who was snooping around and getting in their business.

Give or take a birth or a death, there were about only two hundred people who lived on St. Lucy's year-round, so the community was a tight one.

In the summer, there was an influx of artists who came and took up space and were barely tolerated despite the money they poured into the town before they left at the first signs of fall. But spending a few warm months on the island didn't make you one of them.

Mia wasn't sure growing up there for sixteen years would hold much water anymore, either.

It did mean that out of anyone on the squad, she was the one who stood the best chance of pulling any information from them. Really, Mia shouldn't have been put on the investigation. She knew it, Murdoch probably knew it, and, before long, Izzy would as well. Beyond Mia's personal history with the island, this type of death wasn't even their forte. They worked cold cases, she and Izzy—reading people, plucking out mostly forgotten memories, navigating lies and false narratives constructed out of desperation and weak alibis. That was their expertise. Not this . . . this . . . whatever this turned out to be.

But these people were hers. If anyone spoke their language, if anyone stood the slightest chance in getting them to talk, it was Mia.

She and Izzy stood at the rail in silence as the small port finally came into view. Squat, colorful houses fanned out from the docks, the bright facades a welcome home for the fishers who spent the rough days at sea. Most of the island's population lived in the little village, and the tight cluster gave the illusion that the rest of St. Lucy's was similarly built up.

Beyond the town's center, though, only forest stretched until the lighthouse to the west, until the Bell mansion in the north. The trees were ashy, their trunks gnarled and weathered, and she used to pretend fairies lived in the pockets of space beneath their moss-drenched roots. She knew each path through the woods, the shortcut to the edge of the cliffs, the meadow that was nothing but dandelion fluff in the summertime. She knew the abandoned hut that stood on the southern tip, knew that no matter how many times you were dared to go into it alone, you knew you shouldn't. She knew her name was carved on the underside of the third pew in the one-room church. She knew this place. It was hers, just like the people were.

The ferry was close enough now to make out the individual buildings. The post office, the grocer's on the corner of Main Street, the diner next to Mrs. Winslow's pale peach bungalow. It had been fifteen years, and beyond a fresh coat of paint or two, nothing had changed.

That's how it was on the island. Time stretched and bent and became meaningless beyond how many hours could be spent on the ocean. When she'd been a teenager, it had driven Mia mad. There was a world out there that was moving forward, for good or bad, but moving nonetheless.

Now there was an ache in her chest that she didn't want to name. It wasn't nostalgia, because there was nothing golden or sweet about it. It was threaded through with resentment and fear and a vicious darkness that ravaged any lingering warm emotion.

And yet, still, that ache was familiar.

Home. She was finally home.

———

"Mia Hart, all grown up," Sammy Bowdoin said when he spotted her and Izzy on the docks. He went in for the hug just as Mia held out her hand to shake his, and her knuckles brushed against his chest while his arms froze midair.

The awkwardness passed as quickly as it came. Sammy grinned and clapped a hand on her shoulder, the easy warmth still in his voice, despite whatever professional distance Mia had just worked to put between them. "Big fancy police detective you are, then?"

There was no bitter edge to Sammy's words, not like she'd get from some people around here. For many of the locals, moving to the mainland, wanting something in life beyond the rough existence St. Lucy's offered, was a deep betrayal.

But Sammy was still smiling, so Mia decided to take the words at face value.

"You're one to talk, Dr. Bowdoin," she said lightly, before turning to include Izzy in the conversation. "Sammy, this is Detective Isabel Santiago. She'll be working the case with me."

"Izzy," her partner corrected, holding out a gloved hand.

Sammy's smile turned tight at the corners, the warmth immediately gone. The reaction was predictable and tiresome, but it also wasn't the complete cold shoulder Izzy would get from others. "Welcome to St. Lucy's."

If Izzy noticed the new emptiness to his voice, she ignored it. "Thanks, Doc."

Grabbing the bags from where Mia and Izzy had dropped them, Sammy jerked his head back toward the village. "You're staying at your mama's, right? Do you want to stop there first or see the body?"

"The body," Mia answered without hesitation. She had no interest in hastening that particular reunion. If there'd been a hotel on the island, Mia would have been staying there instead. But the rental options were limited, and one of the few there were had just become a crime scene. They were stuck with Edie Hart's hospitality.

"Course." Sammy started up the hill.

None of them tried to speak further above the wind, as they ducked their heads to fight through the gusts. Sammy took a left off Main Street, and they followed him to a mint-green one-story house that sat at the end of the side road.

They unbundled in the mudroom, stripping layers down until their bodies had shapes beyond vague lumps of fabric.

It was then Mia got her first good look at Sammy. Time had left him alone, for the most part, just like the rest of the island. Except for a few laugh lines, he looked nearly the same as he had in high school, his light brown hair just starting to go silver at the temples, his mouth too wide for his face, his nostrils a bit too flared.

When they'd been younger, he'd been the kind of kid who didn't have close friends but was welcome into any group when he showed up. Partially because he'd always been generous with his joints, sloppy and questionable though they were. Mia hadn't indulged, but sometimes Asher and Cash had, as they spread out on the rocks by the lighthouse, watching stars, their normally clipped cadence turning to molasses as they laughed at nothing.

Sammy's lips twitched beneath her appraisal, and then he was moving on like he always had, never really standing still long enough to be known.

"Back here," Sammy said with a nod toward the hallway. "Welcome to my jack-of-all-trades office."

She fell in behind him, with Izzy trailing. "Do you live here, too?"

"Nah, I took the floor-through apartment above the diner." He pointed toward the wall of the house that was in the direction they'd just come. "Frankly, I don't get a lot of dead bodies in here, but when I do, I don't quite fancy spending more time with them than necessary."

"Hasn't been a murder on St. Lucy's in how long?" Mia asked. Murder wasn't the only way dead bodies turned up on the medical examiner's table, but they both decided to ignore that particular elephant in the room. She couldn't stop her thumb from rubbing over her scar, though.

"Sixty years," Sammy said. "I think it was a domestic. Wife shot the husband after she found another woman in the bed."

"A bit cliché," Izzy called out from behind them.

Sammy glanced back, his eyes hooded. "You need your murders to be original, then?" In a different tone, the words might have been a joke. But it was clear he wasn't teasing her.

Mia pressed her lips together, knowing she should have warned Izzy this was how it would be. They'd twist anything Izzy said to find fault with it just because she was an outsider.

Izzy's footsteps faltered behind Mia, but there was nothing much to say to that. The uncomfortable silence stretched until they got to what was clearly the makeshift morgue.

The sterile equipment, metal examination table, and two side-by-side cold chambers to house bodies were all incongruous with the cozy, floral-printed wallpaper and the lace curtains on the window. For some reason, the contrast of it all fit the Sammy she remembered.

"My predecessor had these custom built a while ago," Sammy said as he gripped one of the thick handles of the cold chambers and pulled. Mia got a quick glimpse of brown hair before the whole tray slid out.

Robert Twist.

Mia tried to cover her rough inhale, but Sammy's eyes were immediately on her face. "Not a pretty sight, huh? Think he was in the water for a few days."

The words slipped out, unchecked. "It's not that."

Izzy shifted beside her. "What's up?"

The slope of the forehead, the nose that had clearly been broken one too many times. The line of his jaw. They tugged at a memory she barely realized had formed.

She looked up, meeting Izzy's narrowed gaze.

"I didn't expect to recognize him."

CHAPTER TWO

Izzy

Detective Isabel Santiago looked between the dead man's face and Mia's. The color had seeped out of both.

The sea had not been kind to Robert Twist. Though she didn't have a good idea of what he'd looked like before spending time in the ocean, Izzy guessed he'd never been particularly attractive.

He was on the shorter side, with the type of chin that slid off into his neck. His face was concave, the sunken cheeks even more pronounced because of the toll the water and its inhabitants had taken on him. A sharp widow's peak was emphasized by the way his hair was plastered back, caked with sediment.

"You recognize him?" Izzy asked Mia, her mouth suddenly dry. She might have been new to the murder beat, but it didn't exactly seem like a good thing for the lead detective on the case to know the victim. Wishing they were having this conversation in private, Izzy took a step closer so that she was blocking the rude doctor and his eyes that saw too much.

Mia blinked a few times, her mouth twitching as if trying to remember how to form words. Then she took a deep breath, shook her head once, a tiny jerk to the side, and looked up from the dead man sprawled out before them. "I've seen him before. I didn't know him, though."

That, at least, was something. The hollow feeling that had taken up residence beneath her rib cage faded slightly. "Where'd you see him?"

"Outside the station." Mia's composure was completely back, professionalism hiding the confusion. Seeing Mia shaken was odd, but witnessing her ability to slip her mask into place so effortlessly wasn't exactly reassuring, either.

The problem was, Izzy didn't know Mia that well. She was still learning her quirks, her tells, when she wanted to be left the hell alone, and when she wanted to be needled into talking. And Izzy wanted to get it right, because it had been a long time since she'd had a partner she thought was going to last.

She'd been unsure about Mia at first. The woman was tiny, for one. A hundred pounds soaking wet. Izzy had met some women who were short but dense, all muscle, but Mia wasn't like that. Everything about her was delicately built.

The woman was too pretty, on top of it, her dirty-blonde hair cut short, framing a pale, heart-shaped face that was all sleek, straight lines.

She spoke only when the occasion called for it and never went out for beers after work.

The partnership had seemed destined to be chalked up as one more failure in a long list for Izzy. But as they'd worked together, her wariness had evolved quickly into respect, because it soon became painfully clear that Detective Mia Hart was a badass. A classy one. But a badass nonetheless.

That didn't mean Izzy understood her, though. Even now, she looked for any sign of distress or anxiety or fear beneath the smooth exterior and found none.

"You saw him outside the station?" Izzy finally prodded as Mia remained quiet.

"Twice." Mia was quick to answer. "Both times at night. It was like he'd been waiting for me. But he didn't . . . He never approached me."

The last bit was said almost beneath her breath, to herself. Izzy waited.

"I noticed him because he was standing under that busted street-light like he didn't want to be seen clearly," Mia continued, her chin dipping down so that her hair shielded her expression from Izzy's view. "I could, though. See him."

"Well, shit, Mia," Sammy cut in. "That's weird."

Mia looked up at that, the corners of her mouth tilting up in a weak smile. There was no trace of real humor in it. "Yeah."

Izzy nudged the doc. "Did you ever talk to him while he was here?"

"No." The answer was curt, clearly meant to discourage any further questioning, and Izzy wondered if it was because she was a cop, because she wasn't an islander, or because it was just habit. Whatever it was, Izzy suddenly had insight into Murdoch's decision to make Mia the lead on the case.

"He must have stuck out like a sore thumb, huh?" Izzy wasn't deterred. Maybe she didn't have a ton of experience working a murder, but she'd met enough assholes in her life not to be put off by one.

The doc's hackles went up, and Mia shifted beside her. Clearly it had been the wrong thing to say, but Izzy didn't know why. That not knowing made her too itchy and too hot. Most everything about her job came down to being able to figure out why people were reacting the way they were, and when she couldn't do that, the world always seemed just slightly tipped to the side.

"What's that supposed to mean?" The doc's chest had gone all big and broad, and his eyes narrowed, the skin crinkling into crow's-feet at the corners. "Just because he was a big-shot mainland reporter?"

Izzy scratched at the crook of her elbow and studied him before deciding brash was the way to go. It's not like she had a lot of weapons in her personality arsenal, to be fair. Bold and unapologetic was pretty much it. "Um, your island is a tiny blip of land in the middle of Bumblefuck Bay, it's so cold everyone's balls have probably set up permanent residence in their bodies, and, oh yeah, even if anyone was crazy enough to actually want to visit, you can't even get here because the ferry only runs once a month."

She'd been counting on her fingers, but she let her hand drop to her side and leveled him with a glare backed by all the false bravado she could muster. "So how about you drop the act and stop being deliberately obtuse. Because there's a dead guy with a gunshot wound through his head, and somehow he ended up in your bay."

Fighting the urge to blink, Izzy held the doc's stare. He looked away first, his brows raised in Mia's direction.

Her partner had settled back against a counter, her arms crossed over her chest, her face impassive. But when the doc looked at her, Mia shrugged. "She has a point."

The pause that followed was loaded, but then the doctor sighed, and when he spoke, the frostiness that had coated his every word to Izzy had thawed a tiny bit. "I don't know what he was working on. Never talked to the guy."

"But your impression?"

The doc glanced down at Twist. "He was squirrelly."

"Care to define 'squirrelly' for us?" Izzy asked, getting the feeling that descriptor would apply to a broad range of behavior when it came to these people. "Not exactly a technical term."

He lifted a hand in a vague gesture that she couldn't interpret.

"He'd come into the bar most nights. Had a laptop and a bunch of journals, but he'd hide them real fast if anyone tried to sit with him." He wiped his palms against the front of his jeans. "Was poking around the lighthouse a couple times."

Mia coughed. "He was at the lighthouse?"

"Yup."

"Did he . . . ?" Mia trailed off, a distinct crackle at the edge of her voice. "What was he doing there?"

Sammy chewed on his lower lip. "Don't know. Jimmy chased him away."

"Who's that?" Izzy asked, and their gazes snapped to her, as if they'd forgotten she was there. The air was strange and charged, and Izzy was clearly at least three paces behind in the conversation.

"Jimmy Roarke," Sammy said, turning toward her. "Our retired handyman slash contractor slash jack-of-all-trades."

"Does everyone have three or four jobs around here?" So much about this place was foreign to Izzy. Living in Maine, after spending her entire twenty-seven years of life in Dallas, was already a struggle. Everything was harsher—the weather, the accents, the people. They didn't draw out their vowels, and they didn't chat at cash registers, and they didn't know what to do with a six-foot-tall girl with brown skin and a sleeve of tattoos.

She'd be forever grateful to Gina Murdoch for giving her a chance with the job. Izzy had been in a rut at her old station, having stomped on the wrong toes her first week out of training and paying for the misstep for years to follow with shitty shifts and bottom-of-the-barrel partners. When Gina, her father's old friend, told her about a position she had open on her cold-case team—a rarity in this era of budget cuts and speeding tickets—Izzy hadn't thought twice.

It just would have been nice if the job had been somewhere that didn't feel like a different country.

The doc shrugged off her question. "When you have fewer than two hundred people on an island, you have to wear a few hats to make everything work."

"Did Jimmy say how Twist reacted when he was caught at the lighthouse?" Mia asked. There was an intensity to Mia that seemed out of step with the rest of the mood of the interview. The lighthouse. She had started getting weird once the lighthouse was mentioned.

"Nope, just that Jimmy had to chase him off the property." Sammy turned around and grabbed a box of latex gloves, then held them out to both of them.

They all took pairs. Izzy always hated the smell of them and the way they never fit her fingers quite right.

"All right, well, here we go." Sammy bumped Izzy out of the way with his hip. "Robert Twist, TOD sometime between about nine p.m. on Sunday, January sixth and Tuesday, January eighth."

"Why that range?" Izzy interrupted.

"He left the bar at that time on Sunday, which was the last anyone can distinctly remember seeing him," the doc said, in professional mode now. "And there are signs he was in the water for about a week. It could push the time of death to Wednesday, but I'd focus on that tighter window."

"Could he have been held outside for a while and then dumped?" Mia asked. "Would that change anything? Slow down the rate of decomp?"

"That's a little beyond my pay grade." Sammy shrugged. "Could be. That kind of thing might need someone from the mainland."

If this turned out to be a homicide, they'd bring in a professional. But for now . . .

"Best guess?" Izzy pressed.

Sammy's hand hovered near the back of Twist's head before dropping to his side.

"I don't think there was much time between when this wound was created and when he was submerged in salt water."

"Why do you say that?"

"There's no frostbite." Sammy shrugged. "No obvious skin death of that sort. I could be wrong, but I think the salt water staved off any damage from the cold."

"He could have been kept inside, then? And then dumped."

"I guess."

"Apart from the circumstances, are there any obvious signs of foul play?" Mia asked.

"No, not really," Sammy said slowly. "Any gun residue or particulates in the wound that might have shown otherwise are long gone."

Izzy had guessed that would be the case. "What do you think?"

The doc tilted his head to each side, clearly hesitant. "The wound is consistent with what you would see if it was self-inflicted."

Which was what both Izzy and Mia had concluded time and again.

But the idea still didn't make sense to Izzy. "But how did his body get in the water if he was planning on shooting himself? Was he too close to the cliffs when he did it, and his body fell? Why would he have been out there in the first place if he was just going to kill himself with a gun?"

Rocking back on his heels, Sammy lifted one shoulder in a lazy shrug. "In case the gun didn't do the trick?"

She couldn't tell if he was being serious or if it was some poor attempt at humor, but she shook her head anyway. There would be no reason for Twist to double up like that.

"Can you get his blood alcohol levels? That long after death?"

"It's not reliable." Sammy stretched an arm out to grab the file from the counter. He flipped it open, his eyes scanning over whatever was written. "But yeah, it was sky high. Lends itself to suicide as COD."

Not necessarily. But Izzy for once kept her mouth shut.

"Did you do a full toxicology report?" Mia asked.

Sammy tossed the chart back where it had been. "Sent it off to the state. Should get it back in a few days."

"So if his BAC was through the roof, that could explain the cliffs," Mia said. "He was drunk, wandered outside with his gun, shot himself. His body ended up in the ocean."

As Mia spoke, Sammy nodded along, his hands shoved in his pockets.

Izzy could see it to an extent. Drunk guys were notorious for doing stupid things.

The thing was, Izzy knew setups. She'd orchestrated more than her fair share in vice—had been the would-be victim of more than she could count, too. They were hard to pull off perfectly, usually with a sloppy detail or two coming back to bite someone in the ass. A discordant note, something jarring enough to pause over, even if it wasn't enough to make an arrest.

That's what this scene felt like.

Maybe her perception was colored by the fact that she would never willingly go outside in that kind of weather in nothing other than a T-shirt and jeans no matter how many sheets she was to the wind. But it was enough to make her stop, wonder. Doubt. Once that snuck in, it was hard to shake.

"Any defensive injuries?" Izzy asked.

"None that couldn't be explained by his body hitting up against rocks at the base of the cliffs," the doc said.

If it *had* been murder and not suicide, the killer was either smart or lucky. Any marks on the body could be attributed to being in the ocean for a week, and the rest had been cleaned up by the salt water.

"He had no possessions on him?" Mia asked while bending down so that her face was level with the metal table. Izzy mirrored her position on the other side. When Mia tipped Twist's chin toward Izzy to get a look at the gunshot wound in the back of his head, his eyelids slipped up so that Izzy could see the cloudy blue of his irises. She took a half step back, sucking in air as she did.

Working vice in Dallas hadn't exactly been an easy gig—there'd been plenty of dead bodies to stumble over. But Izzy had never liked this part: the absent eyes, the pale skin, the lax expression. She was a cop because she liked puzzles; that was why investigating cold cases was so perfect. The reminder of the fragility of life was a nasty side effect she put up with.

"Nothing on him when the guys—that would be Greg Lawson and Brandon Sonder—pulled him out of the water," Sammy answered from behind them. "Doesn't mean he didn't go in with his wallet or phone."

"Brandon Sonder's new," Mia said, and it didn't seem like a question.

Sammy laughed. "Moved here just after you left. So if you consider being here fifteen years new, then yes."

Mia's teeth flashed—a grin that was quick and real. "Don't you?"

"Of course." Sammy's answering smile was one born from a years-long friendship. "Once an outlander, always an outlander."

That hollow feeling was back, the camaraderie between the two of them unsettling in a way Izzy couldn't quite pinpoint.

Too close, too close, too close. Izzy got why Murdoch had given Mia the file, she did. It was obvious just seeing the difference in how Sammy acted when he was talking to her. Izzy wouldn't have gotten anywhere with these people.

But how were they supposed to work the case? They'd both been cops long enough to know that being too close to an investigation amplified all your blind spots.

It was already happening. Izzy could tell Mia wanted to latch onto Sammy's suicide explanation, despite the holes in the scenario, despite the impasse they'd reached earlier on the ferry. Suicide or murder? Not enough evidence to tell, they'd decided countless times.

When had that changed? Was it when Mia had recognized the man? Or was it that she had an ally backing the suicide theory?

"All right." Mia straightened, moving away from the body as she did. "That's a good start. We'll head over to Mama's now, drop our bags. I have your number in the file if we need anything else."

"Sure. I'll be here till six, then will probably dip into the bar for a beer. If you two are in the mood, stop by."

Mia nodded, but it seemed like a dismissal more than anything else. "Thanks."

They all peeled off their gloves, then Mia headed toward the hallway, back to their layers of coats and sweaters and scarves.

Just before they stepped out of the small room, Izzy turned back. "Oh, one more question, Doc."

Sammy paused while sliding Robert Twist's body back into the cold chamber. "Yeah?"

"Was there a suicide note?" It seemed odd that they wouldn't have mentioned it in the report if there had been, but she had to ask.

Sammy's gaze shifted to a spot beyond Izzy's shoulder, where Mia must have stopped, and then returned to Izzy's face. "No."

There it was again. Izzy on the outside, while the two of them had entire conversations with just a look. She knew she was missing something, and it made her fingers twitchy.

When she glanced toward Mia, the woman was already heading down the hallway back toward their gear.

"Hey," she said when she caught up. Mia's hand was tangled up in the arm of her jacket as she tried to shove her foot into one of her boots.

Izzy kept her voice pitched low so that Sammy wouldn't be able to hear even if he was lurking in the hallway. "What was that about?"

Mia's eyes flicked over Izzy's face, and then she sighed, bringing her arm up to her chest, over her heart. She cradled her wrist with her other hand, her thumb stroking the exposed sliver of skin.

"I didn't leave a suicide note, either."

CHAPTER THREE

MIA

The house on Baker Street was pale petal pink with a sunny yellow door. A summer garden, Mia used to think while dragging her fingertips along the edge of the siding before racing toward the woods in the back.

Now, in the gray mist that foretold a rumbling storm, it just seemed sad.

Izzy hovered behind Mia where she'd stopped on the sidewalk, impatience radiating off her in swooping waves that crashed onto Mia's back.

Mia had managed to convince Izzy that the entryway into Sammy's morgue wasn't the place to talk further about suicide notes, but she doubted she'd bought herself much time.

She couldn't think about that now, though. She had to concentrate on making herself take a step toward the house.

That ache was back, the one that was a tangled mess of emotions she couldn't quite name.

Home.

It had been fifteen years since she'd stood on this sidewalk, since she'd walked through that door. Sweat gathered at her hairline despite the cold. *Flee,* her body begged.

"Is that little Mia Hart?" a voice called from somewhere to her right. Mia flinched as sound beyond the buzzing in her own ears returned to the world.

In the dim, fading light of an already-dark day, it was hard to make out more than just a shape standing on the stoop of the house next to Mama's. But Mia knew who it was. "Mrs. Edwards." She lifted a hand in a small wave, then moved toward the house, keeping her head down.

"You home then, dear?" Natalie Edwards had never been one to be deterred from good gossip.

"A few days." Mia stopped on the porch. Knocking wouldn't be appropriate, not on the door of her childhood home. But walking right in after being gone for more than a decade felt wrong, too. Unsure what to do, Mia froze while Natalie's eyes devoured her every hesitancy.

"For that man who ended up in the ocean, I suppose," Natalie called.

Mia pivoted just a bit at the question, the delay almost welcome. "You ever see him around, Mrs. Edwards?"

"We all did, didn't we?" Natalie said in that universally noncommittal way everyone on the island seemed to be born knowing how to do. "A nosy so-and-so."

Izzy shifted beside her as if she were considering going over and interviewing Natalie. "Did you ever talk to him?"

Natalie's gaze flicked to Mia before returning to Izzy, and the pause before she answered felt like a lie in and of itself. "About the weather if I saw him in the shop. Nothing more."

"Who did he speak to?" Mia tried.

"Oh, he tried to talk to everyone, dear." Natalie's shoulders relaxed, her fingers loosening. Back in the comfortable safety of vague answers. "No one was too keen on chatting to him, though."

That, Mia believed. "He never mentioned what he was working on?"

Again, Natalie tensed, her eyes on Mia's face. "He was real secretive, that one. Not that I'm one to speak ill of the dead."

"Squirrelly, you might say," Izzy muttered, low enough so only Mia would hear her.

Mia swallowed a short laugh. "Okay, thank you. If you remember anything else in specific . . . ?"

Natalie flapped a hand in their direction like a promise, but it was one Mia knew was fake. Still, the little exchange had burned off enough of the anxiety holding her hostage that she was able to finally open the door to Mama's house and slip into the dark entryway.

An empty silence pressed against Mia. It was the kind that came with an abandoned house, even though she knew Mama was there.

Izzy followed in behind her. "So everyone's a nosy busybody in this place, or just her?"

Grateful for Izzy's light tone, Mia smiled and then started the long process of shucking off her boots and other layers. Izzy followed suit. "It's a fine balance. They want to know all the gossip but not have to actually give any of their own."

"Yeah, I'm getting that vibe."

Once they were down to jeans and long shirts, Mia nodded toward the kitchen, where she knew Mama was waiting for them. The passive-aggressiveness of the nongreeting was the steel in Mama's spine that kept her upright.

The lights in the hallway were dimmed, the walls lined with photos. Most were the kind that kids were forced to take at school, the ones with jewel-colored backdrops and dead eyes. But there were a few candids scattered throughout as well.

Mia stopped in front of one of her, Asher Lowe, and Cash Bishop.

The three of them were laughing, no space between their bodies to tell where one ended and the next began. Their hips bumped, and their arms knew nothing of personal boundaries as they grasped each other's waists with careless hands.

Her eyes caught on her own face, tipped up as it was toward Cash. There was a desperation, a raw hunger, in the way she had been looking at him that now flushed her cheeks hot. Back then he'd been the only thing she could see.

He, on the other hand, was looking into the camera, the hints of a handsome face lurking beneath a baby fat softness that had lingered into teenage years. She studied his lean frame, the stance that was steeped in a confidence that came from the money in his family's bank account.

She'd known that body then almost as well as her own.

Mia's gaze slid to Asher without permission, and her throat fluttered closed, a breath caught just on the wrong side.

The picture had been taken in the summer, a few months before he'd killed himself. They'd been sixteen, giddy and reckless and cocky, thinking that being on the brink of adulthood actually meant something. Those days had been slow, syrupy, and happy in a way Mia often forgot she'd ever been.

It was the first summer she and Cash had been officially together, clumsily altering the dynamic between the three of them without much thought to Asher.

But the bigger change had come in the form of the Bell girls.

From the beginning of June until the end of August, the Bell family took up residence in the mansion on the north cliffs, which they let stand empty the rest of the year. During that time, they hosted an artist colony, and St. Lucy's was flooded with dozens of hippies who had perpetual paint smears on their hands, flowers in their hair, and a loose grasp of appropriate public behavior.

Mia, Asher, and Cash had never paid them much attention while growing up. They existed as part of the landscape, to be ridiculed, yes, but mostly to be ignored.

That year, though, the Bells had brought their two teenage daughters with them. Lacey and Monroe.

The girls had shown up, all glossy black hair and blue eyes and curves in the places that they were supposed to be. The older one, Monroe, had caught Asher's eye, and so, more often than not, the sisters would tag along, and their trio expanded to five.

They'd spent their days at the lighthouse, sunning on the black rocks at its base, and their nights passing joints and bottles, and once, just once, some heavier drugs the girls had swiped out of one of the artist's rooms.

They weren't inseparable. Sometimes it would just be Mia and Cash who'd crept out past curfew, and on those nights they'd bring blankets and curl up in the lookout tower, their limbs tangling, lips seeking each other's—unpracticed, yet eager.

But most of the time it had been all of them, killing days that had felt like they'd last forever. Seconds, minutes, hours, they'd moved differently then, when all she'd been able to think about was getting off the island that too often seemed like a cage.

In the picture on Mama's wall, Asher was laughing just as Mia and Cash were, but he wasn't looking at the person behind the camera, and he wasn't looking at the two of them, either.

Instead, his gaze was somewhat off to the left. Mia didn't remember the actual day the photo was taken; it was more a snapshot of a moment in time than an actual memory. But she guessed Asher must have been looking at Monroe, with Lacey behind the lens.

Izzy sniffed, overloud in the quiet house, and Mia was no longer in that rose gold–tinted summer before everything went to hell. Instead, she was frozen in the hallway, her pulse thrumming far too fast for just standing still, with her partner watching her, concern cutting a deep line between her eyebrows.

"Sorry." Mia cleared her throat, making sure not to look back at the photo.

"Your friends?" Izzy asked as they started walking again, their socks muffling their footsteps against the hardwood.

"Used to be," Mia said right before they stepped into the kitchen.

It was tiny, like the rest of the house. Outdated, like the rest of the island.

Mama stood in front of an old, baby blue gas-top stove that had been the main feature of the room before Mia's birth. A radio on the counter by the porcelain sink played some country song, and Mama sang along softly, pretending not to hear them come in.

Mia exhaled. "Mama. We're here."

It took another few tries before Edie Hart spun, her hand clutching at her apron, manufactured surprise on her face.

"You actually came," Mama said, her voice flat, before she switched off the stove and slid the cast-iron pan to the back burner.

"I told you I was," Mia said, and before they could devolve into bickering, she gestured toward Izzy. "Mama, this is Detective Izzy Santiago. Izzy, this is Edie Hart."

Mama's gaze slipped over Izzy's lean and lanky frame, taking in the pink undercut, the nose stud, the row of earrings, her light brown skin, and the ink that disappeared up along her forearm underneath the pushed-up arms of her flannel shirt. "Are you a lesbian?"

"Mama." Mia sighed.

But Izzy just laughed. "Why, yes I am."

Edie nodded once and then turned back to the stove. "You'll be in the den. There's blankets and pillows out there already. Mia, same goes for your room."

For a second, Mia wished she and her mother were the type to reach out, hug, kiss cheeks. It had been at least seven months since Mama had been to the mainland for one of her rare visits. But that kind of affection had never been a part of their lives.

So instead of pressing the issue, Mia turned and led the way toward the room across from the study, where Izzy would sleep.

"Will we still be able to talk to the pilot today?" Izzy asked.

"Probably not." The light in the room had lost any golden hue. The days were no shorter here than they were on the mainland, but somehow it seemed like they were. The island had a funny way of distorting time like that.

"Well," Izzy drawled. "Then you have plenty of time to tell me about that little bomb you dropped back at the doc's."

Mia swallowed. The suicide note. *The lighthouse.*

She hadn't been back since that night. But she wouldn't be able to keep the story secret from Izzy for long. *Shouldn't.*

Might as well rip the Band-Aid off. "All right. Grab your coat."

The lighthouse came into view at the same time the sea did.

It was a simple building, a one-story house and then a phallic thrust of stone into air. Painted white, it stood as a reclusive lookout against the nothingness of the world that was beyond the slick black rocks below it.

When Mia had been young, very young, it had conjured up images of explorers setting off to untamed lands, not knowing if death or untold fortune would be their reward.

As she got older, it became a space that protected her rebellion, held it carefully within its walls, and never let it slip out to be devoured by town gossips.

She'd had sex for the first time in the tower, on a Bishop family quilt, her skin sticky from the salt that had dried after their swim earlier in the day.

She'd stood at the railing and touched flasks with Asher, who had lost his virginity three days before her.

She'd watched the sun set and the sun rise and the storms roll in through the glass panes that had been warped and distorted with age.

She'd cut her wrist in the living room of that house, the razor sting-
ing against skin that gave way beneath blade far too easily. She didn't
remember anything else about that day, but she did remember the slice
of metal against flesh. How simple it had been. Too simple.

The lighthouse.

Her cheeks were wet, and she swiped at them with her gloves, only
then realizing she'd come to a stop. Izzy didn't say anything, just let
her be.

"We came out here all the time," Mia said as the wind howled and
tried to steal her words, tried to inhale them for itself, greedy and selfish
as it was. "That night was no different."

What would she even be able to say? Mia didn't know, so she started
forward once more. There was an open expanse—a meadow in the summertime but a desolate plain in winter—between where they stood at
the line of the trees and the small structure on the very edge of the land.

Her head down, Mia pressed forward against the gusts off the
ocean. The wind cut through the layers of clothing, biting at her skin
despite her efforts to protect it. There would be no more talking until
they escaped the weather.

The door was locked, but she knew where the key was hidden. The
third rock in the space that was meant to house a garden. She would
have broken the window if she had to. But thankfully, like everything
else, the hiding space hadn't changed.

The silence of the room was stark after the roar of the wind.

The place was small, with a dust-coated green sofa facing a fireplace
that must not have been used in years. There were maps on the wall,
tinted a tea color and framed like they were actually worth something.

They'd huddled there, they must have. She and Monroe and Asher.
What had they talked about? What had those last words been?

Whenever she tried too hard to reach for them, she was met with
a thick, impenetrable fog.

Mia's stomach clenched and heaved, and she was thankful she hadn't eaten anything that day, because bile she could swallow down. Her ulcer throbbed beneath her breastbone, but the pain was almost welcome as she stared at the floor where her friends had dragged razor blades across their wrists. Where their blood had slid from their bodies only to be absorbed by the hungry wood of the floor.

The stains were still there, copper and clinging to the boards. Or was she imagining it? She was probably imagining it.

Izzy brushed by her, headed toward one of the windows. She was silhouetted by the light pouring through it, her tall, lanky frame a dark shadow that betrayed no reactions.

The move was purposeful, and Mia was pulled back to the present.

"The Bell family owns the mansion at the other side of the island," Mia started, because if nothing else, it was a place to start.

Izzy whistled low. "That huge one?"

"Yes." Mia's eyes tracked to the window as if she could see it. "The Bells always came in the summer, left by fall. Before winter."

"Can't blame them for that," Izzy said, an overdramatic shiver unsettling her body, which she'd otherwise been holding unnaturally still.

Mia huffed a small breath, then continued: "The Bells had never brought their daughters until that summer."

Izzy had gone quiet again. Maybe because she'd heard the tremble in Mia's voice.

"Monroe was the older one, my age at the time. Lacey was only a year younger," Mia continued, tripping only slightly over the names. "Monroe dated one of my best friends. Asher Lowe. They killed themselves here."

Hooking the tip of her finger into her glove, Mia then pressed on the scar there. "And I tried to, as well."

The shifting light protected Izzy's reaction, kept it hidden. Just like she'd planned. There was a sharpness to her voice, though, that wasn't usually there. "You had to watch your friends die?"

Mia's gaze slid back to the floor. "I don't remember it," she said, an answer that wasn't really an answer to the question Izzy had asked. "At all. I'm told it's common for traumatic events."

She didn't bother mentioning that she'd seen the aftermath—Asher and Monroe's bodies, their limbs at such odd angles.

"None of it?" Izzy asked as if she could hear a hint of all the things Mia hadn't told her.

"Afterward," Mia said. "But. Everything else is . . ."

Izzy just waited, and Mia almost wished she wasn't so patient, so she could be prodded into speaking instead of having to admit it herself. Izzy would find out eventually, anyway.

"Everything else is gone. That entire day."

Silence dropped for a beat.

"What do you remember?" Izzy asked then, because she was a good cop.

"Running out of the lighthouse." Mia tipped her head in the direction of the door. "Lacey found me. That's the first thing I remember."

"Lacey? The younger sister?"

"Yes," Mia said. "She was coming to meet up with us, and she found me." That part was clear—Lacey grabbing onto her arms, her fingers digging in, jagged nails catching flesh that was smeared with blood.

"We came back in and found them," Mia continued. She and Lacey had run toward the lighthouse, their thighs bunching, their feet pounding against the uneven ground. Why could she still feel the burn of it, the pull of tendons and ligaments, but couldn't picture how she and Asher and Monroe had sat on the floorboards?

"It was too late," Mia finished, though Izzy would know that from the outcome. Their cuts were too deep.

Mia stopped in front of the fireplace mantel. There was a jewel-encrusted box that sat on top of an ivory ledge. They'd stored their joints there. Sammy Bowdoin and Asher and Cash.

She rubbed her fingertip over one of the pearls that lined its seams.

"Is that all?" Izzy asked.

Pale bodies caught in moonlight. Dark hair spilling over a blood-drained face. Asher's slumped form, his eyes closed like he was sleeping.

Her own skin had been slick, and she'd tried pressing the bottom of her shirt against the wound to stop the flow. Nothing in her had screamed to let it be, to let the life seep out of her, slowly and surely.

So why had she dragged the razor across her wrist? Why had any of them?

The fog slinked in, obscuring even the details she *knew*, she *knew* she remembered.

Mia nodded, almost forgetting the question. *Is that all?* Yes. Yes.

"I was expecting more." Izzy shifted, but she was still leaning against the windowsill, her face mostly hidden.

"They called it a suicide pact." Mia shrugged, as if nonchalant, as if the night hadn't ruptured the very fabric of her being despite the fact that she couldn't remember any of it. She'd talked about this before, with the cops, with therapists, with Mama—though the last one had been filled with uncomfortable arm pats and loaded silences.

When Izzy didn't say anything, Mia licked her lips. "I left the morning after it happened. My aunt lives in Portland. I went to stay with her."

Izzy's fingers drummed against her thigh, an uneven beat. "How long did that last?"

Mia laughed, without humor. She didn't like to think about that time. Didn't like to think about any of this. "A week."

"You must have still been in shock."

That was an understatement. "It was the start of my insomnia," she said, flushing hot despite the fact that Izzy *must* know about it. "I was screaming all the time, too, apparently. Just absolutely out of control. Lena—my aunt—tried to help me. But we barely knew each other."

"What was the breaking point?"

"I locked myself in the bathroom," Mia said, her tongue scraping along the roof of her mouth, finding the ridge there, pressing against it to center herself. More than she hated thinking about it, she hated talking about it. The words were rotten and heavy, and she had to force each one out. "I was trying to claw open my wound."

She held her wrist up, even though her scar was covered.

"I was hospitalized after that," Mia said. That was the word everyone scrambled for. *Hospitalized.*

"Where was your mother?" Izzy asked the obvious question.

Mia shook her head. "She didn't leave the island in those days. The only reason she does now is to see me, and those visits are few and far between."

"Even though you were . . . hospitalized?"

Pretending not to hear the pause, Mia nodded, knowing Izzy wouldn't understand. "She was cleaning up my mess anyway."

Izzy nodded, but Mia could see the impulse to argue still there in the twist of her mouth. She let it die.

"People are going to be . . ." Mia struggled to find the words. She actually didn't know how anyone would react to seeing her again, but she had a good guess. "I'm telling you all this because they might say something. You might hear rumors."

She forced herself to meet Izzy's eyes, her chin up. This was the time for Izzy to bail, if she wanted to.

In the pause that followed, Mia's bones ached with the weight of it all—the confession, the judgment, the nasty gossip that was sure to haunt her as long as she was on the island. The chance that Izzy might change her mind now that she knew the truth. All of it.

Mia had spent so many years keeping these memories at bay, building walls, brick by brick, to prevent the thoughts from digging their claws into fragile skin. The longer she and Izzy were forced to stay on the island, the quicker those defenses would crumble. The darkness that lay beyond those walls terrified her.

It was why Mia didn't ever come back, why she'd stopped talking about that night long ago.

The question of what really had happened that night snuck up on her sometimes—when she was distracted, when she wasn't actively telling herself not to remember—her brain skittering back away from the thought as soon as it caught up. Because she knew, with certainty, that she was terrified of what that answer would be.

Izzy shifted, finally. Cleared her throat. "Yeah, well. Lucky for you, I don't scare off easily."

CHAPTER FOUR

Izzy

Mia had stopped seeming small to Izzy months ago, despite her petite frame. But standing in the middle of the lighthouse, her eyes on the floor, she was nothing if not delicate, fragile, vulnerable.

That starved, desperate quality that had settled into her body over the past few weeks was more pronounced than Izzy had seen before, even with the heavy layers of winter gear.

Izzy sighed. She didn't want to kick someone when they were down, but she needed to clear the air. Mia was already too close, her judgment too compromised, just from having to investigate people she grew up with. Add trauma to that, and it became a knife's edge, one wrong move toppling them in the wrong direction.

"All right," Izzy said. "You should have told me all this days ago when we got the case. We can treat it as spilled milk and water under the bridge and all that jazz. But you can't keep anything from me like that again."

Mia had stilled and was watching her closely. The disorientation of the first few minutes of the lighthouse had faded, and she was once again composed and unreadable, cool, assessing.

A flipped switch and all the walls had come up.

"I should have," Mia agreed finally, more easily than Izzy had expected. "I don't talk about this ever." She waved to encompass the room. "As you can imagine."

"I get it." Izzy nodded, because she did. She got it. But she also needed to trust Mia here, and that choice to keep Izzy in the dark hadn't helped. Mia should have told her back in Rockport, or on the ferry, even. "Going forward, though, if I ask you a question, you need to actually answer it. No evasive maneuvering or anything."

There was a second when Izzy thought Mia was going to balk. Or at least shimmy her way out of a direct promise. But then her chin dipped a half inch.

"I won't lie to you, Izzy," Mia finally said.

"That doesn't mean you'll tell the truth." Izzy was pressing her luck when she'd technically already scored the victory. But she was starting to get it now, starting to understand the way Mia was when it came to all this.

Mia's smile was rueful as she looked down so that her hair slid in front of her face. Always hiding something, no matter how small it might be. "I'll tell you the truth. You have my word."

Izzy knew she couldn't ask for anything else. But as Mia's eyes tracked over the maps, the fireplace, the couch, as they lingered on the stairs, before continuing to the stack of books on the coffee table, the jewelry box on the mantel, Izzy knew she hadn't really won.

Maybe Mia would tell her truths, but that didn't mean she would tell Izzy what she was thinking.

And Izzy had a feeling that the space in between the two was where Mia would flee to hide.

It was fully dark by the time they left the lighthouse behind, and Izzy huddled in on herself, cursing the ferry's schedule that had them arriving on the island so late in the day.

"Hey, the doc said he'd be at his office till six, right?" Izzy asked, the words made shaky by the chattering of her teeth.

Mia slid her a glance. "Yeah."

"Maybe he has the addresses for the guys who found the body." Izzy shrugged, or tried to. It wasn't clear what came through the layers of clothing.

Glancing at her phone's clock, Mia nodded. "Yeah. They're fishermen, so they're probably home. Let's do it."

"Speaking of the doc . . ."

Mia must have heard something in her voice. She stopped, turned, ducked her chin so her cheeks were protected from the cold. "What's up?"

"Walk and talk, Hart, walk and talk." Izzy snagged her elbow to pull her into motion. Mia laughed as she fell into step. "You seemed to be on board with his suicide theory."

It wasn't a test, it wasn't. But they were going to have to work on being up-front with each other.

Even though Izzy hadn't framed it as a question, Mia was good enough to know what she was asking.

"Horses and zebras, right?" Mia shrugged. It was something of a motto for them, that old saying: when you hear hoofbeats, think horses, not zebras. Too often on their cold cases, they were asked to make leaps of logic when evidence didn't exist to back it up. But they both knew they needed to be kept in check sometimes. If either of them ever wandered too far down a path, the other reined her in. Horses and zebras.

"You think we're making this too complicated?"

Mia paused, and this time Izzy stuttered to a stop next to her. "I think you and I, we tend to see murder where it might not be."

The off notes, though. The lack of clothes in winter. Ending up in the ocean. These weren't reaches.

But Izzy knew that the people who thought "zebra" instead of "horse" were also convinced they were right. She nodded once, not an agreement, really, but an acknowledgment, and they started walking again.

"I'm not convinced either way," Mia said softly after a few minutes. "I know I want it to be suicide, though."

Izzy gasped, overdramatic. "Mia Hart is volunteering information? We've really made progress." She wiped at a fake tear while Mia shoved her hard enough for Izzy to stumble a bit.

This was a sore spot, and maybe too soon to joke about. But they couldn't be careful around each other, tiptoeing and cutting off thoughts just to skirt the confrontation. That's not how they worked.

"Why do you want it to be suicide?"

Mia tipped her head back toward the lighthouse that was almost out of sight. "So we can leave. This isn't exactly my favorite place to be." She held up a hand. "I still think it's worth poking around, chatting to some folks in town. We'll check out his notes, too. Try to figure if anyone cracked and talked to him."

They walked in silence until they were nearly at the tree line.

"Murdoch must think it's murder," Mia said, putting voice to the vague idea that had been lurking behind all of Izzy's unease. Why send two of your specialized cold-case detectives out to investigate a suicide? Even if it was because Mia was from St. Lucy's, that didn't warrant sending them out here for anything less than possible foul play.

"Did she tell you why?"

"No." Mia shook her head. "Think she's like you. Gut feeling, a few details that don't add up."

"We work the case then." Izzy shrugged, because that's all they could do. Strip away expectations, be smart about it, but also question anything out of place.

"Yeah," Mia said, but her voice cut off, abrupt enough for Izzy to glance over.

Mia must have been caught midstep, because her position was awkward, wobbly. Her eyes were locked on the line of trees toward their left, the rest of her body rigid.

"What . . . ?" Izzy's gaze ping-ponged between the darkness and Mia's face.

"Quiet," Mia snapped.

Where Izzy's pulse had ticked up a notch before, that harsh command sent it rabbiting, fast and uncertain, as she reached for the gun she wore holstered beneath her jacket.

"Do you . . . ?" Mia rasped out, and then she was gone. Sprinting, full-out, across the short expanse, her boots sinking into the snow without any hesitation in her stride.

Cursing, Izzy followed, her limbs awkward from the layers, her feet unsure of the terrain. Mia pulled ahead easily, slipping into the forest along with the wind.

Izzy swore with each ragged inhale. Branches caught at her arms, at her face, as she tried, and failed, to follow Mia's path. Her foot caught a buried root that sent her sprawling, and the hardpack against her face might as well have been tiny shards of glass slicing into the windblown, raw skin of her cheek.

She shoved herself up, shaking off as she did, assessing for injuries. Her knee throbbed beneath a wet patch, but there was nothing broken. Not that she could tell.

Once she was sure she could, Izzy started running again, desperately searching for prints to follow. While she was prepared to get lost in an effort to find Mia, it didn't prove necessary.

Mia was on her knees on the path up ahead, staring into the void, her hands resting against her thighs. The rise and fall of her shoulders was erratic, but it was slowing even as Izzy came to a stop next to her.

Izzy bent over at the waist, embarrassed by her noisy gulps of air. "What the hell?"

She asked it quietly, despite the fact that Mia's calm posture spoke of a threat unrealized.

"I thought I saw . . ." The words were dragged over gravel. "I'm sorry, that was stupid."

Straightening, Izzy pressed the heel of her palm against the stitch that tugged at her side, a direct result of her erratic breathing. "Yeah, you think?"

She waited for more, but Mia was silent.

"Who?" Izzy finally prodded.

Mia glanced back at her, her chin touching her shoulder, her hair brushing against her cheeks. "It was no one. Just a shadow."

Izzy met her eyes. "Who?"

It was Mia who looked away first, back toward the empty path ahead of her. The whisper, when it came, chilled Izzy beyond the snow, the ice, the wind.

"Asher."

———

"It was the way he moved," Mia said, the first words she'd spoken to Izzy since she'd pushed to her feet in the woods. They'd stopped by the doc's place to get the address for the fishermen and then walked the empty streets toward the small shared house the men lived in.

In all that time Mia hadn't met her eyes once.

"It was someone, then?" Izzy asked, because she was still off-balance, not even sure what had happened back there. *Asher.* Mia had whispered the name like a confession, a penance for the way she'd run off. She'd thought she'd seen her dead friend in the woods, or, at the very least, something that looked like him. Was it her imagination? It had to be. It had to be.

"No, I'm sure it was nothing. A shadow." But Mia said it like she was convincing herself. "Just dredging up those memories . . ."

Why was Mia seeing her dead friends in the shadows, though? *Christ.* Too close, too close, too close. The mantra repeated. Mia shouldn't be back on St. Lucy's. She shouldn't have taken this case.

If Izzy wanted answers, she knew better than to attack from the front, though. This required a more subtle approach. It was how they usually handled their suspects, their witnesses. "What was he like? Asher?"

Mia stuttered a bit, her boot catching in a footprint that had half filled up with more snow. Izzy was almost thankful for the sign of life, the proof that someone else had walked there, that they weren't alone. There was a quiet that had settled into the island along with the storm, and it had Izzy swiveling to check her peripherals every few steps.

"He was my best friend," Mia said, warm, as if it were a familiar vow. "He was kind of a scrawny kid, had bad asthma and allergies. But, God, he never backed down from a dare."

Most of Mia's face was covered by her scarf, but a smile had tucked into the corners of her eyes, the lines there thin but noticeable.

"Did you guys ever?" Izzy let her voice go suggestive so she didn't have to spell it out.

"No." There was no wiggle room in the denial. But Mia was also a good liar, so Izzy didn't trust it. "I was with someone else."

Izzy thought back to the darkened hallway from earlier, the pictures. "Big jock guy?"

A gurgle that was an almost laugh swallowed. "Cash Bishop. We were all friends since we were babies."

"And then Asher started dating Monroe Bell," Izzy filled in. To be young and riddled with hormones. Izzy wondered how those dynamics had played out. Not well, if the end result was any indication.

"People thought I'd be jealous." Mia nudged them toward a side street. Up ahead at the end of the lane was a one-story house, like most of the island seemed to be, its windows bright, welcoming. "But we weren't like that, Asher and me."

"Then he was okay with you and Cash?" Izzy asked.

"I thought so," Mia said quietly, but she'd turned inward now, the wall between them thick and impenetrable.

The part of Izzy that made her good at cold cases, the one that found the out-of-place nugget of information and didn't stop questioning until it made sense—the one that her mother had cursed as her bulldog stubbornness—wanted to dig in, root around in whatever messed-up relationships had been going on in a way that would leave everyone emotionally bruised and bleeding in the process. The part that realized she'd been asking mostly to suss out Mia's current mental state whispered that she needed to focus on the reporter.

Izzy bit back any further questions as they climbed the stoop to the fishermen's house.

Greg Lawson had only an inch over Mia, and the ruddy, chapped skin of someone who worked outside. He smiled, affable and welcoming, when he saw them, and the fondness that lingered in his expression as he invited them inside told of a kind soul.

Brandon was his visual opposite, a tall, thin whip of a boy, who was the kind of skinny where you could see his frame, the sharp points of his collarbones, the jut of his wrists and knuckles. He was not as welcoming, hovering in the doorway of the living room, all angry eyebrows and suspicious frowns, as Greg settled them into an overstuffed yellow couch.

"And you didn't recognize him from his stay?" Mia asked Greg after declining several offers of cookies, tea, ice cream, and, inexplicably, fish. So far, the interrogation had proven mostly useless, a repetition of what they'd already been told.

"Not enough to place a name to the face," Greg said. "He looked familiar, right?"

"Yup." Brandon nodded, his arms crossed over his chest. "Familiar."

"But, like I said, just one of those visiting types." Greg leaned forward a little, the skin around his eyes crinkling with an inside joke. "You know those artists."

Mia straightened. "He wasn't an artist."

Greg leaned back. "Oh," he said, glancing at Brandon, who was watching Mia. "My mistake. I just assumed."

"He was a reporter," Mia said, slowly. But Greg just nodded, accepting it without protest.

"We've been gone for a few long stretches in recent months." Greg shrugged. "Don't even get to church as often as I'd like to, if I'm being honest."

Izzy wasn't sure what that had to do with the dead reporter, but Mia hummed like it meant something.

"And you called Sammy right away? When you found the body."

"Mainland cops first, right?" Greg looked at Brandon for confirmation.

"Yup." The boy's eyes were dark and flinty.

"Then Sammy," Greg continued, his hands relaxed, resting on his belly. "He took it from there."

"Did anyone else see or handle the body?" Izzy asked.

Greg smacked his lips. "Can't say they did. But can't swear against it, either."

Mia smiled her thanks as she stood up, and Izzy followed. "If you think of anything else . . ."

"We'll be sure to tell you ladies." Greg huffed to his feet. "Won't we, Brandon?"

There was enough of a nudge in his voice that Izzy stopped, then glanced between the two.

Brandon shuffled back, shoulders rounded and protective. "It's nothing."

"Sometimes what seems like nothing can actually help us solve the case," Mia said gently, and Izzy could almost see the *Thanks, Sherlock* sitting in the twist of his lips.

"Listen, it's not a big deal," Brandon said, Greg watching him patiently. "When we were leaving the doc's place, though."

"Yes?" Mia prompted.

"He . . . He called someone." Brandon shrugged. "Didn't say a name. Didn't even overhear anything really. I only even know about it because I had stopped to tie my shoe."

"Sammy told the person about the body?" Izzy clarified.

"Maybe, I don't know," Brandon said, his arms coming up again to cross over his chest. "Like I said, it's nothing."

The downward slant of his jaw, his rounded shoulders, his eyes on the floor—he wasn't giving them anything else. Mia apparently read it, too, because she stood without protest.

"Okay, thank you, Brandon," Mia said, and left her card with Greg. "Anything else, no matter how small."

His fond expression didn't change as he patted her on the shoulder and promised he'd call.

"Not much new there," Izzy said, her arms instinctually wrapping across her chest as they stepped back outside.

"Hmm," Mia hummed. It was noncommittal enough to catch Izzy's attention.

Izzy lowered her voice, though there was little danger of being over-heard in this wind. "The doc?"

Mia flinched, almost imperceptible but there nonetheless. She probably didn't want their guy to be someone she'd been friends with, which was understandable, but problematic if the island was as small as Mia advertised.

"It's strange that Brandon noticed a phone call."

That was true. The brain was good at assessing and then dismissing extraneous information. People called it a gut feeling or a sixth sense or hairs raised at the nape of the neck, without realizing they'd just picked up on something about their surroundings that they hadn't even realized they'd observed.

But Brandon had been able to pinpoint what felt odd about the moment. That meant it had probably stood out enough to make it into a memory.

"So the doc goes on our persons-of-interest list," Izzy said, as they passed the morgue, which was closed up for the night.

It wouldn't hurt to swing by the bar, would it? Catch Sammy in a more casual setting, possibly with alcohol loosening his tongue. "You know, I think there was a mention of an adult beverage at some point?"

With an exhale that crystallized into white ice in the night air, Mia stared at the darkened windows of the doc's place. She nodded once, more to herself than to Izzy, and started toward Main Street. "I definitely owe you a drink."

CHAPTER FIVE

MIA

The bar on St. Lucy's was technically called Macky's, but it had never actually been referred to as anything other than "the bar." It was the only place on the island that served liquor, so there was no chance of confusion.

Although she'd agreed to go, Mia was already regretting the decision.

There was going to be gossip now that she was back. At first it wouldn't be terrible, focusing mostly on the fact that she was home after fifteen years. But if she was stuck on St. Lucy's for more than a day or two, those whispers would turn biting, laced as they would be with suspicion and bitterness and a very human hunger for others' misfortune. If she went to the bar that night, she'd kick-start the whole process, and then there would be a ticking clock until she heard the first snide remark that someone didn't bother to hide behind a dropped voice or the back of a hand.

But the little outing was about more than the alcohol that would be sure to take the edge off the shakiness she hadn't been able to soothe following their trip to the lighthouse, the figure in the woods that had seemed too real, the moment she'd blinked and found herself kneeling in the snow without memory of sinking to the ground.

Gossip flowed like water through this town, and she wanted to drag her fingertips through the currents to tell which way they flowed when it came to what exactly had happened to the reporter.

Mia and Izzy finished the rest of the walk in silence, and Mia was left wondering if the lingering, sidelong glances from Izzy were real or imagined. If the situation had been reversed, Mia would have been more demanding about the incident in the woods. She'd run off, without explanation, completely breaking any kind of proper protocol. She'd endangered not only herself but Izzy as well. For what? For an overactive imagination and a hint of terror lingering behind the fog she knew so well.

But maybe Izzy was going easy on her after the emotionally draining day.

The bar was dark, cozy; the neon signs that hung along the wall buzzed, casting shadows onto the faces of the men who perched on the vinyl stools. The light caught the bottles that lined the shelves, the amber liquid absorbing the pink and yellow into its depths. The paneling was deep mahogany and the leather of the booths forest green.

Max Verdon was working the taps, just like he had been when she was sixteen and trying to sweet-talk him into selling her the strawberry wine he'd kept behind the counter. He was a bit paunchier than she remembered, his stomach pressing out against the buttons of his shirt, his jowls shivering while he laughed. His hair had gone gray but was still thick, while the lines around his eyes and mouth had deepened.

"Well, Lord love a duck, look what the cat dragged in," Max called when he spotted her.

The collective gaze of the room snapped to her and Izzy where they'd been hovering in the doorway.

A flush crept up her neck, and she cursed her pale skin for always giving her away.

She ignored the attention and crossed toward the bar, leaning her forearms against the wood. "How are you, Max?"

"Great, can't complain, can't complain." Max smiled all the way to his eyes. "Beth just had her second. My fourth grandbaby."

"Congratulations," Mia murmured. The place was overhot, especially coming in from the cold, and a bead of sweat pearled on her neck before slipping down along her spine. She unzipped her field jacket, then tugged off her hat, shaking out her hair as she did. "Hey, did Sammy make it in tonight?"

"Come and gone." Max was already moving toward the bottles, and Mia snuffed out the flicker of relief his answer brought. "Still an Eagle Rare girl?"

She wasn't. She wasn't an anything kind of girl. At most she had white wine at work parties where it would be noted if she didn't imbibe. But she nodded.

"On the house," he said, winking as he slid the tumbler across the scarred wood.

"Make that two." Izzy, who had lagged behind Mia, probably scoping out the exits, shuffled up beside her. There was a pause, and then Max reached for a second glass, reluctant. On the house was limited to islanders.

"Cheers, love." There was a teasing note in Izzy's voice as she took the drink, seemingly unruffled.

Max ignored her, still looking at Mia. "We'll catch up, yeah?" But he was already walking away. It was the kind of empty promise that dressed up disinterest in kind words. And it worked for her, as she had no desire to chat about her life.

They weaved through the high tops that were set up near the entrance and then made their way toward the back.

"Sammy apparently left already," Mia said quietly, so as not to be overheard. The last thing they needed was for someone to get it in their minds that the mainland cops were talking about Sammy Bowdoin.

54

"Convenient," Izzy said, just as softly.

Mia shrugged as they slid into the second-to-last booth.

"You've got to explain this island, man," Izzy said, twisting enough so that her back was against the wall, Mia mirroring the position almost without thought. This wasn't somewhere she was comfortable leaving herself vulnerable. "It feels like it's got its own set of rules."

She brought the glass to her lips. Despite her hesitancy to drink, there were certain things that were comforting in life, like Michael Jackson on the neon jukebox in the corner and Eagle Rare still tasting like silk and summer nights against her tongue. "There's no explaining St. Lucy's."

"Try," Izzy countered, lifting her own tumbler for an experimental sip. Her mouth pulled back in a tight grimace, but then she shrugged and took a hefty swallow.

They sat in silence for a bit, but it was comfortable. Izzy wasn't pushing, and Mia was trying to figure out where to start.

"Survival," Mia finally said.

Izzy had been watching the old fishermen at the table next to theirs. Mia recognized them but didn't remember their names. They hadn't glanced over once, for which Mia was thankful.

"What?" Izzy asked.

"Everything here is about survival," Mia said, her finger tracing the rim of her glass. "We survive because we rely on each other. The minute outlanders start encroaching on that, we go on defense."

"You're talking like you're still one of them," Izzy commented, though there was no accusation, only curiosity, in the tilt of her head.

"Once an islander, always an islander," Mia recited, the words as familiar as her own name. "It's a tough life out here. I think you could glamorize it."

"Oh, no," Izzy cut in. "No. No, no, no. This is not glamorous. Do you realize I haven't been able to feel my right pinkie toe since we stepped off that goddamn ferry?"

Mia grinned. Her partners before Izzy had been varied. Tony Bianchi, the man Izzy had replaced, had been the worst kind of cop. Lazy but smart enough to fake it, ambitious enough that there was always a threat of her getting tossed beneath the wheels of a bus, but not enough to actually work for anything. Throw in a little misogyny and racism, and it had made for an erratic, untenable partnership. The one before him had fallen asleep at her desk regularly.

Izzy was a vast improvement.

"Some people do," Mia said quietly, the smile fading. Many of the artists who made their home on the island in the summer romanticized the struggles of those who lived there year-round. But winter wasn't rosy cheeks and marshmallows in hot chocolate. It was worrying about supplies and studying weather patterns in case the plane couldn't come in.

"Not me." Izzy shivered, overdramatic clearly for the sake of killing the tension that was coiling in the air. Mia appreciated it, like she had the whole day.

"All right, St. Lucy's." Mia glanced around as if she could see the history written in the very walls of the bar. "The Montrose family came over from the mainland in the early 1900s. They built the mansion on the cliffs on the north end of the island."

"Like the lighthouse on the west," Izzy said, always so good at holding on to the important things and then dropping them into place.

Mia nodded, though it hadn't been a question. "There were already people living on the island, but the influx of cash from the Montrose family building the mansion created a small boom that doubled the population from fifty to about a hundred."

After swallowing the last of her bourbon, Izzy laughed. "You guys have an odd sense of booming around these parts."

"Doubled," Mia repeated for emphasis. "When you're on a small island, that kind of increase is huge. So all of a sudden there was a bar"—Mia gestured to encompass the building they were in—"an actual doctor's office, a clothing store. It was quite revolutionary, or so the story goes."

"Wow, a clothing store and everything." Izzy clutched her imaginary pearls, clearly pretending enthusiasm.

"Before that, people either made everything or had to wait months for shipments from the mainland," Mia said. "The Montrose family changed the island, some say for worse, some say for better. But for the standards of the time, they modernized it at least."

Mia took a fortifying swallow before continuing.

"The Montroses all eventually died off, and, right around midcentury, the mansion was sold to the Bell family," Mia said, tipping her head. "The Montrose family had hosted artists in residence during their summer holidays, and the Bells continued that tradition right up until that summer Monroe died."

"They never came back?"

"No." Her thumb finding the delicate skin of her wrist, Mia traced over the thin line that was there until she found her thready pulse. Her ulcer seethed beneath her breastbone, already angry that she was drinking on a mostly empty stomach. They hadn't had a chance to eat anything, and between the lighthouse and the figure in the woods, she'd lost her already-weak appetite.

"That's about it." Mia shrugged. "St. Lucy's has the basics but not a lot of luxury. The winter is pretty much all one rolling storm, with small breaks in between."

"Oh God, does that mean it gets worse than this?" Izzy pointed toward the door, and Mia couldn't help the gleeful tint to her own laugh, the smugness that was your birthright from growing up in a place like St. Lucy's.

"This is child's play," Mia said, and Izzy buried her face in her hands. "And since you didn't bother to check, I can tell you we have several fronts rolling up the coast toward us right now. There's a good chance we'll get stuck here if we don't solve this in the next day or so."

Izzy groaned, a pitiful wail, not even bothering to lift her head.

"It gets better." Mia leaned in. "Our cell service and internet have the constitution of a fainting Victorian lady. They have a tendency to give out completely at the merest hint of bad weather."

Peeking at her, Izzy pouted. "You're enjoying this."

"Just your abject misery," Mia said, shameless, but then sobered. "But it is something to take into account. We might be cut off from backup. Not able to look anything up, even. Sometimes the hot spots are feeling generous, but more often than not it's a crapshoot whether you get bars."

Finally straightening, Izzy just nodded, seeming to take it in stride. "Okay." She drummed the table.

Max came around with another pour of Eagle Rare, and this time Mia slipped him a twenty that he didn't refuse. He left just as easily, a small pat on her head reminding her that most people here still thought of her as sixteen years old.

"So should we split up?" Izzy asked, once Max had left.

"Hmm?"

"We came here to talk to the locals, right?" Izzy tipped her head toward the rest of the tables, bringing Mia's mind back to the reason they were on St. Lucy's at all: Robert Twist. "I'm guessing I won't get very far, so point me to the biggest gossip here, and you can go for the more subtle route."

Mia swallowed a laugh as she glanced around. There were a few options, from what she could remember. But her gaze caught on Patty Masterson where she perched on a stool by the dartboard. The game would give Izzy an in, and Patty's loose lips would give her a chance to actually get some information out of someone.

She angled her chin toward the back. "Patty Masterson. She'll give you a little trouble, but you might be able to pry some gossip out of her."

Izzy was quiet for a minute, watching the woman in the acid-washed jeans yank darts from the board. Then she gave Mia a two-finger salute, whispered, "Wish me luck," and sauntered off, drink in hand.

Mia watched her go before scanning the rest of the bar. She'd have to be more strategic in her pick. She didn't want to waste time on someone who only wanted to rehash everything she was trying to forget.

She had just decided on approaching Father Williams when the door slammed open with the wind.

"Sorry, Max," a voice called, and Mia stilled. That voice. It was one was she knew well, knew in anger, knew in lust, knew in fear and sadness.

Glancing over toward the front of the bar, Mia locked eyes with Cash Bishop.

CHAPTER SIX

Izzy

Patty Masterson wore neon blue lipstick with a kind of don't-give-a-shit attitude to which Izzy aspired. She immediately liked the woman on gut instinct alone.

"Can I get in on this?" Izzy asked, gesturing toward the dartboard with her half-empty glass.

Patty cracked her gum and popped her hip like a mean girl in a bad '80s teen movie. Her eyes were assessing as she tapped a long, pink acrylic nail against her thigh. "You've got money, sugar?"

There was liking the woman and then there was being fleeced. Izzy had no desire to be just one more outsider who lost all their cash thinking they could hustle a local. She made a show of patting her pockets before pulling out a single bill. "Five bucks?"

For a second, Izzy thought she'd lost her with the paltry offer, but then Patty sniffed and plucked the cash out from between Izzy's fingers. As she slipped it into the overflowing cup of her bra, she cracked her gum once more, then held up the darts.

Up close without the kindness of dim lighting, the woman looked older than she had from across the room. Now, Izzy could see the droop of the skin around her lips, her jawline. Midfifties instead of early forties, if Izzy had to guess. Her foundation was two shades too dark, and gummy clumps of mascara had fallen from her lashes to settle onto the puffy bags beneath her eyes. The blue lipstick had smeared, leaving a waxy streak by the corner of her thin mouth.

After setting her glass aside, Izzy took the darts with a friendly smile and lined herself up at the single strip of duct tape on the floor. Now the question was: Should she throw the game? Would Patty be more impressed or annoyed with Izzy winning?

It didn't matter anyway, because at the exact moment Izzy released the dart, Patty cracked her gum, loud and obnoxious enough for Izzy's hand to twitch just wrong.

"So you're here with Mia Hart."

The metal tip had sunk into the wood just outside the board, and Izzy tamped down her amusement. Patty played dirty.

"Sure am," Izzy said, even though it hadn't been a question. Everyone must have seen them come in together. She lazily lobbed the next dart. It landed dead center. "Izzy Santiago. Rockport PD."

Patty waited until Izzy's arm was drawn back for her final throw before speaking again. "Because of that reporter the boys had to fish out of the bay?"

This time Izzy had been ready for the interruption, and the metal tip slid in next to the previous one she'd thrown. Double bull's-eye. "Heard he came in here a few times."

It wasn't really an answer to Patty's question, though the confirmation was there in the way Izzy didn't deny it. Patty's lips pinched in at the corners, so Izzy figured she'd picked up on it.

They stood suspended in a kind of standoff. Izzy was a prime target for the town gossip, and that town gossip knew she was the same for

Izzy. Each held the upper hand in some way, but one of them was going to have to blink first. Izzy didn't want it to be her.

Finally, cracking her gum again, Patty tipped her head toward the board, a silent order for Izzy to collect the darts. "Patty Masterson," she said, finally introducing herself, as Izzy picked up the chalk to write the score. "And, yeah, he came in here."

"Ever ask you any questions?"

"Sugar, everyone asks me questions. Just like you are right now." There was a teasing quality to her raspy voice, but beneath it was something sharper, not quite a reprimand but a warning shot. Patty wasn't going to be played. As if Izzy hadn't gotten that sense already.

She passed the darts off to Patty. "All right, what did he talk to you about?"

Patty's eyes were locked on her face. "Asked a lot about Mia."

Izzy's heart paused and then thudded too hard as if it panicked at the skipped beat. Mia had recognized Twist. Hadn't known him but had recognized him. And apparently he was asking about her? "Oh yeah?" Even to Izzy's own ears, her voice sounded reedy, too high.

"Everyone asks about Mia," Patty said, throwing it out like it was a careless afterthought. But there was something about her stance, about the pinched corners of her lips that belied any attempts at indifference.

They called it a suicide pact. Izzy could guess what people asked about. The rush of anticipation that came before a good interview turned to charcoal in her mouth. There was always someone to be blamed in those situations, and Mia was the one who was left to shoulder it. "The lighthouse."

Patty nodded. "The lighthouse."

She said it with just enough suggestion to hint at the scandalous, but with enough familiarity for Izzy to know it was a well-worn phrase. It all made Izzy want to sweep Mia out of the bar. Protect her from invasive, prying eyes. But that wasn't her job. This, this was her job.

"Twist was asking questions about Mia?" Izzy reiterated, trying to focus on the important part. The guilt and wariness and anger she could deal with later.

Patty was barely paying her attention, anyway. She'd lined herself up at the duct tape with an exaggerated stance that caused all her curves to press against the seams of her clothes. Predictably, her first throw landed dead center.

"You know Mia was the only one who came out of the lighthouse that night," Patty said, as she aimed her second dart.

"I'd heard something like that." She couldn't stop her eyes from finding her partner across the room, where she was holed up in a booth with a tall, dark-haired man. They were just curves and lines in the shadows, and yet still their body language was textbook: suffocating tension.

Patty followed her line of vision. "Those two." She clicked her tongue before turning back to the board. She landed the second bull's-eye. "They were all over each other as teens."

So that was Cash Bishop, then. Izzy glanced back over but still couldn't make out much.

Patty's third dart sank into a square on the thinnest ring, earning her enough points to not just beat but crush Izzy's score. The swing of Patty's hips was victorious. "Five bucks only gets you one throw, sugar. Come back when you've got something else."

Paying for information was always a gamble, and putting a price on it was even trickier. "What will twenty get me?"

"Oh, you were holding out on me, Detective." Patty fake pouted, but the smugness underneath the exaggerated disappointment was obvious. She knew that she well and truly had the upper hand now. "Throw in a double shot of whiskey and that'll get you a few answers."

Izzy got herself another as well, one she knew she wouldn't actually drink. But it was a simple trick—it enforced the message that they were drinking buddies, could lull whoever was being questioned into a false sense of security.

When Izzy returned to the high top, she slid a twenty across the table beneath the glass tumbler. By the next blink, it had disappeared.

"Twist was asking about Mia?" Izzy asked once again. Maybe she sounded like a broken record, but now that she was paying for the answer, she was going to push until she got it.

One sharp, pink nail tapped against the glass in an uneven staccato as Patty studied Izzy's face. "If you know about the lighthouse, then you know about the rumors."

"People say Mia had something to do with it." It wasn't exactly a stab in the dark. Izzy could see how the leap could be made.

"Police ruled it a suicide." Patty lifted one shoulder, a casual shrug. But her eyes were sharp. "Case closed."

They called it a suicide pact. "Then no need to ask questions about Mia, right?"

Patty rocked the glass onto its edge. "You should hear the conspiracies about that night, sugar."

"Like what?"

"Some think it was an artist who went nuts," Patty said, deftly dodging ones about Mia that Izzy knew must exist. "Was obsessed with the Bell girl. Ended up killing the boyfriend, then her. Started on Mia but chickened out or something."

Wait. Izzy leaned forward. That was a hell of a lot different from people thinking Mia talked them into it. That's where Izzy had thought that was heading.

"People say it was murder, not suicide? That's what you're saying?"

"You can't blame 'em for talking, Detective," Patty dodged. "There's not much else to do out here."

"Did you tell this to Twist?"

Patty's shoulders went taut as she straightened. Insulted. "Didn't have to. He already knew it."

"He thought an artist killed them?"

"Nah," Patty drawled out. "He realized quickly only the kooks believe that one. There weren't any artists that fit the bill at the time it all went down."

"So . . . ?"

"He was trying to be slick about it." Patty's eyes narrowed, and Izzy swallowed her frustration. The woman could answer the questions like a professional, giving just enough to seem like she was telling Izzy something but not nearly enough to make sense.

Irritation must have flashed on Izzy's face, because a smirk teased at the corners of Patty's lips. "All right, Detective, calm down. You'll get your money's worth."

Izzy remained impassive, not even hinting at the fact that she already had. Now they had a better idea what Twist had been looking into on the island.

Mia.

Patty swallowed the last of her drink before setting it aside and leaning forward on her crossed arms. "All right, look. He was asking everyone about suicide, okay—that's not unusual for us. We get someone out here every once in a while, looking to do some book or school assignment on isolation and depression and all that jazz.

"But." Patty paused, her tongue darting out to lick at her lip, a nervous gesture she'd done enough times to work away at the blue gloss there. "He was really investigating that night. Those kids' deaths. Monroe Bell and Asher Lowe. And Mia, of course. You could tell by the way he wouldn't get really interested until someone brought them up."

And with that, all the pieces from the day began to slot themselves together, starting with Mia recognizing Twist. If he'd been investigating the suicide pact, it made sense that he'd try to scope her out first. Why hadn't he talked to her at all, though?

Because. *Because.* Part of Izzy shied away from the thought, but she couldn't. *Because he thought Mia had killed the others.*

"Only the kooks think an artist went crazy and killed Monroe and Asher," Izzy said, slowly. Patty was a hawk, watching the question form behind Izzy's lips. "So what does everyone else think happened at the lighthouse?"

The quick flick of Patty's eyes in Mia's direction confirmed the theory. "That girl has scars from that night."

Maybe that was true. But that girl was alive. The same couldn't be said about Asher Lowe and Monroe Bell.

And now the reporter who, if Patty were to be believed, had apparently been investigating those deaths had turned up in the bay, without ID, looking for all the world like a suicide.

Her thoughts from earlier circled back. If it was a homicide, the killer was either very lucky or very smart. They knew how to hide evidence.

She thought about how Mia had torn across the meadow toward the woods, how Izzy had found her, silent and still, eerie almost, her face pale in the thin light provided by Izzy's phone. How she hadn't really met Izzy's eyes until they'd been back to civilization, how her hand had shaken when she'd stripped off her gloves.

That was what guilt looked like.

Izzy didn't want to let herself start questioning Mia—trust and loyalty were the foundations of a solid partnership, and it was dangerous to create cracks in that for no reason. But what did Izzy really know about the woman? Not much.

Mia always kept to herself, dodging out on station happy hours and softball leagues. Izzy admired her quiet competence, but beyond the very basic facts, the woman was a mystery.

That didn't have to mean anything. A lot of people liked their privacy, liked separating their personal lives from their jobs. But little moments from the day stood out in sharp relief under the harsh light of this new information.

That pause in the hallway, Mia's eyes latching onto that photograph. The quick acceptance of Sammy's suicide theory. The tic Mia had of stroking her thumb over her left wrist. The dip in her voice when mentioning the lighthouse.

I didn't leave a suicide note, either.

There was a question that Izzy had earlier refused to let properly form but couldn't deny any longer.

Was the reason Mia hadn't left a suicide note because she'd always known she'd come out of the lighthouse alive?

CHAPTER SEVEN

MIA

"Mia." Cash didn't say her name like a prayer or a plea. This was accusation, annoyance, and sixteen years of familiarity that couldn't be erased by fifteen years of silence.

He had come over to her booth, though. Approached her despite the way she hadn't said goodbye before she'd left, hadn't answered his calls in the weeks following.

"Cash," she said, meeting his eyes because she was never one to play coy.

He watched her closely. "What are you . . . ?" That's when the realization struck, and something that looked like relief flashed quick as lightning across his face. "The reporter."

The word rippled across the room, a pebble dropped in a lake that had been still. Eyes shifted and bodies leaned, ever so slightly, toward her and Cash.

It wasn't like she was going to confirm it, so she just smiled a little and let that be answer enough.

He grinned, that slow, easy one that used to let loose butterflies in her belly. For a heartbeat, she was disoriented, off-balance. Here was the boy in that photo, laughing into the camera. But gone was the baby fat. That jawline had sharpened and was now dusted with scruff; his shoulders had filled out, but his hips had stayed narrow.

"Let me get you a drink?" Cash finally said when the silence between them stretched to awkward. "Come on."

He walked away without waiting for her.

When Mia had been a teenager, she'd enjoyed the way Cash, a skilled conductor, directed those around him, bodies becoming the music that bent to his will. As a thirty-one-year-old woman, she found it less than appealing.

But he was already four steps ahead, already at the bar. Once he nodded back toward her, Max got the message and reached for the Eagle Rare one more time. Her ulcer flared, but she ignored it.

Mia spared one more look toward where Izzy was attempting to win over Patty Masterson, before she followed Cash to a booth on the other side of the room.

Sliding in across from him, she let her eyes trace over his face. Here was a stranger she knew so well and didn't know at all.

"I should call you Mr. Mayor, I guess," she finally said. Although she hadn't been back to the island, Mama still told her things.

There was no mockery intended, but he grimaced anyway. "Maura Chapman took over after Dad retired, but stepped down a few years back."

"A Bishop back in charge," Mia said. "Seems right."

"Not much changed since you left."

Cash hadn't bought a drink for himself, so he had nothing to occupy his hands.

Mia loved hands; they revealed so much. They fidgeted, they stilled, they picked and plucked, they covered mouths and scratched at scabs. So many tells.

Cash's were lain flat on the table, unnatural in both their position and lack of movement. If he was relaxed, he'd be tapping the wood, his knuckles bent and loose. There was stress in those hands. She wondered if it was just from seeing her again. She wondered if he'd expected her.

"I wouldn't say that." Mia took a swig of her drink before looking back at him beneath her lashes. Not trying to flirt but not opposed to getting information, either. "You've grown."

"Me? You're the big shot now," Cash said without bite. "Detective and everything. Could have knocked me over with a feather when I heard you were joining the police force."

The news must have spread like wildfire. She hadn't asked Mama what the gossip had been like, and Mama hadn't talked about it. But the town's armchair psychiatrists had probably had a field day. "I enjoy it."

"Wouldn't have pegged you for the type, Mia Mackenzie." His smile was genuine, and she was once again off-balance, back in that lookout tower of the lighthouse, their legs entangled, their hips flush against each other's. *I love you to the moon, Mia Mackenzie.*

"What type would you have pegged me for, Cash Montgomery?" she bantered back, because it cost nothing.

He held up his palms. "Don't get feisty on me," he said with a laugh. "I knew you'd take over the world. Just didn't think you'd want to live in blood and guts every day."

Mia studied him. This time he'd dropped his hands to his lap, hiding them, which was a shame. But there were other ways to tell what a person was thinking. Like the worry that creased the lines of his face, or his careful pauses between words.

"It's more about people, actually, than blood and guts," she said, rubbing the rim of her empty glass. She had her own tells. "I tend to work cases that others have given up on."

"Like cold cases?" he asked. "That must be a challenge."

"Can be," she said. "Any hard evidence is gone or useless, usually."

Cash leaned forward, his biceps pressing against the table. "So . . . it becomes about people then?"

Mia shrugged her agreement. "You talk to friends, neighbors, family. Most don't remember anything, but every once in a while, they do."

It took only one moment, one memory, one face in the crowd that shouldn't have been there, one strange visit that was written off because it was only a tiny piece in a larger puzzle. The answers were there, they were. You just had to find them.

"Sounds like a lot of grunt work."

"It is." Tedious with short bursts of excitement is how she could best describe it. But there was something deeply satisfying there as well, something that, if she were forced to admit it, had nothing to do with helping victims' families find peace. The crimes were puzzles, the hard kind, the field of wheat or a bluebird sky that others tended to give up on.

The brain always saw the small differences, the curves and divots, the corner pieces, the slight change in shade. It's just that most people have grown so used to tossing those details out that even when they try to look, even when they know what to look for, they can't find them.

She didn't know what it said about her that she'd never learned how not to see them.

Like the phone call Brandon overheard. Or when Cash's expression had flickered into anxiety, instead of surprise or anger. Or the way the figure in the woods had paused, just slightly, when Mia had said Asher's name.

Each piece of the puzzle she collected, ran her fingers along their uneven edges, tried to figure out where they'd fit even though all of them looked the same right now.

Cash was watching her closely, quiet, until he realized she wasn't going to continue further. "The reporter's not exactly a cold case."

There was something too casual in his voice, the disinterest too practiced to be real.

"Like anyone here would talk to a mainland cop," she said. "My chief isn't stupid."

Cash laughed, and here was that boy again, young and carefree. His entire body relaxed into the amusement. "That's fair."

Mia chewed on the inside of her cheek to suppress a smile. There were times she missed being ornery for no other reason than because she lived on a tiny island in the middle of a bay in Maine.

"The strategy is the same, you know?" Mia said, not sure why she wanted to make the point. But part of her wanted Cash a little on edge, a little sloppy, a little nervous. "People."

She made a show of glancing around the bar. Here on this island where everyone knew each other's secrets, all she would need to do was ask the right questions.

A muscle twitched in Cash's jaw. "I hope you know what you're doing," he said, something like a warning sitting behind the friendly words.

Before he could say anything else, the jukebox switched over. Their eyes met, and they were back in that summer, two stupid kids who thought there was just enough irony in "Love Is a Battlefield" to make it their song.

Mia smoothed her thumb along the scar at her wrist. "Where were you that night?"

Cash blinked, sat back. "When the reporter disappeared?"

She should say yes. She needed to know that more than what she had been asking, needed to focus on the case, the reason she was here.

"The night Asher died," she corrected instead. Maybe it was the three glasses of bourbon.

His lips parted, perhaps a start to something, but in the end he simply shook his head.

"I don't remember any of it," Mia answered the unspoken question. "I don't remember any of that day."

He inhaled at that. "Nothing?" It was stripped clean of any accusation, curious and probing but not threaded with disbelief.

"The last thing that's clear is the evening before," she said slowly. She'd never had any interest in telling her side of the story. It wasn't one she could give, anyway, since the memories had never stuck. Letting the gossips talk always seemed preferable to that simple admission. But that's when she'd thought she'd never be back on St. Lucy's. And here she was. "We snuck out. You brought whiskey."

"It was just the two of us," Cash said.

Even fifteen years later, that memory was there, clear. Smooth rocks and even smoother liquor. Searching tongues and roaming fingers. The solid weight of a boy on top of her, with the air cool against her skin.

But then everything went blank. No matter how many times she'd tried to probe the darkest recesses. Eventually she'd given up.

Some things were meant to be forgotten.

"You weren't at the lighthouse, though," Mia said. During a summer where she and Cash had been inseparable, it seemed almost inconceivable to her that he hadn't been there. "The night he—they—died."

"I was grounded," Cash said, running a hand through his hair. "God, Mia, don't you know how many times I've wished I had gone with you guys? How many times I've asked myself if I could have stopped it?"

She studied him. "Did you ever . . . ?"

"No." The denial was harsh, leaving no room for equivocation. "I never suspected you'd do anything like that."

The "you" was like a brand, hot and searing against her skin, a pain so sharp it brought reality into focus. The few times she'd thought about that night, she'd always put distance between herself and what happened. *They'd* killed themselves.

She pressed her lips together. Their song had long faded into a one-hit wonder from a few years back, and Cash was a stranger once more.

He sighed and glanced at his watch. "Listen, I better go. But be careful, okay, Mia Mackenzie?"

He didn't have to go. He'd just come in. But ever since he'd caught her eye, he'd wanted to leave. She could see it in the way he'd kept his body angled toward the exit.

Mia flicked her brows up in acknowledgment, but she didn't owe him a promise.

As he stood, she thought of something. "Oh, Cash."

He paused, his long, lanky body still slightly crouched from his inelegant slide out of the booth. "Yeah?"

"Did you ever chat with him?" she asked. It was unofficial, how she was doing this, but she had him here, slightly off guard. She'd take it. "The reporter. Did he try to interview you?"

Cash blinked, a long, slow sweep of lashes against his cheeks. "Can't say I ever talked to the man."

She nodded and shrugged, the gesture conveying a nonchalant *thought I'd ask*. But she was watching his hands.

They had curled into fists at his sides.

———

Izzy was quiet on the walk home, and Mia would have been happy to leave her to her thoughts, but the woman also kept stealing sidelong glances, her eyes darting back to the snow when caught.

"Spill," Mia finally prodded. Patty must have told her about the rumors.

"Did you ever consider . . . ?" Her voice was so hesitant, so unlike Izzy. Mia huddled further into the warmth of her jacket, braced. Izzy paused, huffed out a breath as if gearing up for something, then really and fully looked over at Mia. "Did you ever consider it wasn't suicide?"

Mia's boot caught against the snow, but Izzy's quick hand at her elbow kept her from falling. "What?"

"Something Patty said . . ."

Right. The rumors. Mia kept walking, and Izzy's hand fell away. "That crazy artist conspiracy theory."

"Yeah, Patty said it didn't hold water," Izzy said. "But. Okay, let me ask you something. You didn't leave a suicide note, right?"

Mia nodded, though she knew Izzy didn't need it confirmed. She wouldn't have forgotten that detail.

"Did you ever think about . . . ?"

Killing yourself. That was the unspoken question everyone asked. It was the one that played in her head as she'd searched for a suicide note. Had something changed so drastically from the night before? When she'd kissed Cash while lain out beneath the stars on the cool pebbles of the beach?

"Killing myself?" Mia filled in when Izzy broke off. "No, not that I can remember."

"What about Asher, Monroe?"

"No." Her voice came out a hoarse whisper. None of them had.

"Have you . . . ?" Izzy cleared her throat. "Have you ever wondered if there's a grain of truth in those theories?" Her tone was soothing. "Maybe not a crazy artist. But someone else. Have you ever thought through motives?"

"I don't . . ." The fog. That's what Mia remembered so well. That deep, deep fog. "I don't know."

"If you don't remember any of it, could someone else have been there that night?" Izzy prompted. "Cash maybe?"

No.

Mia traced her gloved hand along the edge of her coat, slipping a finger under the fabric. Even though she couldn't feel the scar, it helped. "I don't . . . I don't know. I remember . . ."

Izzy stepped closer, their shoulders nudging. "What?"

Mia wanted to curl up, ignore these questions, these gentle pokes at a wound that was so raw, so tender still. After all these years. She licked her lips. Then she glanced up, meeting Izzy's gaze. "I remember doing it."

Silence dropped. When Edie's house came into view, Izzy reached out, tugged at Mia's arm to get her to stop, to force her to look at Izzy.

"Do you really remember doing it?" Izzy asked. "Or do you just think you do?"

It took a few tries to get the words out, her brain heavy and slow. "What do you mean?"

"Why do you only know that? And nothing else? Why are you so certain?"

Mia looked down toward her wrist. "The pain, I think," she said. "It was sharp, where everything else was blurry. It sliced the moment into memory."

"You're taking it as fact, though," Izzy said. "Come on, think like a cop instead of a scared teenager."

The roughness of Izzy's voice actually helped. Mia had always been so scared about what lay beyond the fog that she'd never tried to clear it, had tried to never even look directly at it. But Izzy was forcing her to.

And, yes, they'd worked enough cold cases to know memories couldn't be trusted. They warped, they shattered, they were put back together in ways that looked nothing like the original. Too many people took them as fact. But memories didn't work like that. They were more of a perception of what happened than actual reality.

"Maybe you remember the sting of it," Izzy said, keeping up the pressure. Part of Mia wanted to shrug her off. Part of her thought Izzy was onto something. "But do you remember holding the razor?"

"It was too easy," Mia said. Because that had always been a truth to her. That had been her reality. The sting of pain. And how easy it was. "The blade. My skin."

"Maybe it was too easy because you weren't holding the razor," Izzy said. And just like that, a different perception, a different reality. Something Mia had never even considered as a possibility. "Someone said it was suicide, and your brain ran with it. You *know* that happens, Mia—it happens all the time."

Everything in her tilted and then righted itself.

Mia had known people thought she was responsible for the pact, that they thought she had talked Asher and Monroe into it. If either of them had been the ones to survive, they would have faced the same rumors. It was just how people were.

But she'd never seriously considered homicide. That was a fringe theory to give bored people something to talk about.

"Shit," Mia said on a breath.

"Yeah. And, so here's the kicker." Izzy glanced toward Edie's house, and there was a bit of longing in her gaze at the warmth that blazed from the windows. "Robert Twist was digging into it. Their deaths."

"Oh." She didn't need Izzy to elaborate. "And look where that got him."

Izzy grimaced. "It could still be unconnected."

Maybe.

Or someone was desperate to keep the secrets of the past buried.

The warmth from the mug against Mia's palms was just on the right side of bearable, and she pressed her hip bones into the counter as she stared out the kitchen window into the night.

There was an old swing set in the backyard that Mama had never taken down. The metal was rusted, and the chains hollered when any of the village kids used it.

Now it was blanketed with snow, the bottoms of the seats brushing against the windblown mounds that piled up beneath it. The white powder tumbled over the edges of the side each time a gust swept through, and the moonlight caught the glint of silver on the top bar. "Your father was so proud of himself that day," Mama said from behind her, her voice pitched low. It was well after midnight, and Izzy was asleep just down the hall. She'd ducked into the den right when they'd walked into the house. Once again, Mia had taken her lack of questions as a gift and hadn't done anything to break the silence herself.

"You refused to swing on it, though," Mama continued. "Broke his little heart."

Mia brought the cup to her lips. "I'm sure he recovered."

She didn't remember the day, didn't really remember the swing set, either. She had never been one for metal when there was a whole forest to get lost in.

It must have been a thorn in her father's side, though, a constant reminder that she was a disappointment, that his life was a disappointment. She wondered why he'd never taken it down. But people were funny that way. They picked at scabs to keep the wounds open and then were angry and confused when they still bled.

"Do you remember Asher that summer, Mama?" Mia asked, because she was no better than the rest of them. She scratched at scabs, too. "Did you ever suspect anything?"

"That he was sad?" Mama poured herself some hot water out of the kettle Mia had put on. "No. Especially not once that girl came around."

That girl being Monroe Bell.

The first time Mia had met her, it had been at the lighthouse. The old building had long been out of use and so became the de facto hangout spot for the older teenagers during the summers. There was a patch of beach near the rocks at its base, and someone always had a bottle of something to pass around.

It had been May and far too cold for bathing suits, but Monroe and Lacey Bell had been wearing bikinis anyway. Mia remembered snickering at the amount of exposed pale white flesh that had been on display.

The boys hadn't laughed.

Mia had been of the age where she should've resented Monroe—for her curves, or her dark lashes, or the way she drew both Asher's and

Cash's eyes when she tugged the bottom edges of her suit from where they'd slipped up her cheeks.

But Monroe had waved at the length of her own body, then tilted toward the water's whitecaps. *Not quite Florida, I guess.* There was something so *adult* about the way she said it, careless confidence tempered by self-deprecation, and Mia had been immediately won over.

Asher had handed over the bottle of Jack. *This will warm you up.*

They'd stayed the rest of the day, swigging the amber liquid and playing truth or dare until finally they were drunk enough to get Monroe to kiss Asher. When their lips had met, Mia had watched closely, the light from the bonfire turning their faces golden.

She'd always wondered if there was anything more than friendship between her and Asher. Despite the fact that she'd had Cash, there was a question, always just sitting in the back of her mind, not really begging for attention but not fading away, either.

Something odd had curled in her belly when she'd watched the two of them, but it wasn't rancid like jealousy, wasn't sharp like anger. It was just . . . there.

Cash's fingers had slipped up underneath the back of her hoodie, stroking her spine lightly, sending shivers out along her skin like slowly shattering glass.

When she'd managed to tear her gaze from the fumbling couple and the way Asher's hand had ridden high along Monroe's sweatpants-clad thigh, Mia had found Lacey watching her instead of her sister. The girl had smiled and shrugged, then stood up and made her way toward the water, an acknowledgment that she was out of place.

Cash's mouth had been against Mia's a breath later, his hand curling around her hip, drawing her closer. And she'd given in to the pull.

"I was so blind that whole summer," Mia said now, breaking the quiet that had fallen. Mama stood next to her, both of them staring out at what should have been a picturesque landscape. Mia found it achingly lonely instead. A forgotten swing set, a hushed forest, snow that was suffocating instead of pretty.

Her stomach churned, growling at the emptiness it found there. She sighed, laying her temple against Mama's shoulder, the night making them both softer, blurring their battle lines.

Suicide or murder? Suicide or murder? Why did that question keep coming up? For the reporter. For Asher, Monroe. The idea that the teenagers' deaths were anything but suicide was too fresh, too shaky in her mind. So she focused on Twist instead.

"If the reporter's death was a homicide, the killer's probably someone you know," Mia said.

Mama just sighed. "They probably accomplished what they needed to accomplish, though. Not really worried about it, to be honest."

Straightening, Mia nudged at Mama's arm. "You don't care?"

"More worried about you," Mama said, and took both their mugs to the sink.

If Patty Masterson's information was to be believed, then there was probably good reason for that concern. She wouldn't tell Mama that, though.

"Tell me something no one else will tell me," Mia said, pushing her palms against the counter and jumping up slightly until her butt hit laminate.

"You're too thin."

Rolling her eyes, Mia let her heels rest against the cabinets below her. "About the reporter."

Mama turned back to her from where she'd been spending too much time scrubbing at mugs that were barely dirty. Her mouth tugged down in a deep frown, but Mia knew that was just her expression when she was thinking.

"The day before he disappeared, he talked to Earl Bishop," Mama finally said.

"Cash's dad?" Surprise turned it into a question.

"Yep," Mama answered, though she hadn't actually needed to. Mia knew Earl Bishop well. Knew the way he'd thought she wasn't good enough for Cash back then. "Not saying it's anything. Just saying it's something no one else will tell you."

It was true. The islanders were protective in general. But when it came to the Bishops, they closed ranks completely. Even she would be left on the outside.

She thought about Cash's fists, balled at his sides. Cash. Who hadn't been at the lighthouse that night.

Mia rested her chin against her shoulder, her eye catching on the shiver of the swing's chain. The house groaned with the wind, then settled. "It keeps coming back to that summer, doesn't it?"

CHAPTER EIGHT

Izzy

They were being watched.

Izzy had been a cop long enough to recognize the sensation of eyes on her back. And, exposed as they were in the forest, it was only more pronounced.

"Feel it?" Izzy asked Mia, keeping her voice low. The trees blocked the wind and the snow soaked up any residual sound, the hush ruptured only by the way their boots broke through the crust.

"Yeah."

Neither of them glanced over their shoulders. It wouldn't do any good—the shadows were deep, the sun still low in the sky.

They were heading toward the small cabin that Robert Twist had rented for the three weeks he'd been on St. Lucy's. There was little need for cars on the island, or so Mia informed her. One gas station kept the population of St. Lucy's fueled all season long. So they walked.

Izzy had been daydreaming of warm leather seats and a well-working heater when she'd first realized someone was trailing them.

"Think it's our guy?" Izzy asked, her fingers at her zipper. She tugged it down enough so she would have easy access to her gun and cursed whoever it was behind them as the bitterly cold air poured into the space between her jacket and shirt. "Or whatever you saw last night?"

Mia jerked her shoulders in what might have been a shrug beneath the layers of fabric and kept trudging forward, her hands securely in her pockets. Alert, but not worried. So different from how she'd reacted after the lighthouse last night. Izzy could still picture the torn-up snow left in Mia's wake as she'd sprinted toward the trees.

"Don't know," Mia said "No one lives down here. It's just the cabin. So whoever it is, they're probably here for us."

She and Mia were heading south of the village and had been walking for about ten minutes now, each step taking them deeper into the forest, away from help if they needed it.

"It's weird Twist rented a cabin so far away from everyone he was here to talk to." Izzy couldn't imagine that had been easy, trekking into town every day in the midst of seemingly perpetual storms.

"Not many options. There aren't any rooms for rent in the village."

Out of all the weird things about this place, that one almost made sense. Izzy couldn't imagine St. Lucy's attracted enough visitors to warrant anyone running a hotel in town, or even renting out a room.

Izzy's thumb brushed against her gun's grip, a nervous habit she'd picked up after that one time she'd worked undercover for six months. The weight of the holster was a security blanket she still hadn't learned to take for granted. "You said the artists all stayed at the Bell mansion, right?"

"Yeah," Mia said, her voice calm and even, despite their tail. There was something about Mia's gut that Izzy trusted—God knows it had saved her ass a time or two—and apparently Mia's gut was feeling okay with whoever was behind them. "There was also an old house near the northern cliffs that used to board the transient workers who came during the boom. The Bells would have their staff get it ready enough for any overflow during the summers."

"Tell me about them," Izzy prompted, even though half her attention was on the woods. Whoever the person was, they weren't making any sudden moves. "The Bells. The parents, that is."

The land started to slope down, and Izzy had to concentrate on redistributing her weight into her thighs. She was ready to be done with snow.

"Charles and Bix Bell," Mia said.

"Bix Bell, really?" Izzy said as the cabin finally came into view. *Rudimentary* was the first description that came to mind. "That's a great name."

Mia's laugh was muffled by her scarf.

"The mother," she said. "She was an artist, hence the residencies. Married Charles Bell of the Boston Bells. Old money there."

"Was she amazingly glamorous?" Izzy asked, and now she wouldn't be able to stop picturing Gatsbyesque decadence—flapper dresses and champagne fountains and untenable love—despite the fact that the Bells would have been decades late to that particular party.

"In a flower child kind of way," Mia said. "All the Bell girls were beautiful. The boys on the island were immediately gaga over them."

Izzy smiled, endeared by the phrase. "Gaga?"

"You know teenagers and their hormones." Mia waved her hand around a little vaguely in the air. "But, yes, Bix was glamorous and gorgeous. Charles was this straitlaced New England Harvard-educated psychiatrist, but he adored Bix—it was so obvious."

"That's cute," Izzy said. "If they didn't come back here, where are they now?"

Mia shook her head. "I assume the mainland. Boston, probably."

Izzy wasn't sure where they fit in, if they did at all. Their daughter was part of the apparent suicide pact, but that was fifteen years ago, and the only thing they had linking that to the reporter's death was Patty

Masterson's gossip. If the Bells had never returned to the island, it was unlikely they had a role in the current case. But she repeated the names to herself to cement them in her memory anyway as Mia fumbled with the lock.

The door opened with a protest, a metallic scream that sent a blackbird on a nearby branch into flight. Izzy's eyes snagged on the sleek, dark creature as its wings beat steadily against the thick gray sky. A shiver slithered across her skin, the fine hair on her forearms standing on end, and she couldn't help the quick glance she threw to the woods behind them.

Just as expected, there was no one there.

She hurried to follow Mia into the cabin.

The heavy, black curtains were drawn, but the sun pouring in through the door was enough to partially illuminate the room. Something silver shimmered on the desk, and Izzy crossed the room in two long strides.

"Laptop," she told Mia, who had moved toward the unmade bed that took up the majority of the floor space. A small stand next to it held a lamp but was clear of any other clutter.

There were notebooks upon notebooks stacked next to the computer, as well as a mostly empty bowl of soup with just a few carrots shriveled at the bottom and a mug with a dried-up tea bag clinging to the ceramic.

A sink, an out-of-place bright yellow mini fridge, and a few cabinets passed as the kitchen, and by the bed was a darkened emptiness that Izzy assumed was the bathroom.

Her guess was confirmed after she flipped on the stark single bulb that hung above the toilet. *Rustic.*

Dandruff shampoo and a cheap generic bodywash sat on the ledge behind the plastic curtain that was more soap residue than anything else at this point.

Izzy turned back to the main room, her eyes touching on the bare surfaces. "Would be hard to tell if there was a disturbance here."

"The owner said the door was still locked when she came in after they found the body," Mia said, her voice muffled since she was searching through the cabinets. "I just checked the windows. They don't show signs of forced entry."

A black bag tucked into the narrow nook between the headboard and the wall caught Izzy's eye. She knelt and inelegantly shoved her fingers into the pair of latex gloves she'd pulled from her pocket. Once they were on, she unzipped the duffel with careful deliberation.

The caution didn't prove to be necessary. Everything was neat and in order, jeans folded on top of a few flannel button-downs, a handful of T-shirts slotted in next to boxers and socks.

"Anything?" Mia called from somewhere behind her.

Izzy shook her head as she stood. "Just clothes. Toiletries kit on the sink in there." She tipped her chin toward the bathroom. "Not seeing much else."

"He must have had his wallet on him," Mia said. She was standing over the desk, the tip of her pen hovering by the corner of one of the notebooks like she was about to flip it open. But she hadn't yet.

"Or someone with a copy of the key cleaned up behind themselves."

Mia's mouth twitched at that suggestion. "They can't exactly just run down to the local locksmith."

"So he probably took his important stuff with him," Izzy conceded. "What do you think are in those?"

"Whatever he was working on." A *no shit* answer to a *no shit* question.

Frigid air licked at the exposed skin of Izzy's wrist when she took the gloves off, and her exhale was a frozen white coil that drifted toward the ceiling. "Can we take those somewhere else to read?"

Izzy's request earned her an actual smile. "Yeah, we'll see if tech has any suggestion on the laptop, too."

"Bless you," Izzy said, swiveling to flip the light switch off in the bathroom. As she did, she noticed something right near the bottom leg of the bed. Bending down, she slid the small object out from the darkness.

"What is it?" Mia asked. She'd moved closer.

Izzy held it up so they could both see.

"A phone."

Mia met her eyes. "That's out of place."

Nodding in agreement, Izzy looked down at the black screen, then glanced back to where the cell had been pushed under the bed. "I think . . ."

"What?"

"Maybe he was trying to hide it," Izzy said, knowing it was a wild leap of logic but unable to silence the thought. "For us to find."

Mia stopped on the path back into town so abruptly Izzy had to sidestep to keep from crashing into her. The messenger bag full of the reporter's notebooks that Izzy had slung over her shoulder wasn't as quick to react and slammed against Mia's side.

A swallowed grunt was her only acknowledgment of pain.

"Sorry, but your brake lights must be out," Izzy said, her eyes flicking toward the sky. Thick sludge clouds had been rolling toward them all morning, and Izzy was anxious to get to shelter before the storm made landfall.

"One stop," Mia said, squinting at the oncoming weather as well. After a few seconds, she nodded, a tiny confirmation to herself almost, and then took the left path instead of the one that took them back to Edie Hart's house. And a roof. And heat. "We'll have time."

There was nothing to do but follow. "Who are we visiting?"

"Martha Lowe." The answer was so quiet it took Izzy a second to catch on.

"Lowe. Like—"

"Asher, yes," Mia interrupted. "Martha is his grandmother."

Izzy studied the side of Mia's face, trying to read anything there. Her expression was empty, though. "Does that mean . . . you do think Twist's death has something to do with Asher's? And Monroe's?"

Mia bit her lip, but that was the only sign that she wasn't completely composed. "I don't know. Probably not."

Probably not. An echo of what Izzy had thought at the cabin. They both seemed to be dancing around the possibility, not trusting it but unable to ignore it. If Twist's story had been about Asher's and Monroe's deaths, there was a chance, likely or not, that he could have been killed over it.

She wondered if Mia's opinion about whether Twist's death was suicide had shifted yet. Izzy knew for herself if the journals confirmed that the reporter had indeed been asking about that night, it would make Izzy more convinced that they were looking at a homicide here.

But where that left Mia, she didn't know, and she didn't have time to ask, either. They came to a stop outside a sky-blue house with a pristine white door.

The woman who answered Mia's knock had the weathered, hardy look Izzy was starting to associate with living in Maine. She was short but stout, not frail, her silver hair braided down her back.

"Mia Hart," Martha said, like she'd been expecting her.

"Ma'am." It was the most deferential that Izzy had ever heard Mia. "This is Detective Santiago. We'd like to ask you a few questions if we can."

Martha's gaze swung to Izzy, and she instinctively straightened under the attention.

"Come in."

There were no pleasantries, no offers of tea or coffee. Martha directed them to sit on an overstuffed two-seater couch as she took the hard, wooden chair that was kitty-corner to it.

"You're finally investigating Asher's murder."

Mia's small inhale was hardly a gasp, but it was noticeable nonetheless. "Murder?"

Martha's eyes narrowed. "Don't waste my time, child."

Izzy saw an opening to play dumb. "I thought it was ruled suicide, ma'am."

"My grandson did not kill himself." Each word was enunciated as if it were its own sentence, and Martha stared them both down, her chin tipped up, her lips pinched.

It wasn't uncommon for family members to refuse to accept the suicide of a loved one. These kinds of assertions were useless to them, as coldhearted as that might be to admit. But it also happened to follow the same path they were tentatively considering. "Did you tell the police that? Back then?"

"They ignored me." The words were loaded with contempt.

"Okay, tell us, then," Mia interjected. "What happened?"

"Asher saw something." The lines on Martha's face deepened as she scowled, everything about her an unmovable fortress. Whether she was right, she had certainly convinced herself that she was. "Something he shouldn't have seen. They were trying to shut him up. They did shut him up."

Izzy tried to follow her. "Who are 'they'? What did he see?"

"Don't know," Martha said, fast and clipped.

"Why do you think someone was trying to shut him up, then?"

She rubbed a thumb over her knuckle, her eyes on her hands. "Haven't seen Bix Bell since before that night."

Bix. As in Charles and Bix, as in Monroe's mother. Again, Izzy was able to plead ignorance.

"I was under the impression they'd left the island in the days following the deaths."

"That's what everyone thinks," Martha said. "But they used a private boat. No one actually saw them leave together."

"Wait, did you say 'before'?" Mia asked, latching onto the part Izzy had missed. "You mean 'after,' right? Bix was there, at the lighthouse."

"Says who?" Martha lifted her thick, silver brows.

That shut Mia up, and Izzy was no help there, either.

Martha leaned forward and swiveled her jaw once, and then again. "Everyone assumes they saw her. But no one actually did. Because she wasn't there. The cops only talked to Charles Bell."

"My mother didn't go to the lighthouse, either," Mia said, almost to herself, her focus turned inward.

"Yes, but I bought a hammer from your mama three days ago at the shop," Martha countered. "No one on this island has seen Bix since before that night. You know that old house on the Bell land where the workers used to stay? It's just sitting there. Abandoned. Makes you wonder why."

Izzy was going to need her to spell it out. "You think Charles killed Bix, and Asher saw it happen?"

"That boy saw something," Martha answered with the same kind of tactic as Patty—not a confirmation, not a denial, but an evasion.

And this, this right here was what had Izzy worried about, with starting down this path. There was a reason fringe conspiracy theories didn't go mainstream. Coming from Martha, the scenario sounded outlandish and leaned heavily on that wisp of an idea that Bix's possible murder and Asher's and Monroe's deaths were connected.

"Did Asher tell you something?" Mia asked.

Martha's lips pursed. "No, but he came home earlier that day all pale and sweaty. Shaking a little. Had a black eye and wouldn't say where he'd gotten it."

Mia shifted beside Izzy, straightening. Something she hadn't remembered?

"He'd been in a fight?"

"Hmm, yup."

"And had he been acting odd at all in the days leading up to that one?" Izzy asked.

"No, he was right as rain until then." Martha nodded once as if to punctuate that. "Then the black eye."

But. But why would Charles have given him a black eye? Even if Asher had seen something he shouldn't have. That didn't make any sense.

The details weren't adding up. They were spiraling here.

"All right, I'm going to give you my card," Mia said. "You let me know if you think of anything else."

Martha took it but didn't look away from Mia's face. "You don't believe me."

Mia paused, and then more tactfully than perhaps Izzy would have managed: "We're just collecting information, ma'am. Haven't reached any conclusions yet."

"You think I'm crazy, just like the rest of them," Martha accused, her voice rising.

Izzy went for the Achilles' heel. "Do you have proof that any of this happened?"

The answer was obviously no, but Martha didn't put voice to it. Instead, she tapped the card against her thigh. "Find what happened to Bix Bell. You'll have your evidence then."

For all they knew, Bix was sipping champagne back in Boston with her ridiculously rich husband. But Izzy plastered on a small smile and nodded. Mia murmured something as equally noncommittal, and then they were back outside, the storm gathering force behind them.

"I don't know which way that swayed me, to be honest," Izzy admitted as they started back toward Edie's house.

Mia barely seemed to hear her. "I would have known if he'd gotten in a fight that day."

"But you don't remember any of it." Not that Mia needed to be reminded of that. Still Izzy felt compelled to say it. For the record.

Mia's shoulder hunched up toward her ears. "I would have known."

"You think she's mistaken? Getting confused?"

Glancing back once, Mia shook her head. "I think maybe we should focus on the murder we're trying to solve instead of hunting new ones out."

Izzy didn't say anything further. But it didn't escape her that just like Martha, just like Patty, Mia hadn't answered the question.

CHAPTER NINE

MIA

The words jumbled, spilled into each other, gentle curves knocking against hard edges, slipping past boundaries, bleeding together. The letters were random for as much as Mia tried to make sense of the gibberish scribbled in the tight lines of the reporter's notebooks.

"Shorthand," she murmured, tapping the smudged writing. Left-handed. Twist would have been one of those people with perpetual ink stains smeared against the outside of his palm.

Izzy glanced up from the journal she'd taken from the pile. They were sitting at the small laminate table in Mama's kitchen, the same one Mia had done homework on decades ago. There was still that crack running along one side, as thin as a spider's thread. Mia rubbed at it with the pad of her thumb.

They had barely made it back from Martha's before the first flakes fell. Snow alone wouldn't have been enough to put Mia off the investigation, but the storm that followed was brutal. Hail pinged against the windows; wind battered all the seams of the house until it groaned beneath the pressure; lightning sliced into the darkness behind Mia's closed eyes.

"Same here," Izzy said, holding up some random pages as proof. "But I think there's a pattern to them."

There had to be. What mattered was if they could see it or not.

The brain so dearly loved patterns, with a tricky tendency to draw lines where lines shouldn't exist. When there was a lack of solid evidence on a cold case, those leaps were needed to push past brick walls that had blocked others.

But there was danger there, as well, a vulnerability to having an open mind be exploited. It was like those children's games, the ones that came on diner menus, the dots that connected to create an image. A bear, a star, a heart. You could almost see the finished product before even laying crayon to paper.

What happened, though, when all the dots were in the right place but you drew the wrong image?

That's what they were always trying to avoid.

"There are dates and initials," Mia finally said. "This one's from early December, before he got to St. Lucy's."

"Ah, you're right, good eye." Izzy looked down at her own notebook, a line digging into the otherwise smooth skin between her brows. "This one's November."

"We need January." Mia pulled half the stack closer. "Or mid to late December."

"Yup." Izzy didn't quite roll her eyes at the obvious statement, but it was there in her voice.

Mia ignored it, her gaze tracing over the swooping scrawl until she found what she was looking for. *There.* January. Twist would have been on the island then.

"Got it," Mia said.

"When was it that you saw him outside the station?"

The way Izzy asked the question was casual, almost like it was an afterthought.

"Late October? Maybe. Sometime in the fall."

Izzy's lips pinched and then relaxed, a quick flash of an emotion gone before it caught fully. "Maybe I'll try to find the one around that time."

"If it's there," Mia said, off-balance. The man's face had already begun disintegrating in her memory, the distinct features blurring. They'd been fresh in that moment of shock, of seeing him pale and bloated, of recognizing him when she shouldn't have. But the nose, the slope of his forehead, his jawline—it had all faded along with the adrenaline.

Now, she just remembered being cold, pulling her jacket tighter, keeping her eyes on the indistinct figure that stayed a shadow until the headlights had swept across his face. They'd locked eyes across the street that first time.

The way fear had slipped into her bloodstream, though, *that* she remembered well. The animal instinct that said *run* before her brain could question why. Something about him had set off her alarms.

Mia pressed her thumb against the thin skin of her temple, running it in circles along the hard edge of bone. It was then Mama set a mug of tea at her elbow.

Nodding her thanks, Mia curled her fingers around the thick cup and blew on the steam. "Did you ever talk to him, Mama?"

"The reporter?" Mama's back was already to them while she scrubbed at a pan in the sink, her shoulders hunched. "Saw him a couple times."

Izzy looked up from the pages she'd been flipping through but didn't interrupt.

"Sammy said he was poking around the lighthouse," Mia prodded.

The pan clattered against the metal drying rack, the sound loud and abrupt. "Might have been."

"Anywhere else he was looking around?" Mia asked.

"Mm-hmm." Mama plunged her hands back in the soapy water. "Went up to the Bell mansion a bunch of times."

The Bell mansion. The lighthouse. These were the dots lining up into a shape, one Mia could see but didn't want to. Mama must have seen it as well.

It keeps coming back to that summer, doesn't it?

"Is the mansion empty now?"

This time a bowl rattled against the pan. "Nope."

Izzy's lips parted, a question in her sharp gaze. But after catching Mia's eyes, she swallowed whatever she had been about to ask.

Mia was thankful. It wouldn't do well to remind Mama there was an outsider with them.

"Who took it over?"

There was a pause. And then Mama stripped off her washing gloves, slapping them against the counter. She turned, thick arms folded across her barrel chest. Mia didn't know what was coming, but she knew she wasn't going to like it.

"Lacey Bell moved in about three years ago," Mama finally said.

Mia inhaled, the swift slide of air passing her chapped lips loud enough to catch Izzy's attention. "Lacey came back?"

Her mother's eyes were hooded, any thoughts there protected by a sweep of lashes. "Three years ago," she repeated.

Sliding a finger against the rim of her mug kept Mia's hand busy so that it wouldn't find the faded white scar along her wrist.

Once upon a time Lacey Bell had sworn she was never returning to St. Lucy's. Mia could see her still, her eyes wet, her glossy black hair tangled around her red, splotchy face.

"What does she do now?" Mia asked, bereft of any other questions from the sheer shock of it.

For the first time since they'd started the conversation, Mama's face relaxed, her lips pulling back in amused derision.

"She's an artist." Mama made quotes around the last word. "You ask me, she's lucky she's rich."

"Does she actually sell anything?"

Shrugging, Mama turned back to the sink, the tension that had held them locked in the moment fading from her stance. "She was featured in a fancy art magazine a few months back. Still runs those hippie communities in the summer."

"Really?" Mia asked, surprised. "Lacey started them again? The residencies."

Mama grunted her affirmative. She'd never been a fan of the artists who flooded in during the warmer months.

"Are there any up there now?"

"One or two cycle through," Mama said after a pause that sounded reflective rather than loaded with the deliberate obtuseness she'd been employing earlier. She shrugged and started for the hallway, clearly done with the questioning. "They never last long."

Mia and Izzy stared after her retreating back for a long moment before a sharp ding cut through the silence Mama had left behind. Izzy jumped and then laughed in that way that released nerves sound.

"Christ." Izzy held her hand to her heart, leaning into the melodrama. It took only a beat longer for Mia to realize what the interruption must have been.

"The reporter's phone," she said, pushing to her feet. Izzy was behind her in an instant as they hovered over it.

Mia had plugged it into a charger when they'd returned to the house, even though she hadn't been hopeful that they'd be able to get anything useful.

The ding had been a calendar notification. They could see the banner bright against the default lock screen.

Quinn Thomas. 4 Baker Street. 12:00 p.m.

"Wasn't that . . . ?"

"The seaplane pilot, yes," Mia finished for Izzy.

"Twist was planning on leaving today."

Mia nodded absently, chewing on her thumbnail as she kept reading over the notification like it would tell her something new. "Probably."

"Or it was an interview," Izzy suggested. "And whatever he was researching had to do with her."

The Bell mansion. The lighthouse. A figure under a busted streetlight. Mia doubted any of this had to do with Quinn.

She didn't answer. Instead, she idly tapped the home button, not expecting anything. But the lock screen disappeared and she was in.

"What . . . ?" Izzy's exhale behind her was just as surprised. "He didn't have it locked? Who doesn't keep their phone locked?"

Everything on the phone was neat, tidy. Barren, almost. There was nothing personalized about it—the background the default photo everyone got out of the box, the apps the ones that came with the phone. Mia's eyes touched on each of the little squares, lingered as if the simple images would offer a clue that she knew they wouldn't.

The absence of social media apps didn't surprise her given Twist's lack of a digital footprint, but what did was that his camera roll was empty. As were his email and text messages.

Scrubbed. The whole thing had been scrubbed.

In frustration, Mia swiped to the second panel, expecting the screen to bounce back as it did when there was nothing else on the phone. Instead, it slid over, then settled, a seemingly empty screen on first glance. Except, there, tucked against the bottom-right corner, subtle enough to be missed unless someone was looking for it, was an image of an old-fashioned voice recorder.

The reporter's notes. Her pulse ticked up as she thumbed into the app.

Like with the rest of the phone, there was little there. Just one recording.

"This was under the bed?" Mia asked Izzy without looking up.

"Yeah, mostly," Izzy said. "Pushed out of sight."

Mia could picture a desperate hand hiding the phone so it would be found later, just as Izzy had suggested back in the cabin. If Twist's death had been suicide and he was trying to communicate with them, would he have really taken the chance that it could be overlooked?

Murder or suicide? Put one more mark in the former's column. It was a tally that was getting harder to ignore. She was beginning to think that eventually it would just be denial to call this anything other than homicide.

"Who doesn't keep their phone locked?" Mia repeated Izzy's question slowly, looking up from the screen. "Someone who wants their notes to be found."

Her thumb was steady as she pressed play.

The message was short, just three words—a lit match that burned out just as quick.

"It wasn't suicide."

The voice pressed into all the spaces in the kitchen. It was high and thin, the vowels cutting short.

Mia closed her eyes and hit the play button again. "It wasn't suicide." The words crawled along her skin, sticking to the sweat slicked into the grooves of her palms, slipping into her nostrils as they flared with her uneven breathing.

She hit play again. And then again.

Each time, that quick flame, then gone, replaced with silence.

After the initial rush, as her pulse settled, she listened to the voice, the way the message was thrown out, careless and easy, like it didn't really matter. There was no fear threaded through it, no urgency beyond a quick note to himself.

"Is he . . . ? Is he talking about himself, do you think?" Izzy asked, when Mia's finger hovered over the play icon once more.

"It wasn't suicide."

The message so closely echoed her thoughts it made her light-headed. But . . .

"I don't think so. Not about himself. Listen." Mia watched Izzy's face as the voice once more tumbled out of the little speaker. Izzy tugged at her pursed bottom lip, but the rest of her was held taut, her eyes unfocused beyond Mia's shoulder.

"He's calm," Izzy finally said, her gaze returning to Mia's. "Doesn't sound like he was under duress."

"Probably not," Mia agreed. So why was the message left on the phone? Why was the device unlocked in the first place? "I wonder if he erased the rest."

Izzy dropped her hand and ran her palm along her jeans. "That would be odd, don't you think?"

"Yeah. Why would he get rid of all his notes in the middle of his investigation?" It would be odd. To do all that work. Interviews, thoughts, impressions. All gone. "Or maybe he wasn't the one who deleted them."

"The killer then?" Izzy shifted so she was leaning back against the counter. Mia didn't move from where she hovered above the phone, her irrational side nervous that they would be locked out if she took one wrong step. "If he was murdered, that is."

It wasn't suicide. Mia almost repeated the words out loud, but she wanted to hold on to doubt a little longer.

"I don't think a potential killer would have done it," she said. Why would they leave a message like that on the phone yet delete the rest of the voice memos? There was no other indication that the person was trying to get caught. "Maybe Twist was getting scared. He deleted the more incriminating recordings in case the killer found the phone and checked it."

Izzy ran a hand through her hair. "That was a risk. By deleting the rest of them, he put a spotlight on that one."

"For us then," Mia said. "Maybe it was worth chancing someone else finding it. Worth it to get his message to us, I mean."

They both stared at the phone as it did absolutely nothing in Mia's hand. Then Izzy cleared her throat. "So. Was he talking about Asher and Monroe?"

Mia gripped the counter to keep from touching her wrist, where she knew she would find her rapid pulse. They were barreling toward something she wasn't even sure her brain was ready to process. Would the inevitable conclusion be more darkness?

"I'll poke around in the phone," Mia said, instead of answering, because she was worried it would come out yes. "You take the journals."

There was a pause, and Mia didn't look over. Her knuckles ached, and she slowly unpeeled her fingers from the slightly sticky corner, conscious of every small movement.

"Sure, will do," Izzy finally said, easily, though Mia could tell she wanted to talk more.

Mia lifted her gaze to the window overlooking the tiny backyard that bled into the forest beyond. Mama's home was at the top of the small incline that sloped gradually back down into the port. There were no more houses behind theirs, just woods and snow. Silence where in the summer there would be birdsong.

The soles of her feet could still feel the press of knobby roots and misplaced stones as she and Asher and Cash played cowboys and robbers in the warmer months. In the winter, they'd had epic wars: their ammo of choice, ice-glazed snowballs; their enemies, the handful of kids home on college break.

The memories were tinted sepia and softened at the corners, like old photographs of someone else's life. She didn't look at these often, but when she did, she was careful, reverent, pulling them out, caressing the smiles, the laughs, the flushed cheeks and giddy glances. Her thoughts always lingered on Asher for a beat longer, searching for an emptiness in his eyes that she may have missed when she was younger.

But then the memory would blink, shiver, move on to the next. And once again, she would have missed any signs.

The pain beneath her breastbone screamed, and she pressed the heel of her palm to the spot, though it wouldn't help. She hadn't eaten almost anything since she'd stepped off the ferry, and yet she was on her fourth cup of coffee for the day.

She tucked her fingertips into the pocket of her jeans for the chalky tablet she'd stashed there, popping it between her teeth with her back to Izzy.

Her eyes were on the trees as she snapped the tablet in two between her teeth as quietly as possible.

———

Although the phone had been mostly wiped clean, whoever had deleted the emails and text messages had missed something. The call history was still there.

Most of calls were just random strings of numbers, not used enough to warrant a contact name. There were a few who had earned one—Peter. Bram. Marlie.

Peter's showed up the most frequently. In fact, the last outgoing call had been to him on the day after Robert Twist had arrived on St. Lucy's. But they all seemed to be missed calls or only a few seconds in length that could have been a voice mail.

Mia wasn't sure if it meant anything, but she made a mental note to have a trace done on the number.

She kept scrolling as she asked Izzy, "Did you find anything useful?"

Izzy looked up from where she was working on the notebooks. The journals were small, holding only a few interviews each, and Izzy was combing through them to create a rough timeline of whom Twist had talked to and when.

"Initials." Izzy held up a scrap of paper. "You can probably help with those."

Wordlessly, Mia held out her hand for Izzy's notes. She scanned the combinations of letters and could pick out CB and EB—Cash and his father, Earl—and JR right next to them.

Jimmy Roarke. Likely.

Sammy had mentioned Jimmy chasing the reporter off from the lighthouse.

"These initials—they were all close to each other?" Mia asked, tapping the grouping.

Izzy flipped through the notebook she'd been working through, humming softly when she stopped on a page. "Yup. A couple pages' worth of gibberish for all of them."

Can't say I ever talked to the man.

That's what Cash had said when she'd asked about the reporter. Why lie? When, with a little digging, Mia was sure she could have proven otherwise through gossip alone.

Why lie? She shook her head even as the question burrowed in, latched on.

Lying was a way of life more than anything else for people on St. Lucy's. Unlike the mainland, where kids were taught not to fib, island children learned a different lesson. Truth wasn't a moral high ground; there were no brownie points awarded for honesty. Rather, they were taught to hoard secrets tight, earning pats on the head for any time they were tempted to tell stories but kept them locked up instead.

Once, when she'd been little, Asher and she had built a fort in his parents' living room beneath sheets that smelled of smoke and lilacs. They'd cuddled as children did, their whispers tangling together way past their bedtime, and Mia had told him about her parents fighting, the terrible words they'd flung at each other when she was supposed to be asleep.

Asher had listened with big eyes. The next day everyone on the island knew about the Harts' problems. Mia hadn't been able to sit down for a week from the smacks Mama had landed on her behind.

She hadn't even been mad at Asher when he'd apologized, his chipmunk cheeks tear streaked and pale after realizing she'd been spanked. She hadn't been mad because she'd known it had been her fault for not lying when he'd asked for her secrets.

Lying had always been their language, their code, their shibboleth. Had she so easily forgotten the patterns of it? They didn't communicate with what they said but rather with what they kept hidden. It was in the pauses, the unspoken words, that the truth could always be found.

Can't say I ever talked to the man.

She didn't want to think about exactly what Cash had been saying in the spaces between his lies.

CHAPTER TEN

Izzy

The alarm on the phone went off again. Quinn Thomas. 4 Baker Street. 12:00 p.m.

It was fifteen minutes until noon now, and Izzy glanced out the window before turning to Mia with a raised brow. "Is it safe to go out?"

Mia pushed to her feet and crossed to the sink. There were still flakes falling—Izzy could see that from the table—but they were large and powdery, gentle instead of the hail of an hour earlier.

"Yeah, let's go," Mia said, and Izzy refrained from groaning at the idea of the cold despite the fact that she was getting itchy just sitting in the kitchen, staring at notebooks full of words she couldn't decipher.

They moved quickly through the process of layering up, and after they were both satisfied most of their skin was covered, they pushed through the door. The icy air sought all the cracks in their defenses: the slips of skin exposed by a rucked-up sleeve, the moisture in their eyes, the gaps between their scarves and the napes of their necks.

"Don't you have to lock the door?" Izzy yelled. The wind had picked up even from that morning's trek to the cabin. If Twist had been alive to make his appointment, there was no way Quinn Thomas would have flown out in this weather.

"We don't lock doors," Mia shouted back, starting toward the sidewalk that would lead them into town, even though it was buried.

"It's almost like you *didn't* just have someone murdered on your tiny arctic island," Izzy mumbled, the words loud against the pocket of silence between gusts. "You know . . . and with the killer still probably running around, locking doors would just be foolish."

"Your sarcasm would be more effective if I could hear it," Mia tossed back over her shoulder. "And we don't know it was murder."

Izzy rolled her eyes, but it was in vain as Mia had already started down the hill. Any attempt at a witty comeback was curtailed by the wind.

They didn't attempt any more conversation as they worked their way past the houses down toward the shops that lined the two streets right off the docks. Quinn's glorified tourist stand with a door was next to the ferry ticket booth.

A small bell chimed as Mia and Izzy walked in.

Izzy didn't bother stripping down beyond her scarf. The office was set to a temperature that favored a low heating bill over human comfort.

The space was long and narrow, just wide enough for the desk that took up three-fourths of the floor toward the back of the shop. A woman with frizzy brown hair held down by a purple hat glanced up at the sound of their heavy boots on her carpet. Her face was pointy, her lips thin. Thick eyebrows pulled together as she looked down at her desk and then back at them. "Ferry office is next door."

"Quinn Thomas?" Mia asked.

There was a pause, a consideration. As if even confirming who she was would be some kind of admission. "Who's asking?"

"Lord," Izzy drawled out under her breath.

Quinn's attention was locked on Mia, though, recognition flickering across her face. "Mia? Mia Hart?"

Mia nodded, just once. "Yes."

The suspicion melted to be replaced by a surprising smile that changed the woman's face from odd to pretty. "Man, it's been ages."

The warmth of the welcome faded. "Ah, if you're trying to get off the island, can't do it. Storm's not done yet. Sorry."

"No, we're here for a little bit." Mia stepped closer to the desk, and Quinn gestured for her to sit. Izzy followed suit. There were maps papering the walls, some obviously antiques, others the kind you could pick up at a gas station, the yellows and pinks and purples denoting different islands. The one hanging closest to them had come unstuck at one of the corners, and Izzy pressed her fingers to the loose bit, trying to smooth it down.

"Ah, well then, what brings you in here?" Quinn asked the question to Mia, still studiously avoiding Izzy.

"Actually, your noon appointment does. Robert Twist," Mia said. "I'm with the mainland police department. We're investigating his death."

There wasn't even a second of surprise. Word really did get around quick.

"Don't know what I can tell you." Quinn shrugged, her fingers toying with the ledger she had open on her desk. Izzy watched Mia watching them. The woman had a thing about hands. Said they gave away secrets every time. Izzy was starting to think Mia knew enough about hiding that she could easily recognize it in others. "Didn't even know the guy. Just talked to him a couple times about some trips."

"That's all I want to know," Mia said, her tone friendly, mellow. "Was he planning on flying back to the mainland today?"

"No. He was headed toward San Sebastian."

Izzy wanted to ask, but just as she was deciding if she could interrupt without causing too much disturbance, Mia tilted her head toward her. "An island about ten miles north of here." Then she refocused on Quinn. "Was it one-way?"

"Yep."

So he'd been leaving. Island-hopping maybe? Chasing his story across the small juts of land that dotted Black Rock Bay. Did that mean he *wasn't* focused only on the suicide-pact story?

"When did he book it? The ticket," Izzy asked.

Mia hummed, a quiet approval of the question.

Quinn's eye squinted as if trying to remember, but then she shook her head and pulled out a big journal. Her finger ran along one of the open pages, before stopping and tapping in place. "Looks like Friday. The one before he disappeared."

So he'd booked a one-way plane ticket two days before his death.

They all sat with that for a beat.

"Can you just . . . ?" Mia paused. "What was your impression of him?"

"The reporter?" Quinn's eyes darted over to Izzy, then back to Mia. "I don't know, he was kind of squirrelly, wasn't he?"

Izzy laughed, an uncontrolled bark. "So we've been told."

The interruption actually earned her a small smile from Quinn. "He was just going around getting in people's business."

"Was he asking about anything in particular?" Mia pressed.

"He talked to Joe—my boyfriend—about the winters a lot," Quinn said. "Like if Joe was feeling sad or depressed and stuff like that. Isolated. The reporter kept using that word—'isolated.'"

That rang true with what Patty had said. But was it a cover, like she'd insisted? Or were they linking the cases prematurely?

"Do you know anyone else who talked to him?" Mia asked. "Were they asked similar questions?"

"Ellen—Ellen Baxter, she's a waitress at the Silver Spoon—had coffee with him," Quinn said. "He paid for it and everything. Said he would *expense* it."

Izzy couldn't tell if the emphasis was derision or if Quinn was impressed.

"She said it was more of the same, though." Quinn leaned forward, her forearms braced against the desk. "That he just kept talking about 'isolation' and death and winter."

"Did he mention anything to you about what he was going to be doing on San Sebastian?" Mia asked. "Even offhand?"

Quinn's eyes went distant, like she was combing through conversations, looking for information. "He was real creepy like. I think he mentioned . . . Do you remember that family?"

"I'm sorry?"

"On San Sebastian, maybe thirty years ago? It was a couple with a toddler. They killed the baby and then themselves," Quinn said, an eagerness in the tilt of her words, the kind that coated the voice when discussing something particularly sensational and morbid. It happened with most people. Izzy was used to it by now, but it still left an unsettling feeling in its wake. "The guy was psycho, absolutely terrible."

Mia shifted as well, and Quinn caught the movement. The excitement on Quinn's face died in that instant at the clear signal that Mia was about to end the conversation. "Oh. Oh . . ."

"All right, thank you." Mia stood before Quinn could get anything else out. The woman sat back against her chair, eyes wide. Maybe she'd been caught as off guard by their abrupt departure as Izzy had. "We'll be in touch. Eventually, we'll need a flight back to the mainland."

"Of course," Quinn said quietly, remaining seated even as Mia and Izzy started toward the front of the shop. "Actually, wait up."

They paused, turned. Izzy's eyebrows raised a silent prompt.

"I don't know if it means anything . . ."

Izzy's attention sharpened. From experience, when witnesses prefaced information with that, it usually *did*, in fact, mean something.

"But . . . ," Mia prodded.

"I'm friends with Bobby Jane, one of Max Verdon's daughters?" Quinn waited for Mia's quick nod before continuing. "Well, she said her dad said the guy had been asking about an artist who had been on the island a few months ago. Tried to keep it real casual like, didn't even mention his name or anything. But Max noted it, so."

An artist. Like one who could have cycled through the residencies up at the Bell mansion. The place Robert Twist had apparently visited several times. The place Lacey Bell now lived. The place Martha Lowe thought Bix Bell was buried.

"That's very helpful, thank you," Mia said, in a way that would probably leave Quinn thinking the opposite. It was a good tactic. The quickest way to kill this kind of speculation was to make it seem boring, useless.

They saw themselves out the door.

Once they stepped outside, Mia stopped, then leaned against the wall of the ferry building, her head tipped back against the brick, the muscles in her throat rippling as she swallowed heavily. When her lashes fluttered open, her lips quirked up, but without humor.

"She had greedy eyes."

There was no need for further explanation. Izzy knew what she was talking about. Quinn had reeked of it, that desire for gossip. It didn't even seem malicious, just borne of boredom with daily life.

Mia looked away, toward Main Street, staring at something. Izzy followed her gaze to a diner situated at the corner of the block.

"Hey," Mia said, pushing away from the wall. "Let's get lunch."

Lunch wasn't just lunch, Izzy realized two minutes later when they stepped into the diner. A perky young woman with Shirley Temple curls and dimples in peachy cheeks that were more freckles than skin greeted them in passing, her arms weighed down with a heavy tray.

Once Izzy caught a glimpse of her name tag, she understood why they were stopping by.

Ellen Baxter. The waitress who had gotten coffee with Twist.

The dip and swing of her voice was nearly melodic as she directed them to take a seat "Wherever you like."

"That's the Ellen that Quinn mentioned?" Izzy asked as they shrugged off their jackets and slid into one of the booths.

Mia peeked over her shoulder and then turned back to the table to grab one of the menus. "Don't ask her anything yet, okay?"

In the light pouring through the window, Izzy could see each sleepless night in the thin veins that crisscrossed beneath Mia's eyes, saw the toll of being back on the island in the downward slant of her lips, in the lines by her mouth. Some of her careful mask worn down after her moment with Quinn.

Trauma and grief didn't have an expiration date, and working this case had to be a shock to Mia's system. It was understandable, but Izzy wondered just how much it was compromising Mia's objectivity when it came to the case.

They waited in silence for the few minutes it took for Ellen to make her way toward the table. After they'd placed their order, Mia stopped Ellen before she could turn away.

"You didn't grow up here, did you?"

The waitress's smile dimmed, the dimples slipping so that her cheeks were smooth. "No, moved here a few years back."

"When I was younger, I lived here," Mia said. "I was just trying to place you but wasn't sure."

Ellen paled further. "I didn't grow up here."

The reaction was out of sync with Mia's casual tone. Hunted. Ellen looked hunted. But they'd barely asked her any questions yet.

By now Izzy was realizing that most people on the island probably knew exactly who they were and what they were after. But this was small talk. Only someone who was hiding something would flinch over it.

"Ah, okay." Mia's tone was still relaxed, but Izzy could tell she was surprised as well. "How do you like St. Lucy's?"

Ellen took a step away from their table, her flight instinct obviously triggered. "If I can't get you guys anything else?" But it wasn't really a question, as she was almost out of range of a normal conversation by the time she finished the sentence.

They'd played the interaction wrong. Mia had played the interaction wrong.

It didn't happen often, not for Mia. But maybe Ellen's sunny facade had thrown her.

"Actually." Mia stopped Ellen before she could retreat to the kitchen completely. "You can get us some answers to a few questions."

Any last traces of warmth that had been left seeped out. "I don't think I have any of those."

Mia sighed and dipped a hand into an inner pocket. She pulled out her badge, held up the leather case, ID facing out. "Now how about those questions."

Ellen's arms came up again, her fingers digging into the bare flesh. Her uniform was inexplicably short sleeved, an old-fashioned-type yellow dress with stiff fabric that never fit anyone correctly.

There was a battle being waged behind those shuttered eyes. The girl could still resist, force them to get a warrant. Or she could give them what were probably half truths and lies anyway. The choice seemed obvious to Izzy.

Ellen's gaze swept the room once, her shoulders tense as she tried to make herself small. "Not here. I'll take my smoke break. Meet me in the alley in five."

Dropping two twenties on the table, Mia slid out of the booth, and Izzy followed. They headed outside and then took a hard right into the small alleyway behind the diner.

It took another seven minutes for the back-entrance door to crack open. Ellen slipped through the narrow opening, bundled up in a heavy jacket and a turquoise beanie that covered her curls.

She glanced at them but didn't say anything as she leaned against the diner's wall and attempted to light her cigarette. On the third try the flame took, and the slim stick shook in her hands.

"I don't know what I can tell you," Ellen finally said, holding the cigarette near her leg instead of bringing it to her lips.

"You know we're looking into Robert Twist's death," Mia started, gentle, like she was trying not to spook a skittish animal.

Ellen jerked her head in a quick affirmative but didn't look at either of them. Izzy had the impression she would sink back into the wall if she could.

"Can you tell us about him? We heard he talked to you. Took you to coffee."

At the last bit, Ellen flinched. Then clearly tried to hide the reaction.

They were all bundled, hands gloved and shoved in pockets, chins dipping beneath the collars of their coats in a vain hope that it would keep their faces protected.

The back alley in the middle of winter left a lot to be desired for an interview space.

"I don't know what there is to tell," Ellen said. "He hit on me when he first got here. I finally agreed to get coffee with him."

"Was it a personal interest, or did he want to talk to you about the story he was working on?"

The girl swallowed, a flush of pink riding along her cheekbones. Embarrassment. Or they were just chapped from the wind. Could be either.

"I thought it was a date until he started asking about you."

And so another confirmation that Twist was digging into that night at the lighthouse.

"What was he asking?" Izzy chimed in. Ellen's attention swung toward her, eyes wide, pupils dilated. It was as if she'd forgotten there was a threat to her right side as well. She stared at Izzy, frozen, then looked back at Mia.

"If I knew you."

Mia's head tipped. "But you didn't. What would there have been to say?"

"Knew of you." It was muttered under her breath.

Izzy was reminded of Patty last night. *People always ask questions about Mia.* No wonder she hadn't returned to St. Lucy's.

"Oh yeah? And what did you know about me?"

There was a pause, and Ellen's arm came up to wrap around her midsection. Comfort, defensiveness. The other hand still held the unsmoked but lit cigarette.

"What people say about you," Ellen said, a tremor in her voice. "That you . . ."

Mia and Izzy waited. In the silence Ellen's chin tipped up. False bravado?

"Did you? Did you kill them?"

The intensity with which Ellen was watching Mia made Izzy wonder what kind of past Ellen had. Ellen's eyes were greedy but not the same way Quinn's had been. This . . . this was tragedy—guilt even—searching for a companion.

Mia huffed out a breath beside Izzy. It seemed more of an *are you serious with that question* than an admission of any kind.

"No," Mia said, and Izzy hated herself for how she listened for any hesitation.

Ellen's eyes went blank once more.

"How often did you see Robert when he was here?" Izzy asked, hoping to right the dynamics of this interview.

"Three times, maybe four."

That seemed like a lot for a date that hadn't turned out to be a date. "You went out with him again after that first coffee?"

Ellen turned to study Izzy's face, searching for a trap maybe. "Yes."

"Did you go to his cabin?"

The blush on Ellen's cheeks deepened, but she didn't blink. "Yes."

"Did he talk to you about the interviews he was conducting?" Mia asked.

Ellen jerked her shoulder. "Just how frustrated he was that no one would talk."

That seemed to be a given.

"No one talks here, though," Ellen continued.

"They talk about me," Mia countered.

"Yeah, well, only when they think I'm not listening." The words bent toward bitterness, and Izzy could relate. It was common ground she could exploit.

"Do people talk about other things when they think you're not listening?"

"A lot of people talking about a lot of things these days," Ellen said, lifting her cigarette to tap the ash. She still didn't bring it to her lips. "Robert stirred up the whole town."

"What were they saying?"

"Just the normal stuff. About that night. Those girls who came to the island."

"The Bell girls," Mia clarified.

Ellen nodded her confirmation. "About their parents, too."

There was an edge to Mia's voice. "What about them?"

"No one knows where they are really." Ellen lifted a shoulder, clearly not invested. But she'd relaxed since the conversation had moved away from her direct involvement. She probably was eager to keep them headed in this direction rather than circling back. "How they'd always been strange."

"Strange how?" Izzy asked, because it didn't seem odd to her that they hadn't returned to the island where their daughter had died.

"Rumors about what they did up in that mansion." Ellen peeked at her beneath heavy eyelashes. "With all those drifters about."

Sex, drugs, and rock 'n' roll, Izzy guessed. That kind of environment was bound to attract gossip like that. Again, none of it raised red flags. "Anything else?"

Ellen stared at the ground, her breathing gone a little shallow. She'd been holding herself so tight, so rigid, that she was almost shaking with the effort. People got this way around cops sometimes, even when they weren't guilty of anything. Those people usually had a past.

"Cash Bishop."

Ah. That name was becoming familiar.

"What about him?" Mia asked.

"He was talking to Jimmy about the Bells."

"Jimmy Roarke?"

That name kept popping up, too. Izzy added him to her list of people of interest.

Ellen rolled her eyes. It was so unlike every other guarded moment that it was almost startling. "Is there any other Jimmy?"

"Okay," Mia said. "They mentioned the Bells? Charles and Bix."

"Cash had asked Jimmy to find their current address." Ellen finally slipped the cigarette between her lips. They were going to lose her soon.

"Why'd he ask Jimmy?"

Ellen didn't answer right away. Instead, she dropped the cigarette to the ground, where it sizzled against the snow. At their curious looks, Ellen gestured toward her hair, her clothes.

"I don't smoke. I just need to smell like I took a cig break."

And that was just as telling as the rest of the interview. Because normal people lying, they don't think that deep. They tell their bosses they're going for a smoke break and then do whatever the hell they're trying to do for fifteen minutes before returning, smelling nothing of ash and burned lungs.

Ellen was hiding something. Ellen was scared. But even after all that, Izzy didn't think it had anything to do with the Twist case. That was just her gut speaking, though, and what did her gut know?

"Anyway, Jimmy was there that night, you know." Ellen started shifting toward the door. "The night at the lighthouse."

A flicker of something crossed Mia's face, but Izzy couldn't read it. Her best guess was surprise.

"Did Jimmy know where they were? The Bells?"

Ellen shook her head. "Told Cash to ask that girlfriend of his."

"And who would that be?" Mia asked.

There was a beat of silence, and Izzy leaned forward, her body recognizing the confused silence from Ellen before her mind processed that she should be braced for a kick.

"Lacey Bell," Ellen said slowly, as if their ignorance was somehow a trick.

Izzy stepped forward, unable to stop herself. "What did Cash say to that? When Jimmy told him to ask Lacey."

Ellen's eyes swung between them, before landing on Izzy. "Said it was a sore subject with her. Didn't want to bring it up. Tragic history and all." There was something about the way she said it that hinted at animosity rather than sympathy.

"You're not friends with her, I take it," Izzy guessed.

"Define 'friends.'" Ellen pushed off the wall. She was done.

"That's a no."

"That's a *your time's up, Detectives*," Ellen said with an authority that was at odds with the abused, frightened persona she'd adopted during most of the interview. There were complexities there, maybe a hardness they might be foolish to discount. "You can take anything else up with my lawyer. Cash Bishop. Think you might know him already."

She was good enough to know not to wait for a response to that perfect parting line.

CHAPTER ELEVEN

MIA

Mia watched the door slam shut as she bounced a little on her toes to restore feeling.

Ellen's perfume still lingered, but underneath it was something acidic. Something that smelled like fear.

"Scared," Izzy muttered beneath her breath.

"Very," Mia agreed. But there was more to it than that.

Did you kill them? No one had ever asked her that before. Straight-out like that.

Mia blinked and swayed, the world going a little hazy. It was happening with more frequency these days, where she seemed to disconnect with reality for a heartbeat.

She still hadn't eaten today, hadn't slept last night. The insomnia was an old companion, almost comforting in its familiarity. Days and nights and eternities were lived in those hours, those hated hours where mindless infomercials and empty streets became her only friends.

Even when her limbs ached, a deep and restless throb, her mind three paces behind, tripping over nonexistent cracks because of exhaustion, her body would fight sleep. If she lay down on the bed, anxiety would slip into her veins and she'd be worse off for even trying. Sometimes the only rest she got was when she dozed off in a chair or at her desk, desperately clinging to consciousness. Her body liked a good fight. Her body liked winning.

At one time in her life, it had nearly driven her mad. Now she was used to it. The not eating was new, though. She tried to pinpoint when it had started, and her stubborn mind supplied a time window around the same week she'd first seen Robert Twist lurking in the shadows outside the office.

"We need to talk to Lacey," Mia finally said. *Did you kill them?* "And Earl Bishop. Jimmy Roarke, too."

Listing them helped. It grounded her in the investigation that she still didn't feel like she had a grip on.

Did you kill them?

"He was the one who took me home that night," Mia said, quietly.

Izzy cocked her head. "Who?"

"Earl," Mia said.

"What exactly was Cash's father doing at the lighthouse?"

"It wasn't strange," Mia said. It wasn't. Not if you understood what life on St. Lucy's was like. "He was the mayor. We don't have cops. Someone had to handle the scene."

"Right," Izzy said, the word drawn out enough so that it was obvious that she still found it strange. Or at least noteworthy. Mia wouldn't argue with the latter. "And he didn't call your mother to come out and get you?"

"No, he took me home, then went back to the lighthouse, I think," Mia said. "Everything is a little piecemeal. Like, I remember drinking hot chocolate at the table at home in the kitchen. The marshmallows were those giant kind that barely fit into a mug." Mia paused. "Weird, right? Hot chocolate in the summer. But I know I drank it."

A beat of heavy silence followed, and Mia knew Izzy understood.

Then Izzy shifted. "So the only things you know about that night, then, were filled in by your mama?"

"For the most part," Mia said.

"And those details were given to her by Earl Bishop?" Izzy asked, slowly.

"Yes," Mia said.

"So the only details we have about that night were provided by the man who was the last person our new victim talked to before he died?"

It hadn't quite occurred to Mia to put it that way. But once Izzy said it, she couldn't believe she'd missed that fact. "By the time I was in a position to request the incident report, I had stopped wanting to even think about St. Lucy's."

"But the police *did* come out?"

"From Rockport, yes." Mia said. "They were gone a day later. Ruled it all suicide."

Izzy muttered something under her breath, but Mia shrugged.

"Quacks like a duck, right?" Mia said. "There was no reason to investigate further." She paused. "There's no real reason to now, either."

There was mutiny in Izzy's expression. She so obviously was building a theory, one that linked the suicide pact with Robert Twist's death. But Mia wasn't sure they had enough information to do that yet. There could be a million and one reasons why someone on the island would want to kill a nosy reporter.

However, one thing they both probably now agreed on?

"I think we can start approaching Twist's death as a homicide," Mia said, even if it was a bit reluctant. She'd been slowly watching her chance of getting off the island quickly fade with each interview.

Izzy rocked back on her heels. "Yeah, I think so." Her eyes narrowed on Mia's face, then she clicked her tongue and pointed. "It was the plane ticket, huh?"

Among other things. "Yes."

"Same," Izzy agreed.

It wasn't unheard of for someone to make plans for the future and then kill themselves anyway. The thoughts could have been triggered by any number of things. But he'd bought a ticket to San Sebastian. His cabin was messy, as if he'd been stepping out for an evening. There was no suicide note. Those weren't the actions of a man about to end his life.

In fact, the only thing that made it seem like a suicide was the bullet trajectory. And that could be easily faked.

Beyond that, there was the fact that Earl Bishop was the last man he'd talked to before he'd disappeared. There was the fact that Cash Bishop kept coming up. So did Jimmy Roarke, Earl's best friend. There was the fact that a lot of people on this island would go a long way to protect the Bishop family.

But that was conjecture.

"Hey, where was Cash that night?" Izzy asked. "Why wasn't he there with you guys? If the four of you were all buddy-buddy."

"Says he got in trouble, wasn't allowed out," Mia said, knowing her voice lacked conviction.

"You don't believe him."

"It's not out of the realm of possibility. His dad was strict with him." Mia shrugged. "But we went out the night before—it was our six-month anniversary." So silly, now that she thought about it. He'd packed a picnic with candles and unbearable sparkling wine that they'd drunk out of red Solo cups. It was hard to fathom that she'd ever been so young, so in love.

"Was he allowed out for a special occasion?" Izzy pressed. "Or does that mean whatever kept him away from the lighthouse happened the day of?"

Mia shook her head. "Earl Bishop didn't care about our anniversary."

Izzy was staring at the door where Ellen had disappeared, but it didn't seem like she was actually looking at it. Her mind was somewhere else. Mia waited.

Finally, Izzy turned to her. "What did he do?"

"He didn't say," Mia said slowly, but she was following where Izzy was going. There were only so many things Cash could have gotten up to in daylight hours that would have been bad enough for him to be grounded that night.

"So either something pretty extreme happened or . . ."

Mia swallowed. "Or he's lying about not being there."

———

They mayor's office was tucked into the back of the rec hall, one of the more sprawling buildings on the island. The venue had been the host to weddings, school dances, graduations—almost any and all events that needed space to accommodate a good chunk of the population. But when the place wasn't being used for a celebration, it was a wide-open basketball court.

Mia's and Izzy's boots clicked against the polished wood as they crossed toward where a door was marked MAYOR CASH BISHOP.

A slip of a woman sat behind the scarred oak desk in the little waiting room, her light brown hair pulled tight back into a severe bun, gold-rimmed glasses perched on a small, upturned nose. She was so indistinct in appearance that she all but disappeared into the rose-patterned wallpaper behind her.

She hadn't changed much since high school.

"Dot, right?" Mia asked. She used to be Dorothy Sherman, though the ring on her hand hinted that might be outdated information. Dot had been a year older than Mia and the rest of them, which normally wouldn't have made a difference to whether they'd hung out. But Dot had never been friendly. Not mean, either. Just more interested in books than people.

"Hi, Mia." The frostiness in the greeting had Mia reconsidering that impression.

"Is Cash in? We'd like to ask him a few questions."

"He's on a phone call right now. You'll have to wait." Dot gestured toward the cushioned chairs. And, yes, she was definitely not pleased with Mia.

"I take it you two weren't friends," Izzy muttered as they settled in next to a tableful of tattered *Us Weeklys* and *People* magazines, all with movie stars who were big about five years earlier.

"Actually, no. But I wouldn't have said we didn't like each other." Although, who knew anymore.

As a detective who worked primarily on cold cases, she knew recall was a crapshoot in the best situations. People put a lot more faith in what they supposedly remembered, thinking of it as verbatim what happened. But that's not how it worked. Where there were gaps, the brain took a best guess: emotions twisted events; random details like a certain smell stayed while other major ones faded away. And all that was if you actually wanted to remember something.

Mia, on the other hand, had spent more than fifteen years desperately trying to forget.

Dot had disappeared into Cash's office, presumably to inform him they were waiting, but was now back, her attention almost compulsively on her computer screen.

By an unspoken agreement that Mia wasn't the best person to be doing the questioning here, Izzy stood up and stretched, then turned to look at a high-tides poster on the wall. After a few seconds, she sidled toward the coffee table that was loaded down with pictures of fishing boats. Then meandered across the room to check out the art near the door. It was all very casual and restless. Careless. If you didn't know Izzy.

Dot was barely watching her until Izzy leaned a hip against the woman's desk.

"You work here full time?" Izzy dropped the question like she was just bored, killing the minutes they had to wait.

Dot's eyes narrowed behind those thick glasses. "Yes."

"You like it?"

When Dot glanced over, Mia picked up a *Highlights* magazine to look busy, smiling at dried and crumbling crayon residue from years past.

"Yes."

"Kind of slow now, huh? Is it usually like this?"

"Not always." Dot sounded reluctant to depart from her monosyllabic civility. "Can get busy."

"Did Robert Twist ever come in with an appointment?"

Dot wasn't an idiot. There was a beat of silence, and then: "You can direct your questions to the mayor, Detective."

Shut down. It had been worth the try.

But Izzy wasn't deterred. "Sorry, sorry." She held her palms up, all *it was an innocent mistake, ma'am.* Then she picked up a pen, started fiddling with it. "You've been working here long?"

"Nearly a decade."

"Cash has been mayor all that time?" Izzy asked.

"No, only a few years," Dot corrected, warming to Izzy again. It was one of Izzy's gifts, usually. When they weren't on an island where no one would acknowledge her, she could get anyone chatting, even when they didn't want to be spilling any information. There was a warmth to her that people couldn't resist. Even Mia had fallen prey to the charm several times. "Earl Bishop, his father, hired me."

"Oh man, which one is the harder boss?" There it was again. Nudge, nudge, *I'm one of you, tell me everything you know without realizing you're doing it.*

"They're different," Dot said slowly. "Cash has his own style, but Earl is—was—a perfectionist."

"I'm sorry, I thought Earl was still alive," Izzy said delicately, latching onto the tense change that had caused Mia's own pulse to catch. Mia gave up the pretense of flipping idly through the children's magazine and turned her full attention on Dot.

The woman's mouth parted several times without saying anything. Then, just as she started to speak, the door to Cash's office swung open.

Cash was shrugging into a thick overcoat as he stepped into the waiting room. Mia's stomach rolled, a mix of disappointment and anger and sadness churning there.

He wanted to avoid them. He was hiding something.

"Sorry, Mia, an emergency cropped up at the Rogerses' place." Cash had put on his best distressed face, but he wouldn't meet her eyes when he said it. "There's a shotgun involved. I gotta get over there."

Mia stood. "Do you need backup?"

"No, no." He waved with the hand he wasn't using to yank open the outer door. "It's just old Stan again. You know him. Probably forgot to take his meds. But I should . . ."

He didn't even finish the sentence before he was out the door. They were left staring at his back as he jogged across the empty court, only stopping to kick a stray basketball out of the way.

Mia watched him until he'd disappeared, and stood there long after.

Behind Mia, Dot and Izzy continued talking, a few stray bits working their way into Mia's conscious, like that Dot had married the owner of the hardware store and had three kids, all boys. But most of it was smothered by the one question that kept getting louder every time she saw Cash—What wasn't he telling her?

She turned around, suddenly enough that the conversation behind her dropped off midsentence. "What were you going to say about Earl?" There was no grace to the question, none of her legendary interview skills on display. Her hand shook slightly, and she shoved it in the pocket of the jacket she'd never taken off.

"Oh." Dot looked between them. But Izzy's easy presence had done its job to thaw some of the iciness. "He was diagnosed with dementia a few years back. It's pretty bad."

It came like a blow, even more so than his death would have.

Poor Cash.

She didn't want to think it but couldn't help the fleeting sympathy. Dementia wasn't pretty, and to watch Earl Bishop deteriorate must have been rough for Cash, who had idolized him always.

Mia found Izzy watching her when she opened her eyes, and she realized what it could mean for the case.

Patients with dementia tended to live a lot in the past. Short-term memory was often interrupted, but the long-term—that was just there to pull from.

Which meant there was a possibility that the reporter might have talked to an Earl Bishop who thought he was living in the time period right after Asher's and Monroe's deaths.

And maybe, if that was the case, they were dealing with the fallout from that.

Izzy tilted her head toward the door, a clear question if Mia was ready or if she wanted to stick around. Mia nodded once, but as they both moved to make their goodbyes to Dot, Mia paused.

It was curiosity and the fact that they'd already probably gotten from Dot all that she was willing to give up that made Mia ask the question. It was a cold, vague fear that made her hesitate. But still . . . "Why don't you like me?"

Izzy made a little surprised sound next to Mia, but Mia didn't look away from Dot. The woman blinked at her, curled in, but then straightened as if chastising herself for backing down.

"You were horrible to me. In school. You and that . . . that Bell girl." She spit the words, her chin quivering with either anger or the urge to cry.

"What?" That cold, vague fear turned jagged, shards of ice slicing into the sun-tinted warmth of those summer days.

"I mean"—Dot's lower lip trembled—"you were fine until the summer before you left." She looked away, shrugged, her face pale. "Once you and Cash started dating, though . . ."

"What did I do?"

With squinting, suspicious eyes, Dot studied her. "You don't even remember, do you? I was that insignificant to your little clique."

Mia was helpless. "I'm sorry. I don't . . ."

"You all . . . you all convinced me . . ." Years-old bitterness turned Dot's voice ugly, small, wobbly. "You know what? The details don't matter. I humiliated myself. And you just laughed. All of you just laughed."

Mia's brain rebelled. Even when prodded, she couldn't pull up the memory of whatever Dot was hinting at. But Mia had never thought of herself or the others as cruel. Maybe careless in the way teenagers were. Never cruel, though.

"I'm sorry," Mia whispered, left with nothing else to say. Dot was blinking too fast, far too fast, and Mia didn't want to subject her to the embarrassment of crying in front of them. She apologized quietly one more time and then walked out the door.

"That doesn't sound like you," Izzy said under her breath once they made it halfway across the basketball court.

Mia thought of that picture in the hallway, summer days and loose limbs, their little group wrapped up in each other. So young, so foolish.

But the moment was only a snapshot, unable to capture the darkness that must have lurked beyond the parameters of the frame. Jealousy, pettiness, all the angst that came with stupid, pointless puppy love. A mean streak, if Dot were to be believed.

And why would the woman lie?

That doesn't sound like you. Izzy had thrown it out, offhand, like those questions she'd asked Dot. The thing was, it was just as purposeful as those had been.

Mia stared at the clouds rolling in, slow and steady. This storm that wouldn't relent, that felt as never ending as their time on the island.

"You don't know me well enough to say that."

CHAPTER TWELVE

Izzy

A spring dug into the space just to the right of Izzy's shoulder blade, the tip of the coil pressing up against her spine. She shifted and the couch moaned, the protest too loud in the silence that had settled into the house.

Izzy and Mia hadn't had much time in the afternoon before the snowfall became prohibitive. They'd managed to knock on a few doors, but with little result. Yeah, the reporter had been in town; yeah, he'd been asking questions about suicide. Yeah, Mia's name came up. Usually, then, whomever they were interviewing would either not be able to meet Mia's eyes or would stare at her, hungry for her reaction.

It had left Izzy slightly nauseated, and she almost welcomed the relief of secluding themselves into the relative safety of Edie Hart's kitchen to tear through journals they couldn't even understand.

Izzy bent her knee up now, her heel dipping into the space between the cushions. The move revealed more metal lurking beneath the thin fabric, this time at her hip.

Giving up on the promise of sleep, she sat up fully, blinking hard to get the indistinct blobs in the room to come into focus as furniture instead of monsters. Moonlight slid over the carpet but wasn't bright enough to fully banish the darkness.

She yawned and then reached for her phone where it was plugged into the wall outlet. Only when she was opening her email did she hear it—a footfall against a stubborn spot on the floor.

Then it was quiet again. This time the hush was different, though, more of a pause than the natural creaks and groans of the night.

If the person had been Mia, they wouldn't have frozen, and Izzy would be able to hear her move toward the kitchen or the bathroom. But there was nothing. Just that one high-pitched whine of settling wood.

Izzy dropped her phone on the couch beside her and reached for the gun she'd kept tucked underneath on the floor. Her fingertips curled easily around the grip, and she breathed out through her nose, controlling the relief that slipped through her from the weight of the weapon.

She didn't stand yet, didn't trust the couch not to betray her. So she listened, her muscles poised to spring into action, her head tilted to pick up on any movement from the hallway.

It was another twenty seconds of silence before there was a rustle of fabric against fabric. If Izzy hadn't been paying attention, the noise would have blended and melted into the static of wind and house and breathing.

But now that she could pinpoint it, the person's steps weren't hard to follow. They paused at the bottom of the stairs, just outside the den. Izzy waited. If they started up the steps, she'd have to act. Mia and Edie were vulnerable, unaware.

Whoever it was continued down the hallway, though. Toward the kitchen. Where all the information on the case was lying about, unprotected.

Izzy pushed to her feet, keeping pressure on the couch with her free hand so that she could better control the groan of relaxing metal.

She'd lost track of the intruder now, the sound of a stranger in the house once again fading into nothingness. Izzy spared a thought toward Mia's insomnia and wondered if she was upstairs staring at the ceiling. Then she put Mia out of her head. If Izzy didn't move quickly, the person could get whatever they came for and leave before she even left the den.

The combination of shock and fear had given her nighttime vision a kick, and the once-blurred shapes scattered throughout the room became chairs and side tables that she skirted around with ease. Blood rushed against the thin membrane of her eardrums, and she spared a precious second calming her pulse. If she couldn't hear, she'd be useless.

Then, counting down from three, she stepped into the hallway. She didn't know the house well enough yet to be confident about what spots to avoid, but smooth, easy strides were better than hesitant tiptoes, so she was at the kitchen doorway in seconds.

She paused, her back plastered to the wall, her shoulder pressed into the crook. Her weapon was a solid presence against her sweatpants-clad thigh, and she slid the safety off. The click was loud, ripping apart the silence.

But she could hear the intruder again, and they didn't pause. The unmistakable sound of a body moving, the rub of arm against hip, the scuff of shoe on tile, the inhales, the exhales. Izzy tracked it all.

When the intruder stepped toward the sink, away from the back door, Izzy knew it was time.

She wished she could close her eyes, center herself once more, but she didn't want to blow her night vision.

Instead, she took a breath, brought her gun up, and stepped into the kitchen. "Hands up," Izzy said, her voice deliberately loud enough to catch Mia's attention if she was awake. "Nice and slow."

The intruder went rigid, shoulders locking up.

Izzy's eyes swept down to the person's grip. *Shit, shit, shit.* A weapon. She couldn't tell if it was a knife or a gun, and she didn't want to fumble on the wall for the light switch.

"Put your fucking hands in the air," she said, using her deepest register. Details were seeping in past her initial fight response. Slim, swallowed by a black sweatshirt, with the hood up. Stance was wide, ready to run. She knew exactly what that little head tilt toward the back door meant. The person was going for it.

"Don't make me tell you again," Izzy said, and this time she shifted into their path. "Drop your weapon. Put your hands in the air."

She kept the directives steady, not letting any of the words slide toward panic. She wasn't, anyway. Panicking. This part wasn't new to her. Scumbags with more firepower than brains were a dime a dozen in vice.

A door opened upstairs; they could both hear it through the thin ceiling. And the distraction was a window of opportunity that the intruder immediately seized.

The person lunged, but not toward the door like Izzy had been expecting. The shift in direction surprised her enough that she was slow to follow, and the mistake cost her.

When the intruder whirled, the flashlight blinded Izzy, the white brightness slamming into her retinas so that she couldn't make out anything other than a silhouette.

Mother fu—she threw her hand up, leaving her grip on her gun unsteady. It didn't matter. She couldn't shoot if she couldn't fucking see.

Izzy ducked low, then shifted as if heading right. At the last second, she spun left, ditching the flashlight's beam in the process. She tried to draw a bead on the intruder again, but her night vision was shot—the person nothing but a shape crouched over the table.

The reporter's notebooks. She and Mia had left them there, out for anyone to find. Stupid.

At the sound of Mia's footfalls on the stairs, the intruder grabbed one of the journals before knocking the rest to the floor, clearly headed toward the door now.

Izzy started moving, yelling, though she didn't know what she was saying. Anything to get the person to stop just long enough for Mia to get there, so the odds would once again be in Izzy's favor.

It wasn't until Izzy reached out blindly, going for an arm as the intruder threw open the door, that she remembered the gun.

While it was true she couldn't shoot without seeing properly, that didn't mean the intruder couldn't.

As the frigid air rushed into the kitchen, she stumbled forward, still determined.

There was a crack, and then hot pain slicing across her shoulder, her fingers still grasping for someone who was no longer there.

———

Izzy stuffed her knuckles in her mouth as Mia poured alcohol into the shallow wound just below Izzy's shoulder cuff. Her teeth dug indents into the flesh of her fingers, but she didn't flinch while the burn unfurled tendrils along her arm.

"Shit," she hissed finally when she trusted herself with words again. Mia was slapping tape on the gauzy bandage, a thin line of rust-red blood running along its center.

"You were lucky," Mia said softly, though there was no need to drop her voice. Edie was awake and standing by the sink, watching the scene with a narrowed gaze. "It barely grazed you."

"If I were lucky, we'd have the bastard in handcuffs right now." Izzy shook her head. "What I was was sloppy."

"You should have come and got me."

There was only a slight scolding in her tone, not nearly what Izzy deserved. It had been stupid to confront the intruder without backup.

For a moment, she wished she was alone so she could press the heel of her palm into the wound, bask in the pain of her mistake. Instead, she rolled her shoulders.

"Whoever it was, they got a journal."

Mia paused, her hands hanging limply. "They? There was more than one?"

"No. I just couldn't tell if it was a guy or a . . ." Izzy thought about it. "Could have been female. They were slight enough."

"So you saw enough to rule out some people?"

Nodding, Izzy prodded at the white bandage. Mia had been right. She had been lucky. The wound was only a smidge deeper than a scratch. "Wasn't one of the big guys."

There was a beat of silence. "Not Cash then?"

Mia had managed to be casual in asking the question, but that almost gave it away more than anything. *Too close,* Izzy's mind took the opportunity to remind her.

"Nope." Izzy shook her head. "Not the doc, either. Or the bartender."

"What about the two guys who pulled the vic from the bay?"

Izzy squinted, trying to call up their body types. "Too tall, too fat," she finally concluded.

Another moment passed, Mia's fingers tapping against the table as she stared out the window. Then she stilled. "Ellen?"

Slim. Swallowed by a black hoodie. Izzy layered the waitress's compact frame onto her memory of that first impression in the darkened kitchen. "Yeah. Could have been."

"Okay," Mia said, her eyes going to the notebooks scattered on the floor. "Any chance you'd recognize which one he took?"

"Actually, yeah." She pushed to her feet, the blood rush sending her head spinning. "But I'm not sure how helpful it will be. It seemed more of a desperate Hail Mary than an actual attempt to steal it."

She reached for her own notes, where she'd been cataloging which interviews were in which of the notebooks—her anal soul giving the number of each corresponding journal to the initials. There had been five in total.

"Was it the one with Cash? And Earl?"

Izzy didn't answer at first. She went through her logs, twice, before humming low in her throat. "No. It was the one with Lacey Bell."

Mia sighed, tipping her face up to the ceiling. "Shit." Her expression was composed, though, when she dropped her chin once more. "Actually, it's perfect. We'll go see her in the morning."

CHAPTER THIRTEEN

MIA

It was still dark when Mia rapped her knuckles against the doorframe of the den. Izzy was a lump of limbs and blankets on the couch, and she burrowed in deeper at the sound.

Her injured arm hung off the cushions, her fingertips dragging along the carpet. Mia had fed her some ibuprofen last night, but by this morning Izzy was sure to be in pain.

If Mia had felt like being kind, she would have let Izzy sleep. But her legs throbbed with the need to go, find, hunt. There was someone on the island who was comfortable shooting at cops, and whether that person was their killer or not, they needed to be stopped.

Mia just foolishly, so foolishly, wished doing that wouldn't have led them to Lacey Bell's doorstep.

There was no pretending she hadn't been avoiding her. Lacey was a reminder of that night, of that summer, of Monroe and Asher, and everything Mia desperately wanted to forget.

But she'd put it off as long as she could.

Mia knocked against the wood again, louder this time, and Izzy lifted her head, her messy pink hair a neon beacon. "Jesus, is it even dawn yet, Hart?"

It was, but only just. "I have coffee made," Mia said instead of answering.

By the time Mia returned with a thermos for Izzy, the woman had managed to slip on real clothes and was attempting to tie up her boots with one hand.

"Does it hurt?" Mia asked, but didn't offer to help. And something told her Izzy wasn't eager to go to Sammy to have him check it out, either.

Protocol dictated that they report the injury. Mia had tried that morning using the landline, and the call had gone straight to voice mail. She'd hung up without leaving a message. If Murdoch tried calling them back and got nothing but an empty house or static on their cell phones, she'd probably send in the Coast Guard to rescue them. Better to wait to explain the situation when she actually picked up.

Izzy huffed, straightening and eyeing the mess that was her laces. "Nah. Just a scratch."

Mia nodded, and then they settled into silence until they were outside, crossing the backyard, disturbing the pristine blanket of white.

This was Mia's favorite part of the day. The snow was still pure in most places, the dinginess of real life turning only some of the fringes gray. The sky was an inky purple that faded into pink and gold. The air was crisp, almost renewed from the night before. It was peaceful.

But Mia liked this time best because it *came*. Every night when her blood went hot and her skin itched and her mind crawled in circles over shards of glass, she knew, knew if she hung on, that morning would come.

Fresh and clean and cool.

She breathed it in, she breathed it out.

There was something romantic about insomnia for people who slept. It was late-night diners and unchecked conversations without inhibitions. It was creativity sparked and the beautiful melancholy of fatigue. Bruises beneath eyes, but a wisdom gained from extra hours of being awake.

Living it was anything but romantic. Still, she thought maybe she was able to appreciate the bright hope of morning more than other people. Certainly, more than Izzy, who was muttering obscenities beneath her breath beside Mia.

The curses stopped only when they rounded the small shed in the backyard.

"We're going on that?"

Mia patted the handlebars of the snowmobile. It was an old model, one Mama had bought when Mia was just a girl. But the thing worked. It would get them to the Bell mansion more quickly than trudging through the woods, and she didn't want to take a car out on the unplowed roads leading out to the cliffs.

Izzy stared at the machine with confusion that evolved slowly into horror. Her eyes were wide, her pupils dilated, and if Mia had been in the mood, she would have laughed. Izzy looked more scared of riding it than she had after being shot at last night.

"It's going to be okay," Mia finally said.

Izzy swiveled her jaw, then nodded, still not saying anything.

Mia tried not to smile as she swung a leg over the seat and then patted the cushion behind her.

"You're going to want to hold on," she said. Izzy hesitated only a moment longer, seemingly talking herself into something, and then climbed on. Once her fingers curled around Mia's hips, Mia revved the engine and maneuvered them toward the forest.

Because Mia was driving slow, it took double the amount of time it should have to break through the tree line on the north end of the island. When they did, the Bell mansion came into view, standing on the cliffs, commanding attention in the midst of the barren, windswept expanse. Where the lighthouse was quiet resilience, the Bell mansion challenged the encroaching sea below, laughed at the dangerous waves that licked at the rocks.

Some islanders had called it gaudy just loud enough for the Bells to hear, but Mia found that it always knocked the breath from her lungs on first view. When she'd been younger, the mansion had reminded her of a life fancier than anything possible on the two square miles of land that was St. Lucy's.

The purr of the snowmobile rumbled to a stop as she parked by the fountain in the center of the drive. "That wasn't so bad, was it?"

Izzy shook her head. "Never again. My ass is officially frozen."

"Never again." Mia let a beat pass. "Well, until we have to go back."

"You're straight up mean, is what you are," Izzy said, backing away from the machine. Then she turned to take in the mansion, whistling low and long as she did. "Moneybags."

"You have no idea," Mia said. Moneybags barely scratched the surface of the Bells' wealth. "Come on."

Ringing the bell seemed like the smarter option than the knocker— a better chance for Lacey to hear. Mia pressed it, then waited. After a few minutes, she pressed it once more, refusing to feel guilty at the early hour.

"If you dragged me out here . . ." But Izzy's threat was cut off before it had a chance to fully land.

Lacey Bell stood in the doorway, her eyes wide, her hand still gripping the heavy wood.

The woman was dressed in an oversize lilac sweater with rolled-up sleeves and black leggings that had roses winding up over her knees and thighs. The blade-thin ridge of her collarbone hinted at a still-slim frame under the loose fabric.

Her black, glossy hair was cut into a bob with bangs that slashed across her forehead in a choppy, asymmetrical line. Where her face had once been angular, it was now soft, filled out with age, making her prettier than she had ever been before. Rows of chunky rings sat heavy on her fingers, and a waterfall of pearls cascaded from gold hooks that dragged on her earlobes. Her lips were slicked red with gloss and her lashes were sooty with mascara, despite it being maybe seven in the morning.

There was a moment before recognition hit that Lacey's face remained neutral and pleasant, if a bit surprised at the early visitors, a polite smile plastered on.

But then her eyes met Mia's, and any color that had been left in her porcelain-white face bled out, her arm coming up across her body as if to shield herself from a blow. "Mia Hart."

Mia didn't know what she'd expected. But it hadn't been fear. Maybe Lacey really was their intruder.

"Lacey." Mia nodded, and neither of them moved to hug or even shake hands. They'd known each other only a few months. They were nothing more than strangers with a shared tragedy.

"I heard you were back," Lacey finally said, though she didn't move to invite them in. Her voice was delicate, cultured, unlike the harsh accent of those who had grown up on St. Lucy's.

"In town," Mia corrected. *Back* sounded too permanent.

Lacey's lips tipped up as if she immediately understood. Could relate despite being back on the island herself. "Of course. Apologies."

They stood there for so long that Mia knew she was going to have to force the issue. "Can we come inside?"

"I'm sorry, yes, please." Lacey said it like it had been an oversight and moved so they could step out of the cold. "I was having coffee in the kitchen?"

Without waiting for a response to something that wasn't really even a question, Lacey turned and led the way across the marble tile of the entryway, her socked feet sliding just a bit against the polished floor.

Mia trailed behind her, Izzy bringing up the rear. "That was a chandelier," Izzy muttered. "In the freaking entryway."

All of the decorations in the mansion were ostentatious, but Mia had been there enough times that summer to get used to it.

There were new additions, of course.

Large, dark paintings hanging without frames followed them on their way back to the kitchen. None of them were actual pictures; rather, they were simply black and gray and white splashed on canvas, all the same style. Mia wondered if they were Lacey's.

She stopped by one. It was midnight black at the center, deep blue swirling from there. Something about it made Mia's body tip forward, a tug beneath her belly button, as if she could be swallowed by the yawning abyss. The desire to sink into it eased only when Izzy bumped her shoulder, her eyebrows lifted. "Are they hers?"

A signature scrawled in white at the corner popped against the darker colors. "Looks like."

The painting was every nightmare that hibernated in Mia's chest, waiting for her to fall asleep.

Neither she nor Lacey had escaped that summer, it seemed.

"Can you tell?" Mia murmured the question, even though Lacey was well ahead of them.

"Not her," Izzy said.

"You're confident?"

Izzy tipped her head. "As much as I can be. Too short. The person definitely had a few good inches on you."

And Lacey was about Mia's height.

But Ellen would fit.

Still, this wouldn't be a wasted trip. They'd needed to interview Lacey anyway, and all it had taken for Mia to stop dragging her feet was Izzy getting shot.

By the time they got to the kitchen, Lacey had cracked a window and was toying with a box of cigarettes.

She didn't ask if they minded when she slid one out of the neat row. Flipping it between her fingers, she tipped her chin toward the long, artsy farmhouse table that ran the length of the room.

Mia slid onto the bench on the far side, so she could lean her forearms on the wood. Izzy propped herself against the wall just inside the doorway. It gave them the observational advantage.

Lacey plucked a gold-plated lighter from the windowsill, the click of the flame the only sound in the kitchen. Her cheeks hollowed as she took the first drag, and then her red apple–painted mouth twisted to the side so she could direct the smoke toward the window. Haloed as she was by the light, she looked like a disgruntled movie star who'd been misplaced in time.

"You're here because of the reporter," Lacey finally said, her fingers holding tight to her own arm, protective once more. No small talk, no catching up between long-lost friends. Mia didn't mind. What else was there to say, really?

"I heard he was bothering you up here," Mia said, framing the question, tilting it, so that maybe Lacey would relax her arm, lower her guard.

The woman pulled again at her cigarette, the thin line of smoke quivering from her trembling hand, coiling, obscuring her face so that for a half second she was held apart from them, a veil slipping into place to let her keep her distance. Then Lacey dropped the cigarette back to her side, and the smoke was gone.

"He was asking about Monroe." Lacey paused. "Though from the look on your face, I'm guessing you already knew that," she continued, even though Lacey had barely glanced at Mia since she'd arrived. "A real prick, that one."

"I'm sorry you had to deal with that," Mia said, and meant it. No matter what she felt about Lacey—and what that was, she was still deciding—her ulcer pulsed as she tried to imagine being cornered and surprised by the reporter, being asked about a sister who had killed herself, a friend who had followed suit.

Lacey's shoulder jerked as if to shrug it off, but the violence of the movement belied the carelessness she tried to wear on her face. "Told him what he could do with his story."

"Did he ask you anything in specific?" Mia pressed.

Lacey crushed the lit end of her cigarette into the ashtray and slammed the window shut. Then she looked at Mia. "Mostly about how they didn't leave notes. Asher and Monroe." A pause. "You."

It wasn't suicide.

Lacey shrugged, and the arms of her sweater slid down to her knuckles, hiding her hands. "Was kind of odd, wasn't it?"

Mia tipped her head. She'd looked for her own when she hadn't been able to sleep after being dropped off from the lighthouse, torn her room apart, trying to guess where she would have left it had she written one. Had been consumed with needing to know what it had said.

There hadn't been a letter, though. Not one that she could find.

"Did Monroe ever seem . . . ?"

"Like she was going to off herself?" Lacey cut in even before Mia could ask the question. If Lacey was trying to offend or shock her, it wouldn't work. The brashness, the audacity, the pretending not to care was not unusual to see in the victims' families. Everyone handled grief differently.

Mia nodded.

"Do you know how many times I've answered that question?" There was a manic bent to Lacey's voice, and she must have heard it herself. Her throat rippled. When she spoke again, her tone had evened out. "She didn't tell me everything. You know, she liked her secrets. But. No, she didn't seem like she was on the verge of slitting her wrists open."

"Did she ever talk about Asher to you? Was she serious about him?"

Lacey laughed, her brows disappearing beneath the curtain of bangs. "Asher? He was just a summer fling. She . . . she liked the chase. He wasn't even . . ."

She paused and licked her lips.

"He wasn't even what, Lacey?"

"I'm not even sure why we're talking about this," Lacey deflected, her fingers tugging at the pearl earring, which nearly brushed her shoulder.

Mia usually liked this part of her job, mostly because she was good at it. Reading someone, trying to find the right buttons to push, when to stay silent, and when to poke a little bit. But Lacey was hard. She was constantly in motion, a fragile, skittish bird poised to take flight. Just as quickly, her gaze would turn direct, her words provocative for the sake of it. A contrast of nervous hesitation and unabashed confrontation.

"We're talking about this because a reporter who seemed very interested in the topic ended up with a blown-out skull after asking too many questions. I'm not trying to dig up the past for the sole purpose of digging up the past."

Lacey went still, and it was almost strange. Even the uneasy vibrations that seemed to roll off her body ceased for a few heartbeats. Then a deep breath brought her back, moving, fiddling. "Asher wasn't her only fling that summer."

Mia rocked back on the bench. Monroe and Asher had seemed well and truly in puppy love.

"Who else was she seeing?"

There weren't many options. Not on St. Lucy's. And all the artists in residence had been adults.

Lacey's fingers tangled in the hem of her sweater, pulling, tugging, shifting. "I don't know. She never told me. But I got the impression he was . . . older."

And that opened a few more possibilities. "Was he someone from St. Lucy's?"

"I think so," Lacey said. "The artists weren't exactly that appealing to her."

But someone from the island was? Mia quickly skimmed through the list of who would have been around that summer. It wasn't long. And certainly no one on it would have drawn the attention of the beautiful, rich Monroe Bell.

"She would sneak out," Lacey said as if it meant something, leaning forward a little bit, her eyes wide. When Mia remained silent, Lacey looked away. "If it was an artist, they had plenty of space here."

"How do you know it wasn't Asher she was meeting?" Mia asked. They all snuck out. Sometimes together, sometimes not. She'd assumed Monroe and Asher had found a place to be alone that summer, just like she and Cash had.

"Little things," Lacey said, picking up the cigarette pack once more. She didn't open it. "A weird, I don't know . . . giddiness . . . she never had around Asher. She'd smell different, too. Like the man wore cologne."

So more a feeling, than anything else, really. Mia trusted feelings. She wasn't sure if she trusted Lacey, though.

"It was kind of a high for her, you know?" Lacey continued, her eyes on the floor. "Playing men. Getting them to do things for her."

That . . . that Bell girl. Dot's wobbly lip, her wet eyes, came to mind. That's how she'd painted Monroe. Mean for the sake of being mean.

"She liked the attention?"

Lacey's face contorted, as if she wanted to disagree, defend her sister, but then it smoothed once more. "I wouldn't say it was like that."

"How would you say it was like, then?" There was a harshness that was emerging beneath the soft memory of Monroe Bell.

Was there something beneath Mia's own skin that would be just as ugly?

Lacey shook her head, looking out the window. "Don't. That's not what I meant."

Mia recognized a dead end when she came to one.

"Do you remember?" Mia pivoted, asking what she'd wanted to know since she'd stood in the lighthouse two days before surrounded by ghosts. "Do you remember finding me?"

Lacey froze, and Mia was starting to be able to read her. It was in the pauses that she revealed her truths.

The silence that followed the question was unnatural. There was no rumble of the dishwasher, no bird chatter outside the window. Just a fragile hush and too many memories of blood-slick skin and wide eyes and the unrelenting roar of waves.

"Yes," Lacey said, a whispered confession falling from reluctant lips. The woman cleared her throat, and then she was back, shifting, hiding. "Yes."

"What . . . ?" Mia started, but the rest of the sentence didn't form, her thoughts too tangled to slot words together.

Mia stared at her own hands, her eyes tracing the cracked skin there. It always got that way on the island.

"Why were you coming out there? Just then?" Mia asked finally, lifting her gaze back to Lacey, who had completely composed herself.

"I didn't know you'd be there," Lacey said, fiddling with her bangs with gentle fingers. "I was meeting someone."

"Who?"

Lacey lifted one perfectly sculpted brow. "You think you're the only ones who were getting some that summer?"

That's not what she'd asked. Mia waited.

It was Lacey who broke first, looking away. "Fine. It was Sammy. It was just a hookup, though. He didn't—he didn't mean anything."

Mia dragged in a breath. Sammy hadn't said anything. Why hadn't he said anything?

It was foolish to expect him to, though. When would Mia remember? Lying was their shibboleth.

"But he never made it to the lighthouse, right?" Mia clarified.

Lacey pursed her lips, the light catching on the glossy sheen of them. "No. We didn't really talk after that, to be honest. But, no."

Mia flicked her eyes to her partner, but her face was inscrutable. For the best.

"Is there anything else from the summer that seemed odd?" Mia asked. "Any of the artists in residence?"

"More odd than usual?" Lacey asked, but it was tinted with fondness.

"Right."

"No." Lacey shook her head, her gaze unfocused on a spot beyond Mia's shoulder. "No one particularly dangerous, if that's what you're getting at."

Mia herself wasn't sure what she was getting at. The ground was unsteady beneath her feet, and she was snatching at anything to try to make it all fit.

Artists. Quinn had mentioned Robert Twist had been asking about an artist who had been staying on the island.

"And what about now? Any artists here now?"

"Not since the fall," Lacey answered.

That would still fit. "Who was that?"

Lacey tugged at a loose thread hanging from her sweater. "Peter. Just went by that."

"Like Cher?" Izzy chimed in, even as Mia's mind latched onto the name. Peter. Peter. She recognized it from something recently. *Peter.*

When Lacey and Mia glanced over, Izzy just shrugged. "Or Beyoncé is more current, I guess."

Lacey stared for a heartbeat longer, then gave a tiny shake of her head, enough to send her bob swishing, before dismissing Izzy again.

"When did he leave? Peter?" Once Mia asked the question, it clicked. *Peter.* That had been Robert Twist's last phone call.

Lacey stilled, her fingers curled around the kitchen counter by her thighs. "Early October? Maybe?"

Peter. Was it the same man? And was the Peter from the phone log also the artist whom Twist had asked about?

"Any reason Peter left?" Mia pressed, scenting blood in the water. "Or his residency was just over?"

Lacey smiled then. "He wasn't a fan of the cold."

Izzy hummed in agreement, and Mia's lips quirked.

Lacey scratched at her collarbone, and the sleeve of her sweater slipped down to her elbow. At first Mia thought there was a splotch of paint on the woman's forearm. Then she realized it was a bruise, fading green at the rim but still a deep purple at the center. It was shaped like a thumbprint, as if she'd been grabbed and yanked. Mia had seen bruises like that before.

She looked away to find Izzy watching her instead of Lacey. Izzy tilted her head, a silent question. Anything else?

Pushing to her feet would be answer enough. Mia patted one of her pockets for a card, then held out the small ivory paper to Lacey. "If you think of anything else."

The sweater had already slipped back down over her arm when Lacey reached out to take it. She pressed the pad of her pointer finger into one of the sharp edges.

"I won't."

Mama had told them last night that Ellen lived in the run-down gamekeeper's cottage behind the island's church. St. Lucy's cemetery stretched out behind the little house, the marble of the crosses catching the midmorning light where they stood out from the snow.

Izzy shivered as they walked by the Montrose family tomb, shameless in its ostentatious design among the other modest grave markers. "Of course she lives in the cemetery."

Laughing, Mia shook her head. "Near."

"Not sure the ghosts are going to be bothered by your semantics," Izzy said.

Mia rolled her eyes as they stopped in front of the cottage, then knocked.

When Ellen opened the door, her bloodshot eyes told a particular story. Guilt.

The woman was dressed down in a baggy pair of flannel pajama bottoms and a worn-out looking hoodie that was probably three sizes too big, her hair pushed back into a sloppy bun so that curls had escaped to bounce around her puffy face.

"Can we come in? We have a few questions to ask," Mia said. There was mutiny in the twist of Ellen's lips and the way her shoulders rounded as she hunched in the depths of her sweatshirt. But her eyes shifted between Mia and Izzy and then dropped to the floor.

"Okay."

The living area fit a two-person love seat, a twin mattress that was set up on the floor, a bistro table with two metal folding chairs, and a lone bar stool. Ellen perched on that, her fuzzy sock–clad toes curling around one of the rungs.

After Mia and Izzy had squeezed together on the sofa, Mia pulled the trigger, so to speak. "Where were you last night, between midnight and four a.m.?"

Ellen's chin tipped up. "I stayed over at Sammy's."

It was a classic mistake, not questioning why Mia was asking, just happening to have an alibi at the ready. The unforced error was another puzzle piece when it came to Ellen. So she had experience lying, but maybe not to cops.

"I didn't realize you two were dating," Mia said easily. Where did the reporter play into that situation?

Pink stained Ellen's cheeks, and Mia sympathized over the fair skin. A giveaway every time. "Off and on," Ellen said, a shrug in her voice.

As if it didn't matter. But she was chewing on her lower lip, her gaze somewhere on the floor several feet to their right.

"He can attest to your whereabouts for the whole night?" Izzy chimed in, a little more demanding than she had been during their time on St. Lucy's so far. But she *had* been shot at.

This time, Ellen met their questioning stares straight on. "Yes." More resigned and exhausted than anything else.

"Do you mind if we take a look around?" Mia pushed a little, testing to see if the fire that they'd seen only in her parting shot was still there.

"I do mind, Detectives," Ellen said. "Now tell me why you're here, arrest me, or leave."

Their hands were tied to an extent, without easy access to a judge to issue a warrant, and not a whole lot of evidence even if they could reach one. What they had was that Ellen possibly could fit the body type of their intruder and the fact that she looked guilty as hell.

It was clear Ellen knew all that, too. Mia considered her options.

"Look, we don't care about whatever you're running from." Unless it was tangled up in their case. But Mia didn't add that caveat. "You're worried we're going to stumble onto it." She held up a hand before Ellen could say anything. "You don't need to respond to that."

Ellen chewed on her bottom lip, eyes wide. The radiator crackled, grumpy and noisy; a cat meowed from the kitchen, hiding from them; the washer rumbled, struggling with the load that had been running since before they'd gotten there.

And Ellen remained silent. Not refuting any of it.

Mia nodded, once. "Does it have to do with Robert Twist's death?"

"No." The whisper was so low it almost got lost to the low buzz of noise from the rest of the house.

"Okay," Mia said. Izzy hadn't stiffened at all, and, if Mia had to guess, she would think they were on the same page. Under any other circumstance, they wouldn't have stopped until they'd arrested whoever was shooting at cops. But if it had been Ellen, the way the bullet had just grazed Izzy even at close range suggested that she'd been aiming for a distraction, not to injure. "Now that we're clear on that, what can you tell us about Robert Twist's time on the island?"

Ellen drew in a shaky breath, then rubbed a hand against her eye. The sweatshirt had slipped down enough to cover all but the tips of her fingers. "I honestly don't know what else I can give you guys."

"Did he mention an artist who had come to the island?"

"Um." This time Ellen scrubbed at her whole face. "Maybe? I think he had a buddy or something come out here before."

Mia straightened. "Did he mention a name?"

Looking up at them again, Ellen shook her head. "Not that I remember."

Disappointment flared, but she tamped it down. Even if Mia mentioned Peter's name now, she couldn't trust that Ellen wasn't just picking up cues from them. That was a good way to get false information.

"Why did you go out with him? Robert, that is," Izzy asked, bolder than Mia probably would have been. Which was why they worked well together when Izzy was free to do her thing. "You don't seem like you're swept off your feet or anything."

Ellen scrunched her nose, her shoulders relaxing for the first time since they'd arrived. "It's not like there's a lot of options here." She shrugged. "And Sammy . . ."

"Sammy what?" Mia prodded.

The question seemed to jar Ellen, and she lost that ease she'd worn, a quick insight into what she'd be like when she didn't have her back up against a wall.

"No, nothing." Ellen's voice was too casual.

"Was he jealous?" Izzy pressed. "Did you want him to be?"

Ellen's eyes slid to the side again; then she drew in a deep breath. "He's been, I don't know, distant lately. More so than usual."

"When did that start?" Mia asked, thinking back to the phone call Brandon Sonder had overheard. Whom had Sammy called after they'd found the body? What had he said that made it stand out enough in Brandon's memory for him to tell the cops about it?

"Summer, I'd say, but maybe earlier," Ellen said. "We've been more off than on these days. So."

Mia didn't want Sammy to be involved; she wanted him to stay Stoner Sammy B., the boy who listened to *The Dark Side of the Moon* on vinyl, on repeat, while lying on the shaggy carpet of her bedroom, talking about life and snails and wondering what color mirrors were. Her ulcer throbbed, and she ignored it.

"You said Jimmy and Cash were talking about finding the Bells."

"I honestly didn't hear much else than that." Ellen brought one leg up to her chest so she could wrap her arm around her shin. She rested her chin on her kneecap and stared them down. The tight lines around her eyes and mouth had relaxed almost completely, and her lids drooped as if fear and tension had been the only things keeping her awake.

"Not why Cash wanted to find them?"

Ellen tilted her head, considering. "Something about the father contacting Lacey again? Or bothering her? Or Lacey being upset about something."

Charles Bell. Mia couldn't forget Martha Lowe's resolute face, her utter and total belief that the reason that Asher was dead was because of something that had happened to Bix Bell. So where did it all fit in?

The unsure half answers were more likely to be true than if Ellen had given them something verbatim, so Mia *almost* trusted them. What she didn't trust was Cash's portrayal of the situation to Jimmy. Overheard information should be taken with a grain of salt at best, and this was even secondhand.

But Mia couldn't deny there was a long line of questions stacking up for Cash Bishop.

The storm had moved in while Mia and Izzy had interviewed Ellen, and the hail had already started by the time they made it back to Mama's house.

Mia had wanted to talk with Cash or Earl Bishop, but even running from the shed to the kitchen had been enough of a challenge that Mia knew she'd have bruises and welts where the brutal ice had pelted her arms, her cheeks.

And Earl's dementia added a complexity to how they approached any questioning. They would have to be sensitive to how they handled him, and a surprise interrogation in the middle of a storm probably wasn't the best option.

"Tell me what you thought of Lacey," Mia said once they'd shaken off the snow that clung to their jackets and stripped down to long shirts and jeans.

The windows protested as the wind pummeled the glass panes, and the lights flickered, a quick blink that always made Mia hold her breath. They had backup generators that would kick in if the power went, but there was something terrifying about the vulnerability that came with the first plunge into darkness.

Izzy had been quiet most of the time they'd talked with Lacey, and then after Ellen's house, too, so Mia didn't have a read on what she was thinking.

Now Izzy settled into the kitchen chair, popping it back on two legs, her arms long enough to grab the counter and keep herself balanced. "Lacey," Izzy said before humming low in her throat, her eyes on the ceiling. "That one's an odd bird, isn't she?"

An echo of Mia's previous thoughts. A bird, poised for flight.

"She's an artist." Mia shrugged. It became a joke on St. Lucy's. If an islander did something strange or outlandish, or broke the strict norms for acceptable behavior, someone would faux whisper, "Oh, they're an *artist* now."

"I think that term can be applied loosely," Izzy said, dropping her gaze back to Mia. "Did you see her paintings?"

"They've sold for more than ten thousand a piece," Mia said, amused at the way Izzy let the chair's feet hit the ground.

"Get out."

"Did a quick search on her," Mia said, nodding toward her phone. Wi-Fi was spotty even in the best of times. But if you stood just right, sent up the right kind of prayers, and threw salt over your shoulder, you could sometimes get a signal of some kind if you weren't in the middle of a storm. "There wasn't much to find, beyond the fact that apparently she's taken over the Boston art scene."

"Man, did I get into the wrong profession." Izzy shook her head, then leaned forward, her elbow on the table, her hand propping up her head. "Anyway, you want to know my thoughts?"

"Please."

"It feels like there's something big we're not seeing," Izzy said. "And we're trying to work two cases, without really working either."

"The reporter's death," Mia said slowly. "And whatever he was poking into."

"What if we keep chasing him down this hole but there's nothing at the bottom?" Izzy pushed her fingers through her hair, disrupting the style so that the pink strands stood on end, a ruffled cockatoo. "I'm not saying we're not onto something. The phone message was strange. I just . . ."

"Don't want to get bogged down," Mia finished for her. There was also an elephant in the room, and Mia was part grateful and part uneasy that Izzy wasn't mentioning it.

Did you kill them?

It was Ellen's voice in Mia's head, but the question flitted across Izzy's face anytime she thought Mia wasn't looking.

Mia scratched at her wrist. That figure in the woods on their first night, the man under a streetlamp, the questions digging into Mia's past—they were itches she couldn't scratch, and they burned beneath her skin. But they had to stop dancing around this. "If we're completely on the wrong track, if he got into a fight with someone on the island and this is a personal beef, I think Mama would have told me."

There was a beat of silence. "Would she?"

Mia thought about their conversation from the first night. "She's worried about me."

"Isn't that what mothers do?" A slight smile turned the question almost teasing, rather than challenging.

How to explain it?

"Living here isn't easy," Mia started, because that couldn't be said often enough. "Everyone here depends on each other in some way. All those people with multiple jobs? It's because people stepped up where there was a need."

Izzy nodded.

"That tight community forces everyone to be kind of in tune with each other," Mia said. "Say someone gets sick. On the mainland, it's not a big deal. But here, one person has the flu, that could wipe out the island. And what if it's the plumber on the same day a pipe bursts in Sammy's office. A few other people could probably do a quick patch job but not enough to really fix it. Then someone has a heart attack, but the doctor's office is flooded because someone sneezed on someone at the wrong time."

They sat with that for a minute.

"People learn each other's rhythms here, better than on the mainland," Mia said, wondering if she was making any sense at all. "They notice a cough days earlier, or a pregnancy, or who's sleeping with who, because no matter how small that thing might seem, it affects everyone else's survival."

"Your mama is worried about you," Izzy said, like she actually understood.

Mia shrugged. "She'd know if Twist's death was because of a fight. But she warned me to be careful. Which means she thinks he was killed because of whatever he was working on."

"Then there's a good chance that's true, right?"

"Yes," Mia answered quietly, admitting it to herself fully for the first time. It was why no one was acting all that worried about a possible murderer on the loose; it was why Mama still hadn't been locking all their windows, which is how the intruder had gotten in last night. People weren't worried, because they knew the target had been Robert Twist.

The lights shivered again, went out, came back. They stared at each other across the expanse of the table while they waited to see if this was the time the power would give up. When it stayed on, Izzy glanced over at the bullet that was still lodged in the kitchen's doorframe.

"She was right to be worried, I guess," Izzy said. "But our visitor last night was probably Ellen."

The waitress had watched them with haunted eyes as they'd zipped into the jackets earlier, leaving Mia wondering if she was running a risk–benefit analysis on fleeing from the island. "She could have been playing us."

"Just now?"

Mia nodded.

Izzy pursed her lips; then her face relaxed. "Do you think she was?"

"No," Mia said, quietly.

"Me neither," Izzy said with a big, dramatic sigh. "Which means we should probably keep going through these, huh?"

They both looked down at the pile of notebooks they'd picked up off the floor after last night's scuffle. When Mia just grimaced, Izzy leaned forward, grabbed one of them, and tossed it to Mia.

"Down the rabbit hole we go."

A frustrating hour of jumbled words later, Mia dropped the notebook she'd been working on into her lap. "Theo."

Izzy glanced up, blinking too fast as she tried to catch up to Mia's non sequitur. "What now?"

Mia stood up without bothering to answer. She couldn't believe she hadn't thought about it earlier.

Mama still had an old-fashioned landline hooked up in the kitchen. It was a step up from a rotary phone, but just barely. Her cell was hopeless at this point, though, and beggars couldn't be choosers.

She hopped up on the counter next to the phone and checked her contacts list for the right number.

Theodore Schaffer answered on the second ring even though it was a Saturday and she was calling from an unknown number. She wasn't surprised.

"Schaffer." He was distracted, she could tell.

"Hey, it's Mia Hart."

"Ah, Mia." There was some shuffling on the other side, and then a door closed. "My favorite detective."

"I bet you say that to all the cops," Mia said, lacing it with fondness.

Theo was currently the editor for the daily newspaper in Portland, but before he'd given in to the call of the North, he'd worked for decades on the politics desk for the *New York Times*.

He also was in a forty-year-long partnership with Gina Murdoch, the Rockford chief of police and Mia's boss. Once, Mia had asked why they'd never married, and Murdoch had laughed for a long time, then insisted she could never be tied down.

"Only the best ones," Theo said now, and Mia rolled her eyes, though she couldn't stop the smile that tugged at her mouth.

"What can you tell me about shorthand?" Mia asked, without any further preamble. Theo would appreciate it, he was a busy man.

"I could tell you more than you ever want to know about short-hand, my dear," he said, his deep, cigar-and-whiskey voice rumbling with leashed laughter.

"Is there a universal one reporters use?"

There was a pause at that. "The Gregg method is popular."

Mia jotted the name down. "I've heard of it. We were taught a bit in training."

"Well, that's part of the problem," Theo said. "Journalists aren't really taught the technique. They just pick it up as they go. So even if the main principles are there, everyone's comes out a bit different."

"Like an accent? But in writing?"

Theo hummed. "More like German and Dutch. You can muddle through, but you might miss some big concepts and some small nuances."

"If I sent you some samples, could you try deciphering it?" Mia asked.

"I can try. Can't promise anything, though," Theo said.

It was something. "You're amazing."

"I bet you say that to all the reporters."

Mia laughed. "Just the best ones. I'll send you some pictures when I can."

Izzy was watching Mia as she hung up. "You going to run down to the FedEx and scan these over to Portland?"

Waving her cell in Izzy's direction, Mia hopped off the counter. "There is this invention called a camera. You may have heard of it? You can even send the pictures via this little device."

A balled-up napkin hit Mia's face. "Smart aleck. You don't have any service."

That was true. She could still save them to her phone, though. Send them to Theo when the Wi-Fi kicked back in. If it ever did.

Mia pulled out her chair. "Hand me the ones with Earl and Cash Bishop, will you?"

Izzy threw her the notebook she'd been paging through. "What's up with them? The Bishops."

"Not counting the Bells, since they only came in the summer, the Bishops are St. Lucy's royalty," Mia said, as she flipped open to the sections with their initials. She lined up the little lens on the phone so she could capture the full page. "Earl is the island's leader for all intents and purposes. Or he was. Now Cash might be."

Mia clicked a picture and then moved to the next part. "Mr. Bishop always made me nervous."

Izzy latched onto that. "In what way?"

"Not in . . ." Mia shook her head, strands of hair falling into her eyes. She pushed them back. "Not in an inappropriate way. He was just stern. Never smiled. I don't think he thought I was good enough for Cash."

"They've lived here forever?"

"And a day," Mia said, thumbing to the page that had the notes about Cash on them. "They claim their relatives founded the port."

"So you think they had something to do with this?"

Mia included the notes on Jimmy Roarke for good measure, then looked up. There was a thought lingering on the outskirts of her mind, fuzzy at the moment but waiting to be fully formed, nudging and knocking for attention. "What Lacey said today."

It was kind of a high for her, you know. Playing men.

Izzy's eyes flicked up and to the right, like she was relistening to the exchange. "Christ. An older man."

"If Monroe was seeing someone older on the island . . ."

"Maybe it was Earl Bishop," Izzy finished for her, and it was a relief that Mia didn't have to actually say it.

For all that he'd scared her, Earl Bishop was an institution. A father figure, even though the last thing she'd needed was another one of those. Her tongue scraped against the dry roof of her mouth, seeking moisture it suddenly lacked.

"How old would she have been? That summer," Izzy asked.

"Sixteen. We were all sixteen," Mia said quietly. The older man Monroe had been seeing could have been someone else. It could have been Danny Acker, who had been home from college on the mainland. A lot of the younger girls had their eyes on him. He would have been a nice challenge. Or Timmy Stern, the man who used to run the plane from the island.

But Earl had been the last person Robert Twist had talked to before he'd died.

She didn't need to glance outside to know the storm had set up shop over St. Lucy's. They wouldn't be going over to Earl's anytime soon.

"So what now?" Izzy asked, her own gaze on the darkness outside.

"Now we wait."

CHAPTER FOURTEEN

Izzy

Izzy had never been good at waiting. Especially when there was a killer out there, and she was trapped in a tiny kitchen, stuck in limbo. Moving might not actually be productive, but at least it would feel like she was doing something.

In the past few hours, the snow had tapered from a rageful blizzard to a steady fall that was almost pretty.

Mia seemed perfectly content with the reprieve from the interrogations. She was hunched over, staring hard at the notebooks, still trying to decipher gibberish despite the fact that she couldn't understand it. *Something to do,* Mia had said a while ago when Izzy had pointed out that it was mostly pointless.

Izzy pushed her chair back, the feet scraping against the linoleum floor. Standing up, she paced to the window. "I've got to get out."

"Antsy?"

Izzy rolled her shoulders to try to ease the itch between the blades. Her wound protested the movement. "Do you think I'd make it to the bar in this?"

Mia's eyes slid past her to the window, then came back to Izzy's face. "Sure, if you're really determined. The hill back up is going to be a pain in the ass."

Right now, being able to escape the suffocating house felt worth the risk. "Think I might pop down," Izzy said.

"All right," Mia said, and moved to gather up her things. "I'm going to take these upstairs. Maybe try to draft a few emails to the uniforms. We need to look into Twist's phone records. Peter especially."

Izzy bounced on the balls of her feet, frustrated that they hadn't had even a blip of reliable Wi-Fi that day to google the guy.

"You want to come for a drink, then?" she asked Mia. "If we can't do anything else."

"No, I'm going to do a little more digging," she said, lifting her armful. "The door's unlocked for when you get back."

"Okay, I won't be long. If I don't return, send a search party."

"That would be a search party of one." Mia pointed to herself. "And it would be a very grumpy search party."

"I'll try not to get myself killed, then," Izzy said, the offhand comment landing with a thud between them. "Sorry."

Mia smiled, but it was definitely out of pity. "Be careful."

When Izzy stepped out into the hushed world, she drew in a breath, her rib cage expanding, rung by rung, as she tasted the hint of salt against her tongue. The muscles at the top of her neck unlocked; her teeth, her jaw, her fingers unclenched.

There was something inherently uncomfortable about being on St. Lucy's. Izzy felt out of step, like she was tripping on cracks, like there were rules and rituals that everyone knew but that she'd never been taught.

The silence that came in the wake of the storm was a relief, was a break from the weight of holding herself so tensely.

The trees were stark silhouettes against the Armageddon-esque orange-and-brown-tinted sky. The world was fresh and yet bleak at once, the pretty coating of snow simultaneously obscuring any ugliness beneath while enhancing the end-of-the-word isolation of the island.

Izzy started down what would be the path toward the bar, her boots sinking in to her knees, her jeans damp and cold against her skin in an instant. Three steps later and she was regretting the rash decision to leave the house.

But she couldn't go back now with her tail between her legs and face a warm, dry, and, more important, smug Mia after only a few minutes of braving the outdoors. She trudged forward, the snow, which was now the consistency of wet cement, grasping at her each time she tried to lift her legs free.

Panic tickled her throat at the thought of coming back up the hill. This had been such a bad idea. But there was light up ahead, a savior in the darkness, and so she pressed forward.

It took her another ten minutes to get to the bar, despite the short distance she had left to cover.

The room wasn't as empty as she'd been expecting. A few men were perched on stools, just like before, and a family with a couple of kids had taken over some of the center tables. Pub food was piled high as little hands grabbed for chicken fingers and fries and mozzarella sticks. Quinn, the pilot, was in a back booth with another woman Izzy hadn't met, and Patty wiggled her fingers at Izzy from her place in front of the dartboard. An older guy was taking his turn, and Patty was pushing up her cleavage to try to distract him. Izzy smiled and raised a hand in greeting.

Instead of joining her, though, Izzy started toward the bar. The same man was working the taps again, his broad shoulders stretching out a simple black tee. His arms were covered in a rainbow of fading tattoos that danced under the lights as he slid a wineglass across the wood to one of the customers.

When the person reached out to grab the stem, Izzy realized it was Lacey Bell, in the flesh. The opportunity was too tempting to pass up. Izzy settled in beside her at the bar, keeping one seat between them.

"Eagle Rare." The bartender pointed at her, already grabbing for the bottle. Izzy didn't have the heart to tell him it wasn't her preference. It was like when she'd been nice about a ceramic frog her grandmother had bought her for Christmas one year, and the next thing Izzy knew, everyone in her life started buying them for her. She'd ended up with a sizable collection that she'd felt too guilty to sell online. So now she was just stuck with hundreds of frogs.

Lacey hadn't looked up during the exchange. She was bent over a bit, her choppy, hipster bob falling in front of her face, hiding it. Once again, she was dressed in an oversize and clearly expensive sweater along with leggings, topped off with a chunky necklace and elaborate dangling earrings.

Her hands were petite but sturdy, with cuts along the knuckles, and chipped black nail polish. She was sketching something on a napkin carelessly.

When she was finished, Lacey pushed it over to Izzy without having once looked up or acknowledging her presence. Izzy grabbed the rough drawing as Lacey lifted the wineglass to her mouth. A glossy red smear coated the rim when she set it back on the bar.

"Monroe," Lacey said, breaking whatever game of chicken they'd been playing. She finally flicked a glance toward Izzy, her dark makeup playing up her eyes.

Izzy picked up the napkin, tilted it so the low ambient light turned the loose, overlapping lines into something resembling a girl's face.

The hair was long and straight, black by default of the pen, but judging from Lacey's coloring, it had probably been that way when she was alive. Most of the other features were similar to Lacey's, as well—a fox face, with a pointed chin and nose, high cheekbones, and a delicate neck. But Monroe's lips were plush, too big for her face, and her eyes sloped down, a seductress in training.

Or at least that's how Lacey had portrayed her.

"Pretty," Izzy said, opening her fingers so the napkin drifted in slow swoops back down to land on the bar.

"She was," Lacey agreed easily, swirling the ruby liquid against the sides of her glass. "We were born exactly fourteen months, two weeks, and fourteen hours apart from each other."

"Nearly Irish twins," Izzy said, and Lacey's lips twitched.

"I hated that she was older," she said. "When I was younger at least. If she was still here, I'd probably never shut up about it."

"I'm sorry." Izzy wondered how long it had been since Lacey had been forced to think about Monroe so much. And here they were stomping through everything that must have been grieved and buried and somewhat healed. Now Lacey was sketching her dead sister on cheap bar napkins.

Lacey played with the pack of cigarettes, her nail picking at the seams of the box, before she tapped it against her thigh and then brought it up to spin on the wood again. So fidgety. After a few seconds, she seemed to make some decision. "Max, I'm lighting up, and you can kiss my ass if you tell me not to."

"Hey," the bartender dragged out the protest as he pointed to a THANK YOU FOR NOT SMOKING sign hung up behind him.

"You want to call the police on me? Oh, wait, they're already here." Lacey tipped her head toward Izzy while digging for a lighter in her little black bag, the cigarette between her lips, the red of them shocking against the white of the paper.

Izzy shrugged when Max looked her way. He grumbled, but when Lacey just raised a perfectly tailored brow and blew smoke out of the corner of her mouth, he rolled his eyes and turned away.

"Thanks," Lacey said, tugging in another hit of the nicotine. As a former smoker, Izzy knew the way it slithered into your veins and made everything that had been ricocheting around go still.

They sat in silence, which was surprisingly companionable rather than awkward, Izzy working through her Eagle Rare that had gotten better by the fourth or fifth sip, Lacey with her vice of choice.

"We both had so much blackmail material on each other." Lacey once again was the one to break first. Izzy recognized the need to talk, the need for someone else to know the person you were missing, even though it was impossible for them to do so. "If either of us had started snitching, we would never have seen daylight again."

"I thought your parents were hippie types," Izzy said, keeping her eyes on the rows of bottles in front of her. It seemed wise not to look at Lacey, not to startle her when she was talking so freely.

"Mom was," Lacey said, and the affection there was clear. "Dad, not so much."

That's what Mia had said, as well. Bix and Charles Bell, a case of opposites attract. Or maybe not.

"Your father was strict with you two?"

Lacey laughed, but there was no humor in it. "Strict. Yeah." She dropped the rest of the cigarette into her almost empty wineglass and pushed it away.

"Lacey," Max muttered, but he blushed when she winked at him.

"Sorry, Max," she said, a throaty purr turned even raspier from the smoke. "Another merlot?"

The tension in Lacey's shoulders seemed to validate Ellen's overheard conversation between Jimmy and Cash—that not only had Charles Bell been contacting Lacey but that it was contentious enough for Cash to go behind her back to try to find him.

"Why did your parents bring you out that summer?" Izzy asked, while Max reached for the open bottle. "You'd never come with them before, right?"

Max also topped Izzy off before leaving them alone once more. Lacey waited until he was at the other side of the bar.

"Monroe was going to be a senior in high school that next year," Lacey said, her eyes on the sketch. "Mom wanted her to work on her painting, and Dad wanted her to have something to write about for her college essay."

"And then you met the locals," Izzy said, trying to imagine what that would have been like for a fifteen-year-old girl. Even as a grown woman, Izzy found everyone on the island intimidating.

Lacey met her eyes in the mirror that ran along the back of the bar. It was an odd sensation, a distorted connection that was tempered by aging glass.

"Monroe thought it was funny," Lacey said. "To play with them. Asher, Mia, Cash. She treated them like dolls. I thought it was funny at first, too. You know how teenagers are."

Her fingers were back to tapping, scratching, pulling at the hem of her sweater, sliding along the stem of her glass. Izzy almost wanted to light a cigarette herself just watching the fussing.

"What happened?" Izzy asked, not really knowing what she was expecting. The question was so broad, so sweeping, it could mean anything. What happened that made it not funny? What happened to Monroe? What happened that night? Izzy would take any of the above.

"Monroe wasn't mean," Lacey said.

Dot's bitter voice echoed in Izzy's memory. *That . . . that Bell girl.*

"Okay."

Lacey shifted on the stool, bringing one leg up beneath her. "She wasn't. It was just . . ."

Izzy didn't fill the silence. There was no quicker way to shut someone up than by doing just that.

"She got bored quickly," Lacey finally said. "Asher was so easy for her, too. Didn't even pretend not to be. I thought maybe Mia and them had some weird triangle thing going on."

They both laughed, nervous, because Izzy didn't know if there was any truth to that, and Lacey probably didn't, either.

"But Mia was always moony eyed over Cash." Lacey smiled, and it wasn't possessive. Her gaze was on the bar, but Izzy wondered if she was somewhere else. There was a softness to her voice that betrayed her as lost in a memory.

Izzy finally decided to poke a little. "And that made you the fifth wheel?"

Lacey shook her head. "I already told you I kissed plenty of boys that summer, too."

There was a smug tilt to the corners of her mouth, which smoothed out as she took a rather large swallow of the wine. She slid Izzy a glance while doing so, her head tipped back, her eyes hooded, her throat exposed. Seductive, but also clearly performative.

Izzy looked away. "So what kind of artist was Peter?"

"Sculptor," Lacey said easily.

"What did you think about him?"

Lacey's eyes narrowed, her gaze suddenly intent on Izzy's face. "You're interested in him. You and Mia, both."

Izzy lifted a shoulder, feigning her nonchalance. When someone kept popping up in an investigation, there was usually a reason for it. Before Ellen's interview, Izzy had been on the fence about whether he'd been important. That had sealed it, though.

"When we work these cases, sometimes it's easier to eliminate options," she said. These people weren't the only ones who could lie. "Helps narrow the field."

"Is everyone on the island a suspect, then?" Lacey asked, batting her heavy lashes, playing at coquettish. "Even me?"

Your boyfriend is, at least. Izzy just smiled, though, keeping it relaxed. "It's good to start with a broader net and winnow it down."

Lacey laughed, throaty and unconcerned despite the act she'd just put on. "You'll do fine here, Detective. No one can give a straight answer on St. Lucy's, either."

"You moved back here, though," Izzy commented, careful to keep any accusation from her voice.

But the subject alone was enough to shut Lacey down. Her fidgeting ceased, and she angled her body away from Izzy, her foot sliding down to the lower rung of the barstool, ready to flee. "Yes."

"That must have been . . . hard."

Lacey shifted even farther away. "Not everything here is tainted, you know."

It seemed like it would be, though. Mia hadn't come back since that night. Even if she wasn't showing it, being back was difficult for her. If Izzy knew anything, she knew that much. But maybe living on the island numbed some of the pain, layered new memories over the ones that were so ragged.

Before Izzy could say anything else, a door slammed in the back, a loud crack ripping through the buzz of low conversation.

If Izzy hadn't been watching closely, she'd have missed Lacey flinch. But Izzy had been, and she saw it. She saw it, and she saw Lacey's fingers tremble against the stem of her glass. And when Lacey looked over, she was blinking too fast, her pupils eating up the color in her eyes.

Izzy held up her palms, because in her experience frightened people like to see what you are doing with your hands. "It was only the door, Lacey."

Lacey sucked in a deep breath, her chest shuddering on the inhale, and then she laughed, and it was too bright, too high like tin wind chimes. "I'm so jumpy. Always have been. Silly of me."

But now the woman was in classic defensive mode, her shoulders hunched, her arms crossed in front of her, each hand holding on to the opposite elbow. Making herself small, protecting organs.

"Lacey . . ." Izzy couldn't not say something.

Predictably, it sent Lacey running. She smiled, a twist of lips that was more concerning than reassuring, and slipped off the stool. Lacey was already zipping up her coat by the time Izzy realized she was about two seconds from leaving.

"You don't have to go," Izzy said, though she knew it was useless.

Waving a hand once more at her empty spot, at the napkin, at Izzy, Lacey shrugged. "Sorry for . . . you know. Have a nice night, Izzy Santiago."

Izzy thought that was going to be it, until Lacey took a step closer, meeting Izzy's eyes. The flight reaction had mostly faded into resignation, the delicate skin beneath her eyes revealing her exhaustion. "Seriously. Don't waste your time worrying about me. I'm not worth it."

"Everyone is worth worrying about," Izzy said.

Lacey's eyes traced over Izzy's face, and then she looked past her to the exit.

"Not me."

———

Izzy snagged her nearly empty glass on her way toward the back of the bar.

"Hey, sugar," Patty greeted when Izzy sidled up beside her. The woman was playing herself at darts. "Want a go?"

"Nah, you cleaned me out," Izzy joked.

Patty hooted and then went back to lining herself up just right. "You want some gossip on her then?" As Patty asked, she threw a thumb over her shoulder toward the exit Lacey had just fled through.

"You have any for me?"

"Not really, no." Patty lifted one shoulder. "She keeps mostly to herself. Dating Cash Bishop, though you already know that."

"Yup."

Patty clicked her tongue. "Lacey's probably not too happy about Mia being back."

"The ex in town," Izzy agreed easily, without giving anything up herself. If she had to guess, she'd say Patty was on a fishing expedition to figure out if Mia and Lacey were about to catfight over Cash. So predictable and disappointing. "What can you tell me about Sammy B.?"

Patty's hand paused, just before release. She lowered her arm and turned to Izzy. "Thought I cleaned you out?" There was a mercenary glint in her eyes, but behind it was interest, confusion. Izzy had surprised her with the question.

"Put it on my tab?" Izzy asked lightly. She'd pull her badge out if she had to, but she didn't want to be forced into that.

Something must have shown on her face, though, because Patty's lips curved up. "All right, sugar. Not much to tell there, either. Nice kid. Left to go to school in Boston but came home as often as he could during it. Moved here a few years back."

"Dating anyone?" Izzy said, playing dumb.

Patty slid her a look. "What do you think?"

"Ellen?" Izzy asked.

"Dramatic, those two." Patty waggled her brows, and something sparked in Izzy's gut. "Like wet cats when they fought. But then the next minute, they'd be canoodling in the diner's storage room."

"Word on the street is that the reporter got coffee with Ellen, though."

"Is that what the kids are calling it these days?"

"So one of those fights caught for good?"

Patty popped a hip. "Now that you mention it, those did die off a while ago."

Perhaps around the summer when Ellen said Sammy had started getting distant.

Izzy hummed low in her throat.

"Did you know Peter while he was here?" Izzy changed the subject. There was a lot to think about with Sammy Bowdoin and Ellen Baxter, and she didn't quite know where to dive in.

"That artsy guy who stayed with Lacey?" Patty tilted her head. "Seemed fine. Didn't make waves."

"Was he . . . 'getting coffee' with anyone on the island?"

Patty laughed. "Think a couple gals were nosing around, but got the impression they were barking up the wrong tree, get my drift?"

Izzy nodded. "Were you here when the Bells still came in the summers?"

Once again, Patty remained unruffled by the non sequitur. "Course, sugar. The Bells were lovely. Bit strange. But lovely."

Izzy thought about the way Lacey had tensed when talking about Charles. Thought about the conversation Ellen had overheard between Jimmy Roarke and Cash Bishop. "Were *they?*"

"You want to know if either of them was 'getting coffee' with anyone on the island?" Patty made the question seem ridiculous, but Izzy nodded anyway. There were threads she was collecting, and sometimes her own brain didn't even realize why until it all came together. Something about the Bells was niggling at her, though. She'd learned a long time ago not to fight it.

Abandoning any pretense that she was playing darts, Patty turned to Izzy fully. "Bix liked to flirt, maybe. But nothing serious."

"With anyone in particular?" Izzy pressed.

Patty tipped her chin back, her gaze going distant. When her eyes returned to Izzy, she shrugged. "Earl, Jimmy, those guys."

"Bishop and Roarke," Izzy clarified.

Patty actually wagged her finger in Izzy's face. "Don't go making that anything salacious. Charles worshipped the ground she walked on."

"What did he think of the attention she got from Earl and his friends?"

Patty just shook her head. "He adored her."

"That's not answering the question."

"Notice that, did you?" Patty turned her back on Izzy, her attention on the board. "We might make a proper detective out of you yet."

———

Izzy kept her jacket unzipped on the way home despite the temperature outside. She didn't feel the eyes on her neck like she had in the woods, but after getting shot at and asking too many questions of too many people, it didn't seem paranoid to be cautious.

The snow had stopped, leaving behind a fresh blanket, her boot prints from the trek down the hill just a faint echo of what they had been. The way back up was tough, but the residual fire in her blood from the Eagle Rare made it slightly more bearable this time.

The quiet let her think, too. Since they'd arrived, there hadn't really been time to regain her footing. The eerie silence gave her time to run through the list of players they'd been gathering.

Sammy Bowdoin. The doc had rubbed Izzy the wrong way, and though he hadn't done anything that raised big red flags, his behavior certainly leaned more toward suspicious than not. Plus, he was in the perfect position to clean up any evidence he'd left behind. The only hesitation she had about him was motive. Why would he have killed Twist? Jealousy seemed a stretch since he'd been pulling away from Ellen for months.

But . . . he might have been an accomplice. That fit with the phone call Brandon Sonder had told them about. She'd have to sit with that one for a bit.

Cash Bishop. Mr. Tall, Dark, and Handsome. Izzy didn't have a read on him yet, apart from watching Mia react to him that first night. Mia had been tense, but that could be chalked up to him being an ex. He had dodged out on their questioning and had been asking about the Bells, but it seemed plausible that he was trying to keep his girlfriend from finding out he was digging into her father just in case she didn't want him to.

Which brought Izzy to Lacey. She was an interesting one. She'd found Mia that night, which sent up alarm bells. Had she seen something she shouldn't have? And was the bruise on her arm and the nervousness in her eyes related to the case? Or was she just haunted by demons they had no business uncovering?

For that matter, where did Bix and Charles fit in? They hadn't been on the island in years; no one had even seen them in that long. Were they even worth pursuing now, when the Robert Twist case was their main focus?

And what about Jimmy Roarke and Earl? They kept being brought up, but was that just because it was such a small town that it was inevitable they'd be included in conversations?

The past and present were blurring, and Izzy was having a hard time keeping them separate. She wanted to follow Robert Twist down the path he'd sniffed out, the secrets he might have revealed about the supposed suicide pact. At the same time, she was here to solve his murder, not a decades-old mystery.

Mia. She was the link between it all. She was the one who'd recognized Robert Twist, the one whom he was asking about. She was the one who'd gone into the lighthouse with two of her friends and emerged the only survivor. She was the one who swayed on her feet and blinked too long and looked, at times, for the all the world like she was simply going to burn to the ground where she stood, float into the air like ash. Disappear.

Izzy trusted her, she did. And more than that, she knew Mia hadn't been to the island recently, so that probably gave her an alibi for the murder. That didn't mean, though, that she didn't have more secrets that she was keeping tucked away. Had that call Sammy made been to Mia? Was it worth it to find out?

All of them, they were all threads. Izzy just had to find the right one to tug. Then those lies they so dearly loved to tell would start to unravel.

CHAPTER FIFTEEN
MIA

At first Mia thought the pounding was in her head, the migraine that had been coiling at the base of her skull finally unleashed. But the pain she was expecting as she blinked awake in the early-morning light was absent.

"Mia," Edie said from the bedroom doorway. "Think you better get down there."

When her bare feet touched cold hardwood, she hissed but didn't pause as she tugged on a sweatshirt and headed toward the stairs.

"Iz," she called down the hallway but didn't wait for a response. There was someone out there, banging on the front door, and Mia didn't know how long the small house could withstand the attack.

When Mia yanked open the door, she ducked, just to the side, in case a fist was headed toward her face. The hit didn't come, though.

Instead, Cash's hand dropped. His eyes were wide, panicked and unfocused.

"You," Cash snarled, an accusation and challenge. He was on her in two steps, his fingers curling into the collar of her sweatshirt, hauling her up to her toes. "You did this."

Her world narrowed down to the two of them, his bared teeth, the anger in his voice. He could toss her like a rag doll against the side of the house if he wanted.

"Let me go." She said it in the firmest voice she could, stripping any fear from it in the process. "Cash, let me go."

Izzy was there. She hit him, hit him hard. But rage was fueling him now, and he didn't go down. Mia tried again. "Cash, let me go."

Over and over the same simple phrase, calm and easy, without raising her hands. The seconds stretched into what felt like hours, but finally Cash released her.

He didn't throw her, like she'd been expecting. But he didn't put her down gently, either. Her feet scrambled for purchase, but it was too little, too late. Mia ended up sprawled half on the porch, half in the entryway.

Izzy had her gun out, pointed at Cash, the safety off the weapon. She had been prepared to shoot, and Mia was thankful it hadn't come even close to that.

Cash was down the stairs, crouched on the cleared path leading up to Edie's house, rocking, his hands up around his head. "He's dead."

Everything was still too sharp, the smell of burning wood somewhere in the forest, the snow against the soles of her feet, the metallic fear lingering in her mouth. The words sliced into her newly vulnerable skin, raw and sensitive from the chemicals flooding her bloodstream.

"Who?" she asked, though she knew. She knew.

"He's dead," Cash said again, broken, pale, and sweaty. His voice was that of a little boy's begging for someone to tell him it wasn't true. "Earl is dead."

"Mia?" Izzy hadn't relaxed her stance, her eyes trained on Cash.

"It's okay," Mia said and hoped it was true. She held out a hand to Izzy, gesturing her to lower the gun even as she kept her eyes on Cash. "It's okay."

They were all having trouble forming thoughts into anything other than basic sounds, repeated until they sank in.

Mia pressed at her temple with her thumb and concentrated on sitting up, unlocking the muscles that she hadn't been able to control as well as her voice.

Eventually the cold cut through the shock, and Mia was forced to push herself to her feet. If she started shivering, she wasn't sure if she'd be able to stop.

Izzy had dropped her weapon to her side, but her shoulders were still tense, her feet still braced apart. She was ready to draw again if needed.

Mia approached Cash like she would a wounded animal: careful, slow, deliberate. Once she realized he wasn't going to lash out, she grabbed his biceps and tugged. If he hadn't wanted to go, she wouldn't have been able to make him budge, but he unfolded himself easily, a puppet being pulled up by strings. "Come on."

She guided them all into the house.

Her hand was firm on Cash's back as she pushed him down the hallway and then deposited him into one of the chairs in the kitchen. She put on coffee.

None of them spoke until she'd placed his mug on the table and then sat across from him. Izzy was behind her, leaning against the counter, her eyes watchful, her gun resting against her thigh.

"Tell me what happened," Mia finally said. Cash's gaze flew to hers, his eyes red rimmed and wet, his lashes clumpy with his shed tears.

He dropped his gaze.

"If you'd just let it go," Cash muttered into his cup. "Christ, Mia, if you'd just . . ."

"What, Cash?" Because she needed him to say it. This wasn't a confession; at least she didn't think it was. But it wasn't nothing, either.

"Left well enough alone."

Mia ran her thumb along the rim of her mug. "You mean, just not investigate a murder?"

His eyes were on the table. "Who even cared about that guy? And now . . ."

A dry sob cut off anything further. Mia sat back against her chair, meeting Izzy's eyes. The woman's lips were pressed together as if she were holding back thoughts that wanted nothing more than to escape.

Mia turned her attention back to Cash. This wasn't the boy she'd known. The boy she'd known was on the cusp of becoming a man with strength and conviction. This person before her was almost unrecognizable. What had happened? A disdain she never could have guessed she'd feel toward him rolled through her.

"He left a letter," Cash said like it was dragged out of him, the words sliding against gravel.

A letter.

Mia ran her sweaty palms against her pajama pants, feeling far too defenseless and underdressed.

"Do you have it?"

Cash reached into his jacket. Mia's heart fluttered, but she remained still. When he pulled out a sheet of paper and not a gun, she relaxed.

He tossed the letter to the table and stared at it, his fists clenched so that his knuckles were white.

Her fingers trembled as she picked it up.

I'm sorry. Forgive me.

Mia cursed on a quiet exhale and then handed the message back to Izzy. Cash hadn't looked up at her to watch her read it.

"This morning?" she prompted.

He nodded once, licked his lips. "He comes down for breakfast every morning at seven sharp. He didn't today."

"How?" She ripped off the Band-Aid they'd all been waiting for her to strip away.

"Pills," Cash said. Not another gunshot wound, then.

"And you didn't hear anyone else in the house?" she asked.

At that he looked up, surprise breaking through the thick lines of anger that had settled into his face. "No."

"Nothing out of the ordinary, then?"

There was a pause. "You think there was foul play?"

"Covering the bases," Mia said, not wanting to agitate him.

Cash studied her but then dropped his gaze once more. "Nothing out of the ordinary."

"How did he have access to that kind of medication?" It wasn't like he could just pop some aspirin. It would have had to be heavy duty. Opioids, probably. Powerful painkillers.

The line of his shoulders broke as he hunched forward a little. "Why the hell is that important?"

"Bases," Mia said, trying not to let it sound flippant.

"He was . . ." Cash cleared his throat, glanced back at Izzy, then finally looked at Mia. "He had Alzheimer's. A couple months ago he wandered off, fell, and broke his femur. He was still recovering."

Mia tapped her finger against her mug before quieting her hand. Her nerves were so easy to read for anyone who looked for them. She nodded to get him to continue.

"I kept them in my medicine cabinet." The guilt in Cash's voice was evident. "Locked. But it wouldn't have been hard for him to get them. I didn't . . . I don't monitor it that closely. Not for this kind of thing. He's never been suicidal."

"A theme with this case," Izzy murmured so low that Mia wondered if Cash had even heard.

"Did you call Sammy?" Mia asked, standing. She no longer worried that Cash was about to go off again. His volatile rage had clearly fizzled into a sad, dampened helplessness.

"No, I came straight here." Cash glanced at Izzy's holster. "You're the police."

He hadn't seemed to be thinking about that when he'd lifted her from the ground, his fingers curled into her sweatshirt. But she didn't mention that. Just nodded and grabbed her phone.

After a quick call to the coroner, she directed them all to the foyer to wait as she threw on some actual clothes. Along the way back downstairs she stopped by a locked drawer and pulled out her own gun.

———

A crisp white sheet covered Earl Bishop's body.

Mia stood in the doorway, blocking the others from the room. She wanted a first impression that didn't involve Izzy's nerves or Cash's grief or even Sammy's surprise.

The furniture was unfinished oak, simple and bare and sparse. There was a dresser and then a bedside table with a half-drunk glass of water, a neatly folded pair of reading glasses, and a tattered paperback book.

A pair of boots, well worn and weathered, were tucked under the foot of the bed.

The walls, though . . . the walls betrayed the true state of the man who had lived there. They were papered in Post-it notes, the yellow and green and pink of them quivering at the mercy of a draft. They were layered on top of each other, a sticky mapping of the inner workings of Earl Bishop's deteriorating memory.

Izzy nudged at Mia's shoulder, and she knew her time was up.

She stepped into the room, and the others were quick to follow. Like Mia, Izzy was captivated by the little messages tacked to the walls.

Sammy and Cash made their way toward Earl's body. They were all quiet, tense.

The handwriting on the Post-its revealed varying stages of dementia. Some had neat block lettering, the exact type Mia would have expected from Earl Bishop. Others were a scrawled jumble of letters that might have made sense only to him.

"Wild," Izzy said.

Mia nodded once, to show she'd heard, and then stepped toward Sammy. "Can you check for defensive injuries when you do your report?" It was strange having to ask one of their suspects to examine the body. But that's how life was on St. Lucy's. They had one coroner, and they had to follow procedure. They had nothing on Sammy other than an overheard phone call and reports of him being a distant boyfriend.

Sammy lifted a brow. "Course, Detective."

It was doubtful he'd find anything. If it had been foul play, it hadn't required strength. Just access. And considering few, if any, residents on St. Lucy's locked their doors, that wouldn't be hard, either. Someone could have easily come in at night and overpowered a sleeping, disoriented Earl Bishop without leaving any signs of struggle behind.

"Wish we had a tech team," Izzy said, her hands on her hips, doing a slow sweep of the room.

Everything was so much harder here. A weariness settled into Mia, achy and sore, dragging on her lashes. When she opened her eyes, it was to find Izzy watching her, her head tilted.

"Yeah," Mia said, and with the way Izzy's lips pressed together, she thought she might have been late on the reply. How long had she slipped behind the darkness of her lids? It had seemed like only a blink, maybe a second longer.

But time had become a funny thing.

Izzy studied her a minute longer. "Are you okay?"

Mia nodded. "Yes. Just tired."

"Sleep helps with that."

"Oh, really? Never heard of that, should give it a try." Mia softened the sting of the words with a small smile as she walked away toward the far wall.

While there wasn't a coherency to the arrangement of the notes at first glance, the most important daily ones were close to the headboard.

Keys. Wallet. Glasses. Earl Bishop. St. Lucy's Island, Maine. Tess died 11/4/2014.

Tess had been Cash's mother, whom Mia had only a fleeting memory of despite the amount of time Mia had spent in and out of the Bishops' house. She'd been a wisp of a woman, slight and pale and reserved. Mama had mentioned her passing, briefly. Cancer, if Mia recalled correctly.

Mia stepped closer, wanting to lift the notes so she could see what lay beneath. What Earl had thought was the most important thing before *keys, wallet, glasses* had taken over. But one off to the side caught her eye. It was on top of three or four others, and the shakiness of the lines in the writing seemed to date it as recently.

Call Jimmy.

Jimmy Roarke. He had been Earl Bishop's right-hand man, his lifelong drinking buddy, and Cash's godfather. He'd also caught the reporter out by the lighthouse.

"Has Jimmy been round lately?" Mia asked, without turning back to the others.

Cash cursed. "I have to tell him."

"Before this, though," she pressed. "Since we got to the island. Has Jimmy come round?"

"No." Cash sounded uncertain. Mia glanced over her shoulder, and his jaw went taut. "No."

The second denial was firmer. But . . . "Why the hesitation?"

"I'm not home the entire day." Cash shrugged. "But I don't think Dad had him over."

"Was Earl upset? That we were here?"

Cash's face flushed, the pink of it crawling up his neck first before slipping into his cheeks. "He was talking about Asher."

Mia turned fully toward him. "What?"

"You just . . . you set him off, Mia." Cash threw up his hands. "Why did you have to come back?"

You think I wanted this? Mia didn't let herself get dragged into that particular fight, though. "Was he talking about that summer?"

"He got confused easily."

"That's not what I asked." Sometimes she thought Cash forgot whom he was talking to.

Cash sighed. "He always liked Asher. Thought he was a good kid. But we'd gotten in a fight. That's why I wasn't allowed out that . . . that night you all went to the lighthouse."

"You and Asher? Got in a fight?" Mia clarified.

"Yeah."

"It was physical?" It was hard to believe she'd missed something so big. But she hadn't realized Asher was planning on killing himself, either.

Cash was considering lying even when asked point-blank; it was so easy to read him.

"Don't," Mia said. She didn't need to elaborate. *Don't lie.*

He glanced up, his eyes sliding over her face. "Yes. I punched him."

The room was still, and Mia almost forgot Sammy and Izzy were there, listening.

Mia licked her lips, and she thought back to that picture in the hallway. The three of them, their bodies like puzzle pieces, so at home with each other. Mia staring up at him like he was the stars and the sun and every happy and sad thought in the universe, a constellation of perfection. But it was the girls beyond the edges of the frame that had held both Cash's and Asher's attention. She'd thought Cash was looking at the camera.

"Monroe?" she finally asked, because, of course, why else?

Cash's nostrils flared, and he wouldn't look at her. He didn't answer, because silence was part of their pattern of lies, and it was enough.

"Shit," Izzy said on an exhale from across the room.

That summer. What did she really remember? She'd thought they'd been tangled together, she and Cash. Blind to anyone else. Hot, slick skin and swollen lips and hungry fingertips. Sugarcoated tongues from the syrupy Coke they'd drunk by the case during the day and alcohol-saturated laughter that spilled too easily from their mouths at night.

The memories felt like a film now, a pretty one, cut with rose and gold and sunburst filters. A melodic soundtrack played in the background as shots of her long blonde hair swirled around bare, tan shoulders and spaghetti straps.

How had it really been? Could she strip away the nostalgia to find the raw footage? There had to be things she wouldn't want to see, bruises and hurt feelings. They'd been teenagers after all.

That first day when Monroe sat on Asher's lap during their stupid game of truth or dare.

When Mia had thought about it earlier, she'd still been able to feel Cash's hand on her back. But what about his face? Had he been watching them? Envious already? Of fresh possibilities, skin that hadn't already been explored millions of times over the years, a body that didn't reek of familiarity.

Why did they see things through prisms rather than as they were? Why couldn't she see his eyes when Monroe straddled Asher? Why couldn't she remember the punch or the blooming green and purple on Asher's face?

"When?" she asked, because anything else was too much, too loaded and fragile and important. *When did you punch him?* That was easy at least.

"That day," Cash said, and there was almost relief in his voice. Like the secret had been eating him from the inside out for more than a decade.

"You were grounded for it," Mia said, her brain slow, so slow.

"Dad was furious that I punched someone."

"Hey, I have a question," Izzy called from her corner of the room. Mia flinched at the interruption. "As, you know, someone who doesn't speak your supersecret language."

Cash just shoved his hands in his pockets, but Mia met Izzy's eyes, a silent go-ahead.

"Why were you the one swinging at Asher? If Monroe cheated on him with you, wouldn't it have been the other way around?"

Cash's eyes flicked to the side to catch Mia's face in his peripheral, and something slid into place. Why hadn't she asked that question? Blind spots. She had so many on this case.

Mia swallowed the saliva that had gathered against the pockets of her cheeks, flushing hot, then cold again.

The spaces between the truths always hid the lies. Cash had punched Asher. Cash had punched Asher over Monroe. Cash had punched Asher over Monroe and been grounded for it.

But none of that meant Cash had been in the wrong. He'd just been acting like that kid she'd known back then, trying to right the world's injustices.

"No," she said quietly, because she was a person sometimes just as much as she was a cop, and she didn't want to let go of her best friend, the one who'd died fifteen years ago. Whatever Cash was about to say, though, she knew just from the way he hesitated that it would be bad, knew it would be a shadow that slid over the Asher she remembered.

Izzy's eyes snapped between them when Cash didn't say anything, but his fingers clenched and unclenched against the sides of his legs.

"What am I missing?"

Cash licked his lips, looked once at Mia, and then turned back to Izzy.

"Monroe was pregnant."

CHAPTER SIXTEEN

Izzy

Mia and Izzy didn't return to Edie's house until midafternoon. They'd helped Sammy deal with the body, then walked through all the rooms, checking each as thoroughly as possible without a tech team.

"So that's convenient," Izzy said, settling into what she was beginning to think of as her chair. "Wraps everything up nicely."

While filling the kettle, Mia glanced back at her over her shoulder. "What do you mean?"

"Monroe was having an affair with an older guy on the island." Izzy pushed her chair onto two legs. She held on to the counter behind her with her uninjured arm. "He finds out about the pregnancy, kills her, makes it look like suicide so there's no autopsy. No one knows about the baby. Boom, problem solved."

"Cash knew," Mia said, leaning against the counter, her arms crossed, not giving anything away about how she felt about that particular revelation.

Cash had sworn that he hadn't been sleeping with Monroe, had said he'd simply been trying to get Asher to step up and do the right thing. The fight had just been a man-up talk that had escalated because teenage boys were teenage boys.

Izzy doubted it had really been that simple, but, for now, she was going to let it go.

"Right."

Mia rolled her shoulders. "And that scenario doesn't account for why they'd be okay with Asher and me as collateral damage."

Izzy deflated further but tipped her head in agreement.

"Actually," Mia continued, the word drawn out, thoughtful, "I was thinking about it a different way. Still convenient."

Izzy waved her free hand. "Do tell."

"The case looks like it's wrapped up," Mia said.

"Isn't that what I just said?"

"No. I mean this case. The reporter's death. With Earl . . ."

"We see Earl's suicide," Izzy jumped in, "and assume he was the older guy involved with Monroe."

"We conclude that he thought Twist was onto him," Mia continued. "Logically, then, it would follow that Earl killed Twist, and both deaths, Twist's and Monroe's, weighed on him so much he swallowed a bottle of painkillers. That gives us a killer for both possible homicides, and a dead one to boot. Our jobs are done."

"Case closed," Izzy said softly. It was a tasty, easily digestible morsel all wrapped up in pretty paper.

"But what if . . . ?" Mia dragged her fingers through her hair, pushing it back into a low ponytail as she stared off at a point way beyond Izzy. "What if . . . ? What if it just *looks* that way."

A setup. That's what had struck Izzy as off about Twist's murder as well. When you were a cop long enough, you learned how to smell a setup. And Mia was right. This whole case reeked.

I'm sorry. Forgive me.

The note, the pills, they told a clear story. But what if it just had the outer appearances of a suicide? "Just like with Twist."

Mia nodded. "Earl *did* leave a note, though. Twist didn't."

"That's easy enough to forge," Izzy countered. What if they were both staged? And the person was getting smarter with each kill. Adding in a note this time to make sure it was clear. "It was typed."

"All Earl's notes to himself were handwritten," Mia said, and, God, she was a genius sometimes.

"So someone is screwing with us."

Mia held out her hand. "Hold up. We're running too quickly with this theory. It's just a thought."

"But think about it. His death could be a cover for the real killer." Izzy let the legs of the chair drop. "Loose ends all tied up."

Their eyes met across the small room. Cases like this were always tough, but this one seemed particularly hard to wrap their arms around. Add in someone planting a narrative in their heads, and it would become nearly impossible to untangle.

They needed a place to start.

"What about Cash?" Izzy couldn't shake the image of him, face reddened, veins popped, teeth bared, holding Mia up on her toes. "He seems like he has anger issues."

"You're not seeing him like most people do," Mia said.

"I think I'm seeing him a bit more clearly than most people do," Izzy countered. "He was about two seconds from taking your head off this morning. And not for nothing, but we both saw Lacey's bruises."

Mia shook her head but said, "I know."

"So why would Monroe go to Cash about the baby? It wasn't . . ." Izzy didn't want to ask the question, but she had to. Mia saved her from having to put it into words.

"I don't know if it was his, but I think he would have mentioned that," Mia said, her arms wrapped around her stomach, her fingers pressed into the bottom of her rib cage. Izzy hated this. Hated it. "He told us about the fight. And back to your original question, why would he have punched Asher?"

That *had* struck Izzy as strange. Cash had tossed it out like it was a reasonable expectation—hit his best childhood friend over a girl he barely knew and had no personal attachment to. "Can you explain that?"

"He was kind of . . ." Mia trailed off, her eyes unfocused. "Idealistic, I guess, is the right word. When he was younger."

"Saw himself as a white hat riding in to save the damsel in distress?"

"You have to understand the way he was raised here," Mia said, nodding. "I told you Earl was the de facto leader of the island and that it means more here than other places. I wasn't exaggerating. He was responsible for essentially maintaining civil order on St. Lucy's."

"Judge, jury, and . . . ," Izzy summarized.

"Not quite executioner, but nearly." Mia huffed out a little breath. "Most people took disputes to him rather than going through any formal methods—he broke up bar fights, got the instigator to pay for the damages, things like that."

"Was the first responder to a suicide pact between three teenagers," Izzy said.

"Exactly." Mia touched her nose, then pointed at her. Izzy didn't know if she should be worried or relieved that she'd begun to pick up the rhythms of this place. "Cash was groomed into that position. So something like this—if Monroe was upset when she went to Cash, it might have seemed like the right thing to do to go talk to Asher."

"And then things get heated, maybe Asher says some not-so-flattering things about our damsel, and our white hat hero throws fists," Izzy said.

"Earl sees or hears about it, grounds Cash, and he can't go to the lighthouse that night," Mia finished for her. "Which was probably a good decision all around, to be honest."

Izzy studied the scenario they'd just drawn out, looking for cracks. Mia seemed to be doing the same.

"You didn't remember the fight because you don't remember that day," Izzy finally continued.

"But why would I have gone with them, then?" Mia said, her thumb finding her wrist like it so often did these days, the pad of it stroking over the scar Izzy knew was there. "What the hell was I doing there?"

The door slammed open down the hallway, and Mia visibly tensed. "Mama."

"Oh, maybe she knows more." Izzy snapped her fingers. Why hadn't they asked her anything yet? Perhaps it was the weird undercurrent between the two women, the way their bodies were like similar magnets, always pushing away from each other no matter how much you forced them in close.

A flicker of something passed across Mia's face, but she nodded a quick affirmative before Edie walked into the room.

"Mama," Mia said again, this time to the older woman. "Can you sit, please?"

Mia's tone must have set Edie on alert. She stopped midstride, her body stiff and unnatural. "I'm getting out of your way."

"No." Mia shook her head. "We need to ask you some questions."

It was then that Edie's gaze swung to Izzy, obvious in the reminder to Mia that there was an outsider there. "Don't think that's a good idea."

Izzy sank lower in her chair, trying to make herself less obvious. The piercings and pink hair probably didn't help. She ran a hand over the spiky strands to try to get them to lie flat.

"Mama."

The two women had a silent conversation in just that one word.

Finally, Edie sighed, poured a cup of tea from the kettle Mia had put on, and then sat in the empty chair, her body angled toward her daughter, away from Izzy.

"You heard about Earl Bishop?"

Edie crossed her heart. "Bless him."

Mia nodded once. "Where did I say I was going that night?"

If Edie was surprised by the abrupt question, she didn't show it. Izzy guessed the words "that night" had never and would never need to be qualified.

"Out," Edie said simply. "You didn't lie."

"Who did I say I was meeting up with?"

"The usual."

Mia leaned forward. "Did I say 'the usual,' or is that you paraphrasing?"

Edie sighed and rubbed her thumb along the space between her brows. "I don't know, Mia. It was a long time ago."

"Okay." Mia relaxed into the counter again. "Did I seem . . . normal?"

Edie's thick brows shot up. "Don't actually know if I even saw you more than in passing. Was at work most of the day."

So Mia could have been out of it already. Was she thinking drugs? That . . . that would explain a lot.

"When Earl Bishop dropped me off here, what did he say?"

"Just that there'd been an incident at the lighthouse," Edie answered slowly, clearly weighing each word. "And that Doc was already there and had bandaged you best he could. That you'd need to be looked at in the morning when everything settled down."

"Do you remember anything about Earl in that moment?"

Edie crossed herself again, and Izzy was reminded that not everyone was as good at compartmentalizing death as she and Mia were. "I'm not speaking ill of the dead, Mia Mackenzie. Take that thought right out of your mind this second."

Izzy tensed and shifted so she was no longer slouching. *Ill of the dead.* That meant there was something to say. Mia flicked a quick glance toward Izzy. She'd picked up on it, too.

"Mama, it could help the case."

"And that's all that matters?" Edie asked, her tone harsh, slipping deeper into her clipped northern accent. "Some reporter no one knew or liked? He matters more than the man who helped keep this town together?"

It was an echo of what Cash had said earlier. An outsider's life meant less to these people than protecting their own. It was a harsh reality but one Izzy couldn't ignore.

Izzy followed Mia's lead in not mentioning their theory that Earl's suicide may have been staged. If she didn't want to bring it up, Izzy wasn't going to rock the boat.

Mia's stance was braced, looking like she was ready for a fight. "What aren't you telling me? What happened that night, Mama?"

"Earl Bishop was a good man," Edie said.

"I know." It was said on an exhale that wasn't quite as impatient as Izzy would have been. Mia knew these people. Knew when to push, when to back off.

Time stretched, the hands on the clock's slow tick forward the only thing marking the passing of the seconds. The sound wiggled and burrowed into the crevices of Izzy's brain, and she wanted to scratch at the soft tissue until she could reach it.

I'm sorry. Forgive me.

What had Earl meant by that letter? And *had* he even written it?

Izzy's legs ached, begging her to push to her feet, walk, stretch, let the pressure that had been tightening in her chest unfurl.

"He brought Lacey here, too," Edie finally said. "Her parents were still at the lighthouse."

Mia's reaction was characteristically muted. "You'd never told me that."

"Because we talk about it so often?"

There was a beat, a nod, a recognition of the point made. "What happened then?"

"He left." Edie picked up her mug, her stubby fingers pale white against the turquoise.

"Then what aren't you saying?"

Edie took a swallow of her tea. "You were a zombie, completely out of it. I would have said you were high, but it was different."

This was what Mia had been getting at earlier. The lost day. Maybe it wasn't just her brain protecting itself. Maybe it had been deliberate.

Izzy leaned forward. "Drugged?"

"Sedated, maybe. Figured Doc gave her something."

"Who's Doc?"

"Sammy B.'s predecessor," Mia answered. "Henry Jackson."

"More info please," Izzy said. Another player, another player, another player. They kept adding up. So many on the island had been touched by that night.

"He grew up here, was friends with Earl and Jimmy." Mia held a hand up before Izzy could say anything. "Everyone of that age was. It's not unusual."

But friends covered for each other, helped hide bodies. What if one of the three had been the father of Monroe's baby and he had snapped? And then he'd called his buddies to come clean up the mess. It wasn't out of the realm of possibility. "Was he handsome? Henry, that is."

"Um." Mia looked up like she was trying to pull up his picture in her mind. Edie huffed and shuffled in her seat. "I guess?"

"Could he have been the older man Monroe was seeing?"

"What?" This time it was Edie who was taken off guard.

Mia's eyes slipped to her mother's face. "There's been talk that Monroe was seeing someone other than Asher."

"No, that can't be." Edie crossed her arms over her chest. "Those two only had eyes for each other that summer."

"You think?"

That wasn't the impression they'd been given. Izzy heard her own doubt reflected in Mia's voice.

"I thought she was bad news at first, God's truth." Edie nodded. "But I'd never seen that boy like that before."

And that was more in line with what Lacey had said. Maybe Monroe had seemed interested at first, to hook Asher, but had gotten bored once the newness had worn off.

"So. I was out of it?" Mia got them back on track, and Izzy guessed her thought process hadn't seemed much different from Izzy's. They knew all of this. "When Earl brought us back here."

"Lacey wasn't much better, still had blood on her," Edie said. "But she was somewhat coherent."

"What did she say?" Mia asked.

The ghost of Edie's earlier assertion hung in the air. *Earl Bishop was a good man.*

On an exhale, Edie put her tea down and then sat back against her chair. "She said she didn't know how Earl had gotten there so fast."

"To the lighthouse?" Mia clarified.

Edie nodded. "She'd run to tell her parents, but on the way back, Earl was already at the meadow. She kept asking me how he'd gotten there so fast."

Mia chewed on her bottom lip, and Izzy kept her mouth shut, not wanting to draw attention to herself.

"It doesn't mean anything," Edie finally said. "He could have been out on patrol. Received the call on his walkie-talkie."

"I don't remember when he showed up," Mia said. "And Jimmy was there?"

"She didn't say anything about him."

"You know he was there, though, right?"

Edie shrugged. "That's what people said."

Mia leaned forward, her forearms on her thighs. "What was the talk afterward? What did everyone think happened? Not what they told investigators, but what did they really think?"

"Don't you mind that," Edie said, her eyes shifting to Izzy once more. So very aware of a stranger in her presence.

"If it's that I killed them, I've already been filled in on that," Mia said.

"People just like to talk." Edie shook her head. "Like the sound of their own voices."

"But that's what people were saying?" Mia pressed.

Edie sighed and reached up to grasp the cross on her necklace. "They wondered why you were the only one to make it out. With only one wrist . . ." She nodded toward Mia's arm.

With only one wrist cut.

What had stopped Mia?

"It looked a lot more believable that you didn't have anything to do with it since you were injured yourself," Edie continued. "Just enough to show you attempted to"—she waved her hand—"but not enough to carry through with it."

"Then I came out, made up some wild suicide-pact story, and got away with murder?" Mia asked. Her face was still relaxed, though she'd gone pale, the flush from the cold long gone.

"People are bored," Edie said, and all of a sudden she sounded tired, so tired. "Not much to do here other than sit around and tell tall tales."

"This isn't a tall tale," Izzy butted in. Annoyed with her, annoyed with these people. Annoyed with herself for the part that whispered the accusation wasn't that far-fetched. "They're calling Mia a killer."

"Oh, they'd never say it so anyone else could hear," Edie said.

Mia met Izzy's eyes across the table, and she knew they had both come to the same conclusion. The reporter.

"But someone did," Mia murmured.

———

"So Jimmy Roarke, Henry Jackson, and Earl Bishop were all buddies." Izzy was leaning back in her chair once more. Edie had gone upstairs a few minutes ago, and Mia was staring off into nothing, her back ramrod straight. "And they all just happen to show up at the lighthouse that night?"

"One of them must have called the others," Mia said, but she wasn't quite present, her words dragging, her eyes still on a point near the door. She blinked, a lethargic droop, and then met Izzy's gaze finally. Her pupils ate up the blue in her eyes. "One of them was there first."

"Which one?" Izzy asked the obvious question.

Mia sucked on her lip, then released it. "Just because Lacey saw Earl first doesn't mean that's what happened."

"Yeah. She was, what? Fifteen? Probably in shock," Izzy agreed. "And maybe she did see Earl first. But one of the others could have called him?"

"Could have been any of them," Mia said. "But if Earl's suicide was staged, then someone wants us to think it was him."

The horses and zebras theory, the one they used to keep themselves in check when tempted to spiral down some wild path on an investigation, snapped into her mind. Maybe Earl had done something all those years ago; maybe he had actually killed himself, the guilt stoked back to life by the reporter asking questions. It was the simplest explanation. But Izzy had seen his frail body beneath the sheet. It would have taken a miracle for him to have overpowered Robert Twist.

Which left them with a killer still unaccounted for, no matter what Earl's death was ruled.

"And maybe that same someone who set up Earl's death wanted the reporter to start looking into you," Izzy said, trying to grab hold of all the threads. There were too many. They needed to start cutting some away. "To get attention off of themselves."

"The reporter was already looking into me, though," Mia said, her toe tapping against linoleum. There was a similar twitch running along Izzy's calves, a need to expel the nervous energy that just kept building the longer they sat around in this goddamn kitchen. "Late October. After Peter left the island."

"Yeah."

Mia pressed her thumb into her temple, another one of those gestures that was becoming commonplace. She'd seemed to have had a headache since they'd stepped foot on St. Lucy's. Not that Izzy blamed her. "I just. The timing? It seems odd. And I know it's a common name, but the fact that *a* Peter was in the reporter's contacts, was one of his last calls . . ."

The timing. *The timing.*

"What if Peter was the one who found something out about that night?" Izzy said.

Mia's eyes focused, alert for the first time since Edie had left the kitchen. "That would make more sense than someone on the island willingly talking to a reporter."

"Yeah, I'd imagine they would have been on guard for a reporter," Izzy said, warming to her theory. "But an artist? You said they're thick on the ground here."

"Dismissed, even." Mia pushed to her feet, started pacing. "Ignored."

"He doesn't know what to do with the information, so he tells his buddy, the reporter," Izzy said. "Maybe whatever it was wasn't enough to go to the police, or maybe Twist saw his opportunity to get a byline in something other than a regional artist magazine."

"Twist comes and checks me out at the station." Mia picked up the conversational ball. "Then makes up some cover about investigating suicides on Maine islands but is really coming here to dig into the night at the lighthouse."

It wasn't suicide. The reporter's voice for his phone recording had taken on an eerie undercurrent for Izzy that hadn't existed in the original message.

"The voice memo," Izzy said. "That was Peter telling Twist, or Twist summarizing what Peter had told him. It wasn't suicide."

"So what about San Sebastian?" Mia asked, her voice low like she was talking more to herself. "The plane ticket?"

Izzy answered her anyway. "He was onto something. The killer was getting nervous, and Twist knew he needed to get off the island. Which was true. He just didn't do it soon enough."

They both paused a beat.

Then Izzy put voice to the question she guessed was sitting heavy in Mia's gut, as well. "So where is Peter now?"

If Robert Twist had come to the island asking if the artist was still there, that didn't seem to bode well for Peter.

Mia blinked a few times, too fast, then flexed her jaw. "We find him. We find him."

"And by 'we' you mean a uniform, right?" Izzy clarified.

Mia grabbed for her phone. "Of course. And have them find Charles and Bix Bell while they're at it."

Mia muttered a curse, and Izzy knew what was wrong without having to ask.

She checked her own cell. No service. She held it up, screen out, wiggling it a little to catch Mia's attention. Her partner looked out the window, sighed. "Landline it is."

While Mia searched her contacts for the front desk of the police station, Izzy pulled up emails. There must have been a blip of Wi-Fi sometime recently because there were two messages from Theo sitting unopened at the top of her inbox.

"Did you see these emails?" she called to Mia before she could start dialing. "From Theo."

Before the question was even out, Mia was hovering over her shoulder, her body curled around the back of Izzy's. "No, what did he find in the journals?"

Izzy clicked into the thread, and they both skimmed it.

"Mentions Earl Bishop's dementia," Izzy said, even though Mia had read it as well. "He thought he was back in that summer during the interview."

"Got agitated." Mia straightened. "Cash was mad, kicked the reporter out."

"Fits with the anger issues," Izzy muttered, earning a nudge from Mia's hip. "What? He's showing a repeated pattern of violent behavior."

"He wasn't at the lighthouse that night, though," Mia said.

"Says who?" Izzy countered. "Look at the fight story from a different angle."

"What do you mean?" Mia moved toward the kettle. The water had to be cold by now, but she just fiddled with the handle, not moving to reheat it.

"No, really." Izzy let her chair drop. They were on a roll now. "Cash makes up some bullshit story about Monroe being pregnant, him punching Asher, getting grounded. He just gave himself the perfect alibi."

"A perfect alibi . . . that no one can corroborate?" Mia asked, disbelief in the arc of her brows. "Not quite perfect, Iz."

"Ah, but that's where you're wrong." Izzy slapped the table, loving the feeling of pieces slotting into place. "Jesus. It makes him look just bad enough, you know? The story? Oh, you punched the victim in the face the same day that the kid, quote, unquote, killed himself. Can't believe you're admitting that to the cops. It must make us believe you and everything else you're about to say. But then he twists it to give us the perfect excuse of why he wasn't at the lighthouse."

Mia didn't say anything; her neutral mask was in place.

"The only reason we know *any* of that is because of him, and he only told us it after the man who had done the 'grounding' was no longer around to call out his lies." Izzy stood up herself, unable to keep still any longer.

"You've said it a million times," Izzy continued. "Everyone here is lying. Why wouldn't he? Don't you think he was a little too upfront with his information today? Quite a different tone than he's been taking with us."

Izzy paused her pacing, but her mind was still stumbling forward, ever forward. "What if . . . ?"

When Izzy didn't continue, Mia kicked out a foot, falling far short of actually tapping Izzy but getting the point across. "What if what?"

Izzy pinched the skin of her wrist, the flicker of pain not enough to silence the thought. "What if Monroe wasn't even pregnant?"

Mia shifted back, an almost imperceptible jerk, but Izzy was watching her closely.

"Why would Cash tell us she was?"

Spinning away from Mia, Izzy stalked over to the small refrigerator and then toward the back door, then repeated the path as her mind shifted through possible scenarios, each more outlandish than the next.

Finally she stopped to find Mia, one lazy brow raised, leaning against the counter, still patient, just waiting as Izzy prowled around the room.

"I don't know."

Mia looked away, her delicate jaw in sharp profile, the dim natural light sliding over her pale skin, so that she looked like a painting— exhaustion, grief, resignation, all caught in a few brushstrokes. But then Mia rolled her shoulders, turning back to Izzy, and she was once again just Mia, a blank slate, all her sticky emotions sloughed off with that one careless move.

"All right," Mia said. "It's something to consider."

Where that left them, Izzy didn't know. She shook off the odd moment, then moved to wake the computer up from its doze so she could get into the second email from Theo.

At the top was a note.

Sorry, this one took me longer. It was more the reporter's thoughts than the interview itself. Looks important, though. Good luck, bucko.

Looks important. The words had Izzy straightening out of her lazy slouch.

"What is it?" Mia asked, sharp and fast.

Izzy read over the short paragraph one more time to make sure and then looked up.

"I think he might have found out who Monroe's older gentleman was."

Mia raised her brows. "Who?"

"Jimmy Roarke."

CHAPTER SEVENTEEN

MIA

The one thing Mia missed the most on this case was an investigation room. There was something about the stripped-down starkness of white walls and a utilitarian metal table that kept people from being able to hide behind carefully constructed masks.

Jimmy Roarke's kitchen, on the other hand, let the man be distracted by, dodge, and dance away from any question that got too uncomfortable. He fiddled with mugs for tea, dug in the cabinet for crackers, positioned himself so that the fading sun created shadows on his face.

Mia watched him now as he flicked off the soap opera that was playing on mute on the small television mounted to the wall near the stove. It was odd to imagine him there, tinkering over dinner, indulging in melodramas. She'd pictured Hungry-Man frozen dinners and TV trays in a living room that needed to be scrubbed of decades of careless eating.

He was a burly man, like many on the island, his shoulders stretching the worn flannel of his shirt, towering over Mia by more than a foot.

Silver now tangled in his red beard and the hair at his temples, but he was so familiar that her chest ached with it.

She hadn't wanted it to be Jimmy, even as his name kept cropping up. Chasing the reporter away from the lighthouse. Ellen's story of him talking with Cash about the Bells. The scribbled, shaky note in Earl Bishop's bedroom.

But Jimmy had always been nice to her, nice to Mama. When Mia's father had passed two years before that terrible summer, Jimmy had shown up to help mow the lawn in the spring, clear the snow in the winter. Sometimes he'd even bring around fish he'd caught, good ones, not just the ones he wouldn't be able to sell at market. He'd never asked for anything in return, not money nor Mama's attention. People whispered about how he was a little slow, didn't always catch on, missed jokes, and turned conversations awkward. But Mia had always just thought he was kind.

He finally sat and ran his palms along the rough material of his well-worn jeans. "I don't know what I can tell you, Mia."

His voice softened on her name, like she was a familiar and lovely ache as well. She didn't often think about anyone on St. Lucy's missing her; she didn't think about the island when she could help it. And since she'd been back, she'd encountered more antagonism than welcome. But maybe she'd been liked, maybe missed. At the end of the day, these *were* her people.

If only she weren't here for the reason that she was here. She wanted to be straight with Jimmy, ask what the hell he'd been doing. But that's not how any of this worked.

"We're just checking in with everyone the reporter talked to, Jimmy," Mia said instead.

Jimmy's foot tapped against the linoleum, an unsteady beat that tattled on the anxiety he was clearly trying to keep under wraps. "Didn't talk to him much, though."

Mia decided to come at it from the side. "Sammy says the guy was poking round the lighthouse." She paused. "And that you chased him off."

"Might have." Jimmy hunched over his mug, his foot still going, filling the quiet room with the dull thud of rubber against tile. "He liked to snoop everywhere."

"Everywhere?"

Beneath his beard Jimmy's lips twitched, pursed, relaxed. "Poking into everyone's business."

Mia waited, but he didn't elaborate.

"Did he say anything when you caught him at the lighthouse?" Mia pushed.

Thwap, thwap, thwap. No pause, no stutter. "No."

Maybe she didn't have an interrogation room, but now she had a baseline for Jimmy's tell. If she could read it right.

"You were there that night, weren't you?"

Jimmy's foot stopped, and the quiet pressed in against her. It was only when it was missing that she realized how loud the tapping had been.

And then it was back. "What do you mean?"

"The night Monroe and Asher killed themselves," Mia said, hating this tactic, hating that she had to put it so harshly. But Jimmy was a suspect, not a family friend. And there was no room for pulling punches here.

"Half the island was out there, Mia," Jimmy said, not unkindly, his hand coming up to thread into his beard, catching in the knots. Everything about him had actually relaxed at the question, the tapping slowing as he sat back in his seat. Mia flicked her eyes to Izzy, who was in her peripheral, then looked back at Jimmy.

"Can you tell me about it? What happened that night?"

Again, there was no sign of distress, just a sadness in the slope of his eyebrows, in the crease between them.

"Don't remember it well, huh?" Sympathy rather than anxiety coated his words. "You were out of it."

That's what Mama had said as well. Drugs. She was leaning more and more toward that option. The therapist at the institution had told her she couldn't remember the night because she'd repressed the memories. It had been too much shock for her brain to deal with, so her body had protected her.

But drugs made sense, too. Which means the deaths had been premeditated. Mia still wasn't sure what she thought had happened, but drugging the victims didn't exactly scream fit of rage.

It also meant that the killer had wanted Mia there, too. It would have been so much easier to turn Asher and Monroe into Romeo and Juliet. Mia ruined that pretty little story, casting doubt on the whole setup. So why risk it? And why just the three of them? If someone wanted to go after their little gang, why not wait until Cash was there, too?

There were too many questions left. Usually by this point in a case she could see parts of the image, what she thought it was going to be, at least. Right now, though, all she had were dots, and a lot of people trying to tell her what picture they should form.

However, she did notice that Jimmy hadn't actually answered. "Who called you out there? Earl?"

"Yup." Jimmy nodded, still tugging at his beard. "Woke me up. Time I got there, it was swarming."

"With who? Who beat you there?" She would have guessed he would have been one of the first ones called.

That's when she noticed the tapping again. It was fast, too fast. "The Bells were there, weren't they," he said, but it wasn't a question.

The Bells. Of course, they'd been there first. But why did Jimmy care? Why had he and Cash been talking about them recently?

"The doc," he continued, and his foot had slowed again. Which meant he had been flustered by the mention of the Bells. Charles and Bix. Why?

"Henry Jackson?" Izzy clarified. "The doc. That was Henry Jackson, right?"

"Ayup," Jimmy said in a clipped affirmative, looking at Izzy for the first time since they'd started talking.

"He'd have access to drugs, though, wouldn't he?" Izzy asked, overly casual.

"Course."

"Is he still on the island?" Izzy asked, glancing between them.

"Moved to Florida, lucky bastard." Jimmy chuckled, the tightness almost completely gone from his shoulders. This was not how Mia had thought the interrogation would go. It was throwing her.

"Have you heard from the Bells since they left the island?" Mia asked, going for surprise.

His fingers dropped out of his beard and curled around his mug, bringing it up to his mouth, which did wonders to help cover most of his face.

Thwap, thwap, thwap. Too fast, too agitated. What the hell had happened with the Bells?

"Nope."

That was it, a quiet, definitive denial.

"Heard you might have been trying to find them," she tried. "That Cash was asking you about them."

"Who said that?"

"Does it matter?"

He'd leaned forward until his forearms were braced on the table, and for a second Mia thought he was going to argue the point. But then he glanced away, toward the window overlooking the backyard. His house was on the opposite side of town from Mama's but was up against the woods, just like Edie's. The snow in his was untouched.

Except for a single track of boot prints leading into the trees.

She thought about the trek out to the reporter's cabin, thought about the feeling of eyes on their back.

Jimmy had sunk deeper into the darkness that crawled ever closer with each passing minute.

But when he turned back to Mia, it was fear she read on his face.

"Were you sleeping with Monroe, Jimmy?" Mia asked, as tempered as possible.

He flinched with his whole body, a visible, shocked recoil. "What."

It wasn't even a question, the way he said it, just an emotion wrenched from his belly.

Mia didn't move, didn't react. Just waited.

"Jesus, no." Jimmy rolled his shoulders like he was trying to shake off the suggestion. "No, never. I'm not . . ."

He trailed off, still looking down, his head twitching sporadically like he had no control over it.

"I don't even know what to say," he mumbled, the words slurring behind thick lips only to get caught in his beard. "Why would you think that?"

The fear was gone when he looked up, and again Mia struggled to adjust to the patterns of the interview. She'd thought he'd been afraid of what they were about to accuse him of. But clearly she'd missed something.

"It was in the reporter's notes," she answered, going with honesty. "What did you say to him?"

Jimmy blinked, slow and confused, his gaze unfocused. "Nothing. I said nothing."

"You must have said something," Mia pressed. She thought back to Theo's message.

Ar w mb (v1). Affair with Monroe Bell (victim one). The message had been underlined and starred in the reporter's journal.

"I barely knew the girl," Jimmy said now, back to tugging at his beard. The tapping had resumed, but it was steady, more a thoughtful beat than anything else. "Talked to her once or twice in town, maybe."

He could be lying. It was in his blood to do so. But he was also easy to read. *Too easy*, one part of her whispered, while the other thought about all she knew of Jimmy. He wasn't particularly clever or manipulative. His tics were numerous and varied—the tapping being the most obvious, but his fingers betrayed his thoughts as well as they pulled at his beard. If it had just been one thing, she might have thought he was doing it to throw her off. But his movements were natural and reactive.

Probably he was hiding something. But just not what they had thought when coming in. So why had the reporter walked away with the impression that Jimmy was sleeping with Monroe?

Then something slid into place. "What about Bix?"

And there. There was his sore spot. He didn't blanch, not like before when she'd asked about Monroe. This was more subtle. A hitched breath. White knuckles on a clenched fist. A tongue darting out to the corner of his mouth.

"She was married," Jimmy said.

"She was," Mia agreed easily.

The silence that followed was weighed down with everything he wasn't saying. It was almost fully dark now, the light from outside all but gone. The echo of cigar smoke lingered stale in the air, along with the secrets, and both stuck to Mia's throat, her lungs, as she breathed them in. They burned away, black dust, with each inhale, each exhale.

"I loved her."

The confession was broken, ugly, almost a sob rather than words.

"Jimmy."

It was all Mia could say. Just his name. Just a plea. *Tell me. Let me help you.*

"It wasn't like that, all right?" Jimmy said, sniffing. "I loved her. But she didn't . . . it wasn't like that."

"What was it like?" she asked.

"She loved him."

"Charles?" Mia wasn't surprised. That's how it had always seemed to her, no matter what anyone now was saying.

Jimmy nodded and wiped his nose against the arm of his shirt, leaving behind a damp, greasy stain. "Don't know why."

"What was he like? Charles." All she remembered was a buttoned-up man. He'd never looked at her like Earl Bishop had, like she wasn't good enough. But neither had he paid any of them much attention. She knew he was a psychiatrist on the mainland, but everyone made it seem more a hobby than anything else. The Bells had no need to work, not with the money that lined their bank accounts.

"Those girls were all scared," Jimmy said, a quiet hiccup cutting off the last of his words. "You saw them."

She had. But she wouldn't have described any of the Bell women as frightened. Brash, bold, witty, and fun, maybe. But not scared.

So was she wrong or was everyone else? Why couldn't she trust her perception any longer? Why did it feel like everything she remembered from those days had been skewed? As if she had been living in a slightly different reality from the rest of them.

Now she knew there was a fingerprint bruise on Lacey Bell's arm and ghosts in her eyes. And she was living here despite everything that had happened on the island. Was she running away? Was it desperation that had sent her back to St. Lucy's? Where was Charles now?

"Did you tell any of this to the reporter?" Mia asked, though she knew he must not have.

"No."

She thumbed at her bottom lip. How had the reporter gotten the impression that Jimmy had been sleeping with Monroe? There hadn't been many notes from the interview itself. But she had assumed Jimmy had said something off the record, maybe. Or offhand that the reporter had interpreted.

"Jimmy, I'm going to ask you something, and I need you to be honest with me," Mia said.

He looked up finally, his eyes wide and red rimmed but dry.

"Was there a chance Henry or Earl was having an affair with Monroe?"

"No," Jimmy said, executing a quick sign of the cross. "No, absolutely not."

Mia nodded like she believed him. But she doubted he'd tell her anyway.

"Hey," Izzy said, a little too loud, a little too abrupt. "Did you ever talk to that Peter guy? The artist who lived at the Bell mansion in the fall?"

"The artist?"

Izzy nodded. "He was in residence during the fall," she said again.

"Never did like that punk," Jimmy said, barrel arms crossed over his chest.

The response didn't feel connected to their question: not quite a non sequitur but also not really an answer.

"Why's that?"

He shrugged. "Caught him sneaking into the old house near the Bell's mansion." He swung his arm toward the window and presumably the north end of the island. "Where the workers used to stay. And the artists, when there are more of them."

Martha Lowe's voice echoed in Mia's head. *You know that old house on the Bell land . . . ? It's just sitting there. Abandoned. Makes you wonder why.*

A tightness gathered at the base of her skull.

That house was right up against the cliffs. If the reporter had been there on the night he'd died, it would have been easy to maneuver his body into the ocean.

"What were you doing up there, Jimmy?" Mia asked, her voice a low rasp.

He was shaking his head before she even finished, a jerky, frantic denial of any implications layered beneath her question. "I go up once a month. Tend to the yard. That's all, that's it. Don't even go in the house."

Mia exhaled, the curve of her spine pressing against the back of her chair as she let the breath out. "Did you tell Lacey he'd been there recently?"

"Didn't want to bother her," Jimmy mumbled. "But I tore into him good. Just like that reporter who was snooping around the lighthouse. No one ever taught them what private property was."

"Was he apologetic?" Izzy asked. "Peter, not the reporter."

Jimmy's lips twisted before going flat again. "Nervous and sweaty, more. Doped out, coked out, something like that."

Or he'd found something, something he wasn't supposed to find, something that was supposed to have been kept hidden. The house was fairly isolated, separated from the Bell mansion by a good deal of land. It was the perfect place to bury a secret.

"When was this?" Mia asked. "When you caught him."

"Think it was about October, maybe, a few weeks before Halloween." Jimmy's voice grew more confident as he spoke, as if the retelling helped confirm it to himself. "Wanted to do one last rake on the leaves before the winter."

October. A figure under a busted streetlight. An upturned collar of a jacket, hunched shoulders. Watching her.

It could be nothing. Or it could mean that whatever the artist had found in that old house had led Robert Twist to Mia Hart.

———

"I wonder why the reporter thought that Jimmy was sleeping with Monroe," Izzy said as they trekked back to Edie's house. It was well into the evening, well into the single digits. Mia was taking them on a shortcut through the woods, rather than having them wind their way back through town, and she almost regretted it.

There was a hush to the forest that she didn't like, an eerie expectation, a threat of violence beneath the quiet.

She picked up her pace, forcing Izzy into a longer stride.

"I'm getting that feeling a lot. People getting the wrong idea about things," Mia finally said. She didn't want to think about it now, didn't want to be distracted. She listened too hard, desperate for anything—a branch breaking, a creature fleeing from their heavy footfalls. There was nothing. Mia concentrated on the weight of her gun against her side, underneath her armpit, and fell back so that Izzy was a step ahead of her with Mia protecting her back.

Was it Jimmy following them? Had he been spooked by the questions?

Asher, something in her whispered. Like that first night. It was a sign of her sleep deprivation that she couldn't immediately shake the thought.

"What do you mean?" Izzy asked. Mia swallowed the urge to tell her to shut up.

"I don't know," Mia said, keeping her voice pitched deliberately low. "It seems like there are a lot of wrong conclusions being made in this case."

Izzy glanced over her shoulder, finally catching on. Her gaze flicked to the shadows trailing behind them, and then back to Mia's face. She wanted to ask what Mia meant; Mia could all but see the question forming behind her lips. But she didn't say anything further, just unzipped her coat enough that her weapon would be easily reached.

They walked the rest of the way in silence.

"Shit," Izzy whispered once they'd stepped into Edie's house. "Shit."

"Yeah," Mia agreed, and the shivers rippling beneath her skin, pulling her muscles tight, had nothing to do with the cold.

"That was creepy as hell," Izzy said, shrugging out of her jacket. "Someone is definitely following us."

Mia locked the door. The dead bolt was rusted and sluggish and protested being put to use after years, if not decades, of neglect. The thud it made when it sank home let Mia relax just a bit.

She hung up her outdoor gear but left her holster in place as she moved toward the kitchen.

"What were you saying about wrong conclusions?" Izzy asked, settling into the seat Mia had begun to think of as Izzy's.

Moving to put a kettle on, Mia tried to attach coherency to the jumbled thoughts that she could barely get a hold of herself.

"Do you know what I told Cash that first night at the bar?"

"Hmm?"

"That these types of cases, the kinds we solve"—Mia gestured between them—"they come down to people."

"Yeah," Izzy agreed.

It was rare these days. With DNA testing and new technology, solving crimes more often than not had to do with waiting for labs to process samples rather than the old ideal of gumshoeing together clues and piecing together mysteries.

"Okay, so wrong conclusions," Izzy prodded when Mia didn't continue.

Mia blinked and swayed, unfocused for a minute, exhaustion seizing on her distraction. "Right." She pressed the heel of her palm against her eye until lights popped behind the lid. "So with Charles, okay? I always thought of him as adoring of Bix. Seemed like a good guy when I was growing up."

Izzy nodded but didn't say anything.

"But Jimmy thinks he was abusive. Or near abusive? If the girls were scared of him, that implies something at least," Mia said, not sure if she was even making sense. "And after you came back from the bar, you had mentioned you got that impression, too?"

"Just a feeling," Izzy shrugged. "Nothing concrete."

"Exactly," Mia said. "And Cash, too. Never would I have said he'd be violent."

"Right up until he hauled you off your feet and almost slammed you against the house," Izzy said. "Don't think that's a wrong conclusion."

"But Mama was shocked," Mia continued. "About his behavior. Which means it probably was unusual."

"And wouldn't you have said Monroe and Asher were all puppy love all the time?" Izzy asked.

Mia snapped her fingers. "Yes. I would have thought they had been pretty serious. Not that she was sleeping with some older guy."

The kettle screamed, and they both jumped, wound too tight from their walk home. Mia reached for the mugs. "It's like an alternate universe. Sliding past this one. One tiny change and everything about reality has shifted," Mia said, wondering if she was toeing the line to delirious.

"So which timeline is the true one?" Izzy asked.

"Hell if I know," Mia said, making Izzy honk out a big, unattractive, yet genuine laugh.

Izzy took the tea Mia poured her, blowing the steam off the surface. "Okay, come on. Say you hadn't talked to anyone on this fucking island."

Mia rolled her eyes at the obscenity, but she saw Izzy's point. They were getting bogged down in everyone else's point of view. They needed to scrape that back, look at the facts.

Mia thought back to the ferry, back to when she'd been standing on the deck, the spray from the sea cutting across her face, her eyes trained on the lighthouse. Thought back to the Bell mansion coming into view through the mist. Thought about the way Jimmy had reacted to the idea of Charles and Bix at the lighthouse that night. Thought about that old abandoned house tucked away on the Bell property. "I think we need to find Charles and Bix Bell."

"Any luck with the uniforms?" Izzy asked.

Mia tucked her fingers in her pocket to pull out her phone, the urge to slam it against the wall barely suppressed when she saw the "No Service" status. "Mama said a storm is coming in. Worst one yet."

Izzy wasn't thrown by the shift in topics but simply grabbed her own cell, holding it face out, like she always did, as if Mia were somehow at fault for the lack of bars at the top. "My brain is choosing not to acknowledge that there could be worse storms than what we've already had. I'm just going to go ahead and plunk my head in the sand and leave it there."

"Denial isn't just a river in Egypt, you know," Mia said, without looking up from her screen, which remained stubbornly useless.

"Boooo," Izzy mock shouted from across the room. "You're better than cheap wordplay, Hart."

Mia lifted her head to flash Izzy a quick smile. "Don't underestimate how cheap I can get."

It was a joke, but the words landed a bit heavy, effectively suffocating the light moment until the only thing left was the knowledge that neither of them knew how low Mia could go.

"So a storm . . . ," Izzy prodded.

This wasn't the time to brood. Mia rolled her shoulders. "Coming in tomorrow afternoon. Will probably drop a couple feet over the next few days."

Izzy huffed out a laugh that was far more distraught than amused. Then she set aside her tea, pushing to her feet. "I think I should go to the mainland."

No. The suggestion sat strangely in Mia's stomach, and the pain beneath her breastbone throbbed in time with her heartbeat. "What?"

Eyes wide, Izzy began to pace. From the refrigerator, to the back door, to the table. Rinse and repeat.

"Look, we need to find information on Peter, on the Bells. We need one of us on the ground, not some knucklehead right out of the academy. And we need you here, so that people will actually talk to you."

It was logical. Even if it wasn't protocol to split up like that, they were in extraordinary circumstances. Their case was growing colder by the day, and they were handcuffed by their lack of access to information, a problem that was only about to get worse. At best, they'd be able to talk to a few more people during the storm, but more likely they'd be trapped in Mama's house, hunkered down just like everyone else.

But Mia didn't want to be left behind, not on St. Lucy's. The rational part of her mind told her that wasn't what was happening, but the irrational side knew how easy it would be to sink into the cloying familiarity of home.

For the first time in her career, she was worried about being able to be objective. She didn't say any of that. She was already too aware of the way Izzy's suspicious eyes sometimes lingered on her when the woman didn't think she was aware.

"Earl's service is tomorrow," Mia said. "Why don't you stay for that. Then we'll see if Quinn can get you back before the storm moves in."

"You'll be okay?" Izzy asked. She was a good cop.

Mia looked away to find her own reflection in the window. It was distorted, but even still she could read the fear on her face. "I'll be okay."

CHAPTER EIGHTEEN

Izzy

Bodies pressed against each other, curves and elbows and shoulders slotting into any empty space, as the residents of St. Lucy's attempted to fit in the one-room church that was desperately trying to accommodate the mourners.

Against the snow and the white clapboards of the church, they looked like ravens, black and sleek and chattering in the early-morning light as they waited in line to squeeze into what Izzy knew must be a tiny room.

Mia and Izzy joined the line, a few back from Patty Masterson. The woman had forgone the blue lipstick for a more respectful cherry gloss, but her dress was cut in a deep V, revealing the lace of her bra beneath the fabric. Izzy gave a little salute when Patty tipped her head in Izzy's direction, but they both kept it respectful, understated.

"You've made friends," Mia said under her breath, amusement in the twitch of her lips.

"I can't figure her out," Izzy mused, letting her eyes run along the rest of the crowd. She recognized Max from the bar. And Quinn, the pilot, had sidled up behind them. "She gave me all the gossip on you but also defended you."

"She's a good resource." Mia didn't sound annoyed but rather fond, actually. And Izzy gave up the hope of ever understanding this place.

"So Earl was popular, it seems," Izzy said as they shuffled forward. How there was still space, she didn't understand. But she wasn't going to question it.

"Ran the island," Mia said, like that explained it. Maybe it did. "I wouldn't call him beloved. But, he was important."

And sometimes, in these kinds of situations, that mattered more. For turnout, at least.

They listened more than talked as they slowly pushed into the church, the joints of the building straining beneath the weight of the collective—and perhaps performative—grief trying to fit inside.

The men behind them chatted about Earl's boat. What was going to happen to it, if Cash was planning on selling it?

The woman in front of them was a sniffler. She even had a delicately embroidered hankie. Her makeup stayed in place despite the way she dabbed at the corners of her eyes every so often.

Izzy caught other snippets of conversations, but nothing stood out as important. People wondered about the house. Wondered about him being buried in consecrated ground. Wondered what Lacey and Cash would serve at the wake.

She and Mia finally breached the entryway and found a spot at the back, against one of the milky windows. Izzy couldn't tell if the glass was warped from age or if it was designed to look like that.

It wasn't until Cash and Lacey walked in that she realized she'd been looking for them. He had his hand at the small of her back, guiding her through the crowd to the front pew. Lacey's face was covered by a birdcage veil, but Izzy got a flash of pale white skin before they both ducked into the pew that had been reserved for them.

Izzy glanced out of the side of her eye to find Mia watching the pair, though she supposed everyone was.

But. There were times when Izzy questioned how much distance Mia had really been able to put between herself and whatever attachments she'd had growing up. First loves were hard to forget.

To Izzy, Cash seemed like the perfect suspect. Violent, angry, big, and loud. For all that people wanted to say Mia was the only one that came out alive, that wasn't true. Looking at the collective dynamics of the group, it couldn't be ignored that Cash had come out alive as well. Just because he supposedly hadn't been at the lighthouse that night didn't mean he hadn't emerged even more unscathed than Mia.

As people continued to file into the small space, Izzy let the scenario play out. What was Cash's motive for killing the reporter?

Had he actually been there at the lighthouse? Had Earl Bishop let that slip during his interview with Twist?

At that moment, Cash turned. She met his stare head-on and couldn't help but note that his eyes were dry, despite the grim set of his mouth. He looked away first, shifting to whisper in Lacey's ear.

The woman stiffened, then glanced toward Izzy and Mia. Izzy couldn't see her expression, hidden as it was behind the intricate design of her veil.

Lacey. Was he protecting her? From whom? Charles?

Izzy itched to be on a plane to the mainland. She didn't even know yet what she would ask Charles or Bix, whichever one of them she found. Why is your daughter hiding away on a remote spit of land where her sister was either killed or committed suicide? Yeah, that might be a start.

Lacey moved so that she settled into the crook of Cash's shoulder, both turning their attention to the front to the priest.

The service itself was short and surprisingly impersonal. Izzy was used to funerals that went on for hours, each family member, extended or not, getting a chance to speak, to pay respects.

For Earl's service, it was only Jimmy who stood up. He rambled on, his sentences never quite ending, just blending into the next as he told one fisherman's tale after another. Toward the end, he broke down, his face flushed and sweaty, his mouth trembling. The crowd fidgeted in a collective mix of embarrassment and commiseration. And then exhaled as Jimmy stepped down to the side, retaking his seat next to Cash and Lacey.

"I don't think he killed Earl," Izzy whispered, leaning close to Mia's ear. There were so many people around them.

Mia's head jerked once, a quick negative in agreement. And if Jimmy hadn't killed Earl, then he probably hadn't killed the reporter, either.

"How bad would it have been?" Izzy asked, confident that her question was masked by the overwhelming bass from the organ, which had just launched into "Amazing Grace." "If Earl had been having an affair with Monroe?"

Mia kept her attention directed ahead, on the priest who was swaying along with the chorus, his arms upraised toward the sky.

"He wouldn't have been arrested," Mia said. "I can't imagine anyone filing that complaint."

"Even the Bells?"

"They were old money." Mia shrugged. "Doubt they would have wanted that bad press."

"So why kill her?"

Mia glanced at her and then shifted straight again. "A baby might do it."

"Yeah, but what if the father didn't know? Or what if she wasn't pregnant? Do you think it warrants killing—an affair with a sixteen-year-old?"

Why hadn't they thought about this before? They'd been focusing all their attention on Monroe, as if she were the obvious victim. But there had been two other people in the room that night.

"What are you getting at?" Mia asked, quietly now as the final chords ripped through the air.

"What if Monroe wasn't the intended victim but rather collateral damage?" Izzy suggested. "What if it was Asher who was the target?"

Mia half nodded to acknowledge she'd heard Izzy, but any attempt at conversation would have been drowned out by the women who surged to their feet in the pews across from Cash and Lacey, belting out an ambitious "Ave Maria."

Izzy waited until the crescendo before leaning closer, her breath hot against Mia's ear.

"What if it was you?"

———

There was a brunch at the Bishop house following the service. Izzy hated to be mercenary about it, but the gathering provided the perfect opportunity to poke and prod at their list of suspects. The entire town seemed to be in attendance.

"I'm going to find Lacey," she told Mia.

Mia nodded. "I'm going to try Cash again. If I can get him alone."

Izzy was definitely getting the better end of this particular deal. "'Kay."

Although the house was much larger than the church, it was still cramped with people trying to hold flimsy cocktail plates and maneuver around small talk and bulky furniture. The place reeked of too-sweet floral perfume that highlighted rather than masked the underlying hint of fish and sea.

After Izzy made it through all the first-level rooms, she admitted defeat. Lacey wasn't downstairs. That's how Izzy found herself ducking into each of the rooms on the second floor. They'd been mostly empty, save for a couple of kids playing hide-and-seek in the guest suite.

She'd already done a sweep of the downstairs and outside areas and knew Lacey wasn't there. That left what Izzy guessed was the attic. The door was already slightly ajar, so it swung open easily on well-oiled hinges.

The room was filled with dusty sheet-covered furniture and duct-taped cardboard boxes with words like "kitchen" and "baby stuff" scribbled on their sides. A bare hanging lightbulb cast a warm yellow glow as it swung on its chain. Lacey hadn't been up here long.

The woman sat on a dilapidated couch beneath one of the skylights that had been carved into the roof. Her head was bent forward, her legs pulled up crisscross style. There was something in her lap and a gentle smile on her lips.

"He had the biggest chipmunk cheeks," Lacey said without looking up, her voice barely a whisper, and then held up what looked like a photo album. It was hard to make out, but Izzy could vaguely see there was a yellowed baby picture slotted into one of the plastic holders. "Cash."

Izzy laughed and ducked under a crossbeam to take a seat next to Lacey. Craning her neck, Izzy tried to get a better look at the album. They were all pictures of Cash as a kid. The affection on Lacey's face was clear. But so was the memory of how she'd looked in the bar, after the door had slammed.

Who are you afraid of?

"You have more questions, Detective?" Lacey asked, most of her attention back on the album. It was funny how they all referred to her that way, always putting distance there.

"Just a few," Izzy said, trying to decide where to start that wasn't *Did your father kill your mother? And did your sister die because she knew it had happened?* It sounded absurd even in the safety of her own mind.

"When you went to get your parents that night, did they both come back to the lighthouse with you?"

Lacey's hand paused mid–page flip. "You've been talking to Martha Lowe."

It was a conversation that had simmered, back-burnered but not forgotten, throughout the investigation. "She has some theories."

Rolling her eyes, Lacey snorted. It was somehow elegant, just a puff of air, a scrape of sound against the back of her throat. "That's one way to put it."

"So they were both there?" Izzy pressed. No one ever seemed to want to answer questions around here, no matter how easy it would be to give a simple yes or no.

"Yes," Lacey said. "My mother came to the lighthouse, but once she saw . . ."

Lacey's voice wobbled, but she tried to cover it with a cough.

"Once she saw Monroe and Asher, she broke down," Lacey continued as if nothing had happened. "My father sent her back to the mansion. That's why I ended up at Edie Hart's place. With Mia."

"Bix went back by herself?"

"No," Lacey said slowly, but it was thoughtful. Like she was trying to make sure she remembered right. "I don't think so."

"Who took her back?"

"Jimmy. I think." Lacey shook her head, her eyes slipping shut. "I don't . . . It's not all the clearest, you know?"

Jimmy. *I loved her.*

"And she was still there the next morning? She didn't leave early?" *She was still alive?* is what Izzy really wanted to ask.

"We all left the island together a few days later," Lacey said. "Martha Lowe needs help."

Grief did strange things to a person. Turned coincidences into conspiracy theories, stitched together snippets of different events to create wild scenarios. And all of this must have been festering in Martha's mind for the past decade and a half.

That didn't mean Lacey was telling the truth, though.

Izzy hummed, not in agreement or dissent.

"Was Monroe pregnant?" Izzy asked, watching her closely.

"God, what?" Lacey was either surprised or good at faking it.

"Cash said he got into a fight with Asher that day because Monroe told Cash she was pregnant."

Lacey's tongue darted out over her lipstick, and her fingers came up to toy with her dangly earrings. "Cash said that?"

"Said he went after Asher, yeah." Izzy nodded. "Do you remember that?"

"I didn't see any of them that day," Lacey said. "Except, well . . ."

"Well?"

Lacey touched her bangs, pushing them to the side, then centering them again. Fidgety. It had only been when she'd been looking at the album that she'd seemed still, calm, peaceful.

"Um, I saw Mia," Lacey said, hesitant. Izzy's attention focused. No one seemed to know what Mia had been doing that whole day. "But not the others."

"Did you just run into her . . . or . . . ?" Izzy waved her hand to prompt the woman to fill in the blanks.

"Look, it's not important. It was years ago."

Izzy waited while Lacey crossed and uncrossed her legs, plucked at the seam of her stockings, slipped her heavy rings on and off her fingers.

"Shit," Lacey finally said quietly, more to herself than to Izzy. "All right. This isn't meant to make her look bad. We were teenagers."

"Sure."

"She came over to the house that day," Lacey said. "She was messed up. High or something."

Drugged. "The mansion?"

"Yeah, um, asked if she could come in," Lacey continued. "She was upset. Talking about Monroe and Cash or something. Maybe Asher, too. I couldn't really make anything out. She was crying and incoherent, really."

"Why didn't you tell anyone this?"

Lacey shrunk back against the couch cushion. "I don't know. She kind of calmed down. Got real quiet. And then left? It didn't . . . I don't think it meant anything. I just think they were all a little emotional that night. It kind of fit, you know? With the suicide thing. Emotionally unstable behavior."

"Did she say anything about Cash punching Asher? Or Monroe being pregnant?"

"No, no." Lacey's eyes were wide, the white stark against her smoky liner. It reminded Izzy of Martha. "Nothing like that. I just thought she'd gotten jealous and was on her period or something."

"Was Monroe interested in Cash, too?" It was still strange to Izzy that Monroe had gone to Cash in the first place about the possible baby.

"Monroe was interested in attention," Lacey said, her eyes flicking away. "But I never saw her make a move on Cash." Lacey paused, breathed in. "I think she liked being friends with Mia. It made her feel . . . important or something."

"Important?"

"Mia idolized her back then," Lacey said. "It was so obvious. I mean, teenage girls want guys to like them, but more than that, they want other teenage girls to like them, right? It makes them popular. And coming here, Monroe was the queen bee of that little gang."

"I thought you were a part of it, too." There was that little-sister resentment that Izzy had heard slip into Lacey's voice a few times. As a little sister herself, Izzy couldn't fault her for it.

"Barely." Lacey shrugged. "Think they forgot about me most of the time. Which was fine. Just . . ."

"But Mia came to you," Izzy said interrupted. "That day."

"Because she was fucked up," Lacey said. Then shot her a look. "Sorry."

Izzy dismissed the apology. "You think it was a pact. You think they killed themselves."

Lacey hugged herself, huffed out a breath. "I mean, they talked about some weird stuff. Whenever we were drinking. Or the boys were getting high."

"Weird stuff like what?"

"Death? But also living forever. Monroe spent too much time around the artists. She just talked that way to sound cool to them," Lacey said, and Izzy refrained from pointing out that Lacey was now part of that group, her look complete with dark clothing, pale skin, and an asymmetrical bob. "I think Asher and Mia took her too seriously, though. They kind of wound each other up or something."

"But not Cash?"

Lacey smiled, that same one that she'd been wearing earlier while looking at the kid's chubby cheeks. "He's always been the sensible one."

Which is how Izzy would have described Mia before this. "Quiet" was the first word that came to mind. But "sensible" was right up there, too. She couldn't align that woman with the one Lacey was describing. But what did Izzy know?

"Mia seems good now," Lacey said as if Izzy had spoken her thoughts out loud. It was jarring. "More stable."

Which was an odd thing to say. Izzy lifted her brows, and Lacey flushed pink. "Not that she wasn't . . ."

Izzy waited, but Lacey seemed to be done. She debated telling the woman about heading to the mainland, giving Lacey her cell in case anything cropped up while she was gone. But the last time someone tried to leave after they'd been poking around, they'd ended up dead. The fewer people who knew her plans the better.

Just as Izzy stood up, Lacey's hand shot out, quick like a snake, her fingers wrapping around Izzy's wrist.

When Izzy turned back, Lacey's eyes were pleading. "I hope I didn't make you think anything bad about Mia. We were all just . . ." She shrugged. "Young."

In that moment, something from one of Izzy's nights at the bar came back to her. Patty Masterson, talking about Cash and Mia. *Lacey's probably not too happy about Mia being back.* It had barely stuck with Izzy at the time; there had been too much other information that needed sorting. But it was there, wedged in beside every other odd thing that had happened in the past few days.

Izzy shook her head. "You didn't make me think anything."

CHAPTER NINETEEN

MIA

Mia found Cash in the middle of the room, surrounded by people who weren't talking to him. His head was bowed as he stared at the watery white dip and carrots someone must have shoved into his hands. When he looked up, they locked eyes above the chaos that pulsed through the house.

She pushed off the doorjamb she'd been leaning against and snagged his arm, just above his elbow.

"Let's walk," she said, slowing down only enough to make sure he was following. They pushed through the tight hallway, and people let them, too uncomfortable with the clear grief on Cash's face to bother him.

When she hit the porch, she kept going, taking the stairs at a light jog. They were near the port, but she turned left instead of right, heading for a seldom-used pier that jutted out into the black water of the bay. It was calm today, the stillness almost unnerving because she knew a storm hovered on the horizon.

Cash followed her out along the old planks, both of them skipping over a board that looked loose. Leaning her forearms against one of the last posts, she kept her gaze directed at the ocean instead of him. "I'm sorry," she finally said. "About your dad."

Timid waves lapped at the wood beneath them, and a seaplane's engine rumbled overhead. There was a shuffle behind her as Cash settled up against the post next to hers.

"Want to know the worst part?" he asked, and she cut her eyes to his face. It was softer than she would have guessed, his jaw relaxed, his shoulders loose. He was staring out toward the nothingness that was interrupted by a single tanker that was moving so slowly it seemed to have stopped.

She made a questioning sound in the back of her throat to get him to continue, and still he didn't look at her.

"The relief."

"Cash," she said on an exhale.

He laughed, just once and without humor, and blinked too fast for there not to be tears threatening at the corners. "That was my first reaction. Relief. How messed up is that?"

His hand shook as he brought it up to scrub at his face. She could tell he hadn't shaved in a few days, his five-o'clock shadow grown out to proper scruff.

"Most of the time he didn't even recognize me," Cash continued when she didn't move to offer sympathy. It was an odd position to be in. Cash and Earl were both suspects, but they were also family of sorts. Even Earl, with his stiff New England coldness. He had been such an institution on St. Lucy's. It must have been devastating to watch him deteriorate, lost in the years that had come before.

As for Cash, Mia was still struggling to reconcile the boy he'd been with the man he'd become. So she didn't comfort him, didn't soothe as might have been her instinct back when they'd been growing up.

Instead, she kept her distance, her arms tucked beneath her breasts, bearing her weight against the post.

"You think I'm horrible, don't you?" Cash asked, a little boy's vulnerability in his voice, like that moment in Edie's kitchen. She turned once again to look at him, her chin resting against her shoulder.

"I think being relieved that your dad's at rest makes you human." She could give him that at least.

"What about the other stuff?"

She raised a brow in question.

"I'm on your suspect list," he said.

"Everyone on the island is on our suspect list," Mia shot back, though it wasn't quite true.

Cash shifted, shoving his bare hands into his pockets. They were both underdressed for the weather, as she hadn't stopped to grab her gear. They wouldn't last on the pier much longer.

"Dad was."

A suspect. She didn't confirm it, just watched the water particles in her breath freeze into visibility.

"You think he killed himself because of it," Cash said, and again that wasn't quite true. She thought he was killed because of it. She wasn't sold on the fact that he was the one who did it. That was a bit more than semantics.

"You said he was living in the past most of the time?" Mia asked. If the deaths had been weighing on his conscience for the past decade and a half, it could have been the heaviness of them that was dragging him back to that particular summer.

"Yeah, but not like what you're thinking," Cash said. "It was mostly from when we were real young. Babies."

There went that theory.

"What do you think he was apologizing for in his note?" Mia asked. Had he been the father of Monroe's baby? How had he gotten to the lighthouse so quickly? What had he been doing out in the woods?

"Being weak."

"For killing himself, you mean?" she clarified.

Cash nodded. It's not like he would have said anything else, anyway. If he'd suspected his father's involvement in whatever had gone down, that was.

"Does Lacey ever talk about it? That night? That summer?" Maybe it was cheap to ask Cash about his girlfriend, but Mia knew Lacey wouldn't tell her what she was actually thinking herself.

He slid her a glance from the side of his eye. "Are you asking as Detective Hart?"

"Some friendly advice. You should always assume you're on the record with cops, Cash." Mia pushed at his shoulder. "You know that."

"Eh, not much criminal law going on around here." He shrugged a little, his grin self-deprecating. "Most of what I handle is contracts and wills."

They were quiet for a beat. Then he broke. "She's had a couple nightmares. 'Bout Monroe, mostly," Cash said, the words drawn out like he was reluctant. This time the pause was longer. He straightened and paced to the other side of the pier, his back to her. She almost thought he'd given up talking, but then he sighed. "And her father."

Her hand twitched in her pocket. Charles Bell. "Does she talk about him at all?"

"Mostly about her mother," Cash said, rolling his shoulders into himself. "Lacey adored her."

"Adored?" Past tense.

Cash seemed to realize. He swung around. "She just . . . she doesn't talk to them anymore. Cut off contact," he said.

"But she's living in their house." Mia tilted her head to make it a question.

"No." Cash shook his head. "It's hers. Her grandmother deeded it to Lacey in her will. The grandmother bought it for Charles and Bix in the first place."

"So, legally, she could keep them away from it," Mia said, and that made more sense as to what Lacey was doing back on the island. Perhaps it was the only safe haven available to her. Especially if she'd cut off her parents' financial help.

"Do you ever think about it?" Mia asked, because it was cold and she was tired and this was the first time since she'd been back that she felt like she was seeing Cash. The boy she remembered and not the violent hothead, not the man lying with every breath. "That summer."

"Mia."

The way her name caught in his throat almost made her wave off her question. But she just waited instead.

"No," he sighed. "I try not to. It was . . . I lost everyone, you know?"

Her, Asher. Monroe, even, though she hadn't thought they'd been close.

"Did Earl tell you that night?" she asked, because she was also still a cop, down to her core.

"Didn't wake me up till he got home. It was early."

Had Earl been cleaning up the crime scene?

"You were gone before I even—" Cash cut himself off, swallowing hard.

They'd never said goodbye, that was true. But of all the things she'd worried about in the past fifteen years, it had been pretty low on her list. They had been high school sweethearts, built to fall apart.

But they'd been best friends before that. Maybe not like her and Asher. Still. He'd run through the woods beside her, just like Asher had. Cleaned up cuts and made up adventures and patted her hand when she cried.

She saw a mirror of the memories in his eyes, glassy and damp as they were. He reached out, his fingers curling around her wrist, his thumb pressed into the jut of bone there. At first she resisted but then gave into his gentle tug, landing against his chest, her arms circling his waist as one big hand pressed against her spine.

Burying his head in her hair, he breathed in. It was a rough inhale, all jagged and shaky, like he was controlling a sob. She barely moved, just rocked, slightly, into his familiar warmth, that same feeling she'd had when she'd first seen the port coming into view. Nostalgia that was burned at the edges.

Home.

Did you kill the reporter? She wanted to ask it, even as he held her, even as his chin dug into the hard plane of her shoulder blade. *Did your father kill Monroe?*

Mia let it go on for another ten seconds before she stepped back. His arms fell away without protest, and awkwardness bloomed in the space where their bodies had been.

She licked dry lips and shifted even farther away from Cash, shoving her hands in her pockets.

A blush rose on the sharp slopes of his cheekbones, and he shifted back onto his heels. "Sorry," he said on a cough. "Um. I better get back."

Nodding seemed wiser than trying to say anything.

"You can, uh, you can come look around again," Cash said, meek now. It was a dramatic change from when he'd plucked her from the ground by her sweatshirt. "At Dad's stuff. I don't care anymore. There's nothing left to protect."

Her stomach contracted. "You were protecting something before?"

He lifted one shoulder. "Don't know. Maybe. I didn't want to look."

"Cash, you can't just . . . That's hindering an investigation." She sighed.

"You gonna arrest me?" He actually smirked at that, a little mischievous. He'd flitted through more emotions in the past ten minutes than he'd had the whole time she'd been back. The ground felt unsteady beneath her feet.

Might have to. But she didn't say it. "I'll come by in the morning."

He'd already started down the pier, but paused at that. "Just you?"

"Izzy's headed back to the mainland," she said without thinking, lulled into the easy rhythm they'd established.

"Leaving you here? By yourself?" The sharpness of his tone had her looking up, reevaluating what she'd just revealed.

"I'll be okay," she said, an echo of her reassurance to Izzy.

The wrinkle didn't smooth from his forehead as he glanced back to the house, his gaze lingering there before returning to her. "Just. Be careful?"

She watched him walk away, and then a movement caught the corner of her eye, a shadow flickering into life before it was gone again. She looked up toward the second floor of the Bishop house, where she'd thought she'd seen something. But there was nothing in the window. Not even a silhouette.

———

The sky was tinted orange brown by early afternoon. Mia stood at the window as Izzy shoved clothes into her duffel behind her.

"Am I going to make it?" Izzy asked, breathy and frantic.

"We have an hour, maybe," Mia said. "Quinn will get you out of here."

"Okay, okay."

Mia turned to find Izzy on the floor, patting under the couch with her good arm. "I'm going over to the Bishops' in the morning. To sort through Earl's things."

Izzy's head popped up comically fast. "Mr. Dark, Handsome, and Angry is cool with that?"

"Yes," Mia said on a laugh. "Invited me actually."

"Jeez, take your gun, okay?" Izzy rolled her eyes and then ducked back down.

"I don't think he killed Robert Twist."

"Why?" Izzy called. "He had motive. Covering up for his father, right?"

Mia nodded but then shook her head, not caring that Izzy couldn't see her. "Earl had severe dementia. Nothing he said would have really held up in court."

"That's . . . actually a good point," Izzy said, sitting back on her heels. She seemed to have abandoned whatever she'd thought she'd lost on the floor. "Covering for someone else?"

"Who else would he be invested in enough?" Mia asked.

"The girlfriend?" Izzy shrugged. "Miss Pouty Artist."

"I am going to miss your witticisms," Mia said dryly. "What was my nickname when you met me?"

"Ms. Badass, thank you very much." Izzy winked, and Mia knew she was lying.

"I don't know." Mia returned them to their topic. "That doesn't seem right, either. Lacey's scared, too."

"So is Jimmy Roarke," Izzy said, and when Mia just stared, Izzy pushed up to her feet. "You know . . . people seem scared in general. That's usually not a good sign."

Mia sighed. "Maybe when you find the Bells." She didn't finish that thought. Who knew if Izzy would actually turn up anything useful.

Izzy wrinkled her nose. "Do you think Bix is buried somewhere on the island?"

"Izzy!" Mia laughed her surprise.

"What? Martha Lowe presented a very reasonable case," Izzy said. "Charles Bell. Even his name sounds villainous. Maybe she's still in the mansion. Hitchcock-style."

They both grimaced.

"Or under the floorboards of that abandoned house up there," Mia said, and any and all humor evaporated. The scenario was no longer far-fetched enough to inspire levity. "I'll swing by and take a look after I'm done at Cash's tomorrow. As the storm allows."

Izzy looked ready to protest the idea, but she seemed to swallow the argument.

"Oh, and Lacey didn't seem to be on board with the Monroe pregnant thing," Izzy said instead. "She didn't say Cash was lying, but she kind of looked nervous that he'd told us that."

"If Monroe found out that day, she might not have told her sister."

"True." Izzy shrugged. "Might have been trying to protect Lacey, too."

"She didn't tell her who she'd been having an affair with, either," Mia said in agreement with that sentiment. "Maybe didn't want to get her involved with it."

"Or," Izzy dragged out, "she just didn't want to tell her baby sister about her love life."

Mia's lips tipped up. "That, too."

"Oh, before I forget, I got an update about that artist Peter guy from a uniform," Izzy said, slapping at her pocket. "But it wouldn't open because of whatever the hell is brewing out there." She pointed to the window. "I'll let you know what it says once I get internet back."

"Might be nothing," Mia said, though it didn't feel like nothing. So many pieces, where did they all fit?

"Enough weirdness to warrant checking out." Izzy shrugged. "And, of course, the fact that he's pretending he's big enough to go by one name."

Mia rolled her eyes, but she was actually going to miss Izzy's relaxed humor. She had a way of breaking tension, which kept Mia just on the right side of sane. "I let slip that you were leaving the island," Mia admitted to be on the safe side.

That got Izzy's attention back on her. "To who?"

This was the part Izzy wasn't going to like. "Cash."

Izzy's eyes narrowed on Mia's face. Her hands were on her hips, and Mia had the distinct feeling of being studied.

"You really don't think Cash had anything to do with any of this, huh?" Izzy swept her hand around, seemingly in an attempt to capture the past, the present.

Did she? *No.* But there was nothing there to back up that gut feeling— just the vague sense that something was off with that picture.

It was too easy.

She could see it: Earl Bishop has an affair with Monroe Bell. Monroe gets pregnant, and Earl loses it, kills her. Stages a suicide pact to cover it up. That part was easy. Suicide was rampant in these parts. Years later, a reporter shows up and starts snooping around. With Earl's dementia, it would just take one wrong word to bring down the man who had been one of the town's most respected leaders. And for what? An outsider? Because that's what Monroe Bell had been. Cash takes care of the reporter. Jimmy Roarke is scared because Earl called him out that night to help cover up the crime. Lacey's scared because Cash has been acting off for however long the reporter has been in town and it's raising red flags for her. Cash was the intruder who shot Izzy, but it had been an attempt to keep them from finding out about Earl's interview more than an actual attack. It had been a flesh wound, a distraction while he slipped out into the night. Earl kills himself over the guilt of it all, which breaks Cash. He figures let Mia find what she will, let the chips fall and all that.

Like that children's game: all the dots were there; they just needed to put pen to paper to draw the final image. She could probably even build a somewhat solid case, depending on what she found tomorrow in the Bishops' house.

She caught the inside of her lip between her incisors and thought back to that photo hanging on the wall just outside the den where she and Izzy were standing—Mia's face tipped up to Cash, like he owned her universe. She thought about the press of his thumb against her wrist on the pier. The warmth of his long body, the way his arms had gripped her like they'd missed her.

Too close. She was too close to this all. It wasn't that she was still in love with Cash. It was that she remembered the give of his hips before he'd grown into his height. It was that she knew he laughed too hard when someone tripped, knew that he liked to be outside when getting high, knew he always failed to account for the width of his shoulders when playing hide-and-seek, and knew that he probably hadn't cried when he'd been told about Asher because he'd always tried to be strong back then.

It was that he was part of her home. And maybe she hadn't realized that meant something to her, but now she did. Now a tiny part of her understood why these people, her people, would have closed ranks to protect one of their own.

You really don't think Cash had anything to do with any of this?

Izzy hadn't moved since asking it, had barely breathed, and was watching her with a kind of reluctance Mia was getting used to. She made Izzy nervous. And maybe the woman wasn't all that far off with her worry.

"I don't know if he does," she finally said, because it was easier than all of that complicated mess of emotions. She'd promised Izzy the truth, but she hadn't promised Izzy all her secrets. And the truth was, she didn't know.

Maybe Mia would have gotten away with it a few days ago. But Izzy was starting to be able to read her, which was scary in itself. Her expression didn't relax; instead, everything sharpened.

"You're going to be late," Mia cut her off. There was nothing to be gained from hashing it all out. "Quinn won't risk it if you wait any longer."

Izzy's gaze shifted to the window beyond Mia and then back to her face, mutinous and resigned at the same time. She wanted to argue, drag it all out, all the complications that Mia could barely put into thoughts, let alone words.

"All right," Izzy finally said, slinging her duffel over her shoulder. She paused in the middle of the room, then crossed to Mia in three long strides. In the next moment Mia was dragged into an awkward hug, with Izzy patting the back of her head. They didn't do this; it wasn't them. But Mia laughed lightly and tolerated the embrace for the few seconds it lasted.

Clearing her throat, Izzy pulled back. "Just watch out for him. He'll distract you with the Dark and Handsome, and you'll forget about the Angry."

"Never," Mia said. "Be safe. Let me know when you get in."

Izzy tossed her an easy two-finger salute and then headed for the door. She'd insisted she didn't need Mia to walk her to the port, so Mia watched her go until her pink hair disappeared around a corner down the way.

"She's gone?" Edie asked, her voice coming from just inside the doorway to the hall.

Mia didn't bother turning around but simply stared at the place where Izzy had been. "Yes."

Edie wrapped an arm around Mia's shoulders, her fingers digging into the bone. "Good."

CHAPTER TWENTY

IZZY

The Rockport Police Station was small and crumbling, just a squat, long building on the corner of a block that was dominated by warehouses and three thriving minimarts.

Izzy swung through the door and breathed in the familiar air with relief. It might as well have been years that she'd been on St. Lucy's instead of just a few days.

She greeted the uniform manning the lobby desk. He was a cute kid, with acne scattered along his hair- and jawlines. He went bright red from the attention but waved back.

It was evening, so the bull pen was mostly empty. In the far corner, Rockport's newest and very eager rookie, Detective O'Malley, was hunched over his computer, his back to her; there was a light on in Murdoch's office, but Izzy couldn't see the woman.

Other than that, she was alone. It was on the later side, and Rockport's crime levels didn't necessitate a robust round-the-clock police detail.

Izzy powered up her desktop as she sent Mia a quick text that she'd made it back to the station and was going to start digging in to find the Bells. It was a crapshoot whether Mia would get the message or not, judging by the storm that had been rolling in as Quinn and Izzy left the island.

Tossing the phone onto a stack of files, Izzy turned back to her computer. She'd have to start with the basics—Google, a scan of the national databases, and anything Rockport had on file.

She realized within a few minutes the futility of looking for such a common name.

There was nothing in the federal criminal system nor in the local ones. As for the web search, there were a couple of society columns, a few mentions of Monroe's death, a few more of the artist residency, and a profile of Charles and Bix from a few decades back that some quirky magazine had helpfully uploaded onto their site. She printed that out.

Narrowing it down to the *Boston Globe* for any mentions garnered only an article on Bix's gallery opening from ten years before Monroe's death and an old engagement announcement.

Izzy clicked on the short piece with the young couple.

Charles Edward Bell, a prominent psychiatrist and the son of Hayes and Eliza Bell, was to wed Brenna "Bix" Connolly, a student at the Rhode Island School of Design. The pair had met in Providence, when Charles commissioned a caricature from Bix, who had worked as a street artist to help pay her tuition. The quick sketch had cost him five dollars, and he'd walked away with her phone number.

It was a cute story, and she wondered if it were true. Probably they'd hooked up in a bar and had made up the rest of it so it would be a good read.

Either way, now Izzy had a real name. *Brenna Connolly.* Somewhat less glamorous than Bix Bell, but somewhat more helpful when it came to searches.

Black Rock Bay

With that, she started getting real results.

Including an obituary.

"All right, here we go," she whispered to the mostly empty room. O'Malley grunted but didn't look up, and there had yet to be any movement coming from Murdoch's office.

The obit was from a paper in Cooperstown, Maine. Izzy tabbed over to a new page, pulled up a map, and typed in the town.

Just outside Portland.

Izzy's pulse stuttered as she scanned the rest of the obit. Bix had died in September—only a month after Monroe's supposed suicide. There had been a fire.

That's all the short announcement mentioned, but there was a link to a full article at the bottom of the page. Izzy clicked it.

There were more details in the full story. The police reported that Bix had fallen asleep with a lit cigarette in the living room, near a stack of magazines and art supplies. Bad luck and poorly stored turpentine had caused it to spread out and consume the entire bottom floor of the house. Firefighters had tried to rescue her but had been unable to get to her in time. No one else had been home.

Officials said no foul play was suspected.

"What'd you find?"

Izzy jolted back, a full-body jump. She panted, her hand on her chest, as she looked up to find Murdoch hovering over her desk.

"Give me a heart attack," Izzy muttered, but was quick to smile up at her boss. "Hi."

"You found something." Murdoch didn't mess around with small talk, never had. Izzy loved her for it.

Izzy tried to think of the best way to shorthand everything that had happened. She and Mia had tried to keep Murdoch updated, but communications had been so limited; it felt like they'd told her nothing. "The reporter who was found dead out on St. Lucy's? Think

243

he was looking into some suicides on the island that involved this family."

"The Bell family?" Murdoch asked, her eyes on the screen over Izzy's shoulder.

"Yeah."

Murdoch nodded for her to continue.

"Right." Izzy snapped her fingers. "Well, turns out the mother, Bix, died in a fire only a month after the family left the island."

"Aah." Murdoch's attention focused, just like Izzy's had. "Do we suspect the husband in both deaths? Possible homicides, instead of a suicide and an accident?"

It fit. "Maybe," Izzy said, and Murdoch studied her, probably picking up the hesitation in the drawn-out word.

"No?"

Izzy tapped her finger on the desk, reading over the details of Bix's death once more.

Those girls were all scared. And now two of them were dead, and the third was hiding out, living among her own nightmares painted on canvas.

"I don't know."

Murdoch only spoke when she had Izzy's attention once more. "Seems like the obvious conclusion. What's bothering you?"

The answer was an itch beneath her skin, noticeable, distracting but out of reach.

Izzy glanced toward the windows on the other side of the room, already knowing what she'd find. The blue tint to the sky had faded into black so that she could see only her reflection in the glass rather than anything outside.

"Think I'll drive up there," she said despite the hour. If she left now she could find a hotel along the way. That would put her in Cooperstown early in the morning. Maybe she could get an address from the local station up there.

"You need company?" Murdoch asked.

Backup. That was the underlying question. Did Izzy need backup? Her eyes slipped back to the obit. "Nah, I'll be okay. More worried about Mia to be honest. That whole island gave me a creepy vibe."

"Creepy vibe?" Murdoch laughed.

"Hey, don't mock the gut," Izzy said. They both knew that lesson too well.

"Touché." Murdoch sobered. "Well, call me if you need rescuing."

"Doubt I'll even find anything," Izzy said, already talking to Murdoch's back. She shut down her computer, grabbed her duffel, and headed for the door, restless to do something, anything, now that she wasn't stuck on a square mile of land in the middle of the ocean.

Her car was a Honda Civic from the previous decade, which often took no less than three tries to start. This was one of those times. When the engine finally turned over, she plugged coordinates into her GPS, thankful that she was back in the world of reliable technology.

The storm was projected to slip up the coast, mostly missing Rockport, pummeling the islands instead. But it still must have scared a few people inside here. The roads were mostly empty, and when she hit the highway, her eyes became unfocused, the hum from the radio interrupted only by the rhythmic slap of rubber against road.

That itch, it was still there, burrowing deeper with each passing mile, and part of the problem was they'd let the teenagers' deaths and Robert Twist's become so entangled that Izzy couldn't stop trying to solve the old murders along with the new one. And they just kept going in circles.

The GPS cut into her thoughts, a calm British voice informing her to take a right soon. She shifted lanes, only half her mind on the road.

Was there any truth to Martha's suspicions? Had Asher seen something? If he had, it would have had to be damning enough for Charles

Bell to consider the death of his own daughter worth the price of covering it up. That seemed implausible.

The simple act wasn't hard to imagine. Izzy had enough experience with rage that she had no doubt that it could blind a man, could lift his control to the extent that he murdered a supposed loved one. But in those cases the killings were close, personal—intimate almost. Usually it involved hands around throats, or weapons that required proximity to the victim. A knife, most likely.

This, though. This was razor blades slashed across the wrists in neat wounds. Izzy had looked at Mia's. There wasn't even a hesitation notch at either end of hers.

Izzy would request the files for the case once she got back to Rockport. Even if the cops had marked it suicide, they still would have taken pictures of the scene, of the cuts.

As a psychiatrist, Charles could have drugged them all; he had access and knew how to use the medicine to make his victims docile, compliant. It could explain the neatness of the deaths.

But not the reason he'd involved Monroe. The drugging meant there was some forethought. Even if Asher had witnessed something like Charles harming Bix, even if he'd then run off to tell Monroe all about it, it still felt like a leap for Charles to kill his own daughter over it. He probably would have been able to convince her it was a misunderstanding. Children were primed to believe their parents, no matter how outlandish the lie.

Killing someone, planning to do it, not just snapping in anger, took a cold, calculating person to pull off.

Had Charles Bell been that man?

A long, rude horn brought Izzy out of her own haze, and she jerked the wheel too far to the right to overcompensate for where she'd drifted into the trucker's lane. The rumble strips protested, the dullness of the sound reverberating in the confines of the car.

Izzy breathed out a curse as she righted the Honda into the center of the lane. Her hands had gone shaky where she clutched the wheel, her knuckles white against the sandy-colored leather.

At the next neon sign advertising gas, she pulled off the road. She popped into the minuscule convenience store and bought the largest size of coffee they had, not caring that it was chunky and tasted of burned toast. Caffeine was crucial.

When she was back on the road, she didn't let her mind drift again. Or mostly not. She was still trying to figure out Charles. He fit better than most, although she hadn't written off Cash covering up for Earl. Was Sammy Charles's point of contact on the island? Is that how the man was still pulling the strings, even when not physically there?

The British voice once again sliced through the frustrated scream in her own head. She'd be in Cooperstown in ten minutes.

With one hand, Izzy reprogrammed the coordinates to find a place to stay in the next few miles. She looked back to the road, squeaked out a distressed sound, and turned just in time for the driveway of a hotel.

The *A* in the VACANCY sign flickered, but the place didn't give her murder vibes and she doubted she could really do any better at this point, so she got a room for the night.

Barely looking up from his newspaper, the old, portly gentleman working the front desk shoved two plastic cards at her and pointed down a long hallway, grunting as he did.

By the time she dropped onto the bed, she was too tired to even strip the comforter off, even though she, like everyone else in America, had watched those stupid exposés that used blue lights to show all the fluids that saturated the fabric. Her body ached, and her shoulder throbbed, no longer bleeding but bruised, and she knew if she tried to close her eyes, sleep would evade her anyway. She spared a thought to Mia's insomnia and wondered how the woman was still functioning. This buzzing beneath her skull was brutal in its subtlety and persistence.

Her email notification dinged on her phone, and it was only then that she remembered she still had an unread message about Peter, the artist.

She patted the bed blindly until she found her cell, and dismissed the junk message that had set it chiming in the first place. There beneath it was the one from the uniforms who had looked into Peter's identity. Another possible missing piece in their puzzle.

Izzy clicked on it and blinked hard to get her eyes to focus as the screen loaded.

While she skimmed the email, the fingers on her free hand tapped out a staccato against her jean-clad thigh, more an expulsion of energy than a nervous tic.

Peter Hughes. An amateur artist out of a small town north of Portland, he was a bartender by night and worked at a grocery store during the day. He also hadn't returned to either position after he'd quit for the Bell residency.

That might not be odd. That's how artists were, right? Whimsical, untethered to reality and things like addresses.

There were a few other small tidbits but nothing earth-shattering. At the bottom of the message, the uniform had attached a profile of Peter that had run in what looked like a tiny artist magazine, if she had to guess by its name alone.

Her phone lagged under the weight of the motel's shitty Wi-Fi, and her eyes blurred, at the point of exhaustion from the long day, the long drive, the long pause of nothing but white screen.

Then the article loaded, fuzzy at first before sharpening with the internet's final push. When the picture at the top came into focus, Izzy sat up fast so that the rush of it caused black spots to pop in her eyes.

Jesus.

Izzy checked the caption three times just to be safe and then thumbed over to her call list. Mia's phone sent her straight to voice mail four times in a row. The storm. The goddamn storm.

She dropped the cell to the bed, bringing up the screen with the profile, her fingertip pressing against Peter Hughes's face.

It was the same one she'd seen just days ago after he'd been pulled from the bay.

CHAPTER
TWENTY-ONE
MIA

The skin beneath Cash's eyes was puffy, and he simply blinked at Mia after he opened the door, as if trying to make sense of her presence.

She shoved the extra cup of coffee she'd brought into his hands and then brushed past him into the house. "Drink up."

There were still discarded paper plates on the foyer table from the service the day before, and she fought the urge to start cleaning. It would send the wrong message.

"Earl's things?" Mia reminded Cash because the caffeine definitely hadn't hit his bloodstream yet. He scrubbed a hand over his face, then cleared his throat, gesturing to the stairs.

"Yeah, bedroom, attic," he said, his voice thick. It was clear he hadn't quite woken up yet or talked to anyone else, and she wondered if Lacey had gone back to the mansion. "Take your pick. I'll be in the kitchen."

He wouldn't meet her eyes, and before she could react, he'd stepped around her toward the hallway.

The behavior was dismissive at best, shifty at worst, the tone change from the pier the day before enough to cause whiplash. This again was the man who had grown into a stranger, no longer the boy she'd known so well and thought she'd caught a glimpse of yesterday.

Had grief been enough to strip the years away? Had it really happened? The world tilted, just a bit, and left her wondering just how fragile her grasp of the truth was.

Mia shook off the heaviness that had settled into her shoulders. This wasn't the time for doubt. That could come later.

When she was sure Cash was puttering around in the kitchen, Mia started for the stairs. The bedroom was daunting, the thought of the number of Post-its she'd have to comb through enough to direct her steps toward the doorway of the attic. There was sure to be more clutter, but there was a better chance that it would be comprehensible.

Not that she was even sure what she was looking for.

A souvenir from the night? The razor blades that had been drawn across their wrists? A pregnancy test from Monroe? Each option seemed more ludicrous than the last. But this was what she had to work with.

Mia checked her phone when she got to the top of the stairs of the dusty room. No service, no data, no nothing. It had been like that since the first flake had fallen last evening. The storm was mild for Maine, heavy and steady rather than wild and raw. Yet, still, it had been enough to knock out the already-precarious communication none of them could rely on. Most people on the island didn't care. They carried walkie-talkies with them all through the winter months, anyone they needed probably in a one-hundred-yard radius.

But Mia hadn't even received a text that Izzy had landed in Rockport, and she knew Quinn, at least, hadn't returned. She wasn't worried, per se. There was an awareness, though, at the base of her spine, that she was effectively alone on the island, cut off from backup.

She shoved the cell into her jeans pocket and then shrugged out of her damp jacket as she crossed the well-trodden floorboards. The dust that settled like a light film over most surfaces had been disturbed in some places, as if someone had been up here recently. Cash? Or Earl?

Light spilled in through the window at the far end, sliding over duct-taped boxes and sheet-shrouded lumps that Mia assumed were furniture.

It was only when she found the box labeled PICTURES that she stopped. With her nails, she ripped at the fraying tape holding the cardboard together until it finally gave beneath her fingers. Inside were stacks of albums—leather, fabric, cheap, plain, designed. If Mia had to guess, she'd say they were the work of Tess Bishop, Cash's mother. She'd seemed the type to hoard moments, tucking them away into plastic sleeves, protecting them and hiding them at the same time.

Mia sat down so that her back was against a couch that smelled vaguely of cat urine despite the fact that Mia knew the Bishops had never owned a pet.

Her fingertips traced the gold stamp on the deep mahogany leather of the first album in the bunch. The *B* in Bishop curved and coiled so that it was more art than letter.

The pictures inside were of Tess and Earl's wedding. She'd worn a high-collared gown, he a cherry-red suit. The former seemed to match the memory of the woman who had been more background noise than anything else during Mia's childhood. But Earl was a surprise. So were the flushed, happy cheeks, the wide grin, the way he was dipping Tess in the middle of the dance floor. Earl had always come across as stern, unbending, allergic to lightness and gaiety. Had he changed so much? Or had she known him only through the prism of a teenager's viewpoint, unwilling and uninterested to recognize that there was a person behind the authoritative mask?

Not for the first time did she wish they'd talked to him when they'd landed on the island.

She placed the album aside and reached for the next one. Soon she realized they were in chronological order, and sped through the ones of young Cash, with a reluctant smile tugging at the corners of her mouth.

When she finally got to his teenage years, she slowed down. There she and Cash were, their smiles wide and carefree.

It was strange seeing the moments caught in time when she knew the real life that had been lived in the seconds, the minutes, the days on either side of the careless candids.

There was the first night they'd kissed. Cash's fingers had brushed along the waistband of Mia's jeans, then hooked into one of the belt loops to pull her closer. Asher had been down at the rocks, too, but neither of them had paid him much attention.

Had they always overlooked Asher? Had he cared at all? She hadn't thought so. But maybe she just hadn't thought at all.

She flipped through a few more pictures, past the winter dance that had been held in the gym of the four-room school. Asher had gone stag, but that hadn't meant much at the time, what with five guys and four girls total in their age range.

There was a picture of the two of them dancing—her and Asher. It must have been a slow song, because her arms were looped around his shoulders, his hands were pressed into her hips.

They weren't smiling. Mia's eyes caught on her own face, and she wondered at the expression there. It wouldn't have been odd for her to dance with him, but she would have thought they would both make it silly, a joke almost, or a warm hug that they swayed through in time to the music.

An odd sense of unease clawed at her belly. This picture wasn't silly.

But. They hadn't been like her and Cash. They'd never been like that.

She turned the page.

Monroe made her first appearance in the albums three pages later.

Mia paused, her hand frozen midair. There was something absolutely captivating about the girl, a quality Mia hadn't remembered, which radiated off her even through faded film and yellowed corners.

Mia let the plastic sleeve fall so that she could see the picture in full.

It was a snap of Monroe sitting on the rocks down by the beach. Her head was tipped back toward the sun, her throat exposed, silky black hair brushing over her hand where it rested against smooth black stone. Cutoff jean shorts barely hid her long legs, and her white crop top exposed a sliver of stomach. The light caught against the jewel that was nestled in her belly button.

The girl had been beautiful beyond her dark hair and pale skin. Mia saw Lacey in her features, but there was something about Monroe that eclipsed her sister's nervous prettiness. Maybe it was the hint of lushness at her lips and hips, a promise that had never been realized. Youth interrupted, caught in time, perpetually on the cusp of being spoiled forever by age and cynicism and a deep world-weariness.

But dying young was glamorous only in rock songs and movies.

Mia flipped the page.

Most of the rest of the photos from that summer were a variation of her, Asher, and Cash, just as she would expect. The three of them and their unbreakable bond. Lacey and Monroe made quick cameos, but Mia sensed their presences offscreen far more than they were captured by a lens. Always the boys' eyes pulled by the two girls who stood beyond the camera.

If there was a better metaphor for that summer, Mia couldn't name it.

By the time she got to the Firefly Festival, the annual town-wide event held to celebrate the solstice, Mia had begun to worry she was wasting her time by indulgently sinking into the past. There had been hints of the dynamics she'd remembered—Asher caught up in Monroe, Mia caught up in Cash—but nothing illuminating enough to warrant the hour she'd spent so far sifting through the static memories.

Except that shot of her and Asher dancing. She pushed the thought aside.

Here, here was something else.

The picture, in front of the hot dog stand at the Firefly Festival, was of Jimmy Roarke, Henry Jackson, and Charles Bell. Charles's arm was wrapped firmly around Jimmy's shoulders, and both of them had their heads thrown back, laughing.

Those girls were all scared.

That's what Jimmy had said, with fear in his eyes, his shoulders hunched. The *of him* had been implied.

But here they were together, Jimmy and Charles, just weeks before the lighthouse night. Their amusement, their comfort with each other, was clearly genuine.

So had something happened to change that?

Or were Jimmy's memories faulty, distorted? And, if they were, how had they gotten that way?

Her gaze snagged on a picture at the bottom right of the page, distracting her.

The photo had been taken at dusk if not later, the lack of light challenging the capabilities of the rudimentary camera. Mia and Lacey were the main subjects, their tipsy smiles apparent even to Mia now. Lacey *had* been very pretty when taken on her own, separate from her sister. She'd worn her hair in a cut that had highlighted all the sharp points on her face, but that harshness was softened by her eyes, which were deep blue and lined with classically attractive, sooty lashes.

Both Mia and Lacey presented a different kind of youth than Monroe had. Where Monroe was out of reach, Mia and Lacey were accessible, attainable. There was a pimple erupting just above Mia's eyebrow, and cheap, too-pink blush smeared in the hollows of Lacey's cheeks instead of on the ridges. They'd grown into those faces, adulthood realized, whereas Monroe had been left behind, unspoiled.

If Mia hadn't been looking for something off in the picture, she would have missed the couple in the background. They were more shadows than anything else, limbs catching the flash at just the wrong angle, faces obscured by smudged ink and time. But Mia recognized the pair easily.

Monroe and Cash.

And just on the edge of the picture stood Asher, watching them. Neon slid across his features, throwing him into sharp relief against the general blurriness of the scene. Everything about his stance screamed anger, from the fists at his side to the tension in his shoulders.

There they were, all five of them, just weeks before Monroe's and Asher's apparent suicides, and Mia's apparent attempt, caught in a tableau of teenage jealousy, ignorance, and lust. The waves of each were so strong they crashed into Mia's chest, catching along the throbbing pulse of her ulcer, slipping acid into the edges of the pain.

Mia had been naive to think they'd been carefree that summer up until that night. The silvery, thin lines of emotion that connected them were all but visible in the photo.

She slipped her finger into the plastic pocket and wrested the picture out into the present. Here. This is what she'd been overlooking with all the pregnancy rumors, the older men, the mysterious artist.

The five of them, the way their lives had touched, intersected, and then blown apart.

Trying to strip away the noise of the past few days, Mia hunched over until her nose was almost brushing the picture, as if getting closer and closer and closer would help her see the answer that lay beneath the glossy patina.

At the center of it was Cash, always Cash. The one who hadn't been there that night at the lighthouse. The one whom Izzy hadn't liked or trusted. The one who'd lied about talking to the reporter, the one who'd cried and made her think he was better than that first quick impression she'd gotten of him at the bar. The one who was talking about the Bells. The one who was dating a woman with bruises on her arms.

What was lacking was a motive. Not for the reporter's death—that she could explain. But for Monroe and Asher, and even Mia.

It was the loop she kept getting stuck in.

Her phone vibrated in her jeans, just as she leaned back away from the picture in frustration. She scrambled for it, even as she realized the one quick ping was just a text, not a call.

Mia breathed out in relief when she saw Izzy's name.

The happiness curdled when she read the text.

They're all lying. The artist was the body in the bay. Get the hell out of there, Hart.

The words didn't even make sense on first read. It took three more tries for it to sink in, and once it did, her pulse kicked up, fast enough that she could actually feel the beat in her throat.

The artist. Peter. A gadfly that had buzzed at the edges of her mind ever since Mia had heard of him.

They're all lying.

Were they? All of them? How many people had seen the body? The guys who had pulled him out of the water. But anyone could have mistaken two middle-aged Caucasian men, especially with his face so bloated with the sea. They hadn't even been to town since Mia had arrived, which made her think they kept to themselves. And when they'd interviewed them . . . hadn't they said the man had been an artist? Should that have been a red flag?

Her brain tripped then, sadness slipping into the new hollowness beneath her breastbone. *Sammy.* He had to have known, there was no way around it. At the very least he was an accomplice.

She thought back to the first day, the easiness of his welcome, the familiarity of their banter.

Was it just Sammy? Was he covering his own tracks or someone else's? It was possible that no one beyond him had seen the body. The men from the boat had called him directly, probably. If he told everyone in town it was the reporter, why would anyone question him? Especially with Mia and Izzy on the way.

They're all lying.

The words focused and then blurred before sharpening once more. She blinked hard, staring at her phone's screen.

Of course, they were all lying. It was the one truth Mia knew, and knew well.

But was there more to it? Did Izzy know something else, something that hadn't come through on her messages yet? Mia's phone lagged, trying to load other texts, but then it promptly shut down.

Frustration coiled in her belly, climbed into her esophagus. *This goddamn island.* Her fingers trembled in her effort not to fling her cell across the room.

She started to push herself to her feet, not knowing what her next move would be yet, but knowing that sitting among dusty memories in the Bishops' attic was no longer productive.

As she rocked to her knees, she realized that Cash was standing there, still and silent, only a few steps away. On instinct, she flinched, her hand going to her holster, as she prayed her distraction hadn't just gotten her killed.

"Mia." Cash's voice was eerie, stripped down of all the bitterness that had turned it rough downstairs.

The fine hairs on her forearms stood on end, her skin pulling tight into goose bumps as the whisper trailed along her nerve endings.

"Cash. You scared me," Mia said, keeping her hand tucked right up against her gun as she slowly, very slowly, stood up.

"Sorry," Cash said, but there was an emptiness to the apology. There was no rueful smile to accompany it, nor did he try to laugh off the uneasiness that turned the air around them brittle.

She toed at the album still lying on the floor, making him split his attention. "Was just looking at some old pictures."

He nodded but didn't say anything further.

"I hadn't realized Jimmy and Charles Bell were friends," she said, because her body might be on the verge of slipping into fight or flight, but her mind was stuck on the dots, the outliers that kept cropping up at perfect places to fit an image that seemed too easy to draw.

Cash's head tipped to the side, and she couldn't tell if his eyes were actually empty or the blankness was because of the shadows from the attic. "I don't think they were. I actually . . ."

"What?" Mia asked, her hand still on her gun, even as he continued to keep his distance. The blood was no longer rushing past her ears, so she could hear the house sigh and settle with the wind, could hear the rumble of a washing machine, could hear any potential shift in Cash's body that signaled an attack.

"I got the impression Jimmy wasn't too fond of the guy." Cash lifted one shoulder, his arms relaxed by his sides. She was beginning to feel foolish for her initial scare.

"How?" she asked.

"What do you mean?"

"I mean how did you get that impression?" The photo of the three of them told a different story. What was the truth? A moment snapped in time, or a gut feeling a decade and a half later. It kept cropping up. That disparity. Mia's memories acted more like pictures because hers were safe, removed, untainted. But everyone else's had bent.

Or was it the other way around? She swayed on her feet, just a little, trying to ignore the question that had started as a whisper and then grown to a howl she pretended not to hear when she stared at the ceiling of her childhood bedroom.

What if her mind had simply supplied her with pretty images to paper over horror lingered in reality?

Cash shrugged again. "Don't know really. Always just was. No one ever said it out loud."

She shook her head. "You noticed when you were a kid? When you were that young? You thought Jimmy didn't like Charles?"

Because she hadn't thought much about any of the adults that summer. Not beyond avoiding getting yelled at and figuring out which house was empty so they could sneak some liquor.

Cash's brow collapsed. "I mean . . . I guess not, no."

Right. Her mind grasped for something that was just a wisp, insubstantial but not nothing, either.

Mia dropped her gaze to the floor, and it caught on the photo she'd pulled out of the album.

"Cash, would you say you were close with Monroe?"

The sound of boots shuffling against hardwood was her only warning, before he was in front of her, too close. She couldn't back up because the couch was behind her.

"What? No? Not really?" Cash said, all questions instead of statements, coming at a rapid-fire pace. "Why? What are you thinking?"

His gaze was locked on her face, searching. She took a deliberate step around him, so that she had a clear path to the exit.

She ignored the last bit and focused on the denials. "But she came to you. With the pregnancy thing?"

"She didn't come to me."

What?

Mia paused where she'd been slowly inching toward the stairs. No fast movements, no obvious tells, and put voice to the startled thought. "What?"

"It wasn't Monroe who told me about the baby."

Everything stopped, the background noise, her heart, her breathing. Her eyes closed as she inhaled. The wisp of that idea solidifying into something she could finally grab a hold of, finally wrap her arms around.

The spaces between the lies.

"Shit," she said on the exhale, then opened her eyes to find Cash watching her closely. "I need you to try to get in touch with Izzy. Try the Rockport police department. My cell is out."

Mia was already running down the stairs, her boots heavy against the protesting wood. She hadn't given him any instructions on what to tell Izzy, but her mind was tangled in the web of lies that had been woven since they'd landed on the island. Her finger ran along the sticky edge of each thread, sliding closer toward the knot in the middle, where she poked, where she dug a nail in and tried to pull it all apart.

She was out the front door before she stopped. Panting, she bent a little to catch her breath and her balance.

They're all lying. Get the hell out of there, Hart.

Did Izzy know enough to put it together?

It wasn't Monroe who told me about the baby.

The last dot slipped into place, the image complete, just as the blow struck the back of her head and the world faded into black.

CHAPTER
TWENTY-TWO

Izzy

Izzy studied her reflection's red-rimmed eyes and the dark circles beneath them in the bathroom's mirror as the morning sun finally spilled into the hotel room.

She hadn't been able to sleep, hadn't been able to turn off her brain, so she'd just paced all night, left with nothing to do but hope Mia had gotten one of her dozens of texts. Best-case scenario: Mia wasn't responding because of the storm. Worst-case? Izzy didn't want to think about that.

Slapping at her cheeks to get a little color in them was mostly useless, but Izzy just shrugged at the result. There was no time for anything else—merely passable would have to do.

Some finagling with the local cop who had been manning his desk overnight had gotten her the last address that was on file for Charles Bell. Izzy grabbed the piece of paper on which she'd jotted it down, then swung out the door of the hotel room, finally able to do something beyond sitting there going slowly crazy.

It was early enough that the streets were mostly empty, and the quiet drive gave her too much time to think.

Why had Sammy lied about the body's identity? And where the hell was Robert Twist, their original victim? Was he still alive?

And if Mia had recognized the person in the morgue, that meant that Peter had been the one to come to the station in the fall, not Robert. That lent credence to the theory that he'd found something in that abandoned house on the Bell land, something connected to Mia.

If he'd told Robert about it, though, why go back? Was he foolish enough to try to solve the mystery himself? Twist *had* been asking about him, or an artist at least when he'd first gotten there. Peter had even been his last outgoing call.

What Izzy didn't understand was Sammy's long-term plan. The state could have sent something back in the full toxicology report; someone who knew Robert Twist could have shown up to claim the body. Rockport could have shipped over the dental records they'd been running.

The only possibility that made sense was that there had been no long-term plan.

Izzy knew it with the same certainty that she'd known Sammy Bowdoin had been pushing the suicide angle way too hard on that first meeting. He'd been casual about it, but even then she'd been able to pick up on it.

A strange thought nipped at her anger, begging for attention, and a tiny part of her, the one that didn't want Mia to be crushed by even more bad news, suggested that maybe this had been Sammy's attempt at protecting Mia.

If they'd wrapped up the case quickly, called it suicide, and left, they wouldn't be in danger from whoever put that body in the bay.

Protect their own. That's what those islanders did better than any-thing else. Had Sammy been protecting Mia?

The address for where the Bells had apparently lived fifteen years ago was three turns ahead. It was a modest two story tucked into a row of modest two stories. The contrast was so stark to the decadent mansion perched on the edge of dramatic black cliffs that Izzy actually checked the numbers on the note she'd written herself just to be sure.

It was right, though. She pulled to the opposite curb, her service-able Honda blending in with the other affordable compact cars. This was solidly middle-class America.

If the Bells had really come here, they must have been desperate to escape whatever they had been leaving behind.

Izzy grabbed at the flimsy coffee cup she'd snatched on her way out of the motel room, bringing the Styrofoam to her lips as she kept her eyes on the front door of the house. The sludge was lukewarm at best, but it was another hit of caffeine, and at this point beggars really couldn't be choosers. She finished it in one gulp.

It was unlikely she'd get anything out of the current owners about where Charles Bell was now, but at least she had a starting point. After she talked to whoever had bought the house, she'd fan out to the neigh-bors, maybe get lucky. Fifteen years or so wasn't that long to live in the same place.

There was something strange about Charles staying in the house where his wife had died. According to the local guy Izzy had sweet-talked over the phone, this had been Charles's last-known address as recently as six years ago. Why had he stayed in it all that time? Wouldn't that have been torture, walking the hallways hand in hand with the ghost of your supposedly beloved wife?

Cold and calculating. That was the kind of person that Charles would have needed to be to kill his daughter to cover up whatever Asher had seen. That was the type of person who remodeled their house instead of moving out when the flames consumed Bix.

Though if Bix hadn't died until she was on the mainland, that meant that if Charles was responsible for Asher's murder, it wasn't because Charles had been covering up Bix's death like Martha Lowe had suggested.

A spiky headache was pulsing in her frontal lobe, so Izzy tossed her empty cup onto the floor and grabbed her bag. Just as she went to step out of the Honda, a car turned onto the street. It crawled past each house until it turned into the driveway of the one Izzy was watching.

There was a woman behind the wheel, but Izzy couldn't tell her age, or much beyond her diminutive build. Izzy ducked her head for a better view while the woman climbed out of the beat-up sedan.

She wasn't young but wasn't elderly, either. Her hair was pulled back into a low bun, the sunlight catching on the silver strands threaded throughout. Both the style and color probably added a few years, but Izzy would guess midforties.

The woman was clad in pale blush scrubs and a white cardigan that she was straightening as she walked the path up to the house.

Izzy made her move.

"Excuse me," Izzy called while still across the street. She glanced for cars and then broke into a light jog.

The woman startled, clutching her purse where it swung at her side. Izzy held up her hands, palm out.

"Hi, I'm Detective Isabel Santiago," Izzy said, as soothingly as possible. "I'm working on a case in the area. I was wondering if I could ask you a few questions."

The introduction was enough for the lady to loosen the white-knuckled grip she had on her strap but also earned Izzy a thorough up-and-down perusal. The woman had thick, straight eyebrows that turned her face severe—a look that was not helped by her tight, pinched lips.

"Do you live here?" Izzy asked when the silence passed the point of socially acceptable.

That earned Izzy a quick jerk of her head. "No," the woman finally said. Her voice was deep, almost surprisingly so. But it fit with the too-broad shoulders and the square jaw. "Let me see your ID."

Izzy pulled the leather case that held her badge, number, and picture, and held it up and open for the woman. She leaned in to study it, her hazel eyes slipping from it to Izzy's face more than once. Izzy didn't mind. She actually wished more people would be as careful when she told them who she was.

Finally, the woman nodded once and straightened. "I don't live here. I'm just the home nurse, so I don't know if I'll be able to help you."

"What's your name?"

"Teresa."

Izzy knew no last name was forthcoming.

"Are the owners home?" Izzy asked, turning a bit toward the house.

In her peripheral, Teresa shrugged. "Yes. But I doubt he'll be able to answer your questions."

"Oh? Why's that?"

"He sleeps more than anything these days," Teresa said as she started toward the stoop, digging in her purse. She pulled out a large ring with more than a dozen keys jangling together. With the efficiency of someone who was familiar with the place, Teresa unlocked the door and began switching on lights in the foyer even as she dumped her bag on a side table.

"Are you here all day?" Izzy asked, for lack of anything better to say. If the owner was out of it, there wasn't much she was going to get from her time here.

"Hmm, yes," Teresa answered, her back toward Izzy. "Vera comes at night. Our schedules are off by about an hour."

Izzy nodded even though Teresa was already heading toward the kitchen. So she hadn't gotten lucky; she hadn't really expected to. "There's no other family then?"

Before following Teresa, Izzy dipped into the living room. No personal touches, no photos, no knickknacks set out solely to collect dust. Everything was clean, neat. But it lacked any warmth.

Izzy continued on to the next room, where Teresa was pouring herself a cup of coffee.

"Vera sets a timer for me." Teresa held up her mug, the smallest smile on her lips. It countered the harsh lines of her face until she was almost pretty. "And, no. No family. No one visits."

"Have you worked here long?"

"Five years," Teresa said. "All right, he's on the second floor. When he's awake, he's aware of what's going on. You can see if he'll answer any questions."

Teresa led the way, and Izzy followed silently until they paused outside a closed door. Teresa knocked lightly and then pushed it open.

The room was like much of the rest of the place. Bare, utilitarian. There was a simple dresser, a nightstand, a single lamp in the corner by a chair. A man was asleep on the bed, his salt-and-pepper hair gone more toward the former than the latter. His body was clearly frail beneath the heavy comforter.

"Sleeping," Teresa said, the *I told you so* evident in her tone.

"Oh." Izzy grabbed Teresa's wrist before she could walk into the room. "What's his name?"

"Charles," Teresa said, shaking Izzy off and heading over to fluff an extra pillow. "Charles Bell."

CHAPTER TWENTY-THREE

Mia

Mia blinked into consciousness, pulled from the darkness by the pain at the back of her skull. She tried to lift a hand to explore, but something caught at her wrist, hard plastic digging into her skin.

Bound. She was bound. And had a head wound.

Panic threatened, a copper tang in her mouth, but she swallowed against it. She brought her tied hands up together and pressed the heels of her palms into her eyes, hoping to dispel some of the fuzziness as she tried to remember what had happened.

The picture.

Mia had been in Cash's attic, going through the photo albums. There'd been that picture of the five of them, her and Lacey in the foreground. Now she was in a small room. But what room? Was she still at Cash's?

She opened her eyes. Wherever she was being held looked like a basement. An old one. The walls were stone, the floor concrete.

Mia was propped up against something heavy and large, and there were small puddles of water gathering in the slight dips of the floor.

Her feet were bound with thick rope instead of the plastic zip ties that held her wrists, and her pulse points fluttered against each other, her heart refusing to steady out. She breathed through it.

Wrists tied, ankles tied. No gun. But that was to be expected.

Her fingers trembled anyway, fear turning them shaky.

One thing at a time.

The rope. That she could deal with. Knots were made to loosen, and she'd been taught every kind there was while growing up in a fishing town.

Her wrists would be next. Once she could stand, she'd be able to get enough leverage to break the plastic.

She'd also been stripped of her coat and the fleece she'd worn underneath it. A distant part of her mind recognized that she was freezing, but even the slight chattering of her teeth didn't make the reality of it sink in. Her blood was on fire, laced as it was with adrenaline.

Barefoot. She was also barefoot, her boots nowhere near her. That was smart of her captor. It would make it harder for her if she did escape.

Had she been out long? Was she still on St. Lucy's? If she was, that meant several feet of snow outside. Dressed as she was, she would be risking frostbite even if she made it out of the room.

The alternative wasn't appealing, either.

Pain sliced through her head, a spike that came out of nowhere. Tentatively, she brought her bound hands up over her shoulder to feel along her hairline for the bump. Her knuckle nudged it and then came away sticky. Blood. The hit had been hard enough that it had broken skin.

What had happened after the picture?

Cash. A quick flash of his face in shadows was followed by a bolt of agony that left her panting. She tried again.

Cash. Shadows. Dead eyes. The picture. Each time she grasped for more details, though, they faded only to be replaced with that piercing ache.

Time passed. She wasn't sure how much, but she started measuring it in the waves of pain that ebbed and flowed with her attempts to figure out what had happened.

Move. She had to move.

Mia maneuvered into a position where she could tug at the knot at her ankle without jarring her head. Two nails broke off, as she worked the rope, the skin around her fingers burned raw, but she kept going. Whoever had tied it had known what they were doing.

They're all lying.

It came like a breath, the memory, so that she almost didn't notice it. It came when she'd been distracted, when her mind had emptied.

They're all lying.

She paused. Who were all lying?

The more she pushed, the more it skittered away. Frustration built, threatened to turn into something more, something that was frantic and wild. It gathered in her chest, pressed against her tear ducts.

It's okay. It's okay. Just keep working. Focus.

Mia dug into the thick threads of the rope once more, her determination costing her another nail. She let her thoughts go static once more.

No gun. No shoes. Rope on ankles. Bound wrists. Head wound. No other pain that she could identify. No broken bones.

The checklist ran on a loop, a manic whirl that she didn't even try to control.

No gun. No shoes. Rope on ankles. Basement. Concrete floor. No windows. One door. One door. One door. How would she get out? It would be locked. One door. No gun. No shoes. No window. One door.

Get the hell out of there, Hart.

She only realized her breathing had gone ragged when she swayed with the lack of oxygen. Dropping her forehead to her knees, she concentrated on pulling in air, allowing her lungs to expand and press against her rib cage. It didn't hurt. That was a good sign. She held on to that as her mind tested the boundaries of the leash she'd just put on it.

Get the hell out. She was trying to. But it wasn't a thought, rather an echo again. Just like earlier. *They're all lying.*

Hart. No one on the island called her that. Who would call her that?

Izzy. Her head throbbed, but this time the pain was bearable, blunt instead of barbed.

She let her eyes unfocus. Izzy had told her that. When? In the attic. The buzz, she'd felt it in her jeans. There was something else there. Something important.

Mia breathed in again. There was a hint of salt, just like everywhere on the island.

Izzy was gone. She was trying to find . . . someone. Important. Someone important.

The artist.

No.

No, she wasn't trying to find him. Because . . .

The artist. The artist.

The artist was dead.

Mia blinked everything back into focus. Her broken thumbnail had been digging into the already-pink skin by her ankle. The pain barely registered.

The artist was dead. So where was the reporter? Robert Twist. If the artist had been the dead man in the bay, that meant Sammy was in on it. Was he the one holding her? Had he knocked her out? But where? The last she remembered she had been in Cash's attic.

She flinched away from what that meant and went to work on the knot again. It was starting to give beneath her desperate fingers.

This time she let herself listen instead of think. It seemed likely she was below ground, but maybe she'd be able to hear footsteps above her—if she could get the blood roaring past her eardrums to quiet down.

Only when sound started filtering in again did she realize how much she'd been missing locked inside her own world. Pipes rattled and protested, a radiator hissed somewhere in the corner, a steady drip of water pinged against something solid. The background noise of a Maine basement.

Then she heard it. Soft, so that it almost faded into nothingness. Mia would have missed it if she hadn't been listening for each groan of the house.

A hitched breath.

There was someone else in the room.

She froze. But the noise was gone. Had she imagined it?

Mia weighed the odds. It was unlikely her kidnapper was hiding down here. She'd been dumped and left bound and woozy. The door was probably locked so there was little chance Mia would be able to escape.

So who did that leave?

A second victim.

As quietly as she could, Mia shifted to her knees, her palms flat on the floor to give her balance. She shifted away from whatever she'd been propped on and scooted toward the shadows on the far side of the room. There was an old dresser blocking her view of the whole wall, and she moved slowly, so slowly, to the left so she could see around it.

A crumpled figure was curled up against the wall. Mia bit her lip until she saw the rise and fall of his chest beneath his thin wifebeater.

"Shit," she whispered, her voice rough from disuse. The man flinched but didn't even look her way.

Broken. He was broken.

272

She edged closer, her movements disjointed because of her bindings. A distant part of her realized that he had no such ties, but he looked so weak he could barely lift an arm, let alone fight off their kidnapper.

"Hello," she said quietly. "I'm Detective Mia Hart. I'm going to get us out of here."

There was a pause, and then that hitch of breathing again. Just when she was about to reach out, the man rolled over.

She covered her quick intake of air with a cough, but her gaze darted from the blood that glued his shirt to the side of his body to his damp, pleading eyes and then back again.

He licked dry, cracked lips. "I can help."

CHAPTER
TWENTY-FOUR
Izzy

"Charles Bell," Izzy repeated, still standing in the doorway, unable to move any farther into the room. Charles Bell's room, apparently.

Teresa glanced up from where she'd been fixing the quilt that draped over Charles's legs, possibly sensing the shift in tone. "Yes," she answered, though it hadn't really been a question. Izzy had heard her the first time. Loud and clear.

This shouldn't have been as unexpected as it was, maybe, but Izzy had convinced herself Charles Bell would have moved on. But beyond that, to think Bell in his current physical state could overpower anyone would be laughable.

Sammy's phone call, though. It could have been to Bell. Maybe Bell was just pulling the puppet strings and leaving the dirty work to the doc.

"Can I . . . Can I try to wake him?" Izzy asked, unsure of the proper protocol.

"Won't work, but . . ." Teresa jerked her chin toward his prone body.

Izzy stepped closer and called his name a few times. No response. She didn't want to touch him, which left her few other options.

When she looked up, Teresa was watching her with a smug smile, her arms crossed over her chest. "I told you." She seemed like the kind of woman who found pleasure in that phrase.

"Can I look around?" Izzy asked. This was a gray area ethically, legally, but she kept her face neutral.

"Don't see why not," Teresa said. "Not going to find anything. Rest of the house is like the downstairs."

"Okay," Izzy said easily and then paused on her way out of the room. "You said no family visits?"

"No. Poor man," Teresa said.

"Who pays his bills?"

Teresa's eyes narrowed on Izzy's face, but her cautiousness seemed reserved just for her own privacy, not Charles's. "It's a trust. His lawyer oversees it."

The mention of the attorney sent Izzy out into the hallway without any more questions.

She wandered through the rest of the rooms, her fingers dragging along the molding on the walls. Teresa had been right. The upstairs was almost bare. An eeriness had settled into the nooks and empty spaces, like there'd been a death in the house.

There had been.

She soon realized that while the house was Spartan, it wasn't completely devoid of personal items. Izzy scoured each of the three bedrooms, digging through trouser- and sweatshirt-filled drawers, pausing over a small jewelry box tucked away in one. It played a haunting lullaby she somehow distantly recognized, but in a way that felt like from another lifetime. Under the beds were cartons of books, thick Russian volumes and tattered romance novels with dog-eared pages; comics, too, carefully preserved in plastic wrap, their bright colors garish. In the closets were dresses, silk and velvet, an era old but in pristine condition like they were just awaiting the return of their owner. Those were the creepiest finds. Izzy grimaced as she went to close the door of one in the last rooms.

A chill had settled in along her spine, and despite an urgency to find *something*, she also just wanted to get the hell out of there. But then her eyes caught on something. In the corner on the shelf was a dark box, pushed mostly out of sight.

Thankful that she kept a spare pair of latex gloves stashed in her jacket pocket at all times, Izzy shoved her fingers into them, then bent to pick up the box before dropping it lightly on the bed.

Carefully, so that she didn't accidentally damage anything, she opened the lid.

Inside was a thick maroon journal, simple but clearly of good quality, and next to it lay a gold ring with an inset pearl. Izzy didn't know jewelry that well, but it didn't look cheap.

She grabbed the journal and opened it to the inscription page.

Brenna Connolly. Bix Bell's maiden name.

Izzy ran her tongue over her teeth, pressing hard against her incisor, dread slipping into the places in her mind where only questions had been before.

The first page was dated in September of the year Bix had died. They would have just left St. Lucy's at that point.

The writing curved and swooped, delicate in a way that Izzy would have guessed just based on the descriptions she'd heard of the woman alone.

But the words were stark.

I will be dead by the end of the year.

Anger and surprise came, a quick double shot of bitterness landing heavy in Izzy's belly. Here, here was her ghost, that echo of a death that haunted the place. It had followed her from room to room until she'd found this.

The entries that came next read like textbook escalation.

I haven't been able to stop crying about Monroe. He gets so angry with me.

He hit me tonight. His palm left a red mark. He cried as he stared at it. I didn't shed a single tear.

It was a slowly ticking bomb both she and Bix would be helpless to stop.

Where was that boy who bought a street painting for five dollars? His ashes were scattered beside our daughter's.

The journal ended abruptly three days before the date of the fire.

Bix's prediction made reality.

Izzy swallowed hard, saliva and trace amounts of blood from where her teeth had dug into the inside of her lip.

The haze of rage cleared enough for her to reread several of the passages. They were almost too damning. She all but expected to find the paper crinkled and water stained from dried tears.

Why keep the journal? Why risk it being found? It told a clear story of Bix's abuse, one that would be hard to misinterpret.

Izzy found herself in front of Charles's bedroom door before she realized she'd even moved, her limbs following some buried command sent along her nerves as her thoughts remained stuck on that first entry.

I will be dead by the end of the year.

There was a detached quality to her movements now. She watched her fingers curl around the metal of the handle, watched them grip and turn and push. Rote muscle memory. Would she feel the same way as those same fingers pressed against Charles's windpipe?

Her gun bumped against her rib cage as she stepped into the room, and the simple weight of it brought her back.

Why keep the journal?

The thought pushed through again, battled the anger, dug shallow roots into the banks of her consciousness so that it would hold firm as she tried to push it away.

She listened for Teresa's footsteps, but she must have gone downstairs. Charles was alone in the room.

Izzy tossed the journal on the nightstand and then stepped even closer to the man.

He was pale, nearly translucent so Izzy could see the thin veins that ran beneath his eyes. There were dark spots near his temple, a discoloration that was unpleasant only because of the way his skin bunched around his neck, pulling taut over the ridges of his face.

The shirt he wore revealed the way his body was nothing but a wasted frame of bones, his muscles having deteriorated to leave behind a sunken hollow where they used to be.

Powerless. Fragile. Sickly.

It was hard to believe this was the same man from the journal, the one who had all the Bell girls scared.

But looks rarely had any role to play in abuse. Humiliation, rage, grief. They all made weak men feel strong.

Izzy was at a loss for what to do, though, other than wait. There was an IV by his bed, a slow drip of something slithering through the clear tubes. If it was morphine, it could explain his vegetative state. Maybe cutting off the supply would lift him out of his stupor. It would probably also cause him intense pain.

She reached for the bag.

As her fingers touched the tough plastic, Charles's eyes snapped open.

Izzy flinched, but his hand lashed out to clamp around her wrist. His palm was fire against her skin, his pupils eating up most of the color of his irises, his breathing swift and frantic. His gaze bounced everywhere from her face, to her weapon, to the side table, and back again.

There would be bruises in the shapes of his fingerprints tomorrow.

"Charles Bell?" she asked.

"You found it." His voice was painful, a rasp dragged out over shards of broken glass. "Of course you did. She wanted you to."

"Found what?"

His eyes slid back to the side table.

"The journal," she said, answering her own question. Why had he kept it? "Who wanted me to find it?"

Charles's fingers tightened against the pulse point that pounded at the inner side of her wrist. His lips worked and twisted, as if trying to form words, but no sound came out.

Izzy leaned forward as Charles took another rattling breath, the crackle of his lungs loud in the quiet room.

He tried again, and this time he got it out.

"Bix didn't write it."

The words hung there, and Izzy imagined them in the same delicate handwriting that filled the journal's pages.

"What, what do you mean? It wasn't hers?"

Tears gathered in the man's pale eyes, spilling over papery cheeks. His mouth was moving again, but fruitlessly, his fingers loosening from around her wrist.

"No," Izzy said, keeping her tone authoritative to try to keep him with her. "No. Who was it then? Who?"

He turned his head toward the window, away from Izzy.

"Her. It's always been her."

CHAPTER
TWENTY-FIVE
Mia

Mia was worried for the man even as he offered help to escape. It was obvious he was in bad shape, though she couldn't see the full extent of the wound on his side.

"I can." He nodded, earnest but quiet. "I can help."

"Okay," Mia soothed, even as she eyed the cut that was still weeping into his shirt, the bright red of the blood mingling with the dried copper from days past. "Yes, you can help. What's your name?"

"Robert," the man said, confirming what she'd already guessed. They were missing a person. Here was their person. "Robert Twist. I'm a journalist."

There was a distinct lack of panic in his voice, and Mia tried to remember what to do with a person who was in shock. She smiled, going for reassuring, despite the way her head still throbbed. "That's great, Robert. I've been looking for you."

"Yeah?" It was hopeful in the way of a child being told he was a favorite by a teacher. "I don't know how long I've been here. Lost track of days."

"Do they come down here at all?" Mia asked, moving to sit next to him so that her ankles were in reach of his hands without him having to move. "Can you start in on that knot there, Robert?"

His mouth pulled back in a tight grimace as he brought his hands up, but he didn't complain as he started tugging at the ends.

"No, put pressure on the point where the rope crosses," Mia instructed. Then asked again: "Robert, do you know who's keeping us here? Do you ever see them?"

Robert paused, looking up. *There* was the fear that had been missing earlier. Maybe it came in waves, the detachment followed by a fresh flood of terror.

"I don't know." The admission was hesitant, almost shameful, and he'd ducked his head once more, hiding.

"They don't come down?" The webbing of old and new blood on his shirt said differently. That was a wound that had been aggravated over time.

His fingers trembled. "I have a pick."

"What?"

"For the lock," Robert said, his lips tugging into a proud smile, that child once again. "Well, it's just a piece of metal. But the lock is old fashioned. I think it could work."

He glanced at her, his eyes bright. "You know how to pick a lock, don't you? I don't. I couldn't . . . It wouldn't work. I tried, but it wouldn't work."

Mia shifted her ankles to bring his attention back to them. "I'll try," she said, though she didn't have much hope. What they needed was for her to have her hands and feet free if their kidnapper came down the stairs.

"You haven't seen their face?" Mia tried a different way into the question.

But Robert just shook his head. It didn't seem like a denial, but she couldn't read him. He was eager and scared at the same time, hopeful and broken.

It took a long time for the bindings to finally give, and when they did, it happened all at once. In one moment the rope was stubborn and unmoving; in the next it relaxed against the tops of her feet. Something in her chest followed, untangling as well. She didn't like being restricted.

Robert cheered lightly beneath his breath as she kicked the rope away.

Once Mia was able to stand, there was a simple maneuver she could use to get out of the plastic zip tie. She brought her hands up above her head and then, in a swift, practiced move, threw them toward the ground. The stress was too much for the restraint, and it gave way beneath the pressure.

She breathed hard as she thumbed over the tender skin where the hard plastic had dug in.

"That was impressive," Robert said.

Mia smiled, a little. "They teach it on day one of training. Just couldn't do it sitting down. Now where's that lockpick?"

———

Mia was still kneeling by the door an hour later, the rusty piece of metal that could only be generously called a pick in this situation clutched in sweat-slicked hands.

The work was made more tedious by the way she had to pause every few seconds to listen for footsteps. If they were found in this position, they would lose any advantage they'd gained from slipping out of their bindings.

Robert had tried standing behind her, his cheek pressed to the metal, but it didn't take long for his weight to sag against the door, against her shoulder. He was too weak to last beyond the first ten minutes. Now he was sitting silently on the stairs behind her, his eyes not once leaving her back.

Frustration ate away at her belly. Her vision blurred, and when she squeezed her eyes shut, bright lights popped against the blackness there.

She shook out her free hand, concentrating on the air pressing against her lungs, on her steady heartbeat, on the ache in her kneecaps, anything other than the searing desperation that threatened to sap all her energy.

This was their only option. There were no other exits, no vents, no weak spots. Just one locked door and a piece of metal fashioned out of an old couch spring.

She started on the lock again.

As she worked this time, the memories came, those faint echoes that barely registered because her attention was focused elsewhere.

Cash coming up the stairs. His dead eyes and empty apology for startling her. Reaching for her gun, thinking he was going to attack. Thinking he was their guy. But he wasn't.

Metal clanked uselessly against metal, and she clenched her fist.

It wasn't Monroe who told me about the baby.

That had been it. The truth that had made everything else slide into place.

Just as the reality of it settled in her once more, so did the pick into the lock. The click was overloud in the quiet room.

Mia wasted no time. "Come on," she said without even turning to Robert. He was behind her in an instant, his breath heavy against the nape of her neck. She shivered, the dampness of each puff unsettling.

The knob gave beneath her hand, the door opening without a protest, the hinges smooth and well oiled. They stepped out into a darkened, narrow hallway, her shoulders brushing against the walls as she started down the long corridor. Servants quarters, her mind supplied. That's why everything was so tight. The place was old.

Her bare feet were silent against the hardwood, and she kept her body angled so that her chest wouldn't provide an easy target. Robert stumbled behind her, all noise and pain and carelessness.

He wouldn't make it long. His body was concave, almost curling into itself even as he struggled with each heavy shuffle, his free arm hovering over his center, protecting his wound.

When they reached the end of the hallway, there was a steep staircase leading up to what Mia assumed was the ground floor. Robert whimpered, low and pitiful.

"Robert, I'm going to hide you here," Mia said, both hands clutching his shoulders for the purpose of keeping him upright more than to get his attention. "I'll come back for you, I promise."

A protest slipped out, scraping against his throat. "Don't leave me."

"I don't think you'll make it up those stairs." This wasn't the time for a debate. If needed, she could put pressure on the right places so that he would go down without a fight. She didn't want it to come to that, though.

"I will. Let me try," Robert said, lifting his chin. "Let me try."

She met his eyes. This was a man who had spent however many days locked in a damp basement. If the situation were reversed, she'd rather do anything than be left behind.

"Okay. But if you need to stop . . ."

"I won't."

Mia took him for his word and started up. She didn't need to turn to make sure he was keeping up; his breathing was loud enough that she could track his progress.

By the time they got to the top, sweat had beaded along his hairline, and his face was nearly gray in the light from the single bulb above their heads.

But he'd made it.

Neither of them smiled in celebration this time.

She held her finger to her lips and then tested the knob. Again, it gave beneath her hand, and in the next second she was in a kitchen, one she hadn't been in before. But she knew where she was. The abandoned house, the one Peter had been caught sneaking into.

The door to the back was right there, only three strides away. But she was frozen.

Too easy. This was all too fucking easy.

Mia glanced toward Robert, who had moved toward the counter with the sink. Not toward the door.

Too easy.

What were the chances they'd make it this far? Almost zero.

Everything slowed down as she watched Robert open a drawer without any hesitation. He knew the layout too well.

In between heartbeats she looked toward the door once more. Three strides. That's all it was. Throw the lock open; then she'd be outside. Free to get lost in the night.

Too easy.

But she had to try.

She ducked on instinct and took one step before Robert's voice stopped her.

"I'm sorry I can't let you do that, Detective," he said, his voice holding enough authority to tell her that he had a weapon.

Mia debated going for it anyway. She doubted he was a good shot. But they were close, close enough that he could just point and maybe hit something vital.

She stilled, turning toward him, palms up. He was holding the gun with two hands like they did in bad movies, his stance wide and all wrong. He wasn't shaking, though, which wasn't a good sign for her.

His side had to still be killing him—that wasn't fake. She'd seen it. But desperation and stress did funny things to the body, and right now they seemed to be keeping him upright.

"Why?" she asked, curious rather than betrayed. She should have questioned why he hadn't been bound. It was a sloppy mistake.

Robert bit his lip and then started to answer before a voice from the doorway interrupted him.

"Oh, Detective," Lacey Bell said, stepping into the room. "I do so hope you liked my game. It makes everything so much more interesting, don't you think?"

CHAPTER
TWENTY-SIX

Izzy

Her. It's always been her.

The echo of Charles Bell's voice drowned out every other thought. Izzy didn't even realize that she was back in her car before she was sliding the key in the ignition. She'd tossed the journal onto the passenger seat, and it stared at her now as mindless pop music blared over the stereo. Its blank face was mocking in its neutrality. The pages held answers, but they were false ones. Just like the rest of the goddamn case.

Bix didn't write it.

Someone set it up to look like Charles killed his wife. Someone wrote the journal, kept it hidden in the back of a closet just in case anyone went looking for a bad guy to blame.

Those girls were all scared. That's what Jimmy Roarke had said.

But why did he think that?

Bruises.

A thumbprint blue-and-green splotch on a pale, delicate arm.

"Jesus," Izzy breathed out, staring, unseeing, out the windshield. Her pulse, a pounding beneath her ribs, almost painful.

Lacey Bell.

The girl's fear had never been anything obvious, had always been subtle. That's why Izzy had trusted it.

That first interview. Her sweater had slipped up, offering a glimpse that had been so quick it was over between one blink and the next.

The first seed planted?

Later, when Izzy had run into her at the bar, she'd done it again. Jumped when the door slammed. She'd flushed and ducked out, with a believable embarrassment of someone who knew abuse, knew how to hide it.

Then there'd been the cutoff remarks about Charles, never fully formed, never truly bitter, but hinting at a strict father who had a heavy hand.

"Shit, shit, shit." Izzy slammed her palm against the steering wheel as every little moment stood out in sharp relief.

Lacey had been the one to tell them Monroe was having an affair in the first place. Nothing concrete, no. That would have been too blatant. Just an impression, a suggestion. Give them enough information to be reliable, not enough to actually figure anything out.

God, the bar. The scene at the bar had been played beautifully even before her fake fear. That napkin, the quick sketch of Monroe as a seductress in training. The sly grin. The pauses and downcast eyes.

Monroe wasn't mean . . . She wasn't.

An insistence that hadn't even needed to be made if it wasn't true, which Lacey would know. It put the idea that Monroe was mean, manipulative, the kind of person who treated others like playthings into Izzy's head even as Lacey denied it.

All of the little dots, dropped seemingly at random, to create a picture of a girl. And it was all lies.

She hadn't stopped at Monroe, either.

I hope I didn't make you think anything bad about Mia.

That had been too brash, too much. Lacey had been slipping. An off note in an otherwise smooth concerto.

At the time, Izzy had paused but had written it off as jealousy of Mia. Maybe resentment for her surviving instead of Monroe.

But it was just another seed. She was setting something up.

What?

I hope I didn't make you think anything bad about Mia.

Just like with her assertion that Monroe wasn't mean, Lacey was putting the thought into Izzy's head even as she denied it, knowing it would stick there, fester, sour and oozing and begging to be noticed.

So what had it accomplished?

Lacey had said Mia showed up at the Bell mansion that day, upset about Cash, about Asher. Then she'd gotten quiet and left.

It hit Izzy then. Lacey was going to pin it all on Mia.

That was the missing long-term plan, the one Izzy couldn't figure out. Mia was going to take the fall for whatever had happened that night. Perhaps there was even a record of her traveling to the island in the last couple of months, one that Izzy would conveniently find at the right time.

A sharp buzzing threatened at the corner of Izzy's brain, and she forced herself to ignore it.

Had this been Lacey's strategy all along? For decades?

Lacey said she didn't know how Earl had gotten there so fast.

That had been Edie's retelling of that night. That's what Lacey had kept saying, even then, even at fifteen. Earl must have been her first attempt at setting up a fall guy.

A sociopath in training.

That Bell girl. The voice of Cash's secretary, Dot, rang bitter and haunting in Izzy's mind. That Bell girl had been cruel to Dot, had goaded her into humiliating herself in front of her peers, had laughed, had laughed along with Mia.

And what had Lacey said about that night? That she was meeting Sammy Bowdoin. When she'd said it, she'd been defiant, all teenage pride and hurt ego that she'd been single in a group of coupled-up friends. It was so well played. Distract, deflect. A master manipulator at work, at ease knowing just how to work the strings.

Izzy licked her dry lips and dug her phone out of her pocket. Nothing from Mia. Had she even gotten any of Izzy's previous messages?

A horn honked in the distance, and Izzy recoiled, her body clearly braced for an attack that wasn't coming while she was still in the safety of her car.

The tangled nerves that sat heavy in her windpipe escaped on a breathy laugh that had nothing to do with humor, then got lost among the radio hosts' inane chatter. Izzy slapped at the controls, her fingers fumbling with the buttons until there was nothing but silence and her ragged inhales that sounded far too close to hyperventilation.

Izzy had to get back to St. Lucy's.

She pulled out onto the road, clearing her mind so that she didn't lose control of the car. The miles ticked by, and she barely acknowledged them. The only thing that sank in was a sign letting her know she was twenty miles outside Rockport.

When she passed that, she reached over blindly, her hand groping for her purse. Without taking her eyes off the road, Izzy dug for the business card she knew she'd shoved in there.

Quinn picked up on the second ring. "Island Hops, how can I help you?"

"Quinn, it's Izzy. Santiago. From Rockport?"

The laugh on the other line was mocking. "Yeah, I remember you from a day ago, babe."

"Right. Are you still on the mainland?"

"Yup, stuck and bored as hell," Quinn said, clearly missing the tightness in Izzy's voice.

"Any chance you can fly me back to St. Lucy's?" Izzy asked, braking hard. She'd nearly blown through a red light without thought.

"No can do, babe," Quinn said. "Storm's still sitting just off the coast."

Izzy pulled the phone away from her ear to keep the string of curses that sat on her lips from reaching Quinn.

"Is there any way to get back to the island? Other than you?" Izzy asked.

There was a long pause, a new kind of silence. Not the bored kind. Quinn must have finally picked up on something. "What's going on?"

"I need to get back to St. Lucy's, Quinn," Izzy said.

Izzy could hear Quinn breathing, but she didn't push. They were on the precipice of something, and Izzy didn't want it to go the wrong way.

"Okay."

Izzy closed her eyes for a heartbeat, afraid she was misunderstanding. "You'll take me?"

"We both might die," Quinn said, and she was back to the careless attitude from before. Izzy couldn't tell if she was just confident or if it was gallows humor. "But there's a small gap in the clouds. Normally I wouldn't risk it, but . . ."

"Thank you," Izzy said on an exhale.

"You gotta be here in like fifteen minutes or the deal's off."

Izzy glanced at the dashboard clock, trying to calculate all the possibilities. The only one that was realistic was driving directly to the docks. And even then, she'd be cutting it close.

"I'll be there," Izzy said, then paused. They weren't going to beat Lacey by charging in, guns drawn. For one, they had no evidence. She'd made sure of that. And two, she was much too smart to be caught off guard. Izzy could bet money that she had a plan on how this was going to end. "Would anyone on the island think you could make it back in this storm?"

Quinn hummed in thought. "Nah. They'll think I'm stuck."

Izzy smiled for the first time all day. "Perfect."

CHAPTER TWENTY-SEVEN

MIA

Mia didn't take her eyes off Lacey as the woman stepped farther into the kitchen, closer to Robert. "Game?"

"The daring escape, of course," Lacey said, tilting her head, a childlike smile on her lips. "I thought you'd appreciate the challenge, Detective. And this pup is so willing to play." Lacey patted Robert on the cheek. "So eager for a treat."

Robert's hand shook, but the gun stayed pointed at Mia's chest. Tears had turned his eyes glassy, and a low whine caught in his mouth as his gaze flicked almost helplessly to Lacey's face. Embarrassment for the man burned hot in Mia's cheeks.

Lacey had done a number on him.

"See, what a good boy," Lacey cooed, her pointed nails scraping along his jaw in a facsimile of petting. Goose bumps that had nothing to do with the cold pulled tight on Mia's arms. "Now you're going to stay right here, and keep the detective where she is, okay?"

Robert nodded but didn't try to speak, and Lacey turned her full attention to Mia. She didn't come closer, though. Instead, she hopped up onto the kitchen counter, just like she had in their interview.

Lacey wasn't twitchy this time. Her body was held in complete control, and Mia realized just how deep her act went.

The pieces still didn't all fit yet. But Mia knew that she'd been played.

Monroe hadn't been the one to tell Cash about the pregnancy that summer. Lacey had. She was the only possibility. It hadn't been Asher, because Cash went to confront him. And it certainly hadn't been Mia.

That alone wouldn't have been enough to set off alarm bells—Lacey could have been protecting her sister, or maybe she hadn't known whom else to talk to so she went to Cash.

Except . . .

Except that Izzy said Lacey hadn't known Monroe was pregnant when she'd questioned her. That Lacey hadn't come right out and said Cash was lying about the baby, but she'd acted nervous.

"Was Monroe pregnant?" Mia asked now, simple curiosity driving the question at this point.

"Sweet Princess Monroe, pregnant at sixteen?" Lacey tipped her head back and laughed, rusted wind chimes. "Can you imagine?"

Mia tried to remember Monroe without all of the suggestions Lacey had planted getting in the way. She'd been funny. Self-deprecating. A little mischievous, but never unkind. At least that's what Mia had thought before a few days ago.

"God, she was a prissy bitch, and you all worshipped her." Lacey's voice was threaded with bitterness, the tang of it metallic against Mia's taste buds as she breathed it in.

"You killed her," Mia said, watching for anything. A flicker of emotion. Regret. Grief. Anything.

And yet Lacey's smile didn't change. The dreamy quality of it would have Mia questioning Lacey's sanity if not for the sharpness in her eyes.

"Uh-uh-uh, Detective." Lacey wagged her finger at Mia. "I'm not a killer. How dare you throw around such slander."

Mia closed her eyes, trying desperately to remember anything past the sharp slice of razor against skin. There was only darkness.

But saliva pooled in her mouth, and she swallowed against the bile that burned at the base of her esophagus. "Asher."

Lacey clapped, a giddy schoolgirl, and kicked her heels against the bottom cabinets in some kind of celebration. "Oh, brava, Detective," she said, her smile turning sly. "And it's only taken you fifteen years to figure it out."

"Why would he have . . . ?"

"Puppies are so easy to train, don't you think?" Lacey asked, reaching out to slip her fingers into what remained of Robert's hair, not even flinching at the sweat and grease. He didn't shift away, almost nudged into the caress even as he stood bleeding from wounds Lacey had inflicted. This was no amateur; this was a skilled sociopath with years of practice.

Everyone's scared. Mia wondered how many people on the island Lacey had worked her manipulation on. Jimmy, who had fear in his eyes. Dot, who still had venom in her mouth. Ellen and her parting shot: *Define "friends."*

Cash.

Mia wondered just how much his memories, his behaviors had been shaped and dictated.

Lacey was watching her closely, continuing: "See, this one here, he's quite weak. Doesn't care about many things. All he wants is for the pain to stop."

"You told him you'd let him go if he played this silly little"—Mia waved to encompass the room—"game. You told him he'd be free?"

Pleasure sparked, quick and gone, over Lacey's face. "No, darling. I told him the pain would stop."

Robert whined, a reedy, broken plea, knowing that was his death sentence, but Mia couldn't spare him a thought.

"And Asher?"

Lacey tipped her head to the side, her eyes hooded, coy and smug at once. "Jealousy is sinfully potent, isn't it?"

"But Cash said he wasn't sleeping with Monroe. Why would Asher . . . ?"

The small smile didn't fade as Lacey just continued to watch her, patient. "It wasn't about Monroe, darling."

Mia shook her head, her memories slotting, reslotting as she caught on to what Lacey was hinting at. But, no. Asher hadn't wanted Mia like that.

"He had Monroe. He loved her." That Mia trusted. "He didn't care about me. About me and Cash."

The look Lacey gave her was genuine pity. "Please. You're not that stupid."

"He didn't," she said again, but this time mostly to herself. He didn't. But that picture lingered behind the denial, the one of them dancing. The one where it hadn't been a joke. Mia whispered the accusation as it came to her.

Lacey straightened. "Do you really understand so little? That's disappointing."

Maybe that was supposed to be a jab, but Mia didn't care. The more Lacey talked, the more time Mia had. "What am I supposed to understand?"

"It's one of those truths that make humans so exquisitely predictable," Lacey said. "Children only want a toy when someone else has it. Asher couldn't just let Cash play with his toy, now could he?"

Mia cringed. "Asher wasn't like that. You made him think that."

"I simply offered him a sympathetic ear." Lacey shrugged. "Is that really such a terrible crime?"

"You planted suggestions." Just like Lacey had been doing this whole investigation. Again, she said, "You made him think that."

"Everyone has buttons you can push." Lacey lazily shrugged one shoulder before pinching Robert's earlobe hard enough to make him wince. The gun still didn't waver. "You just have to find the right ones."

"What are yours then, Lacey?" Mia asked.

"Oh." Lacey let go of Robert and slid off the counter. She edged around the table until she was close to Mia but not within arm's reach. Her eyes were dark, dilated. Mia flushed hot, her pulse thrumming in every soft spot on her body. "That was actually a good question, Detective. I'm almost impressed."

Mia pressed her lips together so that they wouldn't tremble as she inhaled through her nose. The slip of oxygen along her throat steadied her. "Enough to answer?"

Lacey laughed, the serrated edges of it slicing into Mia's skin. She tried not to recoil.

Without warning, Lacey reached out, her hand catching the back of Mia's neck. Her breath was too warm against Mia's ear. "Boredom."

She was gone as quick as she'd come, before Mia could even react. Dancing away, giggling.

"Boredom," Mia repeated, fighting the urge to swipe at the smear of lipstick that Lacey had left behind on her skin.

"That summer was so fucking boring," Lacey said, hopping back up on the counter. "Don't you remember? But you all . . ."

She trailed off and tipped her head back, an undulating shiver running through her body. "All of your petty drama and big eyes and fragile emotions." She met Mia's gaze, her own lashes heavy. "Delicious."

"Was Cash supposed to be there that night?"

For the first time since she'd walked into the kitchen, Lacey's glee flickered. "He was supposed to be. I don't know why . . ." Lacey paused, shook her head. Thrown for the first time all night. When she continued, it was soft, more to herself than to Mia, her eyes on the floor. "But then I saw him."

It was a button to push, and it helped Mia wrap her arms around her own fear, helped her press it down. "Not quite as in control as you thought, huh? You couldn't get him to do exactly what you wanted?"

Lacey's nostrils flared. Anger. That was so much better than the odd high Lacey had been riding. Anger made people lose control.

"Pup, give me the gun," Lacey said to Robert, her palm out, her gaze locked on Mia still. Mia's heartbeat tripped, that panic she'd just reined in snapping at its restraints, begging to be let free.

She eyed the door. Too far. The table would provide some cover if she could be quick about it, but it would be a risk.

"Please don't think I won't shoot if you so much as breathe wrong, Detective."

Dead if she did, dead if she didn't. At least Mia could try. Go down with a fight. Her thighs tensed, and she shifted her weight to one hip, ready to fling herself sideways.

"Oh, calm down, I'm just going to have pup here tie you up," Lacey said, waving toward Robert. He took his cue and crossed the room, his eyes on the floor.

Mia gauged his slender frame. She could take him, but a hostage was only as valuable as their worth to whoever had the gun. Mia guessed Lacey would shoot through his body to get to her. She held her hands out.

Robert slipped a zip tie over her wrists, and Mia thanked God for small favors. As long as she was standing, the plastic was easy enough to overcome. But then he bent and began tying a rope around her ankle, to the base of the heavy bench of the kitchen table.

Lacey watched, patient and assessing, until he stepped back. Then she held out the gun for Robert to take, crossed the room in three long strides, and slapped Mia so hard she ended up on the floor, with nothing to break her fall. Her elbow caught most of her weight. Spiky, white flashes of pain radiated out from her arm, her nerve endings begging for relief that didn't come.

When Mia was finally able to blink her eyes open, Lacey was hovering over her, gripping her chin. Mia tried to pull away, but Lacey held firm.

"Everyone does what I tell them," Lacey said, her voice disturbing in its calmness, a stark contrast to the violence of her handprint on Mia's cheek.

It was a remarkable study in Lacey's tight control of her own anger. Mia had provoked her over Cash so long ago, and yet she'd sat, unperturbed, through Robert's fumbling attempts to bind Mia. Only when it was safe to act did Lacey let loose her rage.

Mia didn't move, her eyes slipping over each of Lacey's features, cataloging the twist of her lips, the sigh that escaped when she sat back on her heels.

"Asher wouldn't have hurt me," Mia said, taking advantage of being so close to Lacey. Without her constant fidgeting, she was so much easier to read. Before, her tells got lost in a constant barrage of little movements. Now they were amplified by her stillness.

Lacey was thinking about lying.

Mia could see it in the tug of her mouth, caught between a smirk and a grimace. She could see it in Lacey's eyes, the way they darted to the side and then flicked up—so fast Mia almost missed it. She could see it in the press of Lacey's knuckle against her own thigh. The truth or a lie? Mia waited.

Lacey leaned forward, her delicate hand pulling at Mia's wrist until she was no longer sprawled on the floor but rather sitting up, in danger of tipping into Lacey's lap. Thumbs dug into Mia's flesh as Lacey maneuvered her forearms within the tight confines of the plastic zip tie. She didn't let up until Mia's left wrist was showing, the razor-thin scar almost terrifically beautiful against Mia's pale skin.

Ducking her head, Lacey pressed her lips to it like it was a cherished child, lingering at Mia's pulse point when she drew back.

This should have been the moment where Mia moved, kicked, lashed out, grabbed Lacey's hair or necklace or hands, which still cradled Mia's. But her muscles had locked up with the gentle touch of mouth against scar, her lungs refusing to drag in air, her vision blurred with tears.

"Tell me," Mia whispered into the hushed room. "Who did it?"

Lacey's fingertip traced along the smooth line, again, and again, and again. But her hungry, greedy eyes were locked with Mia's.

"You did, darling." The words dripped, poison coated, from slick cherry lips.

Everything unlocked. Oxygen was followed swiftly by adrenaline, and her body throbbed beneath the onslaught of chemicals. "No."

It came out as a raspy exhale instead of the denial she'd intended.

Lacey scrunched her nose, as if unbearably fond of an endearing pet. "You, you were the best of all of them."

"No." It was firmer this time.

Lacey smiled, and it was that same dreamy one she'd worn earlier. "Memories are funny, aren't they? They only show us what we think happened, not what really did."

Without warning, the tip of Lacey's nail burrowed into the end of the scar, and the pain that licked up Mia's arm brought with it glimpses of that summer, the rose-gold nostalgia stripped away.

At the beach—the bonfire that first night. Mia had turned to find Lacey watching her instead of Monroe and Asher.

Mia stood up, the edges of Cash's fingers trailing over the frayed hem of her jean shorts, and walked toward the beach. Lacey was sitting on the slick black rocks, the ocean teasing at her feet.

"Don't feel bad. No one can take their eyes off her," Lacey said as Mia sat, pulling her legs up to her chest.

"What?"

Lacey threw her a pitying look that, coming from the younger girl, jangled at Mia's nerves. "Your boys there."

Mia glanced back toward the bonfire. Cash's gaze was still fixed on the scene across from him, the intertwined pair.

Lacey waited for Mia's attention to shift back and then raised one perfectly plucked brow, the corner of her lip lifting in nothing resembling amusement. "You'll see."

"We didn't . . . We didn't ever talk," Mia stuttered, gasping out of the memory. "You and I. We never talked."

"Is that how it went?" Lacey asked.

Mia never climbed up to the lighthouse's lookout tower by herself. But tonight she went up the stairs, holding tight to the bottle of Eagle Rare she'd nabbed from the bar when Max wasn't looking. She'd leave him a twenty in the register later, but she'd needed the numbness it had offered, and Mama had run out of her supply.

Mia went out onto the metal grating that circled the tower, her legs slipping through the bars, her butt at the very edge. When she looked out, there seemed to be nothing beneath her, nothing in front of her. Just water and emptiness.

"You gonna share?" Lacey asked from the doorway. She must have seen Mia, must have followed her. If it had been someone else, Mia would have been annoyed. But Lacey didn't know her, didn't give a shit about her. Right now, it was what Mia needed. Someone who didn't give a shit.

She took a too-big swig, then held out the bottle.

Time passed until it became meaningless. Only after what had to be hours did Lacey ask what happened.

"Didn't get the scholarship." Mia shrugged, as if it didn't mean anything. As if her world hadn't shattered. "Means I'll be stuck here after school. Forever."

"You fucked it up?" Lacey asked, in that blunt way of hers that was just on the wrong side of painful.

"Yup."

"We can be fuckups together."

Then there was that picture of Lacey and Mia in Cash's attic, at the festival, a mini tableau of jealousy and anger playing out behind them.

"Here, smile big and pretty," Lacey said, smooshing her cheek to Mia's, holding the camera at arm's length, tilted just enough that she was probably capturing Cash talking to Monroe, too. Probably capturing the scene from which Mia had just ripped her attention.

Mia plastered on something that must've looked like a grimace, the flash blinding when they had adjusted to the dark. Lacey's fingers dug into the flesh of Mia's upper arm, painful and bruising, and Mia pulled away.

But Lacey didn't let her get far, her eyes locked on Mia's face, unwavering in their intensity.

She leaned in, quick, a snake striking, and pressed her gloss-sticky lips to the hollow of Mia's cheek, the smack of it loud and exaggerated.

"I told you," Lacey whispered, her mouth now at Mia's temple, as if comforting a child. "I told you he'd get tired of you."

Then she was gone, lost in the festival's crowd, Mia left once again watching Cash watch Asher and Monroe as they walked away from him together, just like that first night at the beach.

Mia blinked back into the present, even as the memories of a million little barbs wrapped around her, slid into her chest, her belly, every empty, aching part of her. Lacey had chipped away at Mia that summer, slow and methodical, patient and vicious.

Lacey leaned forward until her nose brushed lovingly against Mia's cheek. Her lips came to rest along Mia's hairline, so she could murmur in her ear, just like she had that one night. "You, darling, are my masterpiece."

And maybe Lacey was too used to the way she could make her puppets dance to worry about Mia. But Mia wasn't a scared little girl.

She deliberately let out a shattered breath, one that made it sound like she was on the verge of giving in completely.

Then, without hesitation, Mia brought her bound hands up and over Lacey's head so that her wrists rested at the nape of Lacey's neck. There was only a second to savor the flash of surprise on Lacey's face before Mia used the leverage she'd just gained to slam her forehead into the woman's nose.

The crack that sliced through the quiet was satisfying, though Mia knew she wouldn't go down completely. The hit had done enough that Lacey went a little limp, her hands clutching at her face. Mia unlooped her arms from around Lacey's neck and pushed her, hard, so that she went easily to the floor.

Then Mia rolled up to her feet and repeated the motion she'd executed in the basement, bringing her arms up and then down quickly. By this point her wrists were rubbed raw, bleeding in spots, but it didn't matter. The plastic snapped.

She glanced at Robert, who was staring back wide eyed. When his finger didn't twitch against the trigger, Mia bent, and with a few easy tugs the knot around her ankles relaxed. Not only had it been tied by inexpert hands, but as Lacey had been talking, Mia had been slowly working it loose with small movements.

Mia had two options: Either fade into the shadows of the house in the hope of getting lost in the vastness of its long hallways and empty rooms. Or risk the temperatures outside, the snow, and the ice with her damp jeans and T-shirt.

Get the hell out of there, Hart.

Without hesitation, Mia ran to the door, flung it open, and fled into the safety of the night.

CHAPTER
TWENTY-EIGHT
Izzy

The wings of the plane tipped precariously against the wind. Izzy clutched the handle of the door, her fingers numb from the strain of it.

"Almost there," Quinn yelled out, but there was a smile on her face. Maybe someone had to be slightly deranged to fly in this weather.

Izzy flashed her a quick thumbs-up with her free hand and then concentrated on swallowing the extra spit that was gathering in her mouth.

Soon enough, Quinn was directing the nose of the plane toward the water. The little thing was so light that Izzy thought it might just get taken away by a strong gust, but they did manage to land. It wasn't smooth, and Izzy had been praying even though she stopped praying years ago.

"Quinn, don't tell anyone I'm back, okay?" Izzy said after she'd crawled out onto the dock. She wanted to just lie there on her back, feel the solid ground beneath her weight. But she indulged for only the space of a heartbeat before she was on her feet again. Moving.

"Aye, aye, captain," Quinn shouted at her back. Izzy shook her head, bemused by the woman but also so grateful to her that Izzy spared the moment to turn and wave.

Then she started up the hill as fast as the freshly fallen snow would allow. Izzy would start at Edie Hart's house, then go from there. Mia had mentioned searching Cash Bishop's place for things Earl had left behind. That would be her next stop.

The minute she stepped into Edie's pale pink house, Izzy knew it was empty and wrong.

Izzy had spent the morning keeping the worst-case scenarios at bay, but they started circling now, prowling at the boundaries of her self-control.

She went through the rooms, but each confirmed her initial impression. There was no one there.

But. Nothing was overturned. Nothing broken or in disarray. This was not the scene of a crime.

Before leaving, she jotted a quick note, just in case Mia came back. When she was done, she started down the hill at a near run, anxiety not so quietly pacing along the inside of her skull.

Not yet, not yet, not yet. The mantra kept it at bay, each boot fall drilling in the point.

By the time she got to Bishop's front door, Izzy was panting, in a combination of exertion and fear. She pounded on the wood with both fists, just as Cash had done days earlier when he'd found Earl.

The thought gave her pause. Lacey had probably killed the older Bishop. She'd been in town that night; she'd been at the bar. She must have stayed with Cash after.

One more victim. The tally kept ticking up.

The door gave way beneath her hands as Cash ripped it open. Izzy hadn't yet figured out if he was involved, but she had to risk it.

"Is Mia here?"

"Izzy," Cash said, which wasn't an answer. She wanted to grip him by the collar of his shirt, haul him into the air, just like he'd done with Mia.

"Is. Mia. Here?" Izzy repeated, patience long ago worn thin.

"She was. But she left. Maybe an hour or two ago?"

"Shit." The curse was wrenched from her, and Cash shifted back as if it had been a slap.

"Did you ever see the body?" Izzy asked, her eyes on his face.

He blinked, but in surprise. "From the bay? The reporter's? No."

Izzy glanced around. There was no one to overhear the conversation. She weighed her options. There was a good chance Mia was at the diner or at the store or back at Jimmy's. But there was an uneasiness in her gut that was telling her that wasn't the case. If Lacey had Mia, Izzy would need help. She licked her lips, turning back to Cash.

"I need you to tell me where you were that night," Izzy finally said. "I need you tell me, and I need you not to lie. Do you understand?"

Cash swiveled his jaw, opened his mouth, closed it. His gaze flicked past her, out to the bay. They stood like that, in silence, for far too long. But she didn't push.

Finally, he nodded once.

"I was at the lighthouse."

CHAPTER TWENTY-NINE

MIA

The snow gave way beneath Mia's bare feet, the frozen crust shattering so that it sliced at her skin. She knew it should hurt, but it was nothing more than a nuisance—the crimson drops a breadcrumb trail that would make her easier to follow.

Mia tripped, went down on a knee, and the world spun out from underneath her even as she remained still, frozen where she'd crouched. Her chest was tight, her head thick, filled with heavy words and blurry thoughts. The heartbeat that should have been thundering at her pulse points was weak, thready when she found it with the tips of fingers that scrambled at clammy skin.

Soon everything would be numb. Then warm.

It was animal instinct more than anything else that had her stumbling back up to her feet, to keep moving forward, even as her palms caught, ripped along the sharp barbs of the fence lining the gardens.

The dramatic black rock cliffs fell off into the ocean to her left, the Bell mansion stood in the distance to her right.

The forest. It wasn't far. She could lose herself in it, find some kind of shelter.

The lighthouse, her traitorous mind whispered.

And she was running again.

Wind lashed against her, a whip biting into flesh. Her skin burned. She kept running. The trees would protect her. *Get to the trees.*

A wall of silence slammed into her when she made it to the woods— the waves, the wind, her blood all silenced.

The hush was not welcoming, though. It wasn't the pause after a sigh of relief. It was the breath that was bated while watching prey scamper from predator. It was the silence right before a kill.

Mia kept running.

CHAPTER THIRTY

Izzy

"It's not what you think," Cash told Izzy, as he closed the front door behind them. "I was at the lighthouse. But I didn't hurt them."

Izzy pressed her palm to where her headache throbbed, vicious in its relentlessness.

"You have one chance to tell me everything," Izzy gritted out. "And then I'm arresting you on obstruction charges."

Cash smiled sadly when she opened her eyes. "You guys keep forgetting I'm a lawyer."

"You really want to test me right now?" Izzy asked, and his face slipped back into an impassive mask once more.

"I was grounded that night, like I told you," Cash started without preamble. "But I snuck out. The window in my bathroom is right above the back porch's roof. It wasn't hard. I think Dad even knew I was going."

"Okay."

"Lacey had told me to meet them all at the lighthouse. I was . . ." He sucked his bottom lip between his teeth. "Hesitant. If you can imagine. I'd punched Ash earlier."

"But you went anyway?"

"I got there too early. No one else had showed yet," Cash went on. "I went up to the tower—there's some grating up there. Sat and watched the sunset."

"Can we stick to the pertinent details here, Bishop?" Izzy rolled her finger in a *get this moving* gesture.

Cash sighed. "Asher and Mia showed up first. They didn't see me, and I didn't go down. They could be weird sometimes."

"Weird how?"

"I don't know," Cash said, but he wasn't meeting her gaze. "Think it screwed both of them up."

"What did?"

"Us. Me and Mia." Cash shrugged. "Asher and Monroe. Mia always said she wasn't jealous, but . . ."

If the question even had to be asked, there had probably been truth to it.

"Anyway, Monroe showed up after a while. They talked a bit, but I couldn't hear what they were saying." Cash shoved his hands in his pockets, rocked on his heels, and stared at a spot just beyond Izzy's shoulder. "I just remember not wanting to be there, wanting to be home again."

"Did anyone else come in?" *Lacey. Did Lacey come in?*

"No, just them," Cash said, and she didn't know if she believed him. Or if he thought it was the truth.

But Lacey must have been there at some point. If Izzy was right about her.

"When did you realize something was wrong?"

Cash pressed his lips together before taking a deep breath. "It went quiet. I'd never felt that kind of quiet before."

"What kind?"

"The kind that feels like death." Cash finally met her eyes. Sweat beaded along his upper lip, and he licked at it, his tongue dragging along the skin there. "I ran down."

The truth? Maybe. "You did?"

He thumbed at the space between his brows, and she wondered if his headache mirrored hers. "Believe me, I didn't want to. Back then, though . . ."

They both paused. They both knew Izzy could see what he was now, could see the cracks in his character that everyone else seemed to gloss over.

"Back then I thought I was brave." The corners of Cash's lips tipped up in self-mockery.

Izzy stayed still.

"There was so much blood. God." He pushed his fingers through his hair. "I, um . . . Mia was on the floor, and when she looked at me . . ."

His eyes dropped down to his lap. The tick of a clock somewhere behind him counted the hesitation, each second more damning than the last.

When he drew in a breath, Izzy's pulse tripped because he still hadn't mentioned Lacey being there. But Izzy had to be right about it. Who else could Charles have meant? *Her.*

Except . . . Except there was another *her.*

"When Mia looked at me. She said"—Cash paused, glanced up—"she said, 'They weren't supposed to cut that deep.'"

Izzy's brain tripped. "What?"

Cash shoved his fingers through his hair, yanked. "God, I ran over to her—she'd just done the one wrist—it was pretty shallow. I took the razor from her, and she just smiled up at me."

"It was just the three of them?" Izzy clarified again. Lacey. Where had Lacey been?

Her. Her. It had to be Lacey. Everything else fit.

For the first time since Izzy had stepped into the house, Cash's attention really focused on her. "Who else would have been there?"

She shook her head, a dismissal she didn't know if he'd let her get away with. "What happened after you found her?"

"I don't know, I think I was yelling at her," Cash said. "It's kind of hazy. But I remember I was terrified. I grabbed her shoulders at one point, pulled her to her feet, and shook her a little. She looked doped up on something, so I slapped her across the cheek like they do in movies." His cheeks flushed red at the admission.

"Did that work?"

"Yeah, it was like a light had switched." Cash nodded. "She went wild, thought she could help the other two but . . ."

It was too late.

A fucking suicide pact. This whole thing had been an actual suicide pact. Or at least an attempt. *They weren't supposed to cut that deep.* What did that even mean?

Her.

"When did you leave?" Izzy asked.

"After she ran out, saying she was going to get help." Cash shrugged. "I couldn't stay there. You don't . . . you don't know." His eyes snapped to hers. "There wasn't anything else I could do."

Something slid into place. *She kept asking how Earl had gotten there so fast.*

"You called your dad."

He nodded, just once.

"Henry Jackson and Jimmy Roarke weren't helping cover up a crime Earl committed," Izzy said slowly. "They were helping clean up after you."

"I didn't . . . I didn't do anything," Cash said, his voice small.

"Right. You didn't."

Cash flinched, the blow squarely landing. He didn't defend himself.

So where did Lacey come in? "There were just the three of them," Izzy repeated, almost without putting sound to the words.

"You keep saying that," Cash said. "Why?"

Izzy made a decision. "Because, if I'm right about everything else, there should have been one more."

CHAPTER THIRTY-ONE

MIA

Lacey was behind Mia.

Mia could sense it more than hear it, as she dodged through the branches. Broken, brittle limbs caught at her exposed arms, and blood trickled from her hairline, dripping off her jaw into the hollow of her collarbone.

The lighthouse was close. It had a door. She could lock it. Maybe the phone line was even working. She couldn't picture it. Everything that had happened before this moment, this chase, this consuming desperation for survival, was lost to adrenaline.

There.

The clearing. Up ahead. Her thighs bunched as she picked up her pace, careful not to stumble again, careful not to give up her seconds—minutes maybe—of advantage.

A meadow stretched out before her, open, wide, and exposed. It was what stood between her and the relative safety of the lighthouse. The potential vulnerability scared her, terrified her so that panic throbbed along with each step she took closer.

It was evening, but early evening, so there was no bright moon to betray her movements, no silver to catch on pale white flesh. Just a blue-tinged darkness that should shroud her in shadows. If she was lucky.

She paused just at the edge of the tree line, the animal in her whimpering at the thought of going out in the open. But the only other choice was to stay and be caught.

And she was not prey.

Mia took off. Her mind cleared of anything other than the siren's song of safety.

Time stretched, like it always did on the island, stretched and became meaningless beyond the distance her feet ate up. It stretched, it stretched, and then it snapped back. And she was there. In front of the door, grasping at the knob.

It refused to budge beneath her numb, frozen fingers, and the frustration nearly took her to the ground.

Key. It was a shout inside her own head, loud and demanding.

There was an extra key. She'd used it when she and Izzy had come.

Mia did drop to the ground then, but it was only to scramble in the drifting snow for the fake rock. It took two tries to get it out, the metal eventually falling into her trembling hands.

But it had taken her too long.

A gun pressed against the base of her neck, and Lacey's silky voice cut through the wind. "You know I'm not a killer, darling, but even I have my limits. Open the door."

It wasn't over, it wasn't over, the animal howled, pacing beneath the pressure of the barrel.

Still, she stepped into the little room, didn't try to take Lacey down in the open.

In the lighthouse, there was so much more to work with than there had been when she was bound on the floor in the abandoned house's kitchen.

The fear quieted, the roar of it, which had been so loud while she had been fleeing, settling into a buzz beneath her skin, bringing everything into focus. The rustle of Lacey's coat as she moved, the pungent must thick in the air, the splintered boards against her feet.

Lacey came in behind her, shutting the door as she did. She pouted at Mia. "You ran away. But we were having so much fun."

Mia didn't respond, didn't fall into the trap of engaging with the woman. Instead, she started to assess items as potential weapons or dismiss them as useless.

"Well, I can't say I'm disappointed," Lacey continued. "Back where it all started, huh? Fitting, I guess."

The jewelry box had sharp edges. The table was too heavy to lift.

"It actually adds a bit of poetry to my plan," Lacey said, her voice going singsong to try to goad Mia into answering.

If she broke one of the pictures on the wall, she might be able to use the glass. The poker by the fireplace was perfect, but far. The books were probably too light.

"You don't want to hear my plan?" Lacey pouted again, her lip slick with spit in the thin light filtering in through the window.

They were standing in shades of darkness. At least outside, the snow had helped a little. Now it was nearly pitch black. Lacey paced closer, probably wanting to see each emotion flick across Mia's face. "All right, you don't want to play? You'll just have to wait and see, then."

Before Mia could say anything at all, Lacey pulled out her cell phone. Mia thought of her own useless one, probably filled with messages from Izzy.

Lacey held the gun up to her own mouth in the *shhh* gesture, before winking at Mia.

She grinned, a flash of white teeth, when whomever she'd called picked up. Then she began to whisper, a quiver turning the words frantic, terrified, urgent.

"Oh, Detective Santiago, you have to help me. It's . . . It's Mia. She's . . . I think she's going to hurt someone. We're at the lighthouse. Please come. Fast."

CHAPTER
THIRTY-TWO

Mia

"Izzy's not even on the island, you know," Mia said, with a calm she actually felt. The chase was over. This was no longer about predator and prey but rather opportunity. And Mia was good at opportunity.

Lacey tucked the phone away into her jacket pocket. "My sources say otherwise, darling."

Mia hid her surprise beneath a question. "Sources?"

"You know, when you have a past to hide, it doesn't take a lot of persuasion to agree to certain favors."

"Ellen," Mia said, and it wasn't a guess. "You blackmailed her."

"Oh, darling, that's such a dirty word." Lacey's smug Cheshire cat smile was back. So pleased with herself. "She wasn't even a challenge."

"But I was?" Mia asked, because beneath everything else was an echo, faint but clear. *You are my masterpiece.*

"Deliciously so." Lacey stepped toward her but then seemed to think better of it. There was still blood smeared in the dip between her nose and mouth from where Mia had slammed into her. "Even more now. Harder to read. But everyone has their buttons."

"What are mine?" Mia asked. Izzy was on the island, Izzy was coming. There was no way she'd believe Lacey. All Mia had to do was stall.

"Hmmm." Lacey tapped the barrel of her gun against her lips, thinking. "Asher. Always has been."

Mia sucked in a breath, something slotting into place. "It was you, in the woods that first night."

"Did you think you were going crazy?" Lacey's voice was gleeful. "Did Detective Santiago think you were going crazy?"

Yes. To both.

"No." Mia shook her head.

"Don't lie, precious," Lacey cooed. "I heard you call out his name." She leaned forward. "It's the guilt."

"What else?" Mia said, ignoring the taunt. "My buttons, what else?" It was an obvious delay tactic, but Lacey didn't seem to mind.

"Hmm, Cash," Lacey said easily. "Though he should never have been. You were so much better than him. But he's still there, isn't he? Under your skin."

Mia just smiled. "If you think so." Anger. It was so much easier to work with. Maybe she could even provoke her enough to drop her guard.

"Oh, darling, don't try to lie," Lacey said smoothly, but she stepped closer. "I saw you two on the docks."

Were you jealous? But Mia swallowed the question, loath to be predictable. She bet Lacey loved when people were predictable.

"Does he know?" Mia asked instead.

"Oh please, he's an idiot." Lacey's lips twisted, dismissive. "You know he was there that night? He's the one who stopped you from going through with it."

Mia's vision tunneled, her mouth tangy with her surprise. "What?"

"Then he ran off like a coward dog. He's been absolutely eaten up with guilt ever since. It makes him so fun to play with." She paused. "It's the only thing interesting about him, you know."

Lacey leaned in, her eyebrows raised. "Do you want to know what's even better?" There was that giddy, dreamy quality to her voice again. "He saw me, outside, before you did. He thinks I've been keeping his secret for all this time."

She giggled then, and somehow the girlish pleasure in it was worse than the rusted wind chimes.

Something Cash said on the pier came back to Mia. "You made him think your father was contacting you again. The nightmares."

Lacey grinned, that Cheshire cat smugness making her features hard, ugly. "Can you imagine? If he'd gone off to find my father? Who, by the way, is a rotting vegetable. But Cash would find a little present there, just enough evidence to cement his belief that dear old Daddy Bell killed my beloved mother."

Mia's nails dug into her palms where her fingers had curled into fists as Lacey laughed again.

"He'd finally have something to do with all that exquisite guilt," Lacey continued. "He's quite slow on the uptake, but I was finally making headway with him. The nightmares really sold it, I will say."

Playthings. That's how Lacey saw people, not as humans but as dolls to be used for her enjoyment. Appealing to her humanity would be pointless here.

"Really," Lacey continued, "it was the only thing keeping me entertained in this joke of a place."

The disdain dripped from the words. "Why did you come back here, then?"

Rage rippled across her face, before it smoothed out again. "Daddy Bell isn't as dumb as he looks sometimes."

"He cut you off," Mia guessed. The Bell mansion was deeded to Lacey, but the rest of her life would have been funded by her parents. The punishment of banishment was perfectly cruel for the little sociopath.

Lacey pouted. "I should have solved the problem before he discovered my games. I would have inherited millions. But he gave the money away. To charity." She practically spit the last word. "The only thing that was left was enough for that shitty little house he's rotting in and his medical care. I can't get to that trust he set up."

"That must have really pissed you off, huh," Mia said, goading. She wanted Lacey as angry and sloppy as possible by the time Izzy got there.

But instead of sinking further into her rage, Lacey smiled, all sunshine again. "That's where Cash came in. My little guilty white knight, trying to save the day."

Mia sighed and shifted tactics. "Izzy's not going to believe you, you know."

Straightening, Lacey dabbed at the blood beneath her nose. In the dim light, Mia could already see bruises forming beneath her eyes. "Which one of us looks like they're the victim here?"

Mia didn't call attention to her state of undress, but Lacey must have noticed the way Mia couldn't help but grip her own arms, her body hungry for warmth. Lacey shrugged out of her own coat and tossed it to Mia. "Put it on," she said, with a little jab of the gun.

Despite whatever part the jacket was about to play in the scene Lacey had planned, Mia was grateful for it. The heat from Lacey's body lingered in its fabric, and Mia sank into it, ignoring the intimacy of the action. Tears gathered behind her closed lids at the reprieve from the cold.

Lacey tilted her head to study Mia, then nodded once, satisfied.

They both heard it at the same time. A tiny scrape of boot against stone.

Izzy.

Lacey flashed her one more bright smile and then whispered, "Catch."

On instinct alone, Mia grabbed the gun from the air, the weight of it so welcome and familiar that she didn't stop to think before she pointed it at Lacey.

In the next heartbeat, the door swung open, and Izzy was in the room.

———

Mia knew it looked bad. It was designed to.

"Drop the gun," Izzy said, as she charged through the door, her fingers fumbling for the light switch. The bulbs buzzed to life above them. The glow wasn't enough, but at least they were no longer dealing with shadows.

"No." Mia stayed calm, her gaze mostly tight on Lacey, but she couldn't help glancing at Izzy's weapon, which was firmly trained on her.

Lacey's eyes were wide, her breathing shallow. There was blood on her face, smeared across her cheek, while blue and green spread out from the bridge of her nose. She blinked at Izzy but didn't try to say anything.

A picture of the perfect victim.

Christ, she was good.

Izzy's tongue darted out over her bottom lip, her hands trembling around the grip of the gun. "Just drop the gun for now. Okay? We'll get it sorted, Mia."

"Don't—" Mia's voice was tight, harsh, when it came out. "Don't talk to me like that."

"Like what?"

"Like I'm the crazy one with a gun."

The silence was damning. *Come on, Izzy, fucking trust me.* She tried to say it with her eyes, but Izzy's were completely shuttered. It was the

322

same way she'd watched Mia throughout the case—a little wary, a little secretive.

Mia wondered what memories were flashing through Izzy's head, wondered how they'd be viewed under the light of Mia now holding a gun.

"Iz, I'm not going to drop it," Mia started, trying for calmer than before. Lacey had something planned, she was sure of it. And that plan involved Izzy thinking Mia was out of control. Mia needed Izzy firmly back on her side, and acting erratically wouldn't do it. No matter the hurt that ached like a wound in her chest. "I need to make sure she doesn't try anything."

A low chattering filled the quiet that followed. Lacey's teeth, and they both shifted toward her. With Mia wearing the coat, Lacey was dressed in a tank top and leggings, nothing more.

Helpless. She looked so tiny, so vulnerable, so helpless. But she'd called Izzy here. She'd thrown Mia her gun. There was definitely an exit strategy cooked up in her devious little mind, and it probably involved both Izzy's and Mia's deaths.

Mia's gaze flicked between Izzy and Lacey. "Here's what we're going to do," she said. "Izzy, do you have handcuffs?"

"I do," Izzy confirmed slowly. Then she deflected. "How about you place the weapon on the floor, and then we'll sort it."

"Izzy, she's been playing us this whole time." Mia switched tactics, even though it sounded desperate, like she was grasping at straws. That's why she hadn't said it before. "She's playing you right now."

"Funny, because she hasn't said anything," Izzy countered. "And you've done a lot of talking."

Frustration licked hot in Mia's belly, crowding out that hint of sadness. "Right before you walked in the door, she was holding the gun on me."

It sounded absurd. She *knew* it sounded absurd. That, coupled with the assertion that Lacey was playing them, was denting Mia's credibility with Izzy. But it was all she had left.

"Mia" is all Izzy responded with.

When Mia didn't say anything further, Izzy looked back at Lacey, whose lip trembled as if she were trying to speak, but no sound came out. "All right, come here, Lacey."

"You're going to cuff me?" There was a quiver in Lacey's voice that slipped like an itch beneath Mia's skin, burning and just out of reach. She wanted to slap her, see her crumple to the floor.

Instead, Mia remained where she was, not wanting to do anything to derail getting handcuffs on the sociopath.

Lacey stepped toward Izzy, her arms coming away from her body so that her wrists were held out, the picture of compliance.

"You're going to cuff yourself," Izzy said.

Lacey chewed on her lip but then moved closer. Mia could see the sweat that beaded along the line of her hair.

"Thank you for coming," Lacey whispered, loud enough for Mia to hear. The words meant to be a punch in the solar plexus for Izzy as Lacey took the cuffs.

In the next breath, Lacey looped the metal chain over Izzy's hand that was holding the gun. She twisted and then yanked it down, hard, so that the weapon clattered to the ground.

Lacey was quick to retrieve it, quick to move out of Izzy's arm's length.

"Don't even try, Mia," Lacey said, without taking her eyes off Izzy. "It's just blanks."

It had happened so fast Mia hadn't had the chance to pull the trigger, but she'd been lining up the sight.

Mia called her potential bluff, a loud crack shattering the silence. But no one fell, no blood spilled. Lacey just grinned at both of them and held up one finger. Then she dug her phone out from where she'd tucked it into the waistband of her leggings. It was lit up, and Mia got a glimpse of squiggly, electric lines. She'd been recording the exchange.

Lacey pressed stop.

"Just need to cut the end bit off," Lacey said to herself. "But that won't show up as tinkering when the tech guys check it."

"What?" Izzy was a step behind, but Mia could see what Lacey was planning. It was almost brilliant.

"I'm going to shoot you, Izzy," Mia said, her voice devoid of all emotion. Izzy flinched, her eyes going to the weapon, even though she knew there weren't actual bullets in the gun. Instinct. "And you'll have no choice but to take me out. Tragically, your wound will prove fatal."

Lacey did a silly little clap, her eyes lighting up, before aiming the gun at Izzy's chest once more. "See, Mia. That's why you're my masterpiece."

Shame spread across Izzy's cheeks, a red stain obvious even across the room. It did nothing to ease the anger shredding Mia's control. "Why the hell didn't you believe me?"

"Oh, don't be too harsh, darling," Lacey said, her voice honeyed, gleeful, clearly reveling in Mia's near tantrum. "Lesser souls have fallen prey. It's just so easy, don't you see? Barely even a challenge anymore. Though, I have to admit, this was particularly fun."

Lacey pointed the gun at her. "Detective, if you would so kindly cuff yourself. And then be a dear and step closer to Mia over here."

Izzy didn't even put up a fight, simply stepped around the sofa until she was all but shoulder to shoulder with Mia, locking the metal around her wrists as she went.

The docile response was the first thing that slipped through Mia's haze of rage. It was strange. There wasn't even a quip to accompany Izzy's surrender.

"That's close enough," Lacey said, words going sharp. She might just be realizing that it wasn't a good idea to have them this near to each other. "Now, Detectives, I have one more thing to take care of, and I'm going to need you to be dead silent for it."

Mia huffed out a disbelieving breath, and Lacey's eyes snapped to hers. "I can shoot you in a very painful place, or I can shoot you in a not so painful place, precious. Your choice."

The threat was meaningless. Mia didn't plan on going down without a fight either way, and Lacey wouldn't be able to control her aim in the chaos.

Lacey's attention was divided as she dialed some number and then held the phone up to her ear.

"Don't do anything stupid," Izzy said under her breath.

Mia went stiff as the words hit her, but she didn't acknowledge the warning in any other way. Was Izzy planning something? Or was that just a general request?

Just then, Lacey let out a wet, broken sob. It tore through the room, pressing into all the corners and hidden spaces.

"Gina? Gina Murdoch?" Lacey struggled to get out. "I . . ."

Her voice wobbled, collapsed into sobs again. "They're dead. They're dead."

There was tinny shouting on the other end. But it wasn't clear enough to make out.

"Mia shot . . ." Lacey wavered again, breathed deep. "Detective Santiago. I tried. I tried to save her, but I . . . I . . ."

She heaved in a breath, as if she were trying to stop a panic attack. "I'm sorry," she cried out. "I'm so sorry. I couldn't save her."

And then she pulled the phone away and ended the call.

When she glanced back at them, she sighed happily, her eyes dry, her smile too big for her face.

"Isn't it all just so perfect?"

CHAPTER THIRTY-THREE

Izzy

Izzy could practically smell the tang of Mia's rage, but it was layered now. Confusion lingered in the tightness of her shoulders.

Don't do anything stupid. Izzy thought it again, not willing to risk another warning.

"Wait," Izzy called out, even though Lacey hadn't moved to shoot them yet. "You have to tell me something. Before you, you know"—she gestured to the gun—"kill us."

It was a distraction, and Lacey was going to fall for it. Because, Izzy guessed, if there was something Lacey loved more than anything else, it was talking about how clever she was.

"Hmm, you're not exactly in a position to be making demands, Detective." Lacey trailed one finger along the barrel of the gun. But that wasn't quite a no.

"What was up with Peter?"

"Ah, Peter." Lacey sighed. "He screamed so beautifully."

Izzy cringed.

"Peter, Peter, Peter," Lacey hummed. "He was very naughty, that one. He liked to snoop and found all my souvenirs."

Mia shuddered beside Izzy. "Souvenirs?"

Lacey smiled at her. "My mementos. I have a razor blade from that night. It has your blood on it, darling."

Izzy's stomach rolled, then clenched. Beside her, Mia bent in two, her body heaving as she gagged against nothing. As soon as Izzy shifted to help her, though, Lacey swung the gun on her. "No."

Straightening, Mia waved Izzy off anyway, before wiping her mouth with the back of her hand. The mask was back in place only seconds later.

"I'm not mad at him, though," Lacey continued. "At first, I was very angry, of course. Especially when he left the island. But then he came back. And I knew what I was going to do."

The final pin dropped. "He was bait," Izzy said.

Lacey's mouth dropped open in delighted surprise. "Detective, I knew I liked you. Your brain is so clever. I wish you weren't so easy to toy with." Lacey batted her lashes at Izzy. "We could have had such fun, you and I."

"Bait?" Mia asked. "For me?"

"Hmm, yes," Lacey said, her eyes focused on Mia. "That reporter came and messed everything up. But I like to improvise. I had been trying to figure out a purpose for Sammy, anyway. He needed a bit of direction in his life."

"Why switch their identities, though?" Izzy asked. She got why it would have been risky to have Peter turn up dead that close to when he'd been staying with Lacey. She would have been the first suspect they would have looked at. But it all seemed unnecessarily complicated to have Sammy lie about the identity of the body. "Why not just kill Robert and use him to get Mia here?"

Lacey's lip tipped up, and she raised her brows, a teacher waiting for them to figure out the solution.

It was Mia who finally answered. "Because Peter was the one I recognized. He must have told you he tried to contact me."

"Brava, precious." Lacey sent her a fond look that had saliva pooling in Izzy's mouth once more. "He disclosed that little fact . . . right before his very timely death."

When they simply stared at her, Lacey laughed. "Oh, come now, Detective Santiago. You have to admit that it made you look at our dear Mia here differently. When she recognized the body."

Izzy couldn't deny it. Lacey knew she couldn't deny it.

"Yes, Sammy filled me in on that delicious moment," Lacey purred. "It set everything in motion. 'The Unraveling of Mia Hart'—a tragic but satisfyingly logical tale. You, Detective Santiago, acted your scenes beautifully, darling. You are the fruit of my labor."

Izzy's skin went itchy and tight, and she wanted to dig her nails in, scratch until the memories of those words were nothing but red track lines on her arms.

"So you killed Peter?" Izzy asked bluntly.

"Killed is such a dirty word, isn't it?" Lacey said. "I helped him ease his pain. He had some ugly wounds from our time together."

"Ease his pain with a gunshot through his palate," Izzy said.

"Hmm, no. I've never killed anyone, Detective," Lacey corrected. "I simply gave him options. That was the one he chose."

Suicide. The case had always been an odd combination of murder and suicide. Now it made sense. It had been both.

"What about Earl?" Izzy kept pushing. Mia shifted toward the mantel. The jewelry box, with its hard points. That's what Izzy would go for if she were Mia.

Don't do anything dumb. Please, Izzy tacked on, even if the request was trapped in her own brain.

"I heard Earl found some pills." Lacey pouted. "So tragic when they aren't kept locked up tightly."

Izzy tapped her foot once. She could tell Mia's attention wasn't on them.

"And your mother?"

Lacey flinched, visibly.

"Mother smoked," Lacey said finally, and this time the waver in her voice actually seemed real. "Nasty habit."

"I wonder how she fell asleep, though," Izzy said in a faux-curious tone. "With a lit cigarette. Seems awfully irresponsible." Izzy paused. "And don't you have a penchant for dipping into Daddy's medicine cabinet?"

Lacey glanced at Mia, furtive almost, then back to Izzy. "Mother was depressed. She took all kinds of pills to help her sleep."

"All right," Izzy finally said, easily. "Then what about us?"

"What do you mean?" Lacey asked, off balance for once. Izzy did a mental fist pump over what she was going to count as a victory.

"I'm not going to shoot Mia, and she won't shoot me." Izzy shrugged. "You're going to have to break your streak and actually get your hands dirty for once."

Lacey's mouth twisted as if she actually hadn't considered that. Which was strange seeing as how every other thing had been planned with such immaculate attention to detail.

Her face cleared, and she lifted one shoulder. "It has to be done."

Izzy's breath hitched. "So you're going to shoot us?" Izzy asked again. "Dead."

If Lacey thought about it, the clarification would seem odd. But she was too far gone for that. Or at least Izzy hoped.

"Gold star for following along, Detective," Lacey said slowly, but the skin near her eyes had gone tight. She was realizing it was an off note but seemed unable to stop herself from continuing. "Yes, I suppose I'll have to do it myself."

And there was their confession.

The world slowed down, the heady cocktail of stress and endorphins turning everything sharp and clear.

Izzy tipped her head back. "Now," she yelled, so loud that the waves of it crashed against the walls and pushed out into the night.

Lacey's eyes were wild, darting over their faces, to the door, to the stairs, back to Mia. Her finger tightened on the trigger, and Izzy could see the confusion, the hesitation, and then the slow and steady press of flesh against metal. The barrel was still aimed at Izzy's chest.

The door crashed open to her right, the wood splintering and then slamming against the wall. Voices yelled things that made no sense to Izzy, not in that moment.

And still they wouldn't be fast enough.

Lacey's eyes were bright. She hadn't even glanced toward the bodies flooding in from the outside.

Before Izzy could move or react, Mia stepped in front of her just as Lacey pulled the trigger.

The bullet slammed into Mia, and then Lacey's body hit the ground.

Izzy had been right. They hadn't been fast enough.

CHAPTER
THIRTY-FOUR
Izzy

Izzy hated hospitals. Maybe it was a cliché, but maybe she didn't care. The too-bright halls, the lemon disinfectant that burned her throat, the gray pallor of the nurses' skin. She couldn't stand any of it.

She smoothed her palm over her arms, a gesture she easily recognized as self-soothing, as she stepped into Mia's room.

It was empty save for Mia stretched out on the bed. Tubes pumped liquid into her veins; wires kept track of the fluttering heartbeat beneath her rib cage. Both served only to make her slender body appear all the more fragile. Utterly breakable. That's what she was.

Izzy pulled the visitors' chair right up next to the bed and watched the steady blinking light on the heart monitor.

Alive. That's what the rhythmic beeping told her. Mia was still alive.

Izzy held on to that, wrapped greedy arms around that certainty and kept it close.

Time passed, because that's what it did. Izzy didn't mark it, didn't note it. There was sun in the room and then there wasn't. A nurse tsk-tsked at her, tried to kick her out, but Izzy didn't budge, and the woman eventually relented.

All Izzy could do was hold her breath in the spaces between the little dings—the ones that spoke and said *Mia is alive.*

Izzy inhaled on one. Exhaled on the next.

When the machines went wild, Izzy straightened from her slouch too fast, the exhausted muscles in her neck pulling so tight that white-hot pain throbbed in her shoulder, up along the base of her skull. Nurses shoved into the room, pushing Izzy back against a wall.

She only realized she was shouting when someone grabbed her, fingers digging into the sensitive spot above her elbows.

"Honey, she's waking up," the nurse said, her voice firm, her body blocking Izzy's view of Mia. "We need you to wait in the hall."

So Izzy was left with nothing to do but pace, guilt crawling up from the deep recesses of her gut where it had been kept at bay, its unrelenting claws digging in. Sweat turned her palms slick as her stomach twisted, untwisted, twisted again. They'd got a confession. But at what cost?

There was a quiet sickness that came with the thought that Izzy had slipped into Lacey's role, the manipulator, the puppet master pulling emotions like strings. Maybe it was the only way Izzy had been able to think of to get Lacey to talk like they'd needed her to. But justification was rarely difficult. What Izzy would have trouble with for a long time was not only the hurt that had slipped so easily into Mia's eyes but also the resignation she'd worn only a minute later. As if she deserved the betrayal.

By the time they came to fetch her, Izzy had sunk to the ground, her forehead resting on the knees she'd pulled close to her chest. Her grease-heavy hair hung limp over her forehead, and she could see the paleness of her face, the shadows beneath her eyes, in the concern the nurse wore without any subtlety.

"You can see her, hon," the woman said, the wrinkles on her forehead deep and rigid, her voice softening to almost a whisper.

Izzy stood on shaky legs, focusing on relief instead of the onslaught of self-loathing that had been battering not so gently at all her defenses.

She blamed the whiplash of it all for her lack of brain-to-mouth filter when she walked into the room. "I said not to do anything stupid, you jerk."

Mia's face was gray and drawn, her lips white at the edges. But still she laughed. "Sorry."

"I had a vest," Izzy said, the guilt tugging at her with those talons. "I had a vest on, you idiot."

That brought color to Mia's cheeks. "And I was supposed to know that how?"

"I was supposed to step in front of you," Izzy said. It wasn't a real answer. She didn't actually have one. "If it came down to it."

One corner of Mia's lips pulled up. "Sorry to steal your thunder."

Dropping into the chair, Izzy couldn't help but stare at the bandage that peeked out through Mia's gown.

"I'm sorry." It was just a quiet apology, stripped bare of arguments and justification. It was what Izzy had to offer. "I'm so sorry."

Mia's lips twitched, an almost but not quite sad smile. "I'm not sure I can say I would have acted differently if the roles had been reversed."

"Were you ridiculously pissed?" Izzy asked, trying to break the tension. She forced an easy grin, the one she wore often, the one that was now faked but still probably also appreciated.

"Unbelievably so." Mia laughed weakly, and Izzy was proud of herself until it triggered a coughing fit, Mia's small body curling into itself as it heaved and bucked. Izzy was helpless to do much other than watch Mia's oxygen levels drop. She was just about to call a nurse when Mia settled back against the pillows. "How long have I been out?"

Izzy pressed her lips together. "A couple days."

Mia blinked but didn't seem surprised. "Tell me what happened."

Izzy leaned forward, her arms braced on her thighs.

"Did you get any of my texts?"

"One." Mia nodded. "The body in the bay was Peter, not Robert."

"Yeah, you were right about Peter being important to the case."

Mia shrugged. "Not how I expected." She shifted on the bed, her eyes on her wrists. "I met Robert when I was being held."

"We picked him up. He didn't put up a fight."

"No, he wouldn't have," Mia agreed, and when she looked up, the neutral mask was back. "Did he tell you anything?"

Izzy chewed on her bottom lip, debating how much to tell Mia in her weakened state. If she were in that bed, though, she'd want to know everything.

"All right, so this is what we've been able to piece together. Peter Hughes applied for the Bell artist residency over the summer. Just like we thought, he found Lacey's"—Izzy didn't want to say *souvenirs*, the memory of Mia's hunched-over form still clear, so she couched it, knowing Mia would follow along—"collection of things that pointed to her penchant for . . ."

"Killing people," Mia supplied. "Or sort of killing people."

"Yeah." They grimaced at each other. For a minute, it felt normal, like they were talking about any other case. "Anyway, he, understandably, flipped the hell out, booked it out of there. This part gets a little foggy, but it seems like he was going to try to report it to you? He must have heard stories about the suicide pact, and your name was in the little notebook Lacey kept with all the items."

"She cataloged them?"

"Yeah." Izzy sighed. It hadn't been the most pleasant thing to go through that list. "Not a lot of detail besides name and cause of death."

Mia shivered beneath her thin hospital blanket, and Izzy knew it wasn't from the cold. It was going to take them both a long time to forget those haunting eyes, the playful voice.

"Anyway, Robert says Peter chickened out, thinking he didn't have enough evidence." At Mia's eyebrow raise, an implicit question about what Izzy wasn't saying, Izzy laughed. "Yeah, I think he's full of bullshit. Robert probably just wanted to break a serial killer story himself. Probably saw a book deal in it or something."

"Why did Peter go back to the island?"

"He was playing freaking Columbo, I swear to God." Izzy shook her head. "Robert couldn't make a trip to the island until December, and Peter was worried the evidence would get destroyed by then. By Lacey, obviously."

"It would be hard to break a serial killer story without any proof."

"Right." Izzy nodded, acknowledging the truth of that. "But this time Peter wasn't so lucky."

"Handed to her on a silver platter." Mia sighed. "Jesus, she didn't even have to work for that one."

"Nope," Izzy agreed. "She held him for a bit, probably trying to decide what to do. I think the torture thing is new for her. There were two other deaths marked down in the notebook that we didn't know about from her time on the mainland, but from a quick glance at the files, those women hadn't been kidnapped like Peter."

"She was escalating, then."

"Seems like," Izzy said. "Especially with the state Robert was in, for how short of a time he was held."

"Peter was her trigger." Mia met Izzy's eyes from across the room. They both knew the implications of that, what would have happened if Lacey had been left unchecked. She had never been violent quite like that before, but then had tortured two victims in the span of a few months. How many more would have died if they hadn't stopped her?

"So Robert starts getting worried," Izzy continued. "He hadn't heard from Peter in a while, but also sometimes the guy would get flaky like that, so he's not ready to call in the cops quite yet."

Mia smiled, but it was small and tired. "I think you're right about that book deal. He'll probably still get one."

"I'm still thinking of charges for him," Izzy muttered, and Mia shook her head.

"He was in intense pain," Mia said. "Turning on me was the only out he saw."

Izzy grumbled but dropped it. "Robert goes to the island, makes a big show about writing the isolation-suicide article. He figures it will make good B matter in the serial killer story anyway."

"Lacey figures everything out," Mia filled in.

"Yup. He seems to have thought he could withstand her persuasion, so he actively sought her out to talk to." Izzy shook her head. "Then what followed was what you'd expect. Lacey kidnaps Robert, gets Peter to eat a gun, and then lobs him off the cliff."

"It was a risk, having Peter identified as Robert," Mia said.

It did seem like one, an unnecessary risk at that. So many things had gone wrong. But then Izzy thought about the way Lacey had smiled when she'd thought her plan was coming together. "Did she tell you why she did it?"

"I think . . ." Mia's eyes unfocused, her lips pulling back into something between disgust and pity. "Well, the logical reasoning was that she didn't want the death tied to her immediately. She wanted to play us longer."

"If the body was identified as Peter, she would have been our main suspect because he'd just been her artist in residence," Izzy followed. "The game wouldn't have been nearly as fun for her."

"Yeah."

They sat with that for a minute before Izzy shifted. "You were going to say something else."

Mia bit her lip.

"You said, 'I think,' but then switched gears," Izzy pressed.

Sighing, Mia looked back over at Izzy. "You know, I asked her what her buttons were. The ones she said everyone had, the ones she could push to manipulate people."

The smile. The smugness that so clearly lived in the deep marrow of her bones. "I don't even want to guess."

"She said . . ." Mia paused, the slow, steady beeping of the heart monitor filling the silence as she swallowed hard enough for her throat to ripple with it. "She said, 'Boredom.'"

The word sat sour and rotting against Izzy's tongue as she repeated it. "Boredom."

"To be honest, I think part of the mixed identities was for, as they say, shits and giggles," Mia said. "For the dramatics. The fact that I could recognize Peter was probably just icing on the cake."

Izzy shook her head, but not in disagreement. A bored sociopath on an island alone could tangle herself in all sorts of webs just to see if she could get free of them.

"Actually, they might not have even sent me," Mia said slowly. "Murdoch knew the broad facts of what happened when I was younger, knew the Bell family was involved. She might not have risked having me on the case if it was that closely tied to Lacey."

"So she calls up Sammy once the body is found . . . ," Izzy said.

Mia's eyes were on the window, distant. "Sammy."

Sighing, Izzy scrubbed a hand over her face. "I'm sorry, he was definitely involved."

"I figured."

"Yeah." Izzy tried to be gentle, though the blow probably paled in comparison to everything else Mia had found out. "Apparently, Lacey looked him up when he went to college on the mainland. He was kind of a part of your friend group, and she really seemed to fixate on you guys."

"Who would have guessed a budding sociopath would have been dropped like a lit match into our particular powder keg."

"You guys did not catch a break on that one," Izzy agreed. "Anyway, they dated a bit a few years back, and then, uh, 'reconnected' over the summer."

"When Ellen said he started getting distant."

"Exactly." Izzy sighed. "He seems a little baffled by his own behavior, to be honest."

The beeping from the heart monitor kicked up a notch. Neither of them acknowledged it.

"I don't get why he did it," Mia said. "Why he'd agree to switch their IDs, why he'd go along with it at all?"

"My guess?" Izzy debated actually saying it. She wondered how much of her was just trying to make Mia feel better about her friend. She wondered if it mattered that that was her motivation. When Mia nodded, she made her decision to continue. "For some reason he was in too deep with her to come clean to you completely, so he thought the best course of action to get you off the island was to kind of go along with her plan at first."

"How do you mean?"

"Well," Izzy said, drawing the word out, still piecing together the idea that, until she'd put voice to it, had been half-baked at best. "In his interrogation, he swore to us he was trying to protect you. Do you remember when we first saw the body?"

"He leaned toward suicide," Mia said. "When we asked. He leaned toward suicide."

"Right." Izzy nodded. It had made her doubt him, doubt Mia, too. She hadn't been wrong to do so, apparently. "I think in his own way he was just trying to close the case, get you out of there before it all went to hell."

Mia huffed out a breath. "Yeah, he did a shit job of that."

"Well, he was still dealing with Lacey." Izzy wasn't trying to defend him, wouldn't ever try. But Izzy also couldn't forget that, even if it had been for only a few moments, she herself had not been completely immune to Lacey's manipulation. And Sammy had been exposed to it a lot longer. "Lacey really knew how to zero in on things, you know. People's most vulnerable instincts."

Mia met her eyes, must have heard the self-recrimination in Izzy's voice. "She played everyone. Not just you."

"Yeah," Izzy said, but it didn't feel like an agreement. She should have known better. That night at the bar, Lacey had orchestrated the whole scene. Drawing on the napkin, the smoking argument with the bartender, even, a ploy to cement Izzy as an ally. The flirting. The fear when the door slammed, the big eyes when she promised she wasn't worth saving. Izzy could only imagine the ease with which she'd swayed anyone who hadn't already been suspicious of everyone.

"I'm not fishing for absolution," Izzy said, even though it was something she wanted desperately. "But I can picture Lacey slowly putting thoughts in Robert's head, you know? Before she took him. Maybe she even convinced him Peter was crazy." Izzy paused. "Monroe's pregnancy."

"Making Robert think Jimmy was the father," Mia followed her easily. "There wasn't anything in the interview about it. Jimmy said he didn't say anything to make the reporter think that."

"It was Lacey," Izzy agreed. Splicing reality and lies with impressive skill. Robert had been a testing ground for everyone who came after him.

Mia shifted so that her cheek rested against the pillow. "Tell me."

And Izzy got it. "My plan."

Mia nodded.

"I found Charles alive," Izzy started. "Not doing well but . . . alive."

"I think I was surprised when Lacey told me that he was," Mia said, blinking heavy lashes. "Knowing Lacey, I kind of expected him to be dead."

"Two parents, dead in mysterious accidents? It was probably too much, even for her." Izzy shrugged. "I'm shocked she didn't go through with her plan to frame Charles for Bix's murder, though. The seeds were all there."

"Mmmm, I can help there," Mia said. "Lacey filled me in when she was waiting for you to show up at the lighthouse. Apparently, she was going to get Cash to put the pieces together, have him go to the cops with all the evidence. That was what she was using him for."

"Lovely," Izzy said, the sarcasm thick. "Anyway, Charles couldn't say much, but it was enough to imply that it was another woman who had been involved with Bix's death. It got me thinking about who was around then."

"Obviously Lacey." Mia tipped her head down, a tired, half-hearted nod. "She was always there, wasn't she? The night at the lighthouse, but before it, too. The beach, the picture. Just out of frame, but always there."

"Manipulative little . . ."

"And you had to play her game." Mia cut off Izzy's tirade, watching her with an understanding Izzy wasn't sure she deserved, considering their positions.

"Couldn't exactly go in guns blazing, could I?"

"No evidence," Mia said, her eyes slipping shut. "All you had was kidnapping. You wanted murder. Or attempted, at least."

"Quinn flew me back to the island earlier that day," Izzy continued. "Asked her to keep quiet."

Mia hummed a small sound. "Did she tell someone? Lacey said something about sources."

"No. When I was ready, I took a gamble."

It took a second. "Ellen?"

"She has things to hide," Izzy said, looking up. "I figured that made her attractive to Lacey. And yet she's also the type to sell her soul to the biggest threat. At that moment, it was me. So she told Lacey I'd just landed."

"Meanwhile, you had already called in Murdoch for backup."

"And tried to set up a semblance of a plan," Izzy said. "I knew she had you. I was guessing she'd want me there in some way for her little scenario to work out. I just had to get everything in place for when she made the call."

Mia huffed out a little breath of air. "Brilliant."

Izzy straightened, her back hitting her chair. The praise sat awkwardly on her shoulders, ill fitting and uncomfortable. "It got you shot." Even she could hear the flatness in her voice.

"I don't go down that easy," Mia said.

The fluorescent light over Mia flickered, then went dead, the whole room going softer with it, shadows slipping in where there'd been only harshness before. Mia licked dry, cracked lips, and Izzy knew she wanted to ask. Knew she wouldn't.

"I thought about believing her. About you," Izzy said, the truth as her penance.

"You thought about it," Mia repeated without placing particular emphasis on any of the words.

"She was good." Izzy swallowed before plunging in. "And you're still hiding something."

"I promised I'd tell you the truth," Mia said, the weak smile accompanying it showing an awareness of the way she'd just dodged a question Izzy hadn't even bothered asking.

Izzy dropped it, because Izzy had made her point. And when it came down to it, she'd decided to trust Mia. "The doubt . . . it was only for a minute."

Mia slid a little farther down into the bed, her eyes staying closed longer each time she blinked. She'd be out soon. "She was good," Mia parroted. A forgiveness, and gratitude, maybe. For letting her keep her secrets.

Footsteps rushed by outside the door, and Mia waited for them to pass. "You got her, right?" The question was slurred, a last thought at the edge of sleep. This time when she went to blink, her eyes stayed closed.

"Head shot right after she pulled the trigger," Izzy said. She probed at that, a grubby finger nudging at the ripped edges of a wound to check just how deep it went. But there was only relief there. A monster had been taken out of the world. Maybe it wasn't her place to play the judge and jury, but sometimes you had to live in the gray areas that provided the best net outcome for humanity.

"Good," Mia said, her face reflecting the same satisfaction. "She would have gotten out of it somehow."

The words were barely out before Mia slipped back into unconsciousness.

Izzy sat guard a little longer, content to live in the space between the beeps.

CHAPTER
THIRTY-FIVE
Mia

Black Rock Bay, Maine
Friday, February 22

Mia stood on the deck of the ferry as St. Lucy's slowly materialized from the mist, as was her tradition. She was alone this time, hadn't told Izzy she was going back.

There were only a few other passengers belowdecks, and she doubted they were getting off at the island.

No one bothered her.

Like a month earlier, the cliffs came into view first, then the Bell mansion on the north end. It would be only a few more minutes before she'd see the lighthouse.

Her thumb found her scar, and she still felt Lacey's lips there, against her skin. Maybe she always would.

She forced herself to watch the lighthouse as it became a shape instead of blurred lines. The clean white tower, the little house, the slick black rocks below that gave the bay its name. She forced herself to watch.

The water churned beneath the ferry's engine, a rumble that reverberated in the hollowness of her chest, and she had to stop herself from pressing into her healing wound just to feel the pain. It was a bad habit she was trying to break.

Soon, the town appeared.

Home, it still whispered to her, though the sourness of it lingered in the crevices of her mouth.

There was no Sammy to greet her on the docks this time. She ducked her head low, just in case anyone was watching, and started up a small, hidden path that most people didn't know about. It stretched all the way out along the cliffs to her destination.

The day was calm, the waves gentle, the sun hot against her cheeks. It had been a while since she'd been allowed free rein outside. So much of the previous weeks had been spent in hospitals or therapy or in bed, resting. There had been an itch building up beneath her skin because of it, and one night she'd scratched so hard she'd left droplets of blood on her shirt.

Mia didn't think about any of that as she walked. She thought, instead, of the years before that terrible summer, running along this path, barefoot and pink cheeked in the warmer months, careless of the plunge just a few feet off the trail. She thought of Asher's small hand in hers, both of their palms sweaty, crusted with mud at the fingertips where it was starting to dry. She thought of the way they whispered as they built a fairy house, right up ahead, in that one tree that had a gnarled knot at its base.

She thought of each golden-tinged memory, holding them gently in her hands, caressing them, soaking in their warmth.

And then she let them go.

By the time she got to the lighthouse, her face was wet with tears she hadn't realized were falling. She swiped at them, an angry jerk, annoyed with herself that she was crying over it.

She hesitated only a heartbeat before pushing the door open and stepping inside. Averting her gaze from where there was still copper on the floor, now fresh instead of from years ago, she headed for the steps.

Mia didn't stop until she was outside again, leaning against the railing. The same place she'd been when Lacey had sat beside her, taking shots of Eagle Rare.

It was still odd to her how much Lacey had become a ghost in her memories of that summer despite how cruel she'd been, always on the periphery, outside of frame. But Lacey had never really talked about herself, had never become vulnerable, never become real. So she stayed that girl on the beach with the sad eyes and dark hair and slightly off sense of humor, never fully forming into a person beyond that.

Maybe that's why she was so good at it. Manipulating them. She figured out the dark, terrible things they all whispered to themselves at night and then became that voice. No longer her own person but a malicious twist of a knife into an already-formed cut.

Memories are funny, aren't they? They only show us what we think happened, not what really did.

Lacey's words had replayed in Mia's head each night as her legs twitched and twisted, restless beneath the blankets, her body exhausted from the endless waves of pain but unable to be still.

Repeating, repeating, repeating those words. Until they slowly started making sense.

Mia's hand dipped into the jacket of her pocket, sliding along the lining until she found what she was looking for.

The sun hit the metal of the razor blade she'd slipped out of the evidence room. She blinked against the glare, even as her fingers pressed into the tip. Her flesh gave but didn't rupture, and she let off the pressure.

They only show us what we think happened.

The thing Lacey hadn't realized was that she fell prey to that, as well.

She hadn't been in the room with Asher, Monroe, and Mia. That's what they realized when Cash had started filling in the blanks in the story.

Lacey had set everything up, but she'd been waiting outside. Ready to intercept Mia.

Only one person really knew what happened that night.

The memories hadn't come back slowly but rather all at once. A thick fog peeling away, a bandage ripped off hard enough to take skin with it.

The night was blurry enough at the edges, their behavior strange enough, that it confirmed a suspicion Mia had been holding in a firm grasp. Lacey, for all her confident bravado, for all her scheming ways, had drugged them into complacency. It didn't erase Mia's role in what happened, nor the guilt she'd wear just as permanently as the scars on her wrists, but it blunted it.

Mia and Asher held hands like they'd had when they were kids. It was too hot, but their palms pressed together anyway, sweat slicked and uncomfortable.

Everything felt soft and distorted, anyway. Slow and disjointed, like a dream, when you ended up in impossible places doing impossible things for no reason at all.

"I can't stay here," Mia whispered, already thinking of the metal in her pocket. They were flat on their backs on the floor of the lighthouse. Mia didn't know why they weren't outside looking at the stars. They should have been looking at the stars. "I can't be trapped. Can't end up like them."

"Who?"

"All of them," Mia said. Like she knew Cash was going to be. If she did nothing, she'd end up married to him, babies on the way, one after another.

"What if . . . ?" Asher started, squeezing her fingers tighter. Neither of them acknowledged the intimacy, the way their bodies touched at the hips, shoulders, thighs. Some part of Mia told her it was strange to be here like

this with Asher, but that voice came from a distance, muffled so that she only caught a few words of warning. So easy to ignore.

Mia was already shaking her head. "No. I don't have any money saved up. Mama doesn't have any money. I didn't get the scholarship. I'm stuck here."

They were silent, and Mia shook off his hand, sat up. The blade was just waiting for her fingers. Lacey had given it to her earlier with a whispered "you'll thank me."

"What if she wants to keep the baby?" Asher asked. "I can't. I can't do it, Mia. I can't."

"You haven't talked to her about it yet?"

"No." Asher said. "She doesn't even know I know about it, I don't think."

The vise that had gripped her heart since Asher had turned up, swollen face and wet hazel eyes, relaxed as the point of the blade caught against the tip of her finger.

"I have an idea."

It was stupid, so stupid. But everything seemed possible in that moment, floaty instead of tethered to reality. She had read about these cuts; they were like a high. They'd make Mia forget her life was going nowhere, make Asher forget his would be over soon, too. Mostly, though, it might be a solution to the baby. "Get her here."

"She's already coming," Asher admitted. "I told her we needed to talk."

"Perfect." Mia's lips tipped up. Her sluggish brain had latched onto the idea. If Monroe bled enough, surely she'd miscarry, surely. Wasn't that what Lacey had said? Lacey knew. Mia could trust her.

They waited, Asher sitting up, Mia still sprawled on the floor.

"When the time comes, just don't go too deep," Mia said, and Asher's head dipped to avoid her eyes. He was scared; she could smell it on him, sharp and unpleasant and very boy.

But he took the blade.

The power she had over him was a shameful thing, and it buzzed along her nerve endings.

Asher licked his lips. "Not too deep, okay?" He watched her in that way of his, that way that saw down to her marrow, that knew her for sixteen years, loved her for what felt like longer.

Everyone had always whispered that Mia was jealous that Asher had a girlfriend. That he was no longer a lovesick puppy following after her. She'd always said that wasn't true.

That first night at the bonfire, though, she'd watched Asher's hand slide under Monroe's sweatshirt, his fingers tracing the curve of her spine. She'd turned to find Lacey watching her with big, sad eyes, and their gazes had locked across the distance.

The ghost of a girl who saw too much, who saw the demons you couldn't even admit to yourself.

Mia remembered leaning into Cash's body, remembered that she hadn't been jealous, only tipsy and amused. But had that been reality? Or just what she wanted to have happened?

The picture in the hallway. Her watching Cash, Asher watching Monroe. But even standing in her mother's house years later, she'd felt the pinch of something she'd pretended wasn't there. The boys' eyes had always been on Monroe.

When Monroe got to the lighthouse, Mia handed her the blade. "It's like a high. Trust me."

"It's just a little cut, right?" Monroe shrugged, silk hair sliding over her shoulder as she sat down beside Asher. Always inserting herself between Mia and him, even now.

"You can do it together," Mia said, her gaze steady on Monroe. "I brought more." Also from Lacey. "Look, I'll go first."

Before fear could still her fingers, Mia laid the metal blade against her own wrist.

Not too deep, not too deep.

The line she drew was thin, so thin it barely stung. "See."

As she held it up to show Asher and Monroe, a drop of blood pearled and then slipped over the edge of the cut. They all watched its slow progress until it nestled into the crook of Mia's elbow.

"My turn." Asher flashed them a grin, all bravado. But the mask made him cocky, careless, because the blade sank down into his arm, far beyond the thin tip. He dragged it up away from his wrist instead of across, and something about that was so wrong Mia could do nothing but blink.

Not too deep. She'd warned him. Not too deep.

A white fog curled and paced at the edges of Mia's consciousness as blood soaked into Asher's jeans. He met her eyes, no longer smiling, and his lips moved. No sound came out.

Mia tried to say something, anything, to warn Monroe, to comfort Asher—she didn't know. But it was in vain. Her tongue was too thick—heavy and clumsy in her mouth.

Monroe had already copied Asher on one side, dragging the blade up along her forearm instead of across her wrist.

The cut she'd made was thin, though, and shallow. Weeping, but not uncontrollably.

Mia shifted closer, desperate, her eyes locked on dull steel meeting pale skin for a second time. She wanted to stop Monroe, she tried to stop Monroe. But Mia's hands were shaking, and black hovered at the edge of her vision.

When Mia reached for the razor, she knocked into Monroe's arm instead, an accident that in any other second of any other day would have been overlooked, forgotten in the next breath.

Monroe cried out, in surprise more than anything, as the blade burrowed deeper from their combined force.

"Why did you?" Monroe asked, staring not at Mia but at her own slick hands where the blood pooled in her palms. There was too much of it. There shouldn't have been that much.

I didn't mean to, Mia thought. I didn't . . .
But the words still wouldn't come.

Mia traced the edge of the razor against her scar, a shiver following in its wake. Then she flung the blade into the bay.

The metal sank beneath the black water, taking the memories with it.

ACKNOWLEDGMENTS

I'd like to thank my wonderful editors, Charlotte Herscher and Megha Parekh, for their always-thoughtful guidance, spot-on edits, and endless encouragement.

Thanks also to the top-notch team at Thomas & Mercer, who work so tirelessly to make an idea into reality. I am so grateful this story is in such capable hands.

As always, a huge megathanks to my agent, Abby Saul. I couldn't have asked for a better partner in crime. You go above and beyond, and this would be a lesser book without you.

Thank you, dear readers. You keep me on my toes, make me smile, push me to grow, and support me with such trust. I am very blessed to have you.

Abby McIntyre and Katie Smith forever have my gratitude for being the best, most faithful first readers a person could ever ask for.

And, finally, thank you to my friends and family, who are so endlessly generous with their enthusiasm and love. It means the absolute world to me.

ABOUT THE AUTHOR

Born in Harrisburg, Pennsylvania, Brianna Labuskes graduated from Penn State University with a degree in journalism. For the past eight years, she has worked as an editor at both small-town papers and national media organizations such as Politico and Kaiser Health News, covering politics and policy. Brianna is the author of the Amazon Charts bestseller *Girls of Glass*, and *It Ends with Her*, as well as the historical romance novel *One Step Behind*. She lives in Washington, DC, and enjoys traveling, hiking, kayaking, and exploring the city's best brunch options. Visit her at www.briannalabuskes.com.